SKIN RIVER

Steven Sidor

SKIN RIVER

ST. MARTIN'S MINOTAUR
☙ NEW YORK

www.minotaurbooks.com

Book design by Jonathan Bennett

Library of Congress Cataloging-in-Publication Data

Sidor, Steven.
   Skin River / Steven Sidor.—1st St. Martin's Minotaur ed., 1st U.S. ed.
      p. cm.
   ISBN 0-312-32949-0
   EAN 978-0312-32949-5
   1. Bars (Drinking establishments)—Fiction. 2. Young women—Crimes against—Fiction. 3. City and town life—Fiction. 4. Wisconsin—Fiction.
I. Title.

PS3619.I36S55 2004
813'.6—dc22

2004046784

First Edition: September 2004

10 9 8 7 6 5 4 3 2 1

For Lisa

ACKNOWLEDGMENTS

Writers are wrong to think they work alone. If that were true, my book would be a stack of papers in a drawer. I want to thank the people who helped me on this one.

Mom and Dad, who gave me the chance.

Br. Bob Ruhl, who taught me to read and write.

Brian Padjen, who critiqued the drafts early and often.

Pete Przybylinski, who saw what I didn't.

Jamie Howard, my pal in Galway.

Ann Collette, my agent.

Ben Sevier, my editor.

My wife, Lisa, from the minute I saw you at the drinking fountain.

I have a thing
for this cold swift water.
Just looking at it makes my blood run
and my skin tingle. I could sit
and watch these rivers for hours.

—Raymond Carver,
"Where Water Comes Together with Other Water"

There will always be one more river.

—Edward Abbey, "Floating"

SKIN RIVER

1

Flashlight beams play in the dark spaces between the trees as the search party fans out. Its movement forward is slow. The men stop to check the uneven ground, regain their sense of direction, and brush moths from their faces. The air hums. On all sides mosquitoes spin together in patches, and walking through them is like breaking through a series of thin nets. Here the forest is choked with weeds, and their decomposition smells polluted. Floating particles make the air fizz. Breathing in stings. Faint through the moisture, a wisp of marijuana smoke drifts like the mark of a sailboat in an otherwise empty harbor.

Hidden ten feet beyond the reach of the flashlights, a man who calls himself Goatskinner sucks the last life from a joint he holds daintily on the end of a toothpick. The tiny paper flares and disappears. Comfortable in the dark, he stretches back on the hood of the car. He rubs the warm tip of the toothpick with his thumb, then tucks it between his molars, biting down and tasting the smokiness in the wood. The man relaxes, and as the car takes his full bulk, the shocks creak. Large bugs land and walk on his powerful chest. They travel in erratic paths across him. When they buzz, the electricity in their feathery legs and wings tickles like new hair growing beneath his shirt. The lights approach, sweeping the trees that form a lush, broken fence between him and the men aiming the beams. For a lingering moment, splintered light enters through the gaps in the leaves, making the car seem to glow.

With his eyes half-open he witnesses the transformation. The plant life surrounding him changes to black and haunted shapes. His body and the stolen Pontiac turn a faded, milky green. He thinks that he can hear, in the distance, the ocean. Impossible because they are more than a thousand miles from salt water.

Inside the Pontiac, the girl has regained consciousness. He perceives her terror as if it were a vibration in the ground or colored smoke gliding through the car's open windows. The men with the lights are calling out her name. Neighbors' voices mixed with the hoarse shouts of her father, brothers, and boyfriend. The man has confidence in the rope and tape holding her quiet across the length of the backseat. The inevitability of what will happen during the rest of the night is so fixed it feels like the past to him.

"The only one not afraid of the woods tonight is me."

His voice is loud but drowned out by the noise from the search party. It isn't clear if he's speaking to the girl or to himself. He stares with true interest at the insects settling on him, the flat ones like buttons on his skin. He wants to laugh, but the lights move on.

Instead, Goatskinner sleeps.

•

Buddy Bayes' cabin faced Dark Cloud Lake to the south, and to the west, past the one cabin wall that had no window, the Skin River fed the lake and provided a good location for fishing all year long. It took Buddy ten minutes to negotiate the path, overgrown with summer brush, as it hooked and dropped gradually from the side of the cabin to the river mouth. If he had wanted to, he could have taken a hatchet and cleared the intrusive branches, made an easier walk for himself, but he preferred the look of the path the way it was. Just worn enough for the passage of a stocky man carrying two fishing rods, a clear plastic tackle box the size of a hardcover novel, and a soft cooler that fit a ham-and-cheese sandwich, two beers, and a blue ice pack.

From early spring to late autumn, Buddy would hear the river before he saw it. The sound of its rush made his approach more tantalizing. The trees ended a couple of yards short of the riverside. At the place where the path led out, a clump of white birches grew. Buddy slipped past the final, waist-high green branches, and felt, as he always did at this point, like he had entered a private spot. Rocks lined the near bank. Buddy set down his equipment on a flat square boulder the size of a delivery truck. As he bent over, he saw the curlicues of snipped fishing line and muddy boot prints that stamped the rocks along this side of the river. It was no remote site, the water hardly pristine. Fallen branches and trash rolled along twenty feet down in the brown water. The number of vacationers using the Skin River increased every year.

But this morning Buddy was alone and would not have to come up with small talk about weather changes, bait, and how pretty the sunrise looked. From his tackle box he chose a lure and picked up the longer of his two rods. He pushed the sleeves of his windbreaker back to his elbows. Buddy tied on the chartreuse spinner and cast it along the dark, submerged cracks in the rock.

Light wind stirred the already warm morning air. To his left, the lake's tinsel waves sparkled. Buddy worked the lure smoothly as he walked toward the river mouth and back again to where his equipment lay. He kept his attention on his hands, feeling the action of the spinner blade as he pulled it through the water. He waited for the *rap-rap-rap* signifying a fish.

The sun burned off the last traces of fog close to the ground. Across the lake, the sound of an outboard droned then vanished. Slow tension drew Buddy's line taut and bent his rod. He snapped his arms upward and heard the loud clicks from his drag as line continued to go out. It didn't feel like a fish. He opened the reel to free spool. The rod straightened. Buddy watched his line peel away and sink into the current. Probably a snag. The river carried debris for miles.

He waited a few seconds more. Sometimes the hook freed itself, untangled in the slack. Buddy broke his line there at least once a week. The river was tricky. It sucked your lure down between rocks and cut the line, or tied it fast to a hundred pounds of dead wood floating south. Buddy started to reel in. First the line came back easily. Warm drops flew off the reel onto his forearms. Then he felt what might have been a pull, and he yanked back. The resistance lessened. Buddy knew a large northern pike or a musky could be mistaken for a snag. Guides told stories about catching giants they thought were logs until the surface water blew up into froth.

Whatever he snagged was coming in. Slowly.

A cardinal exploded from a thicket behind him. The blur of red feathers passing overhead zapped Buddy's concentration. By instinct, he slammed back on the rod. Bitten or stretched to the point of breaking, the end of the line whipped out of the river and sailed over Buddy into the space where, a second before, the bird had flown.

As he gathered up his line to replace the lure, Buddy saw the cardinal spying on him from the vantage of a long spiral branch on the opposite bank. The cardinal's slurred whistle dropped in with the sound of the flowing water. Its red body mimicked the shape of a flame. Buddy imagined the bird's tiny eyes shimmering like oily beads. A jittery life poking the grass searching for the tips of worms. With small tools the creature met its needs. Buddy knelt next to his open tackle box and when he stood up, he noticed another fisherman, upriver.

The man came nearer, keeping his head down and switching his gaze, back and forth, from the river to the trees. Buddy saw the man carried no sporting gear but gripped a two-way radio in his left hand. The other hand he raised to wave hello. The two men recognized each other.

"Good morning, Vic."

"Wish I could say so, Buddy. I take it you haven't heard the news about the Teagles girl?" Vic closed the remaining distance between them.

"No, I haven't."

They shook hands. Vic's tone of voice said the situation was critical. He kept his smile in check. Both men skipped the protracted greeting of friendly neighbors in deference to the matter before them. Vic judged it to be serious, and Buddy trusted Vic enough to follow his lead.

"Melissa. That's her name. A good girl from what I've heard. Home from college on summer break. Last night she goes out to Pee-Jay's Pizza Shack to pick up dinner. And she never came home. Len and Marie drove to Pee-Jay's. The kid working there said she didn't show. He still had their pizza in the warmer. That was two hours after she left the house. Len went home, dropped Marie off to call the sheriff, then he rode around hoping he'd spot her car. He stayed out till eleven o'clock or so. Marie called her boys and some friends. We were all there when he got back. We divided up. Searched all night long. Nothing. No car. No Melissa. Nobody who remembers seeing her." Vic coughed. "That's about where we're at this morning."

Vic Presser owned a service station in town, and he was still wearing his uniform shirt. Sweat stains looped under his arms. The smell of engines clung to him. Buddy guessed he hadn't changed shirts since the previous day. Above Vic's breast pocket, black cursive letters spelled out his name. Vic reached into the pocket and withdrew a cigarette from a flattened pack of Winstons. One day's worth of grizzled beard roughened his chin. He clicked a green plastic lighter, sucked smoke deep into his lungs, and dropped one hand to his side. His other hand returned the lighter and pinched softly at the cigarette filter he held between his lips.

"There's no chance she just took off on a road trip without telling anyone? Maybe she went to meet a boyfriend, and they lost track of the time," Buddy said.

Vic shook his head. "Len says everything was normal. They were going to eat pizza and watch a movie on TV. She's dating Bill Harkin's son. Bill and his boy helped us with the search. The boy says he last talked to her yesterday. Noonish. They went swimming at the sandy beach right around the corner from here. He says things were good between them. Guess we can't know for sure. But something sure happened to her."

Buddy would have put his money on an ordinary explanation. He had seen small-town parents underestimate their kids' ability to develop adult problems. They came into his place still trying to figure out what happened. To fathom how they got blind-sided by children who grew into the strangers living in their house. But there was probably an equal share of parents who lived apart from their offspring, numb to their problems, distracted, overcome by their own dissatisfaction with life. Blame cropped up on both sides. Either way, Buddy suspected that the girl was safe, if not sound. And her predicament, when it became clear, would probably be a familiar one.

Both men let their gazes wander over the burnt blond grass at their ankles. Vic used his pinkie to dab at a speck of tobacco sticking to his tongue. The cardinal's whistle repeated. Buddy asked if there was anything he could do.

"Somebody who stops in at your place for a beer might've seen something on the road. I'll get you her picture to post at the bar. Putting the word out might help. But, to tell you the honest truth, Bud, I really don't know what we can do. Wait and see. That's about all at this point."

Buddy figured Vic to be the type used to fixing problems. A

leaky trans, maybe a rattle in the exhaust, or a worn tire. Cars were mysteries he could solve. Vic fidgeted. Buddy guessed that looking for the Teagles' daughter made him feel inept.

Then Vic admitted he'd been thinking about his own little girl, Tina, who lived with his ex-wife in Traverse City. Last Christmas she served him invisible food on miniature china plates from Santa Claus. He remembered the careful way she bent her wrist to pour him a cup of imaginary coffee. How he pretended to stir and drink it. The thought of losing a daughter was too horrible.

Buddy felt Vic might be jumping the gun. It was still early. The Teagles girl hadn't been gone long.

"Anyone check along this river yet?" Buddy asked his question as though the flowing water had materialized a moment ago.

"Nope. I think I'm the only one that's been this far away from town. I've been over this stretch back to Ketchel Road, where I parked, but I'm pretty tired. I might've missed things. Hell, everything's starting to look out of place to me. I thought I saw something next to a stump way back there," Vic jerked his thumb in the direction he had come from, "and, goddamn it, I swore I'd found that girl's body. Curled up naked in the dirt with her little knees and elbows sticking out. When I walked up to it . . . just a patch of wild mushrooms." Vic massaged the side of his head with the palm of one hand. "Uh, Len and Marie must be going out of their minds. If it was my Tina . . ."

Buddy detected Vic's fatigue, and the guilt he was trying to push away. Buddy figured it was hard for a man like Vic to accept the secret gladness he was experiencing, knowing his own child was safe in another town. He offered to take up Vic's part of the search.

"Why don't you go home and sleep. I'll look around this side of the river from the sandy beach to the bridge, then I'll cross and walk back along the other side."

Vic nodded his thanks and said he'd drop off Melissa's picture at the bar. He handed over his radio, and Buddy watched him walk off until he rounded a big curve in the river.

·

Augustus Bodine uses his finger to scoop maraschino cherries from a jar. He adds them, one by one, to a drinking glass filled with Jack Daniel's. Country music jangles from a cheap radio propped on the windowsill. He sinks the fourth piece of fruit, and the whiskey brims, the brown fluid swirling with cherry syrup.

Augustus leans forward and, without touching the glass, sucks the top of the sweetened whiskey through his lips. He is at home, relaxing in his kitchen.

Freshly showered, Augustus wears nothing but a soft, raggedy pair of jeans. His bare feet leave damp prints on the linoleum when he walks to the back door. There's a lake breeze. But the stirred air is hot like a blow-dryer pointed in his face. He pushes his nose against the screen. His tongue darts out and licks the metal.

A muffled clinking of musical chimes. Augustus steps back and turns to the interior of the house.

"Just a minute," he says. He reaches for a clean shirt draped over one of the kitchen chairs. He puts it on and fastens the buttons as he walks into the living room. From a tin on the coffee table, he picks up a mint wrapped in a twist of plastic. The chimes ring again.

"I'm coming," Augustus answers. He scans the room for signs, but there are none. As he opens the front door, he crinkles the plastic off the candy and slides the mint into his mouth. A sheriff's deputy stands waiting in the cup of shade beneath his awning.

•

Buddy concealed his gear in the brush near the path's opening. When he backed his way out of the woods, a loose branch slapped the knuckles of his left hand, and a row of thorns nipped him. He used his handkerchief to wipe the dots of blood. The two-way radio clipped to his belt crackled with static, followed by the voice of a man and an engulfing swoosh of interference. Buddy couldn't make out what the voice said. He unclipped the radio, turned the volume down, and transferred it to his bleeding hand.

New droplets replaced those he had cleaned away. He kept the handkerchief pressed down over his wound and felt foolish, strolling along the river's edge holding his hands out in front of him like a prisoner.

The sandy beach turned up nothing. At the grass fringe, the County Park Service had stationed a blue garbage barrel. Beachgoers overfed it the remains of their picnics, perforated inflatable toys, and spent beer bottles with sand molded to their bottoms.

Litter mounded next to the can. Down the slope of the beach, the discarded items were more singular.

Buddy located an aqua pair of toddlers' swim trunks, a tower of sun-bleached Pepsi cans, and a punched-in chicken box from Hardee's. Inside the box were chicken bones, napkins, two empty peach wine coolers, and a condom wrapper.

The land slanted into the water, and the sand washed away in the shallows. The remainder of the lake floor seemed to be composed of little burgundy stones shaped like internal organs. Half of a sopping-wet, gold Nerf football bobbed on the lake's easy wavelets. Farther out, a gutted watermelon took on water and capsized in the reeds.

Buddy kicked through a cluster of white and brown filters from extinguished cigarettes. He found a heads-up penny and put it in his pocket. The ripe stink coming from the trash can chased him back to the river.

He retraced his steps to where he'd been fishing. From there, he followed the dirt trail Vic had come down. Soon he reached a lane stamped in the weeds, veering off to a turnaround on the edge of Ketchel Road. Vic had parked here. Two grooves in the white gravel showed where he had steered his truck in and out. Buddy abandoned the lane and kept close to the river. A bass jumped in the cagey branches of a lightning-struck willow. The dead part of the tree hung in the water.

Buddy never had a sister, wife, or daughter. In fifty-two years, no occasion called on him to rescue a woman or defend one from the violence of a man. He had argued with men over the subject of women but not once had he fought another on a woman's behalf. Women were, in his experience, a source of finite pleasure and lasting perplexity. He sought their company on rare occasions. Margot, the girl who lived above his tavern with her baby, was an exception. He didn't know how to classify their relationship. Friends, he guessed. It could be more. She was young, fit, and her sly smile said *game as hell*. He didn't need that kind of trouble. Not that trouble ever stopped him. But she was too young and he'd make a fool out of himself if he made a play and she declined. Seeing it go that way in his mind's eye was enough to slow him down. Women in his life were scarce as vacations. A few he remembered well.

Grandma Nan raised him and his younger brother, and her spirit hovered over his childhood memories, her scent a mixture of talcum powder and baked bread. Marti Logan became his first love, a girl remarkable for no other reason. She eloped with a truck driver from Janesville when she turned eighteen. Then there was Cassie, a leggy strawberry blonde grad student at UW-Madison. He met her when he was taking a few classes paid for by the GI bill. A more beautiful woman than he was capable of attracting before or since, she taught him about drugs and free love. He had a soft spot for hippies because of her, though she'd been too smart and realistic to be a true hippie. For those same reasons, he made a poor soldier. Their relationship was an exercise in exposing the hollowness of the people they were pretending to be. Mostly they got high and screwed on the shag carpet.

Of course there were others. Tight skirts, well drinks, nylons skimmed off in a haze. Buddy lifting up quietly from sheets smelling of cigarettes. Ducking out. Skies still showing stars. The physical part was like exercise, a good run on the beach. He didn't go to the beach often enough. Always working. Making rain.

Buddy wondered about Melissa Teagles. Would he recognize her if she walked into the bar asking for a draft? Probably not. He didn't want to think about seeing her body floating by, her face turned away underwater, the bones in her neck broken. He blinked sweat out of his eyes and trudged on.

Northward, as Buddy approached the bridge, he clambered up a steep incline. Below him, the river tapered between ledges of rippled gray rock. In the shade of the rock walls, the river surged black, except for where the water creased between two jutting stones, or where, for a short stretch, it thinned over the caps of rocks lodged in a sickle pattern—there the water glittered silver as though chains were pulling just beneath the surface. The air in the narrow gap filled with spray, and the misting river water carried the thick smell of minerals, tangy and greased, like a box of old nails.

Buddy slid a beer can from the pocket of his beige nylon wind-breaker. He had taken it out of the cooler earlier. He popped the tab and drank. The beer was warm from riding on his hip. Per-spiration slicked his chest and dribbled down his spine. Buddy tilted the can, drained it, and put the empty back in his pocket. Then he removed his jacket, folded it neatly over the bridge rail.

A half-century's accumulation of names, initials, and dirty insults gave the wooden bridge character. The fresh carvings were the plain color of toothpicks. In certain places the older words were illegible, worn smooth, giving the illusion that the grain had repaired itself, the way a river did.

The bridge was wide enough for a single car to pass. Buddy seldom witnessed anyone using it in the daytime, but he knew local teenagers dared to speed over it in the middle of the night. With their headlights doused, they followed the shallow ruts, looking for a hiding place to drink and smoke, searching for privacy so they could mess around with each other. He had seen Vic's yellow wrecker up there on a couple of rainy mornings, dragging junks out of the sticks and leaves.

Buddy peered over the rail into the water. He leaned far out over the edge to see under the bridge. Halved Firestones were lashed around the pilings to bumper boats passing through. Down there, a nest of fallen branches jammed against one of the pilings, suspended, for the moment, from its inevitable journey downstream—delayed by one dry black limb curled over the lip of a tire. In the center of the branches, a ball of clothing rested, inches above the Skin River.

Buddy skidded down the embankment, trailing his hand along the underside of the bridge supports to keep his balance. The long grass blades flattened and ripped, squeaking under his boots.

Beneath the bridge, the river was as wide as a neighborhood street, the water too murky to judge depth. Buddy crouched and extended his hand to the tangle of branches. They wobbled in the current just short of his reach. In the knotted clothing he could see denim—he couldn't tell if it was a jacket or pants—a torn shirt of green-and-black flannel, and a dingy white towel. Vic hadn't told him what Melissa was wearing. Buddy blamed himself for not asking. He grabbed a tuft of fat weeds with his left hand, anchoring himself on the shore. Then he stretched the right half of his body out over the river. His fingertips grazed the branches, but he could not take hold. The weeds uprooted, Buddy teetered, and he dunked his knee in the tepid water. Almost falling in.

No long sticks lay under the bridge or along the bank. Buddy didn't want to chance the time it would take to walk back and get one of his fishing rods or even to go up to the tree line and break off a bough. The river soon would work the branches free and swallow them, the clothing, too, as it made its churning progress south. Buddy removed his belt and wrapped the end with the holes twice around his fist. He hoped the square buckle would catch in the branches so he could to drag them closer.

On the fourth try, the buckle caught. He wrested the branches off the tire. They began to jumble and sink. Buddy hauled them in the best he could. Their network interlocked deep beneath the surface. The washed-away ruins of a beaver dam.

He plucked the ball of clothing from its basket not a second too soon. Snapping and clicking, the pile moved against itself and plunged from sight.

Buddy shook water off the silver buckle. Then, tucking the ball of clothing under his arm, he threaded the wet leather through the loops of his jeans. When he finished, he let the ball drop to the ground. And with his boot, he toed it onto a whorl of hard dirt. In the broken shade of the bridge beams, he crouched again and tried to convince himself that unraveling the clothes would reveal nothing. The vomit-covered remnant of some kid's drunken night in the woods.

But he could not push down the acid rising at the back of his throat or ignore the nerves bristling in his fingers. Buddy touched the pant legs, distinguishable now and bound at the knees. A simple knot held the bundle together.

The sun cut golden knife shapes on the riverside around him.

He loosened the jeans.

•

Augustus pats the large folded knife in his back pocket. He unlatches the screen door. He frowns. His mouth opens and the deputy smells mint.

"What can I do for you, Officer?"

"Are you Augustus Bodine?"

"Yessir, you bet I am."

"Well, a friend of mine tells me that when you mount a fish, it looks so real that a person might swear it would swim off the wall." The deputy says this and smiles at his cleverness.

He sees the taxidermist is smiling too.

•

The copper starburst spread across the seat of the jeans was a bloodstain. Its dark center shone wet, almost black. Buddy's pulse drummed. His vision blurred, cleared. With gentle pulls, he unfolded the towel wrapped inside. The cotton was sticking. He pried it apart. Long bronze finger-smears radiated to the towel's edges. In one corner were the marks where someone had wiped a sharp tool clean.

Buddy inhaled the chemical smell of acetone rising from the bundle. He heard no sound. The air was warm, breezeless. He fought the urge to stand up, walk to his cabin, and forget this shit. Forget it because it did not yet involve him. He wanted to enter the familiar space of his rooms, to see his things as he left them, to sit in his chair and read the paper. Maybe entertain the idea of Margot making pancakes for him some cold morning. Red flannel shirt, bare legs, and an over-the-shoulder smile.

He started at what he thought were maggots squirming in the bundle. They were wood shavings and sawdust, trembling from his touch. He sensed coldness and found two cloudy ice cubes snuggled at the center of the package. They dripped over a raw chicken breast.

No.

It was a hand.

The fingers were clenched, making a small fist. A lock of long curly hair wove, up down, up down, between the knuckles.

Red hair.

Buddy remembered that Melissa's mother had red hair. And cinnamon freckles like the ones dusting over the delicate blue veins on the back of this hand, trailing to the wrist. Touching only the towel, he turned the hand over. The fingernails were short, dull. They had broken through the skin of her palm. Buddy wavered. The final sticking bits of cotton released. He stared down at the unmistakable abruptness of bone.

On his knees, he laid the opened bundle in the grass. Squeezed his thighs to stop their shaking.

•

Deputy Carl Sherry opens his cruiser's trunk. The Styrofoam cooler screeches when he pulls the top off.

A twenty-pound northern pike lies straight and cold on a bed of ice. Augustus dons half-moon glasses to inspect the length of the fish. Specks of blood mar its open eye. The small dent behind the eyes came from a billy club hit. Pulpy holes through the upper lip show where the hooks from a black bucktail cut through and held. He runs a finger rapidly over the slimy scales. Pushes his hand into the belly and fondles the thin bones there. Bends forward. Lowers his face in close, kissing distance.

"Color's gone out a bit. When did you catch her?"

"Friday night. In Flambeau. Right in the weedbed off Medicine Rock. She slammed my Mepps like fucking gangbusters. First cast."

Augustus nods. "More than twenty-four hours. You should've wrapped her in a wet towel. Or newspapers. She would've preserved better that way. For next time, now you know."

His fingers invade the gill slit. He lifts.

"C'mon baby." Walking back to the house, he tells the deputy, "I'll have her ready for you in three weeks. Come back tonight for the meat."

Though he can't figure out why, Deputy Sherry is no longer excited.

He's suffered a strange loss.

2

The Black Chimney Tavern has served fresh fish, steaks, and beer to its patrons for thirty years. Buddy's owned the place the last year and a half. Driving west through the woods of northeastern Wisconsin on Highway 70, a person will come upon the pleasant small town of Gunnar, and a few miles past the two stoplights, the tavern's namesake stands tall above the treetops. On cool evenings, and most are, woodsmoke scrolls skyward. The sight of the smudged brick column looks ominous in the rain.

Two months ago, in late June, Buddy found the partial remains of Melissa Teagles. Searchers discovered her parents' car, the one she had been driving, submerged to mid-windshield in a local pond. The rest of her body was never recovered. The sheriff brought in for questioning Louis Soft Owls, a middle-aged Chippewa plumber with a history of beating his girl-friends, but everyone knew Louis couldn't have done this to the Teagles' daughter. He was a violent loser, not a psychopath. The feeling around town was that a stranger was responsible. A drifter traveling between Chicago and Canada. He had dropped in and was gone. At least, everyone hoped so.

•

Buddy sat at the bar eating Italian sausage and crusty bread. He'd fried the spicy link in beer with red peppers and an onion. Throughout the tavern, the air smelled garlicky and delicious. The front door was unlocked for business, but Buddy was alone. He had an hour until the lunch rush started.

Raining outside. But Buddy didn't notice. Blinds pulled shut. The air conditioner running. A Brewers game on the radio. Buddy liked to listen to baseball. It reminded him of his boyhood, freed him to do things in the tavern. If customers came in he'd turn on the Sony over the bar.

When he bought the place a year and a half ago, it was in a shambles. The roof was saggy and dripping under a heavy snow. He saw puddles on the nicked, brandy-colored wooden floors. Frost glared in the windows. Thick icicles crowded the glass, as if the building were on the verge of being swallowed by some enormous winter beast.

The bar itself displayed an ancient hunk of mahogany more like stone than tree. The booths were torn-up. Tables rocked on unsteady legs. No two chairs matched. Even in the cold—with no fire burning in the huge-mouthed, grimy fireplace—the air was fusty.

From the road, the place gave the impression of a large house whose owner had built additions over time to entertain a growing number of friends. The dark brown wood, bordered with tan trim, represented simplicity in contrast to the hodgepodge of add-ons that extended in three directions away from the central rooms. The tavern's appearance was telling.

Built as a weekend retreat for a man whose wealth came, truck by truck, from a granite quarry blessed with deep and wide deposits, the house stood empty even when it was new. Relaxation, solitude, Wisconsin—the man saw little value in these. He had purchased the land on a whim, encouraged by a lumber salesman while the two men hunted deer. Spurred by the excitement of shooting a six-point buck, he hired a contractor who'd put up summer homes for three fellow businessmen. The quarry owner insisted on the oversized fireplace and the spacious square footage. He called his retreat "The Lake," but the property offered no direct lake access. The number of lakes he passed on his drive stuck in his memory. With his three sons and wife in tow, he made less than a dozen weekend trips to the cabin, each one rife with boredom and bitter monologues concerning his investment.

After his death, the Lake passed into the hands of his least-loved son. Out of favor with his father—because he wasn't competitive, hated sports, and liked to share—this middle son had many friends. They made up for what his father withheld. As a final gesture, half insult, his dead father gave him a house in the cold.

Russ Boorman threw great parties. Beer and fried fish. Tequila when the moon rose. Summertime, he'd move a jukebox onto the deck, weather permitting. People danced in its sugar-candied glow. Russ reveled, but he had to worry too. Money from his mother wouldn't go far. It went far enough. He transformed the Lake into the Black Chimney.

Russ served modestly priced hearty fare to stout folk. The tavern thrived.

Russ died on his seventieth birthday. It was a good run considering all the booze, smoke, and beefsteak. Death came on a sunny November morning, his heart stopping before breakfast. A carload of pals and an orange-frosted carrot cake, en route, arrived to find him slumped at the table. A celebratory shot of ginger schnapps, poured but never tasted, beside his ear.

The business traded hands and took a downward slide. Regulars stopped going. Tourists didn't bother. But sustained failure never closed the doors. The establishment lacked the energy to perish. Days passed where the fry cook and barkeep ate the only meals, uncapped the evening's only beers. Stoned drunks banned from every other Gunnar watering hole formed the new clientele.

The old tavern, mired in neglect and decay, was perfect. Exactly what Buddy had been looking for, and he wrote a check and called his lawyer an hour after stepping through the door.

During the remodeling, Buddy lived in the two-bedroom apartment on the second floor. The living quarters were worse off than the bar. The previous occupant was an alcoholic snow-plow driver. He totaled his truck during a freaky September storm and was forced to move to North Carolina, where his sister kept a trailer. He sold the kegs in the basement to buy his bus ticket.

After lunch, Buddy fished a cigar from his shirt pocket. He peeled away the wrapper and dropped it in the pebbled glass ashtray resting on the bar. He bit the cigar tip and rolled the Honduran leaf against his tongue. He struck a match and puffed until a small gold cloud formed around his head. Buddy opened his wallet and removed a folded Xerox of Melissa Teagles' picture. He spread the page out on his thigh, pinned it there with his thumb, and stared down through the smoke at the black-and-white photocopy of a student looking up from her college books, obviously caught off-guard, but smiling, happy for the diversion.

Most of the time, Buddy was too busy to think back on the murder. He knew no way to comprehend it. Maybe it was simple. She talked to someone she should've run from. The sheriff's investigation turned up nothing promising. Some maniac killed a girl. Fed a fantasy with her pain. Girls have always died for such reasons. The beast born in men's minds had to touch flesh to come alive. End of story.

Buddy wanted no part in it.

Before news spread of his grisly discovery, but on the same day, Buddy arrived at the tavern and opened late for lunch because the sheriff detained him to get a statement. It was clear the sheriff's list of suspects would include him. The Guy Who Found the Hand. Problems with Sheriff Rafferty were a growing hassle in Buddy's life.

Buddy had no suspects. He wasn't a cop. Far from it.

Finding the hand of a dead girl was doubly unnerving. It occurred to Buddy that a connection with his past was possible. Not plausible, he decided, though he pondered the thought for several nights from deep beneath a reservoir of Glenfiddich.

Late in the afternoon on the day of the search, Vic had come by to drop off the flyers showing Melissa's most recent photo. He carried them in a brown grocery sack. Buddy hosed water down the steps and watched Vic approach through a hot slanting sun.

He hadn't been told.

Buddy filled him in on the sad facts. They weren't sure yet that it was Melissa. Tests had to be performed. But the odds were bad. A young woman's hand had been snatched from the river. Melissa was dead. The sheriff wanted volunteers to help look for the rest of the body. Vic turned away, pale and speechless. He braced himself against a porch column. Buddy sent him home with a cold beer. After rewinding the hose, he took the flyers in the office and tossed the sack of copies in the garbage.

But one he kept.

Several times since the homicide, he took the paper out. As if by studying the girl's likeness, he could conjure up her killer. All he saw was a pretty girl.

Buddy got up and walked behind the bar. He dragged the wastebasket from the hollow beneath the cash register. Pensive, locked in bloody thoughts, he stood still while cigar smoke feathered up his arm. He picked up a pen from next to the register and scribbled circles over Melissa's picture until he covered her image. Rings of blue ink screened her off, let her fade. Buddy's stogie burned down an inch, and he tapped a cylinder of white ash in the round, dark green, metal can, then lit the crumpled sheet of paper and watched it burn. He heard the door at the back of the kitchen open and close.

"That cigar smells like crap."

Margot Ladd, the twenty-five-year-old woman who lived in the upstairs apartment and waited tables six nights a week at the Black Chimney, rushed in and dropped her car keys on the bar. The key chain was a pink-haired troll. On the ring were four keys and a Swiss Army knife.

"My child doesn't need his new clothes smelling like a poker table." She deposited her son on the end of the bar, tucking a tie-dyed beach towel under him.

They were both dressed in pool clothes. The two-year-old wore navy overalls sporting rows of tiny white tugboats. His mother filled out a peach one-piece under sea-green running shorts. Margot had her damp chestnut hair pulled back in a ponytail. Her cheeks were pink from swimming. The boy stood up on the bar and looked at Buddy. Big green eyes like his mom. Smiling eyes.

"Bud-dee!"

Buddy snuffed out his cigar.

"Watch it there, little man." He put a hand on the toddler's elbow.

"I've seen you serve fishermen who couldn't walk half as well."

Buddy reached behind the bar for a pint glass. He pulled out the dishrag and emptied half a dozen crankbaits onto the counter. He'd already cut off the hooks and split rings.

Duncan cried out, "Fishy, fishy, fishy!" He scooped up a clown-pattern Shad Rap and put it in his mouth.

"I think your son's part bass." Buddy eased the lure away from the boy and swam it through the air.

"So he's half fish and not a paying customer. We can take care of one of those complaints." Margot slapped her palm down. "Bring us two shots of Cuervo!"

Her eyebrows wrinkled when Buddy turned to fetch two shot glasses and a tequila bottle. She went along with his joke. He split a lime with his pocketknife and produced a saltshaker from a slot under the bar.

"You two been swimming in the river?"

Margot shook her head. "We're taking lessons at the high school. Duncan is learning how to hold his breath underwater."

"Not easy for a bass boy."

Buddy sprinkled the salt onto the web of skin between his thumb and index finger. He held Margot's free hand, salted it likewise. Her son rattled a plastic perch. Buddy raised his shot glass. *Twenty years ago, babe, you would've had my full attention.*

"To the little man and his good-looking momma," he said.

Margot met his glass with hers in a midair click. She tried to read his thoughts by looking in his eyes. A romantic notion, but she'd been short-changed on romance so far, hadn't she? Buddy's dark eyes were a pleasant place to go until you had to turn around because they were dead ends. *You can't get there from here*, they said.

She ate salt, downed the liquor, and sucked her bitter wedge of fruit.

•

He wakes in sunshine. The rain weighed him down. Goatskinner hasn't been out of bed. A halo of urine has blossomed underneath him. On his nightstand, empty bottles of White Horse scotch and Gordon's vodka stand attendant: his nurses. A baggie of pot and box of Zig-Zag rolling papers sit between them. Comet showers of hot matches and lit cigarettes have burnt a spatter of brown eyes into the top of the nightstand. The clean window glistens with the look of sheeting water. His belly hurts. He coughs and aggravates his raw throat, sore from smoking and dehydration. Goatskinner craves a hot fudge sundae. He can't remember burning his thumb, but a watery blister throbs in the center of it, the size of a dime. On his bed, twenty or more unsleeved records lie scattered. They rub when he shifts on the mattress. He swings his legs over the bedside, and a pile falls to the floor. Some are scratched to the extent they're unplayable. He rummages through the collection, selects one, and brings it over to the turntable pushed against the wall opposite where he sleeps. His fingers shine with calluses, the digits misshapen like blunt horns, knuckles bulging from being broken in small accidents and a touch of arthritis inherited from his mother. He's chewed the nails to the quick and infections redden the corners. After a few seconds of fumbling with buttons and knobs, the tinny sound of an alto saxophone dodges haphazardly through the beginning of a solo. Goatskinner goes to the grocery store. But he'll have to return because he's forgotten his wallet, his money.

All the while, Dixieland jazz is streaming through the empty rooms.

●

Margot plugged in the jukebox, inserted six quarters from the tip jar, and punched in numbers from memory. Springsteen, Neil Young, Emmylou Harris, Tom Petty, The Pretenders. She finished with a honky-tonk ballad by Jerry Jeff Walker that she knew was a favorite of Buddy's. The first song cued up. The sad vibration of a harmonica triggered a vision of deserted highway cutting between cornfields, stalks wind-bent, all washed in rusty sunset. She used an old butter knife to pry hard gum and crud from the undersides of the tables. Squatting under the furniture made her feel girlish. A fossilized hunk of Wrigley's spearmint popped off into her palm.

Her mom watched Duncan in the evenings. She'd helped out since he was born, after Margot quit the junior college. Pre-Duncan, they hadn't been getting along too well. Now they were both women, both mothers without men, and that seemed to level things. Make them an even pair.

Margot peeked through chair slats at Buddy, who leaned on the bar top talking with Vic Presser about outboard motors.

Buddy was a natural listener. She thought he had a priest's face, a priest who played a lot of golf. His skin was a weathered handsome–dusky, sun-worn, and creased as a shell when he frowned or smiled. He followed people's stories right along, picked up the telling details, knew when to laugh at small mishaps, when just to shake his head, keep quiet, and pour another drink. His moods frightened Margot a few times. Anger spilling over like gasoline sloshed past the lip of an unsteady drum. She learned to read his signs, and, when necessary, gave him the room and solitude he required to resurface. He had waves of gray in his black hair. To Margot, he looked Greek. Once she told him so. He said his grandparents came to America from Eastern Europe. As always, he left out the specifics. Buddy gave up little about his past. He loved to sit down and talk over a beer, but he limited conversations to the outskirts of his life. Margot knew that he had lived in Chicago for more than twenty years before moving north, he was not gay (she could tell), and as far as she ever witnessed, he had no one close to him. Just a brother whose calls Buddy took with the office door closed.

She overheard the conversation Buddy and Vic were having.

"...the cheap flywheel breaks, and when the cord whips out, it takes off the tips of two of his fingers." Vic held up his hand to show which two were maimed. He continued. "The doctors couldn't reattach them because they landed, plop plop, out there in the lake. Okay, well, Dwyer says he didn't really care." Vic paused for a sip of beer. "Now Mrs. Dwyer? She's got an altogether different opinion. I'll tell you that for sure."

Buddy smiled, delivering a bottle of Pabst between Vic's fluid-stained fists. Vic had his arms spread out, buttressing the weight of his torso, as two boilermakers merged with his bloodstream and he swayed upon a precarious high-padded stool. The red-orange crumb of a cigarette glowed in his right hand like a flashy gemmed ring. Buddy relit his own dead cigar.

Margot often wondered why Buddy guarded his solitude. She fantasized exotic schemes to fill in his past: retired diamond thief, rogue spy, billionaire jaded by high society. Ultimately, Margot fabricated his biographies around a tortured love affair. What femme fatale wounded him? At idle times in the bar, she projected herself into the role of this vixen. But in a more frequent, and more realistic, scenario, she was able to see herself as the woman who would resuscitate Buddy. Seduce him back into the vital world.

*

"Glory, Laurie, what's your story?" Augustus asks the waitress as a smile bends the corner of his mouth into a fishhook. Her red name tag reflects sunlight from the windows and shines bright enough to make him wince. Augustus notices her hair's hennaed and sprayed stiff into glassy curls. Her lipstick is a shade of cherry too black, too thickly applied. She has an ugly smile, he thinks, like an open cut.

"Honey, you don't have enough time to spare, and I wouldn't want you to lose your appetite," the waitress croaks and dances her fingertips on his upper arm.

Augustus has forgotten the question she's answering. He orders a perch filet sandwich and french fries. He flips his coffee cup and she fills it. Automatic. She ignores his trembling hands as he broadcasts sugar grains across the counter, tearing apart six packets in succession. He can't hold on to the stainless-steel creamer. It clanks down on his saucer and spills out a puddle of half-and-half. She brings him extra napkins and disappears through swinging doors into the kitchen to put in his order.

Tropical colors pepper the air. Oil stains miraculously inject into space. They bloom from nothing like cartoon-sized monster flowers. Gaudy smears paint objects.

"Dying," he thinks.

Afloat, iridescent tendrils are enveloping him, gripping his body like the suckered arms of a giant squid. He listens for the wolf bark of a god he believes in. Purple bats fly wild, crisscrossing as they approach. The floor gapes.

"This is mine. I'm dying." He is sure as he waits for the frigid washing-over of pure fear. Plummeting. Entering a kaleidoscope the same way waste finds a sewer. Well walls veer past him. In his folded arms he carries a dead dog. Dizziness attacks him. He feels like he's choking. Choking in a restaurant.

"Yes, I am in a restaurant," he speaks aloud to himself. He counts. The chromatic nightmare subsides. Piecemeal his normal vision restores itself, each image joining its partners, snug as cardboard puzzle cutouts.

Sweaty, clammy as a salamander, Augustus stares at a foil balloon that jerks its face in the window. A yellow string connects downward to a kindergartner's wrist. Two mothers are talking. The cement sidewalk beneath them is buckled and craggy. In one crack a lost Hershey Kiss melts. The blonde child, a girl, pinches at ants in between her shoelaces. Augustus can hear the women through the glass. Underwater voices.

"Some girl got killed. He found part of her in the river behind his house."

"What part of her?"

"They're saying it was her hand."

"Sick."

Augustus waits for more. In his mind, his ear touches the cool window. He concentrates. But the child is shrieking and the voices are lost.

"Would you like water?" The waitress is back from her smoke break.

Augustus nods.

•

"This the place?"

"One of them."

"Kind of rundown."

The two men's eyes were adjusting to the change in light from outside. They picked a table away from the music. Both men carried guns, but only one of the four pieces was noticeable to an untrained observer. They ordered beer.

"She's fine," the out-of-towner said as the waitress went for their drafts.

"It's the land."

"Something in the soil makes the girls here sexy?"

"No. Before. What you said about it being a rundown dump?"

"Oh, yeah."

"Well, this spot is prime. Woods on three sides. River at the bottom of the hill. Easy access from the highway. Once the leaves fall, it's a clear view to the State Park. Winter wonderland, if you're into that."

"Enough people are."

"Snowmobilers. Cross-country idiots. We've got miles of trails. Miles. And you know what was big last year?"

Their beers arrived. The man with the blond mustache sipped his while he thought of an answer.

"You'll never guess," the other said. He usually knew all the answers to the questions he asked before he asked them. It was a strange way to have conversations.

"Okay."

"Goddamn snowshoes."

"No kidding."

"Never catch me out there. Below zero. Freezing my nuts. Watch them turn black and fall off."

"Pretending you're some kind of mountain man."

"Exactly."

Both men had badges. One wore the badge on his chest. The other had it clipped to an ID in his jacket pocket, riding along-side a Marlboro hard pack and two sticks of clove gum.

"So he outbid you," the out-of-towner said. He took out a Marlboro and tapped it, unlit, against the worn tabletop.

"He overpaid. You think it looks bad now, you should've been here."

"Looks like business is hopping."

The lawman with the badge on his chest and the gun belt pointed to the door swinging out from the kitchen. "That's him."

The detective, who was also a cousin to the man sitting across from him, used a match from the clean ashtray. He took a long drag on his cigarette. Studying the owner in the kitchen light, he squinted. He leaned forward on his elbows. "You're not going to want to hear this."

"Tell me."

"I know him. Name's Bayer, no, Bayes. Buddy Bayes, right?"

Sheriff Rafferty nodded. The beer in his mouth turning warm as he waited to swallow. He set the glass mug aside.

"We questioned him a couple years ago. Armored cars. This crew took down three in two weeks. Got a tip Bayes was the chief. It went nowhere. These guys were smooth. Clockwork jobs on those cars, man. Nice payout. No hitches. Heat came on and they quit. Took discipline, pulling them off so fast and close together."

"And what happened?"

"Shit. Nothing happened. I mean he's standing over there mixing drinks, right?"

"So he's a fucking thief."

"Word was he was a heavy-duty planner. Big jobs and big risks. But there's no recent paper on him, so that says something too."

"What's it say?"

"Says he's smart."

Rafferty finished his beer in silence. His cousin from the Chicago Robbery Investigative Unit eyed the girls coming and going. Rafferty stood up. He motioned that they were leaving.

"So am I getting this one?" his cousin said. His hand sliding over to the pocket of his duck pants.

Rafferty shook his head. "Let him put it on my tab."

Both men smiled, walked out.

•

The phone rang. Margot was busy with customers. Buddy didn't want to pick it up. He was watching. Phone again. Watching Rafferty and the Chicago cop walk out on their check. Chicago had pulled him in, sweated him about the armored cars. Buddy remembered. Ring, ring, ring. Margot looking back at the bar, catching his eye, her face sent him a question. *Why don't you pick that thing up?* Eyes still on the closing front door, Buddy went for the receiver. He got an earful of his own voice. The office answering machine taking the call. He hung up the receiver. He'd catch the message in a minute. No, he'd get it now. In the office. Alone. He excused himself from the drinkers across the counter. Signaled Margot, making a phone with his fingers. Pointing to the office. He had to get in there and think. His tripping hammer heart telling him life was about to get ugly again.

He shut the door. Left the light off.

Blinking green button.

So it wasn't a hang-up. Jab. And it's a different voice from the past, bumper to bumper with the face that had just stiffed him.

Buddy thumbed the volume higher. His brother, on his cell, another Chicago hookup.

"We gotta talk. Something's wrong. It's about that girl who got killed by your place. You need . . . (A hand on the phone, muffling . . . *No. That's Zo you're looking for. Over by the speakers. In the yellow. He'll help you out.* Distorted guitar starting up, molasses-slow. Drumbeats rolling in, a man shouting into a microphone, *Hell yeah . . . bring it. Bring it on.*) Sorry. Bud, that girl . . . she's . . . there's some complicated stuff, okay? You call me soon as you can. Call."

Buddy hit *Erase*. Wished he had that one working on his life.

•

Margot boosted a tray loaded with mugs and two pitchers of red beer above her shoulder and headed for a table of out-of-towner college students. They all wore corduroy baseball caps, men and women alike. The longest hair at the table belonged to one of the men. He stood up to help Margot with the beer. Tall. Smooth, lean, rock-climber muscle. Onyx crosses dangled from his ears.

"Hey, thanks," Margot said, letting him take the tray out of her hands.

He flashed a perfect smile, glossy white. Rather than turning to give his friends their drinks, he paused holding the tray. His biceps were flexed, cocoa-brown against his white cotton tee shirt. Margot was close enough to be enshrouded by his cologne and the piña colada sweetness of his suntan lotion.

"I have a question for you. We're retreating back into the woods when we finish off this beer. I know that won't take us long. We have a huge cabin. Our jet skis are over on Dark Cloud. And, anyway, we're going to have an intimate party. It'll probably last until morning. I'm inviting you. I think you'd have a good time, and I personally want you to come and enjoy yourself."

Margot bent forward and whispered in his ear, "Sorry, I can't. I forgot to take my pill this morning and I'm strictly a bareback girl." Giving no further explanation, she walked, extra feline, into the ring of shadow around the bar. Laser holes burned in the pockets of her Levi's.

"Maybe one more lap. His eyes haven't fallen out of his head yet," Buddy said. "Never mind, there they go." He waited for the slow smile. Hot blood lighting up her bad angel face. There it was. *Oh, a smile like whiskey in a hard driving rain.* He tried to concentrate on that smile and shut the door from Chicago that was opening again, letting all kinds of misery backwash into his new life.

Margot selected a red plastic sword from a glass full of novelty picks and straws, stabbed an orange slice from the garnish container, and ate it, peel and all. In the mirror behind the bar, she watched Tommy Plunkett come through the door. The glass in the mirror was smoked and marbled with thread-thin bronze streaks. But she could see that Tommy had been drinking, and now he was looking for a brawl.

Tommy was Duncan's father.

Buddy noticed him, too. He motioned for Tommy to approach. It was a friendly wave, summoning him to step closer so they could exchange words with a degree of privacy in the crowded room. Tommy drifted over. His face remained stony, numbed by half a case of skunked beer. Jaw muscles twitching. A current of anger racing through him.

Margot flitted among the cozy tables at the other end of the restaurant. She passed him. He did not look. Buddy pulled a frigid Rolling Rock from the cooler that ran perpendicular to the length of the bar. The cooler's metallic hood slid off his wet elbow and banged shut. He fit the bottle into Tommy's slowly uprising hand. Tommy unscrewed it, killed half without taking a breath.

If it got physical, Plunkett had the advantage in size and strength. He'd been an All-State tackle in high school, drank his way out of a football scholarship to Michigan State, and since then he punished himself with weights and Nautilus machines. Buddy won in the category of experience, but he wanted to avoid the test. Besides compounding an already fucked-up evening, he wasn't sure he'd win. A nastier owner might whack Tommy with the aluminum bat under the register, but Buddy was trying to forget the blood on his hands, not dip into more.

"Tom, that one is on the house. Finish it and go. I don't want a repeat of the last time you were in here. I'm offering good advice. Take it and move on." Buddy spoke in a level tone. Left the man a man's way out of trouble.

Tommy stared back, speechless. Perhaps his soggy brain was trying to make sense of Buddy's warning. Then again, he might be coiling. He knocked off the rest of the Rock. Earlier in the night, he'd lost his cap, and now his hair stuck out in all directions, hay-colored blond, whitened where the sun bleached it dry. His gasflame-blue, bloodshot eyes ignited.

"Bet you never thought you'd be getting such a prime piece of ass at your age, Buddy." He rapped his knuckles against a wooden beam set in the wall. "You two do it with my son in the room, or does she shut him up and turn on some music?" Tommy acted out an ugly, distorted dance, his feet planted while he attempted to grind his hips and shake his arms over his head, writhing. People in the restaurant sitting too far away to hear thought he was telling a dirty joke. Those nearby tensed up.

"You're so hammered, Tom, you don't realize the lack of respect you're..."

Tommy spit in his face.

Forget the bat. Buddy was moving fast. He'd take his chances. Feel bad after he pounded Tommy's thick, polluted head into the floor.

Before Buddy could unhinge the section of bar top and step around, a massive figure rushed in, scooped Tommy up by the seat of his jeans, and turned with him, propelling their wedded bulk through the double doors.

"We're going to get a little air!"

They were gone into the warm night. Buddy breathed deeply through his nose. He made a gradual descent from the liquefied-bone, brain-flattening effects of an adrenaline high. Conversations picked up where they left off. Somebody punched up a song.

Buddy peered through the glass porthole in the door like a sailor checking on a storm. The storm was over. He saw Tommy, sitting, legs splayed, on the river rock–strewn parking lot. He was nodding, apparently apologizing. He held up his hands, as if to fend off blows striking from above. An oversized halogen lamp shed lime-silvery beams on the two men, Tommy and the man towering over him. The man demanded something. Tommy hesitated, and a Red Wing workboot stomped his knee. Tommy yelled and dug into his pocket. Buddy caught the glint of car keys as the bigger man hurled them far into the bushes. Then the man snagged Tommy by his collar, steered him toward the road, and kicked him, low and vicious, in the back. Tommy stumbled downhill to the highway. The other man returned to the bar. Buddy held open the door.

"Glad to help you out, Buddy."

"Weren't you a little rough?"

"No rougher than you were about to get, friend." A smile broke through his dense beard. "He's tough, he'll get along just fine. Needs to sleep it off."

"Let me buy you another whiskey."

"Don't mind if you do."

"How's business?"

"Enough to keep me busy and pay the bills," he answered, and acted shocked when Margot pulled herself up, using his arm for leverage, to give him a kiss on the cheek.

"Thanks," she said. "Buddy needs the backup. Tommy leave okay?"

"He went home to bed."

"Thanks again, Augustus. You're just a big teddy bear."

"Too sweet, darlin'. Hey, Buddy, where's that whiskey?"

●

Denver Denver Denver–Goatskinner flashes on gray slabs of rock with squiggling water falling off their edges. The gothic mountains brightened him. He killed a woman in a ditch there. Icy burning snowmelt seething at his hips. She had a dry sort of beauty, papery taut skin, frazzled wild hair that opened like a sea fan when he plunged her head under. Wilder and prettier in her drowning than when she tried to escape from him. At that time in his life, years ago, his actions were impulsive and sloppy. He was unaware of guiding voices. Early on, he felt only abysmal sadness. Now he embraced his impulsivity, saw it as improvisation. He could cut through the fog. A compass had entered into his possession. He had knowledge of cycles. Cycles powered his life. Never repulsed by what he did to people, he learned to be comfortable with his difference and to cherish his individual perspective. *Are we not just water? Change the direction of water, that's all I do,* he thought. *I kill no spirit. I play. The horror I cause is temporary and for me it is sweet peace. Give up my peace? I will not. A smart man lets the world presume him stupid.*

How far will the waitress go? Goatskinner bets all the way. From the back wall where the liquors are illuminated on tinted glass shelves, she seizes a hammer. It hangs by a black leather thong. She rings a bell and announces, "Last call!"

●

Margot turned the chairs upside-down on the tables.

The bar and restaurant were empty of patrons, door locks were bolted, and the kitchen help clanged pots and pans as they finished their nightly cleanup. Moths adhered to the window screens, fluttering their petal wings. Buddy pulled the chain switches on the neon beer signs and collected dirty ashtrays. He whistled songs Margot didn't know. His mind traveled elsewhere.

Margot felt tired, not sleepy but drained. Her feet ached from standing all night. She slipped off one of her scuffed loafers. She wondered if Buddy gave good foot massages.

The cook and dishwasher emerged from the kitchen, said goodnight, and let themselves out. For a few minutes, Buddy fiddled with the evening's receipts, sorting checks and charge slips, logging figures in a red vinyl-covered ledger, securing thin stacks of bills with rubber bands. He retreated into the coat closet he had refashioned into an office. As was his habit, he opened the safe alone with the door to the office closed. Buddy trusted Margot, but followed his routine. He had shut the safe and was about to spin the dial when he heard a shattering of glass in the bar. He rose from his crouch. One long stride crossed the tiny office. He hurried through the doorway.

He saw no one. Panic flared inside him. Then Margot's slender hand sprouted up from between the edges of two tables on the other side of the room. She waved.

"Broke one of the pitchers. Sorry."

"No problem. I'll get a broom." Buddy wondered if she noticed how jumpy he was.

He found a plastic broom and dustpan in the supply closet. Margot picked up the largest broken shards and piled them on the corner of a table. She moved them cautiously, avoiding the jagged edges.

"Look," she began, "I'll finish cleaning up this mess. It'll only take me a couple minutes."

"I'll help."

Margot swept the glass from under the table. She said, "Duncan's over at my mother's house tonight. We're taking a ride to Uncle Bill's farm tomorrow. They haven't seen him lately, and he likes the animals. Soon as I'm done here, I'm going upstairs."

Standing close. Buddy squatting with the dustpan, Margot bending into the broom. He looked up. She held his gaze for five heartbeats.

"You wouldn't want to stop up for a cognac, would you?" she asked.

Buddy cocked his head as if he hadn't made out the words.

"You know cognac?" she said. "It tastes like candy and smoke and it r-e-l-a-x-e-s you. People drank it like water in the seventies."

"When you were in grammar school."

"Hey, that's not fair."

"No?"

"I wasn't even in school." She grinned.

Buddy sat back on the floor, knees out. He took a deep breath and ran his fingers through his hair. "I'm a little . . ."

She arched an eyebrow. "Not sure?"

"No, I'm pretty sure. Just thinking. Look, I'm tired. Shot. This is . . . you caught me on a bad night, that's all."

"We could, maybe, improve it?"

"Oh, you're not making this easy. But that's good. I want to . . . ah." His hand was chopping slowly in the air.

"Give it a try?"

"Yes. Definitely. But not tonight, because . . . because I want to be at my best with you. And tonight my head's in a crazy place."

Margot look away, nodding, smiling. She put a hand down to help him off the floor. She squeezed. Let go once he was standing. Touched the buttons on his shirt. *"At your best, huh?"*

"Is that okay?"

"It is." She picked up the pan of glass, brushed in the large pieces from the table. "I'm wiped out, too. Soon as I hit the pillow, lights out."

"For me it may take a little longer."

•

Buddy felt great. Exhausted, anxious, horny, but great. The Chicago heat, the hassles with Tommy, and the swarm of weekend customers had taken a toll. The tension of the night left him edgy, wilted. But Margot's offer put him, mind and body, into overdrive. He was whistling as he gravitated to the plush seats of his burgundy Caddy parked in the far end of the lot. A little voice in his head said, *"She's still too young for you, pal."* He told the voice to go to hell. His brake lights flashed crimson in the window like the eyes of a dragon. He made his turn and sailed away.

•

Whoo . . . whoooooooo . . .

The owl hoot resonates in the vacant bar, sounding nearly like a person.

Whoo . . . whooooooooo . . .

Winding-down-machine noise.

Whooooooooooo . . .

The tail end swallowed up in a human mouth, and Margot hears it.

"Buddy? You back there?" she asks, her voice low, whispery, hoarse with fear, almost too soft to be heard in the darkened kitchen. Inching to the door's threshold, eyes bugged open, unblinking, she swipes at the light switch, misses.

Whoooooooooo . . .

"Tommy, that you?" she snaps. Accusing, shouting, doing her best to sound solid. Failing. Redness floods her throat and cheeks.

Whoooooooooo . . .

"Fuck you, whoever you are. This isn't funny. I'm calling the cops. I'm doing it right now, so you better get the hell out." Margot feels a warm breeze whiffling past. The wide kitchen window stands open like an oven door. Inside its frame, she sees only blackness, night air, nothing. She sniffs the perfume of wildflowers and the stench of weeds growing in the wooded lot. She backs away, a cautious shuffling, and raises the broomstick, gripping it tight in her fists, ready to swing. The bristles poke her ribs, but she's too charged to notice.

Goatskinner hides behind a freezer. His chin presses against the dimpled steel. He tosses his gift into the light pooled at Margot's feet. She chokes on a scream, studies the object causing her confusion.

A dead barn owl.

Heart-shaped face. Blank, killing eyes.

Using the broom, she jostles the bird.

Goatskinner lunges.

Margot smothers in a bear hug. He's squeezing, keeping her face pinned against his brawny, furred chest. Dull cracks pop within her; her rib cage starts to cave, and when he releases, she crumples to the floor. She's still breathing, and he's quick to cover her mouth and nose with a pea-green washcloth soaked in ether. He clamps down to defeat her coughs. When she's motionless, anesthetized, he gathers her up. Flops her limp body down on one of the tables. Her nose is bleeding.

Margot stirs. He tapes her wrists, her ankles. Slaps a silver patch over her mumbling lips. She's ready to travel. He slides off her shoes, chooses a little toe with pink polish. With his thumb and forefinger, he breaks it.

*

Buddy realized he forgot to spin the safe dial. He knew there'd be troubled sleep if he didn't go back. U-turn on the quiet highway. He lowered the window so the fresh night air would hit him. Half-wondered if he was going back for Margot. A second wind kicked in his sails. Gas pedal down, he spotted the alien eyes of a doe watching from the tree line.

*

The rear doorway explodes outward. Goatskinner lowers his boot, exits.

He scans the sky, clamps the owl under his arm. Starpoints stitch the heavens. Wispy gunsmoke clouds mask and unmask a pitted sickle moon. The moon: a rip in the sky, two-headed claw. Insect white noise sizzles in his ears. He punts the owl into a faraway thistle snarl.

Almost as if he has forgotten and then remembers, he reaches back into the kitchen, and with a single hand grabs Margot by the ankles, drags her over the doorsill, feet first, into the gravelly lot. From inside a deerskin pouch, he spills out an assortment of chalky tablets and motley capsules. He dry-swallows the bunch, drinks afterward—tiny nips from a bottle of Bombay gin stolen from the bar—he doesn't want to vomit the pills. Bored for the moment, waiting for the drug mix to kick in, he closes his hands and stares through latex-covered fists. He inspects Margot. He gawks again at the moon.

"Let's go there. Seas of dust and lonely gray mountains. You and me together setting up camp on the moon. All my ladies, too, for company. What do you say?" He doesn't look down but continues his lunar gazing. Space rock. Out of the clouds, it's free-floating—the jack-o'-lantern's carved eye.

Candlelight flickers in the trees.

No . . . *headlights.*

Rocks crackle under rolling tires. A car door creaks; Buddy steps out. He leaves the Caddy running. Goatskinner peeks around the corner of the building. He spews a stream of gibberish and wonders if Buddy might be a hallucination. No. The man's real presence alters his designs for the night, churns juices.

He hears Buddy calling the waitress's name. Sees him pace the floor, recognizing blood and beginning to piece things together.

Who has sent this man after him?

Answers multiply, a choir shrieks in his head, forcing Goatskinner out of his dream.

•

Buddy cranked the safe handle. He removed the unregistered S&W .38 from its holster, the leather suspended inside with strips of Velcro. He loaded the chambers. For eighteen months, since he left Chicago, he hadn't picked up the weapon with the intention of firing at anything but paper targets tacked to trees. His body felt compressed, thrust backward in time. So much running, so many private changes transpired. Yet the distance seemed negligible. Habits and old scores always found a way to reach him.

Keeping his eyes on the doorway, he gathered up the phone in the crook of his arm. He punched in Margot's number upstairs. No answer. He dialed the Sheriff's Department.

"This is Buddy Bayes, owner of the Black Chimney. We've had a break-in. Somebody's busted up the back door. Looks like they might've come in through a window. The girl who waitresses for me is missing. There's blood. This just happened. I left here a half-hour ago." The dispatcher told him officers and paramedics were on the way. He hung up.

The bar appeared deserted. Buddy went to the kitchen. The wooden door swung awry. Screws from the hinges lay scattered in the gravel. The intruder had rammed it from inside. *On his way out.* Buddy considered the possibilities. Vandals or Tommy returning after hours in a rage. He inspected the jimmy marks and splinters on the outside windowsill. Under the window, he found a crowbar in the dirt. He was careful not to touch anything.

No obvious trail emerged from the woods. The scrub grasses and weeds parted along footpaths. Ten or more lanes. Walking in offered bad odds and plenty of risks. Buddy heard sirens blaring, miles away. Despite his uncertainties, the familiar weight of the Smith & Wesson electrified him. Thoughts of Margot out there hurting pushed him on. He gambled, picked a path no thicker than a bicycle tire. After a minute, it was impossible to tell where he had gone in or even that he'd been there at all.

●

Reach the river. Reach the river. Goatskinner hears this mantra in his head.

Branches clatter as he bulls downhill, trampling everything, sinking into a smokeblue valley. Margot receives a savage lashing. She bounces on his big shoulder. Unseen barbs dig out flesh. He huffs like a bear. His ankle twists on a nub of powdery rock, and they crash through ropes of wet, greasy vegetation. They tumble over steep ground. Human shovels scraping together leaves, twigs, nuggets of deer scat, and other timberland detritus. The jarring assault stops on the bank.

Moonlit, the murmurous river glides by like an oozing brook of tar.

●

The cruisers wheeled up dust and flashed their carnival lights. Buddy almost turned back. He was making slow progress as he wormed ahead in the dark. He lifted his boot and set it back down, one short tentative step following another. Any evidence of a trail had disappeared, and the hidden ground dropped away by unpredictable degrees. In the canopy of branches overhead, chunks of deadwood dangled from straps of bark. He paused at the lip of a valley. The silver moonlight detailed an illusion of shrunken treetops ten yards straight ahead; he was a giant in the little people's forest. But really it was the land dropping sharply, then, across the valley, pitching upward forming an opposing ridge. He stood there, hesitating. Somewhere down in the middle of the valley, the Skin River unraveled.

Thunder in the trees below him, in a direct line to his left. Thrashing.

Buddy poked his way down the slope, zeroing in. He descended, the gloom thickened, and he became enmeshed. He flicked his revolver back and forth. Unlocking his arm from a wreath of saplings, he almost discharged the weapon, its barrel inches from his chest. Lacy spider webs encased his head. He rubbed them off with his free hand. He withdrew a penlight from his shirt pocket. Using it meant revealing his position, but not using it meant struggling in the maze of undergrowth. He twisted the mini-flashlight and aimed the light cone. He disentangled his legs. Traced the beam downhill. Drizzled blood stained a passage smashed through the forest clear to the river. There, two human forms lay side by side and unmoving.

Buddy focused his light on Margot. Her face was badly swollen. Only the whites of her eyes showed. She had duct tape over her mouth and blood leaking from her nose. He watched her rib cage, wanting to see her breathe. He saw stillness.

He moved closer.

The other figure roused, sat up, and turned away from him.

"Don't move," Buddy said. He pointed the light and the gun at the man's back. The man bent forward into his chest, concealing his features, a headless torso coming to life. One arm shifted, traveled into the folds of his denim jacket.

"Get your fucking hands in the air!"

But it was too late.

The man spun and snapped out his wrist, his fingers rigid and spread like a sideshow magician casting a spell. Buddy's flashlight caught the flicker of a twirling knife.

Sucker punch. Keen steel pierced his shoulder. Cutting through muscle and tendon, a blade whacking the joint. Bone handle protruding from his armpit. Buddy felt a gentle tugging as his blood spurted in quick warm jets. Stag's bone turned sticky red. Buddy couldn't steady the pistol. He fired two shots into the ground. His attacker dived headlong into the river. Buddy never got a good look.

•

Black water eddies at his throat. Hides him, conveys him. The river opens and holds him like a lover with many mouths. *Take me,* he pleads. Goatskinner floats under its veneer, drowning, submerged like a deadhead log. He rides over beds of rocks until the turbulent waters shove him to the surface where he guzzles back his life.

He lost a favorite knife.

Nothing will be forgotten or forgiven.

3

Dr. Hal Genesee entered Buddy's hospital room, closed the door, and pulled a chair from the corner to the bedside. The chair was embroidered with sunflowers, rubbed to faintness through use and age. Though the room had two beds, Buddy occupied it alone. The doctor sat down, saying nothing, reading another patient's chart he had brought with him. He wore square gold-framed bifocals. Buddy rested, propped up with extra pillows, sedated and temporarily subdued.

Morning sunlight pried at the bent, dusty metal blinds.

"How's she doing?"

"The same. She's still unconscious. Broken ribs, punctured lung, a hairline skull fracture. Lacerations and bruises on her chest, face, upper back, and neck. She aspirated vomit, nearly asphyxiated, when she reacted to the ether he used on her." The doctor paused, running his fingers through salt-and-pepper hair in need of a trim. His droopy mustache gave him the look of a movie gunfighter. Buddy noticed the bulge of a meerschaum pipe in his coat pocket. Dr. Genesee took it out and nibbled on the chipped stem. He smelled of cherry-blend tobacco and cough drops.

"How's the arm feel?"

"Like I almost got it chopped off."

Genesee smiled and thumped the bowl of his pipe on the bed sheets. "How'd it go with Sheriff Rafferty? The night nurse told me you two had a shouting match. He was making accusations?"

"Glen Rafferty was true to form last night. If you're looking for a moron good at hassling teenage Indians, then he's the man. Pouring free beer for men with badges? Call him in, pronto. Rafferty's as useless as a pecker on a priest."

"Well, if it's any comfort, most people around here would agree with you." The doctor's shirt collar was frayed, but Buddy noticed the crisp knot in his pale green necktie. Genesee's skin looked waxy and yellow like church candles. *Maybe it's the drugs I'm on,* Buddy thought. The painkillers made him feel buoyant, afloat in warmth. He licked his lips and tasted pennies in his mouth.

"I'm thirsty."

The doctor lifted a brown plastic pitcher from the nightstand and went into the hall. He returned after filling it half with ice chips, half tap water. "Drink slowly," he advised. "I'll come back to visit this afternoon."

When he was gone, Buddy washed down two cups of the cold slush in quick succession. His thirst abated. He shivered, his front teeth rang hot with pain, and a dull ache crept behind his eyes. Afterward, he settled into the hospital version of sleep.

Dreaming of Margot facedown in the river as he fished around her still body.

•

"Is this Kurt?"

"Yeah. What can I do for you?"

"Kurt, this is Augustus. I need some help, man. A guy cut me with a bottle in a bar fight in Hurley, and I've got no insurance, but I need somebody to stitch me up. You know I'm good for payment. And bring some of your friends by, the ones I met at Josie's wedding."

"I wish you hadn't called me at the hospital. Don't make it a habit, okay? My shift ends in about fifteen minutes. You at home?"

"No, I crashed at the Rainy Days. It's on Highway 63 south of Spooner."

"Shit, man, that's almost a two-hour drive for me one way. I ain't driving way the fuck out there. I gotta be back here to work a double starting at midnight. Clean the cut with peroxide and tape it up with butterflies. You'll be fine."

"No. I want you to do this for me, Kurt. I'll pay you two hundred. Cash. I got the bills right here. You sew me up and they're yours. That's easy money, friend."

"Nothing easy about it."

Silence.

In the mildew-spotted bathroom mirror, Augustus reexamines the wicked diagonal gash across his forehead. Scales of dried blood flake into his eyelashes. He blinks and waits for Kurt's response. He's got an ice pack made from two pillowcases saddled on his head. They're wet and turning pink.

Kurt says, "Okay, I'll be there. Gimme three hours. I've gotta go to my place to pick up some supplies first."

"Great. The best, my man Kurt comes through in the clutch. Room 14. Second-floor terrace, on the end."

"Hey, you got any beer?"

"Fresh out."

"Well, I guess I'll be bringing that, too."

"Right, great. Buy a case, okay?"

"You owe me."

"I gotcha covered." Augustus rustled two hundred-dollar bills into the phone. "And I hope to see you real soon."

"I'll be there. Bye." Click.

•

Vic stopped by to deliver a fresh shirt and a box of cigars. Buddy had called the gas station at lunchtime, explaining that the paramedics had cut up his shirt. The White Owls were a get-well present.

Buddy changed into his street clothes, preparing to go home. Genesee brought him a sky-blue cotton sling and showed him how to wear it. Then he wrote a prescription for codeine. Left-handed, they shook and parted company.

Buddy looked in on Margot. It was like she was sleeping in a nest of dreary linen and plastic tubing.

Anger crackled in his head and he had to shut it down. It was no good here. His shoulder was killing him. He was teetering like a drunk. Pissed and staggered.

Margot's mother had gone to the vending machines for coffee and a package of cheese and crackers. Myrtle Ladd was a lady who had survived dirt yards and two abusive husbands. Margot's unplanned pregnancy recalled her own mistakes. They broke from one another, not even speaking during the nine months. Two floors up in the Maternity Ward, while Margot was screaming and pushing, Myrtle began, in her awkward, halting way, to forgive her daughter. Now her baby girl fought to survive. Myrtle returned, shuffling, with the stoop and wrinkles of sixty years. In October she'd turn forty.

Buddy held the door with his good arm, as much for balance as to be polite. Myrtle's baggy red sweater caught on the knob and it took her a few seconds to free it. Buddy saw the shadow of someone hovering outside the doorway. Myrtle spoke up, "Deputy Sherry wants to know if you need a ride home."

●

"Can I smoke in this car?"

"Sure, just crack the window."

The deputy would never wear out a set of brakes. Buddy lost focus of the landscape as the car hurtled along. His shoulder throbbed.

"I know my boss gave you a hard time last night. He doesn't like you much."

Buddy raised his eyebrows, unimpressed with the obvious. He resumed looking out the window. Dull golden sunrays lit the grass fields between stands of skinny pines.

"I don't know why that is. Do you?" the deputy asked.

Buddy didn't bother to turn around. The smoke moved like vapors rising off his skin.

"Do you want to tell me what's going on?" he asked again.

Buddy regretted accepting the ride. He wished there were a radio playing so he could raise the volume. Drown out the deputy's questions.

The deputy said, "Okay, fine."

Serpentine blacktop vanished beneath the tires. Heat radiated off the road in shimmering waves. The deputy gulped lemonade from a wet bottle that had no label. Ice cubes, seeds, and peels whirled inside.

"I wonder if you could describe to me, to the best of your recollection, what happened after you returned to your restaurant and called for emergency services." Deputy Sherry did his best to sound professional.

Smoke blown from Buddy's lips hung in the deputy's face before it carried out the window into the cruiser's slipstream. "In light of my conversation with your boss, I feel better not saying anything without my lawyer." Buddy turned in his seat now and stared at the side of the deputy's shaved head. He had a trio of tiny red moles on his earlobe.

"Mr. Bayes, I really don't give a shit about your beef with Rafferty. I have a personal stake in this investigation. I don't know if she told you, but Margot and I had, you know, a relationship for a while. She used to pal around with my kid sister when they were in high school. I had a big-time crush on her. But I was quiet. And married. After my divorce I figured what-the-hell. Called her on the phone and asked her out." Sherry paused long enough to cross the solid double yellow lines and overtake a semi battling uphill. "Girl can drink, I'll tell you that. We spent some nights at my house. Pretty nice. But nothing earthshaking happened. We still dated. Saw each other when we had free time. Then we ran out of things to talk about. That bothered her. Neither one of us was looking for love, so not finding it wasn't huge. No regrets, is what I'm saying. Not for me, anyway."

The deputy shifted in his seat, making himself taller in the confined space, and said, "It really hurts to see her. Like she is now, I mean. She told me you have feelings for her. Listen; maybe I can help you with Rafferty. But in return I'm asking what you saw. Then you stand back. Let me do my job." He loosened his grip on the steering wheel. But the tension never left his neck. If he were straining to break a collar button, he was doing fine.

Buddy gritted his teeth. He'd never even seen Margot with Carl Sherry. People must have known about them if she'd been staying at his house. But Buddy hadn't heard a whisper. They traveled in different circles, shared few acquaintances outside of customers. Still, he figured he would have picked up on something. Jealousy folded his thoughts into ugly shapes. Margot kept a few secrets too. Buddy didn't trust Sherry, and he wasn't in the mood to explain the unregistered .38 he had chucked into the river.

He started lying.

"There's not much to tell. I went out behind the Chimney to look at the damage. I heard someone walking in the woods. So I followed. The guy who had her—and I'm guessing he was alone because I didn't see anyone else—he was heading for the river. I tackled him. The three of us fell. He had a gun. We went down. Struggled. He fired into the dirt. Then, I guess the pistol jammed or he panicked, because he pulled a knife and stabbed me. He jumped in the river. The gun went with him."

"So you saw this scumbag up close?"

"It was pretty damned dark..." Buddy's voice trailed off. He studied his cigar.

Let the deputy dangle.

The cruiser barreled down a straightaway.

"You can't give a description?" Sherry asked, sounding unconvinced. His eyes were turning pink from the smoke.

"Not unless I make it up." He wondered if the deputy would buy his story. Fought the urge to salt in a few more lies.

Deputy Sherry almost missed the turn to Buddy's cabin. He had to pull the car around a sharp left. Buddy pressed hard into the door. Pain torched his shoulder. The hidden entrance, without a signpost and veering under a canopy of trees, was easy to overlook. The gravel road divided several times into private driveways. Buddy's driveway was the last before the deadend. Railroad ties defined a lane.

Sherry aimed his cruiser between them.

A storm line was blowing in from the west. Fast-moving, black-and-pewter thunderclouds charged across the evening sky. Distant lightning strikes reached the ground and incandesced like bare wires. Huge raindrops snapped the leaves. After getting out, Buddy hurried to the cabin. The deputy's voice followed with a reminder.

"Keep in touch."

•

Kurt knocks on the motel room door. He carries a twenty-four pack of chilled Bud. All-American colors plastered on cardboard. Over his shoulder, a red duffel bag, its canvas mottled by bleach stains. He nudges his sunglasses so they rest high on the bridge of his nose, touching the slope of his sweating forehead.

They're cheap. The lenses bulge out like shiny black bubbles. Kurt thinks they make him look like a human wasp. *Waspman.* He wears his hair combed back with a lot of gel, and it's gritty from a long stretch between showers. The hot water isn't working in his building. He knocks again.

Augustus searches the thick brown curtains, paddles a divide between the folds, and peers out. He sees Kurt, disengages the deadbolt, and jerks the door open so forcefully that Kurt's first thought is he's been stung. Drug bust is the last thing he needs. Augustus calms him, gets him inside.

Three injections of Lidocaine. A couple of "friends" tapped out of a smoke-gray vial labeled: Hospital Pharmacy. The stitches go in easy. Augustus collapses his third beer can and interrupts Kurt's sewing to reach over and claw another one from the case. He pops the tab and a tiny geyser foams to meet his whiskered upper lip. Kurt soaks cotton balls in Betadine, uses them to clean the wound. Rusty stains dry on Augustus' forehead. Kurt waits for his patient to take a drink, keeping his gloved hands positioned away from his body, his wrists relaxed, swiveling limply like those of a hairdresser in the middle of a dye job. Augustus leans into the mirror, grins, looking up and admiring the coarse bug-leg threads of each finished stitch.

●

The doorbell.

Buddy picked up a short-handled axe from the woodpile next to his stove. He looked through the glass and the rain. Embarrassed, he dropped the axe behind his sofa. He opened the door and the wet man outside took up most of the doorway. The wet man had a bottle of Glenfiddich and new stitches. He also had Buddy's mail taken from the box on the road.

"Thought you might want to blow a little steam," Augustus said.

"What happened to your face?"

"I drink too much."

"Not a bad idea. Let me get us glasses." Buddy moved off to the kitchen.

Augustus put the mail on an end table and waited where he was. There was no door between them, just an arch. Cabinet doors creaked and thudded shut. Buddy tossed a hand towel in his general direction. Augustus dried the rain from his face and the bottle. Buddy sat down, coughed, and almost dropped the glasses from his weakened hand. Augustus saved them.

"You better pour," Buddy said.

"Bastard did a number on you, huh."

Buddy took the offered drink, knocked it back. "I'll live."

"Where'd you get cut?"

"Shoulder." Buddy shrugged. "It hurts, but fucking everything hurts these days."

Augustus wore hand-tooled leather bands around his wrists. Snakes biting their tails. He wore heavy earrings in both ears. A blue, rain-soaked bandana noosed under his beard. Today, his hair was braided. Stray hairs frizzed out electrically, wildly around his head as if the air crackled. His eyes were blood-speckled, unfocused.

Buddy guessed he was drunk or high. Or both. The man was

a slow-motion train wreck. Buddy knew you couldn't stop a train. Augustus was going to have to find the brake himself.

Augustus cleared his throat. "Margot's not gonna die, is she?"

"Don't know."

"That bad, huh?"

"I'd say so. Fruitcake whacked her around. Drugged her. God knows what else."

"Lucky you came back."

"Yeah." Buddy tried to refill his glass and ended up slopping scotch on the table. "Goddamnit." He screwed the bottle cap on. "If she pulls through, we'll have something to feel good about."

"She'll make it."

Buddy stared at the empty woodstove. Scotch and codeine were a sleepy one-two combo. The rain didn't help. Augustus shifted, and Buddy smelled a wave of damp sweat and stale marijuana.

"Hey, man, I gotta hit the road." Augustus was on his feet, stretching. He ducked by reflex when his fingertips brushed the low rafters of Buddy's cabin. "Fulfilling my Christian duty, you know, *visit the sick*. Give drink to the wicked."

Buddy tried to get up, but his legs insisted he'd be happier in the chair.

"You just sit there. I'll let myself out."

Augustus waved. Shut the door behind him against the rain. The bottle was close by. Buddy couldn't come up with a reason not to have another drink and go to sleep.

In his drunkenness, Buddy didn't notice the pile of mail. He woke up an hour after Augustus left. He flicked the kitchen light off, rinsed the glasses, and put away the Glenfiddich bottle. The floor tilted as if the cabin were drifting out to sea. Buddy shuffled into the bathroom where he conducted his business quickly in the dark. He didn't remember climbing into bed.

He came upon the stack of envelopes in the early hours, sober, when he went looking for water. Buddy didn't get personal mail. Just the usual bills and junk. But here was a cream envelope. His name handwritten in red ink. No return address. A Chicago postmark. The only person from Chicago who sent letters was Robbie. But Buddy never opened those, not since Robbie's visit to Gunnar. Buddy tore into the envelope. He read the one-page letter. Afterward, while dry-heaving in the bathroom, his bloodshot eyes rose to the glass, and he tried to deny the condemned man he saw staring back.

The Last Days, 20–

Dear Mr. Secrets–

Time's running out. Do you think you're fooling anyone with your good citizen act? I know about you. Didn't your parents teach you any morals?

I did the girl in your backyard creek. I almost got your whore/waitress too. Surprised?

I'm having so much FUN FUN FUN.

I think the sheriff likes you for these killings. Isn't that hilarious? I wonder what would happen if somebody called him and told him where to find Melissa's body? I wonder what would happen if it was under your house?

Happy Digging.

•

The evening sky mirrored the river's colors: dirty rain and clay. Birds were scarce, quiet. The forest seemed shut down. Mud sucked at Buddy's boots, offered dangerous footing, interchangeably locked and slippery. Hypnotized by the swift flow of the Skin, he walked its very edge. The floodwaters of his outlaw days burst through a wall of decent living eighteen months thick, rising.

He had taken a shovel with him into the crawl space. Worked his way underneath the surface soil, starting in the corners. Each time he went a foot deep, the shovel blade struck firm ground. Wall to wall, he turned up nothing but rocks. The trapped heat under the cabin was suffocating. Buddy's hangover banged and slithered before it finally died out. He took a shower to wash off the alcohol sweat. The letter was a bluff, but the questions it raised were real.

Was somebody going to try to frame him for Melissa's murder? Was Margot a victim of the same man who killed Melissa? If the attacks were connected, then what message were they trying to convey? Who wrote the letter? Every question spawned more. All the answers were bad.

Buddy didn't want to think about it, but he had enemies incapable of letting things go. Since getting out of Chicago a year and a half ago, feelings of safety, already lost, never returned. Buddy monitored his world with low-level paranoia. Parked cars signified triggermen. Behind the wheel of his own car, when he turned the ignition key, part of him braced for an explosion. Buddy knew his imagination exaggerated the power and number of his old enemies, but not by much.

Among them were vicious men who practiced retribution.

Time didn't heal transgressions. No scars formed over their memories. They would circle and circle around his life, scavenging, until he begged them to tear him to pieces. Soulless hyenas, they laughed as they lit people's worlds with pain.

Men intimate with grisly corpses.

It burned to think they hurt Margot because of him, and that she might be picking up part of the tab for his sins—that Melissa might've been sacrificed just to get to him. But these men were casual about loss: other people's loss.

A voice in his head rattled a list of names. Mug shots of hard faces matching the names flashed in his mind. *Buck Mendenthall, Archie "Chiller" Mercer, the Porter brothers, Angel Jimenez.* He'd stolen from them all, but they'd shorted and skimmed his cut more than enough to make up the difference. They had their angles. He had his. Unpleasant endings, but everyone profited. No one was totally happy. It was good business, shaved deals that finished square because all the players cheated. Ultimately it was a wash.

Otis Broussard, Sean Tingley, Cliff Strand. Doing time. Stateville, Menard, Pontiac. *Dickie Hoyt.* Shot in the face outside a honkytonk near Nashville. *Guy Fantozzi.* Got his neck broken in a fight at Fenway Park. *Big Mike Hollis.* Scorched himself trying to set fire to a lumberyard in Gary, Indiana. *Morgan Jaspers.* A girlfriend fixed him a hotshot and fed him hamburgers laced with ground glass.

Who was still around?

Buddy stopped walking, noticed the mud splattered to his knees. A wet black dog rambled toward him from the tree line uphill. A stray. Buddy had seen him off and on since the spring, though he hadn't looked as bony or as mean as he did today. A patch of hide torn from his haunches flapped against bloody fur. One ear stood rigid, the other was crimped over like a seashell. He didn't bark. Some kids had wound kite string around his tail, and he dragged three soup cans clunking through the grass. His manhood swung intact. No one had taken that yet. Maybe he had a few lucky days ahead of him. When he got closer, Buddy could see the dimness in his cloudy eyes, the snaggled rotten line of his dog smile.

"Come here, Boy."

The dog edged in closer, then dropped back a few feet. He repeated this ebb and flow, juggling fear and the need to interact. Buddy unwrapped a strip of beef jerky he was carrying in his pocket. He held it out between his fingertips.

"It's okay, Boy."

The dog's taste for meat overrode his caution. He ate the jerky, holding still for a pat on the head and a rub behind the ears. Buddy gathered slack from the kite string and cut it with his pocketknife. The dog bent around and chewed the knot from his tail. Then he whipped his shaggy head back and plucked the jerky wrapper from Buddy's fingers. The dog hunkered down in the reeds a few feet away, clamped the greasy plastic under his paws, and went to work ripping it apart. His tail swatted reeds back and forth.

Buddy remembered another dog, a skeletal Doberman who roamed the alleys behind Rush Street. That dog weathered freezing rains and snowstorms with the resilience of a savvy, drowsy hooker, always lingering in a vacant doorway or under an inch of awning to stay dry. Every so often somebody would feed the pooch a sack of leftover french fries. Around Christmas, if she was lucky, some coked-up bimbo would toss her an untouched steak. She'd feast and lie down in the snow, panting. One of the bouncers at Mother's named her India. Her two-toned coat, sand and oil, matched the cowboy boots worn by the man who kicked her to death: Red Mizel.

Nicknamed for his temperament, not the color of his hair, Red hated dogs. He had no love for Buddy, either. In Red's opinion, Buddy was the man responsible for his brother's death. And Red was the reason Buddy left Chicago.

Lester Mizel, Red's older brother by five years, lived on amphetamines and the juice he got from stealing sports cars. He had a rap sheet of drug charges and auto thefts that led up to the night he was killed. He boosted a gold Trans Am from the floor of a suburban dealership to use as the get-away for a job he was pulling with Buddy. When he picked Buddy up in the rain outside a Greektown bar, blue nuggets from the showroom's shattered window sparkled in the bumpers. Lester was flying, the stereo blared a techno-coke soundtrack, and against his better judgment Buddy went ahead with the job. It was a favor to Lester. They'd known each other since they were teenagers, swiping hubcaps in Lincoln Park. Before Lester turned into a junkie vampire.

Tonight they were taking down an Egyptian diamond peddler who fenced jewelry from North Shore home invasions. Buddy had a tip from a second-story man that the Egyptian, whose name was Sammy Rauf, would be carrying hot merchandise, in particular a high-priced necklace, back to his apartment when he left his Wabash offices. The necklace–a sleek, Art Deco, platinum chain studded with emeralds–should've fetched more than fifty grand from any fence in town. Now the burglar knew this fact because Rauf had hustled him, paying two thousand for it the previous week. When he brought the necklace to Rauf, mixed in with items from another heist, the fence singled out the emerald necklace. He trashed the quality of the rocks, calling the workmanship of the setting substandard.

Total bullshit, and Rauf knew it. The choker, simply patterned, unembellished, achieved a stunning effect with little motion. Rauf remained belligerent. Said he'd never agree to pay top dollar for the piece. His act was convincing. The second-story man acquiesced.

Rauf bragged to another fence about how he low-balled the Cuban Gnat–the acrobatic wetback who risked so much sticking himself outside Gold Coast condos, only to throw it away when he heard the first offer over a hundred bucks.

Fences talk to thieves and other fences. Word filtered down to the Gnat, and now he was getting back some respect. He offered Buddy an extra five hundred, out of his pocket, to break Sammy's jaw.

Sammy was a small, angular man with deeply sunken cheeks, a sparse mustache, and a nose like a curled-up vanilla bean. But Buddy recognized him by the red crocodile attaché case handcuffed to his left wrist.

They followed him home, keeping three or four cars behind Rauf's white Lincoln. Rauf pulled over on a Wrigleyville street crammed with two-story brownstones and the somber ghost-gray facade of a revamped former residential hotel. Water stains crept up the hotel's brickwork. From the building's foundation seeped the damp aroma of wells. Sammy lived in a corner penthouse unit with another man.

Buddy hadn't researched it any further. He wanted to hit Rauf on the street. Fast and hard, scare him and get the goods.

On Buddy's command, Lester doused the Trans Am's headlights and coasted up alongside Rauf's Town Car. The rain fell steadily, and Sammy's keys were slick between his fingers as he leaned out the driver's door, struggling to open his golf umbrella, its canopy painted to look like a gigantic sunflower. Buddy exited from the passenger side of the Trans Am, and when Sammy's sunflower bloomed to meet the falling drops, Buddy smashed him in the face with a leather blackjack. Rauf's ugly nose got uglier. Blood spritzed over the steering wheel and dashboard as his stringy body reeled backward across the front seat. Buddy climbed on top of him. The umbrella pin-wheeled down the street. One blackjack slap under the chin broke Sammy's jaw, loosened his bridgework, and satisfied Buddy's promise to the Gnat. Sammy couldn't breathe right with Buddy kneeling on his chest and a broken mouth. He gargled blood and tooth chips.

Buddy said, "Hold still, you fuck."

Buddy retrieved the bolt cutters tucked in his waistband. He jerked up Rauf's limp left arm and drooped the handcuff chain between the blades. Rauf moaned and spewed a red mist as Buddy scissored the man from the merchandise. Panic made Rauf squirm, and Buddy hit him, the chin again, with the cutters. Pain sent Rauf into a private oblivion.

Buddy pushed himself off the unconscious Egyptian. Rauf

had pissed and shit in his eight-hundred-dollar suit. The Lincoln's interior smelled like a dog kennel. Lester revved the Trans Am's powerhouse engine. Buddy dropped the bolt cutters onto the floor of the passenger side.

The first bullet tore a gash in the hood.

Steam from a severed radiator hose blew through the ruptured metal, whistling like a teakettle. Lester jammed the gas pedal and left Buddy standing in the street holding the attaché. No gun. Buddy's .38 was stashed under the seat of the Trans Am. The car took two more hits, losing the rear window and a tire, before it made the turn around the corner. Buddy hugged the case and rolled under a parked van.

The shooting stopped.

Sammy's male companion, a husky, blond twenty-four-year-old Marine reservist and artist's model, appeared from nowhere. Bare-chested and wearing only sweatpants, he swept the line of parked cars with a nickel-plated, smoking .45. Buddy flattened himself to the street. He could only see gray legs, kneecaps.

"Sam? Are you all right? What'd they do to you, baby?" The words didn't fit the clipped farmer's voice.

Buddy judged that he couldn't squeeze out on the curbside. No space. He would have to crawl forward under a rusty Peugeot or make a break for the street.

"Jesus, aw, Sam, d'you let 'em kill you? Fuckers! Say something, Sam. Lemme know you're alive. You can't be dead. How could they do you like this? I told you! I told you this shit would happen! Talk to me!"

Buddy remained still. He heard the Egyptian coughing. Farmer reacted, folded himself into the front seat with his battered lover.

Buddy slithered from under the van. He dragged the case. The middle of the street was his. Now he had to get up and run.

Headlights bore down on the scene: Lester gunning the Trans Am, illegal and lethal down the throat of the one-way. Buddy caught on his belly still working up the nerve to stand. No time to get his feet under him. He waited for the smell of hot rubber, the bone-crushing weight passing over his body.

Lester swerved. Wild-eyed—more for murderous intent than to save Buddy's prone ass lying in the street—Lester fused the two cars.

Farmer screamed, but his scream was lost in the shriek of metal ripping on metal. Windshields dissolved, and a blanket of scorching oil set fire to Lester's face. The steering column staked him to the driver's seat. The Trans Am ate up the Lincoln to its own destructive end, like a tiger swallowing a live grenade.

Buddy straightened. His legs felt loose, like he'd drop if the wind blew. Instead, he staggered over to the wreckage. Farmer was out cold with a broken spine. If Rauf wasn't already dying before, he was certainly dead now, pinned under the weight of both engines. Lester's skewered carcass smoked and sputtered as fire ballooned from the gas tanks.

Heat blasted the street. Buddy held up the battered case. Croc leather kept the flames off him. He walked. He lowered the case and kept walking. The hellish barbecue blazed. Flames reflected and multiplied in the dark apartment windows. Sirens. Buddy zigzagged between brownstones.

He rode a bus back to Greektown.

The next morning, Red put out a contract on Buddy's life.

Months and miles away, a thief who fought back, ran, and thought he had constructed a new life, walked slowly away from the riverside, leading a stray dog, wondering if Red Mizel still wanted him laid out on a mortician's slab.

4

Goatskinner's cock fattens whenever he watches something die. Grows hard faster when he's doing the killing. Dogs to humans, he's made the progression. Twenty-one women killed since he turned twenty-one. Ripples in a river, garbage in a flooded trench.

Seventeen years of playing God.

He guides his boat into an empty, foggy bay. Drops his jig, baited with a live leech, into the quiet water.

Now the future is important. He has to remind himself to stay focused on tomorrow, to keep moving forward, not to dwell. He opens a black spiral notebook, rests it over his knee. His handwriting fills the pages, margin to margin, without paragraph breaks. The penmanship is narrow, slanted, written with a black felt-tip marker. Diagrams and rough drawings border the text: a hieroglyphic of hate. He reads it out loud, *"The future is unmade, clear of memories. A place of fresh starts. An open field where senseless women stroll through tall wild flowers. I am the lion in the grass, Ladies, the shark up from the deep, the cobra under your blanket. You cannot expect me, but there I am. Naturally, water will seek a low spot. I am waiting there for you."* He stops to rearrange the Polaroid companions to his journal. With the edge of his shirtsleeve he pats beads of condensation off the pictures.

"Hey, asshole, you should buy a *Hustler* if you want to jerk off."

Goatskinner startles at laughter coming from the invisible shore. He struggles to buckle his belt. No, they're not on the shore but right behind him. A rowboat materialized and in it two teenage boys. From their looks, one's Indian and the other a trash whiteboy from the trailer parks. They're giggling and spilling their Lite beers. No motor on their boat. They rowed out from the campground. That's why he didn't hear them until they glided up so close.

The Indian fumbles with the oars. They slip through his wet grasp and bang against the aluminum bench. He swears at a splinter in his palm, picks at it with his dirty, long nails. The other boy scuffles his feet, mindlessly tangling the yellow snarl of anchor rope bunched in the nose of their johnboat. Goatskinner watches his skinny blue jean thighs and hears the grit under his gym shoes scrape metal, the rasp of the sliding rope.

The Indian stands up. He's shaped like a teardrop. Bare stomach exposed under a too-small tee shirt, a soft caramel roll of fat sags over his belt. Bending forward, he drops to his knees. His legs seem to be melting under him, the joints going elastic. He attempts to regain his equilibrium. Overcompensates. He topples backward, nearly overturning the boat. The whiteboy rides out the turbulence. With their boatload of empty beer bottles disturbed, it sounds like they're skateboarding the fourteen feet from bow to stern. Cigarette smoke dribbles from the whiteboy's mouth, a haze within the fog. He belches, scattering smoke, and pitches bottles into the lake. No one talks.

The two boats drift together. Touch.

Whitey leans forward to push off. His thin, pale forearms are spotted with cigarette burns. A Y-shaped scar blurs his lips. He hides some of it with a blond mustache. Eyes of lightless chalk gray, hair hanging in them. Nothing about him shines. His life is smeared. Smudged. All the lines are rubbed out.

Goatskinner pretends to fish. "I was taking a leak," he says.

No response from Whitey, who's busy hunting for his smokes. The Indian mutters, packs wintergreen tobacco into his cheek, sucks, spits in the water, uncaps another beer, takes up the oars again, and rows sluggishly back into the fog.

A minute later, a brown glass missile shoots through the mist, its arc carrying over Goatskinner, its flight dying in the weeds.

He shuffles his photographs into a manila envelope and sandwiches them inside the black notebook, marking the spot where his writing left off.

●

An unfamiliar, older woman's voice picked up. "Merrymakers."

"Can I speak to Robbie?"

"Just a sec."

Buddy cradled the phone under his jaw as he ground pepper over a cheese omelet.

"He ain't here. Jerry says try callin' over at Pinboy's."

"Thanks."

Buddy looked for the number and found it, the fifth one down his list. He tapped the number and let it ring. He was about to hang up when a man answered.

"Hello, Pinboy's Lounge, this is Mike. How can I help you?" A voice like a cracked ashtray.

Buddy swallowed a mouthful of eggs and cheddar. Washed it down with coffee.

"Hello?" Ashtray Mike said, still on the line.

"Excuse me. I'm trying to get a hold of Robbie Bayes. Is he around?"

"Robbie stepped out. Can I give him a message?"

"When's he due back?"

"Half-hour. He went across the street to eat breakfast. Usually done by nine. You should catch him anytime after."

"I'll call back."

"Sure thing, buddy."

Buddy felt a jolt at the coincidental mention of his name. Tracking down his brother had been easy. Robbie keeping to his old haunts. Places where, five minutes after Buddy walked through the door, Red's phone would ring.

In the Black Chimney's kitchen, he washed his plate. The repaired door was propped open, and morning light warmed the room. The stray—it had hung around for the past week, riding to and from the tavern in the backseat of Buddy's Caddy—lounged on the sunny gravel just outside the doorway. Buddy fried half a pound of ground beef, drained the fat, and mixed it with leftover rice the cook was saving to make pudding. He dumped the beef and rice into a salad bowl. The dog appeared on the threshold when he heard the spoon knocking against the side of his dish. Buddy grabbed the new leather collar and backed him up. Outside, he set the bowl on the ground and let Boy at it. In only a week, the dog had put on weight and his eyes had come to life. He was a champion sleeper. But Buddy didn't mind having him around, feeding him. It gave him a set of safe ears to talk to.

Buddy pitched a grimy baseball into the woods. Boy went after it. Returned the slippery ball to Buddy's open palm.

"What a good Boy." He threw the ball again, as far as he could with his healthy left arm. "Go find the ball, Boy, go find it." The dog marched off. Buddy stepped inside to make his call.

He got through to Ashtray Mike at Pinboy's and, as promised, Robbie was there. Mike put the phone down and the next voice was Robbie's.

"What do you need?"

"Gimme a yard on the Cubs. Whatever you're layin' is fine."

"Cubs don't play today."

"Oh, and what, my money's no good?"

"Earl?" Robbie picking up on the joke, using Buddy's given name as he always had since they were kids.

"How you doing, Robbie?" The brothers had not spoken since Christmas. Buddy still sore about Robbie's one visit to Gunnar.

"Good, real good. Hey, what took you so long?"

"So long for what?"

"I left that message. Said it was important. Jesus fuck, Earl, you never return my calls like you should."

"I had trouble."

"No kidding. Why you think I called?"

"Since then. After you called. I had . . . an incident."

"You should've called me."

"Forget that. I'm coming into town on Tuesday. Meet me at

O'Hare. United Baggage. Noon. Just hang around the carousels and I'll come up to you if everything looks okay."

"You flyin'?"

"No."

"Then why the airport? Drive over by . . ."

"Robbie. O'Hare. Noon. Okay?"

"I'll be there."

Buddy hung up. The airport was a safe place to meet. No sense in getting rid of his paranoia when it might be the only thing keeping him alive.

*

Augustus has tools.

They hang from a pegboard, filling out in three dimensions the outlines drawn behind them with a thick pencil. The whispering caged head of a fan blows near the door. The concrete floor gleams. Augustus spends hours working in his shop even when he's hungover. If he can't get to work in the daytime, he stays up through the night. There have been days he's missed work. Interminable, gray, dismal days. Sick days. Speakers are mounted against the four walls, carrying music from the stereo in the house. Adjacent to the wall of hanging tools is a steel workbench, and above it, three levels of shelving.

The stock—epoxy, an assortment of drill bits, turpentine, crimped tubes of oil paints, artist's brushes, grocer's twine, cotton, a pickle jar of glass eyes, glycerine, sulphonated neat's-foot oil, powdered borax, an airbrush and compressor, aluminum foil, balsa skulls, chloroform, a sharpening stone, ether, denatured alcohol, tweezers, scalpels, a tray of rasps and files, dextrine, formaldehyde, a spool of galvanized wire, a hypodermic syringe, various lacquers, thinner, linseed oil, needle-nosed pliers, a tin of paraffin wax, canisters of plaster, stearine, calipers, a bar of soap—is a taxidermist's combination of hardware, chemicals, household supplies, and medical instruments arranged carefully, labels facing forward, with attention paid to frequency of use, size, and easy access.

The third wall, opposite the tools, provides two doorways. One is standard-size, windowless, and double-deadbolted. Stacks of old newspapers turn yellow on either side of it. The other is a two-car garage door, opened and locked by an electric pulley and chain with a power-switch wired inside the house. Switch it off and four strong men would have difficulty lifting the half-inch-thick, solid-steel door. Closed, the sturdy door settles into a groove six inches down in the concrete. No good way to pry it open; it would be easier breaking in through one of the walls or the roof.

Augustus has stapled squares of dark brown cork to the fourth wall. A gallery of animal photographs stick to the cork with silver pins. On the floor, a topless shoebox holds more pins.

One large photograph, clipped from the pages of a glossy wildlife magazine, shows three griffon vultures rummaging through an exploded piñata of guts. The viscera erupt out of a horselike carcass. Dipped in blood, the birds tug the wet taffy of innards. In the periphery, over a hillside of tall dry grass, Augustus has written the word *LOVE*.

•

As it came to be on most nights, Buddy ended up by himself after closing time. The tavern darkened except for the weak rays cast by the office light. Buddy's shadow popped out, grotesque and bending on the wall.

A jingle of keys and the thump of tired footsteps as the shadow slow-danced, pushed chairs around, moving toward the kitchen. Buddy was mopping up. Bleach water and spilled beer.

He sensed the quiet apartment above him, couldn't put it or Margot's absence out of his mind. Buddy had a landlord's key. He stored the mop and bucket and went into the office, where he lifted the key off a screw inside a locked drawer. In the claustrophobic plywood stairwell, he never even paused to consider what he was doing. Key went into lock, man entered room. He used a flashlight just in case somebody might drive by and see him backlit through the gauzy curtains. Used it because it was second nature. Normal people felt guilty when they were trespassing, snooping around in places where they weren't supposed to be. Buddy wasn't normal. He was a thief.

He started in her bedroom.

Yellow walls Buddy had painted himself before he let the rooms out. Lime green cotton blanket flung across an unmade queen-size bed. A white wicker chair in the corner piled with clean laundry waiting to be folded. Sandals crossed beside the nightstand. A Stephen King novel with a gray feather bookmark. Reading lamp. Helen Frankenthaler prints hung on opposite sides of the long horizontal window facing the bed, the only window in the room. She had a closet, a dresser, and a cedar chest.

Buddy went through her clothes. On the floor of the closet he found shoes, more shoes in boxes, and a plastic bin filled with photo albums. Most of the photos were of Duncan, but there were high school snapshots, and student portraits taken when Margot was a young girl. She may not have been the class beauty, but there was liveliness about her and a certain narrowing of her eyes that said she saw through your bullshit but might like you anyway. She played softball, was a swimmer, and she dated a football player.

Tommy. She kept three photos of Tommy. They were apart from the others, folded inside a poorly taped lavender envelope along with a Valentine's card he'd signed in pencil. No letters from anyone. No evidence of her affair with Carl Sherry. No diary. No little black phonebook. She'd lived in Gunnar her whole life, and it wasn't hard to remember the handful of numbers she called.

He checked the bathroom and kitchen. He found what he expected to find in the home of a healthy, small-town, single mother.

What he didn't find was any reason to believe Margot had somehow provoked her attacker. Or any evidence to link her to the rural underbelly of the county. No pipes, no needles, no rubber-banded stacks of cash.

He searched the living room quickly. People didn't hide things in their living rooms. For the same reason, he never went past the Winnie the Pooh sticker on Duncan's door. When he was finished, he sat on her couch in the dark and closed his eyes.

It was his fault.

Or it was random.

The nutjob who attacked Melissa Teagles could be the same one who tried for Margot at the Black Chimney. But Buddy didn't believe in coincidences. And what was the coincidence? Buddy had been involved in both crimes. If he hadn't gone back to the tavern that night, then it was likely he would've discovered Margot's body in the morning. How would it look to the cops? Two murdered girls and he was the common factor. Not a coincidence, but a message.

Like the letter. Like Robbie's call on the machine.

Somebody could've attacked Margot to get to him. Taking advantage of what happened to Melissa or, maybe, doing her, too. Red or a creep he hired. It made no sense, but it made the most sense of anything he'd come up with so far. If this was directed at him, that meant it was Red pulling the strings. Margot was just another way to squeeze him. Make him bleed. Set him up for a hard fall. He had to go to Chicago to talk to Robbie. Find out what, if anything, he knew.

Buddy opened his eyes. The dim room. Toys on the floor. Margot's leather jacket on a wooden peg below a round mirror. Something in the trash can under the kitchen sink had gone rotten. But above the foulness, her scent persisted. Perfume, shampoo, the soap she used, the detergent. Would she ever come home? Or would the hospital be her home until something else finally whisked her away?

He took the garbage out. If anyone saw him, anyone asked, he'd say that's why he was up there among her things.

●

Boy leapt down the stairs and ran circles in the gravel. A little moonlight sneaked through the front entrance and lay like a row of silver dollars leading to the bar. Buddy locked up for the night, then, with Boy at his heels, walked to his car. He had Margot's tied-up trash in his hand. Under his arm he carried a soft bundle. He dropped the trash in the Dumpster. He put the bundle in his trunk, and Boy went to his usual place in the Caddy's backseat. They went home.

•

At sunrise, Buddy pulled into a wayside to relieve himself of the pot of coffee he downed after midnight. Hours earlier, sitting up knowing sleep wasn't going to come and resolved to the fact, he thumbed through a collection of Edward Abbey's essays and began rolling around the idea of escaping to the West. Buddy had never been to a desert, but the solitude appealed to him. He'd lived in a desert his whole life. First he had to clear up his Chicago problems. Help Margot, too.

The sky pinked. But the coolness of the night persisted. Buddy parked the Caddy and surveyed the wayside parking lot. A semi grumbled at the other end. An unlit cab, the driver likely asleep.

Buddy adjusted the sling on his shoulder as he passed the bumper of the only other vehicle in the lot, a sturdy, weather-beaten camper. Two retirees, a husband and wife he guessed, were seated in the front, splitting a cinnamon roll and a thermos of coffee. The driver's window was down, and the husband's suntanned arm dangled a cigarette between thick, bronze fingers. His wife was laughing at something he was saying. Buddy nodded hello and got, in return, a polite wave.

Looks pretty good, Buddy thought. Hard work behind you and you're riding with someone who still wants to hear your stories. Buddy didn't have that, probably never would.

Buddy opened the glass door to the rest area. Stale air tinged with citrus disinfectant. He walked past a rack of colorful tourist brochures and a giant roadmap of Wisconsin. Alone, he entered the tiled gloom of the men's toilet.

Back outside again, the camper was gone and the trucker was awake, stretching his legs. A couple of squirrels chased each other under the picnic tables. They slalomed through a row of trash cans. One snatched up a potato chip, and then the two of them dodged away from him. The way those squirrels moved in sync, one connected to the other and following, reminded Buddy of himself and Robbie as kids.

Grandma Nan was a saint. She saved them from the state orphans' program after their parents were killed in a car wreck. Coming home from a New Year's Eve party, the couple's silver Ford drove off an icy bridge and landed upside-down on railroad tracks. A freight engineer found them at sunup. The bodies frozen by the time daylight arrived.

Police report said they left the party drunk and arguing. Witnesses told the cops Frank Bayes threw a punch at a man in a brown chalk-striped suit. Others said Lily, Frank's wife, had been kissing the same man—tall, blond, same style suit—in the hotel lobby.

One woman, who knew Mrs. Bayes from the days when they both were barmaids, said Lily was "falling down drunk" and she'd "puked shrimp cocktail and a pitcher of Gibsons" into a potted palm by the hotel fountain. The man in the brown suit helped Lily walk to the ladies' lounge. No one could identify him. His name didn't seem to matter. Frank and Lily had reputations. When the firemen cut Buddy's mother from the car, they found a shattered bottle of gin in her lap. Her underwear was missing.

Buddy was three, his brother less than a year, when they came to live in Nan's house. Their grandmother loved them, did her best. Her only child, their father, was dead, and she took part of the blame for his recklessness. A TB widow, she had raised Frank alone and without much discipline. She fared no better with his orphaned sons. The boys had the run of the household. Nan prayed for their souls.

She worked all day at a butcher's shop. Nights she washed floors at a Loop law firm. Left alone, the boys stuck close together and avoided the other neighborhood kids. Grandma couldn't afford to buy them toys.

Buddy remembered making guns from clothespins. Cowboys and Indians in the alley. World War II in the gangway. When Buddy got tired of his little brother's constant company, he'd put him in jail under the back porch, blocking the hole in the lattice with a sheet of scrap wood and a brick. But the little convict always escaped.

Buddy made decent grades but had no friends. Robbie couldn't handle being separated. Their double fraternity–shared blood and a common loss–drew them tighter than either could understand.

Robbie was a fat kid who took abuse. But he surprised everyone, especially himself, when he matured into a fine athlete. Speed, balance, and quickness that defied his size. In his freshman year, he discovered the weight room and a coach who persuaded him to wrestle.

Bullies got wise and those who didn't got hurt. Sports changed Robbie. Gave him confidence and an identity apart from his brother. The wrestling coach volunteered as the offensive assistant on the school's football team. He had no trouble convincing Robbie to live out his destiny as a lineman. Junior year, Robbie arrived for his first varsity practice just under six feet tall but about two T-bone steaks shy of three hundred pounds. Thinking in X's and O's came to him naturally. He digested the playbook like it was a short stack of pancakes.

From the senior sports banquet, he brought home trophies in both wrestling and football. Scouts were calling by the house. But his glory days were short-lived. A broken femur and a bone infection that ate up a hundred pounds of muscle ended everything. Now he hitched his right leg when he walked. He woke up crucified by pain. He took long baths and felt, somehow, that it wasn't his bum leg that betrayed him. It was something outside, like Fate or God or luck.

If he couldn't play football, he could still talk a good game. Bartenders gave him free drafts just to shut him up. But Robbie had something to say, to prove. He analyzed players and coaches and devoted hours to breaking down weekend matchups. He made notes, he preached. No one listened.

Not until there was money involved.

For the next thirty years, Robbie lived and worked in barrooms, his mammoth ass parked on an uneasy stool or spreading the width of a cramped vinyl booth. Nursing a beer usually gone flat and inhaling drippy cheeseburgers, Robbie took bets. He was a corner bar legend in the making. Up from nowhere, Robbie became the most profitable non-Outfit bookmaker on the North Side.

In his spare time, he banged a used set of drums. He hit the skins in after-hours dives, calling out the beat for unhealthy strippers. *Christ*, Buddy thought, Robbie really fell hard for some of those girls. He would slide into the strip lounge circuit, watch them shake and shimmy to the vibrations of his snare. Catching dollar bills in their G-strings. Robbie got a small cut of what the room brought in, and an occasional free blowjob.

Between breaks, he would work the club for bettors. Half his income quickly coming from money counted out on his drum kit under pink lights. When live music died on the club scene, Robbie gave up playing. But the clubs were now permanent fixtures on his bookmaking orbit.

Buddy opened the Caddy's trunk and removed the sawed-off shotgun concealed beside his tool chest. The gun was rolled in a khaki sleeping bag. He'd carried the bag and gun out of the Chimney the night before. He hooked his finger under one of the bag cords, shut the trunk, and carried the bundle to the front seat. Holding the twelve-gauge in his lap, he broke it open and loaded two double-aught shells. He had a full box hidden under the spare tire. Two extra shells went into his glove compartment. He inserted the loaded weapon into the center of the roll and tucked it behind the passenger seat.

Buddy was going to Chicago because he knew he could count on Robbie. Knew his brother would swallow a fistful of roofing nails if he asked. Knew he needed him if Red was coming out of the woodwork hungry for blood.

❋

"Well, if it ain't the Virgin Mary. How the hell are ya, babe?"

The woman sitting at the bar swivels around to give Augustus a friendly kiss on the cheek. Her breath is sour mash and Kools.

"Same shit, you know." She draws her lungs full of mentholated smoke. "Where you been hidin' lately?" she asks, blowing blue-white fumes.

"Never too far away." He signals the bartender to bring him a draft.

The bar is called the Muskets. Dozens of gun replicas decorate the walls. They hang over gritty stucco crossed with wood beams. The room is a cramped, warm, rectangular box. Trapped air fails to circulate. Through uncovered windows, the falling orange sun boils. Regulars pound their beers. A few suck the rims of their happy-hour-special Long Island iced teas. A popcorn-popper radiates like a stove in the corner. Rancid oil drips from its underbelly, and there's a burnt smell coming from its core. Augustus braves the heat to scoop a bowl of popped kernels. He rains salt from a cardboard shaker into his bowl.

"*Phew!* Sweaty bunch in here today," Augustus says.

Mary O'Connor shrugs. She's gotten drunk with Augustus before. She's gotten drunk with a lot of men. He stands beside her, munching popcorn. "Let's get out of here. Black Chimney's got air-conditioning that works."

Mary hesitates. Hopping bars wasn't in her plans for tonight.

"C'mon, I'll drive. All you have to do is walk to my truck." Augustus cocks his head toward the door.

Mary clicks open her teal cigarette purse and finds a lighter. She is shaking her head. "I don't feel like gettin' up and goin' nowhere. Why can't you sit down, drink your beer, and make a little pleasant conversation?"

Augustus sits down and washes back Budweiser. Mary runs her pinkie under his chin. "You got butter in your beard, Gus."

With her greasy little finger, she swirls around the ice at the bottom of her drink.

"I also have a pint of homemade blackberry brandy under the seat of my truck." He makes the offer, raises his beer, and finishes it.

She studies him and comes to a new decision.

"You win. But I gotta pee before we go bouncin' down the lonesome highway." Mary pulls a purple handbag up from between her feet. "Be a sweetie. Pick me up out front."

Augustus watches her wobble to the ladies' room. He leaves a ten under his glass. Nobody pays attention to him as he walks out the door.

Augustus drives a black Chevy Silverado cankered with rust. Scratches uncover a former coat of gold. An amateur job he did himself. The cap over the bed has slender, tinted windows. At a Madison body shop, they sprayed on the bed liner. It's durable and washes clean with a hose.

When Mary gets in, she peers through the sliding window to the back. She sees a spade caked with dried mud and a coil of blue nylon rope, a pair of deerskin gloves and, beneath them, the crescent blade of a hatchet. She thinks she sees a lady's formal evening gown, bagged in plastic. But Augustus closes the window and with his other hand delivers the brandy flask to her parted lips. She assures herself she's made a mistake. Her eyes are playing tricks. The blackberries print a deep blue stain on her mouth. Truck in gear, they're rushing through lengthening sunset shadows. Mary sips.

●

O'Hare traffic forked around a stalled limousine. Drivers rolled down their windows and breathed in exhaust so they could shout obscenities as they passed. The black, middle-aged limo driver worked with a screwdriver on the engine. Buddy changed lanes.

Where did all these people come from? Buddy wondered. *Middle of the day. Didn't they have jobs?*

He motored alongside the limo, noticed the man had a handkerchief wrapped around his bleeding knuckles. In the rearview mirror, Buddy watched him climb behind the steering wheel, wiping sweat from his creasy forehead, talking to himself. Traffic resealed, pushing forward with urgency. Fast taxis weaved in and out of the stream.

Buddy entered the parking garage lane. He found a spot in the middle of the concrete monolith. Before he got out of the car, he shrugged off the sling, folded it, and put it in his pocket.

He rode down the garage elevator with a brunette in a silk suit that smelled like wine. Outside the elevators, in the corridor connecting the terminals, a street saxophonist was playing a mangled version of "Danny Boy." Buddy found the escalators up to Baggage Claim.

No sign of Robbie.

Buddy had arrived early with a purpose. He strolled the claim area, checking out the banks of pay phones, searching for the idle stranger's eyes that were looking for him. Skycaps tooled overburdened luggage carts. Packs of disheveled travelers herded to the carousels. Nothing out of the ordinary.

Someone touched his arm. Buddy stiffened, fingered the brass knuckles in his pocket. Adrenaline pumping.

"Earl, it's me."

The man was standing too close, and Buddy didn't recognize him. Mirrored sunglasses, buzz cut, a chunky gold chain hanging outside a V-neck tee shirt emblazoned with pineapples. The chain rested between taut pectorals. The guy's biceps were the size of cue balls. Capped teeth smiled through a weekend goatee and a face overcooked in the tanning booth. The guy took off his glasses. Bags under the wet blue eyes . . . Robbie's eyes.

Buddy couldn't manage words. Finally he said, "When did you get skinny . . ."

Robbie laughed. He was wearing spandex biker shorts and sandals.

Sandals, for crissake.

He left-hooked Buddy in the arm. The pain bolted through his tender shoulder. Buddy was too stunned to cry out. A gold earring twisted from Robbie's left ear. A seahorse. Higher up his ear, a second protuberance, an eight ball, was studded in a niche of cartilage. Buddy rooted himself to the floor, blinking.

"Hey, I didn't hit you that hard." Robbie took a step back and rocked on his heels. His legs were shaved baby-smooth. He was chewing gum. Buddy caught a whiff of cinnamon.

"What the hell happened to you?" It was the best Buddy could do.

"Been losing weight. Everybody else says I look tight." Robbie clapped his hands together. He hustled Buddy out the door. "We'll talk in the car. I'm parked in a tow zone." He draped his sinewy arm around his brother's shoulders. "You look like shit. Sure you're not sick or something?"

"I was gonna ask you the same thing."

Robbie's blushing face had all the colors of a side of bacon. Buddy tried not to stare. In his peripheral vision, he soaked up his brother's new image. Maybe it wasn't new. After all, he hadn't seen Robbie in months.

"Over there. The white Camaro." Robbie pointed with a jerk of his chin. An immaculate set of wheels. The car's surface gleamed as if it were thawing. Buddy heard the lock release chirp. They got in.

Cool air knifed through the vents as they sped away from the airport. An awkward silence hovered. Each brother had questions he wanted to ask. Robbie jumped on the Tri-State going south.

"You ain't been so thin since..."

"Since I busted my leg. Yeah."

"You still walk like Ahab."

"Better than the White Whale, man."

Orange-and-white sawhorses blocked the center lane. A bulldozer and a gang of orange-vested road workers appeared in the distance. Robbie switched over to the ramp for the Ike, heading east. Traffic crawled at the Hillside Strangler, a bottleneck named for the suburb they were passing through, where all the cars and trucks clogged up. Chicago was that kind of town. Half in love with criminal images, deeply in love with its tough-guy persona.

The skyline came into view. Smog wrapped it in gauze.

Buddy sized up his brother's compact frame. "You look like you're down to about two and a quarter."

"Two flat, in my Jockeys."

"Really? You don't look it."

"I'm a hard-packed sonofabitch."

Buddy frowned. "So you haven't told me how you dropped down from four hundred pounds of Jell-O."

"Your sensitivity is touching. Really. Tears in my eyes," Robbie said. He pretended to wipe a few away. "Doc says I have anxiety issues. Hypertension, too."

The man sitting next to him was his brother, though physically he was the antithesis of the Robbie Buddy remembered. Now this alien, rebuilt version of Robbie was telling him he had *anxiety issues.*

"You never told me any of this."

"Yeah, you ever read the letters I sent you?"

Buddy had no answer.

"My doctor put me on a diet. I eat rabbit food. Fruits and veggies. And fish, no butter. Tuna cakes and protein shakes. I'm off grease. I drink a lot of water so now I'm always having to take a piss. I'm getting up three, four times a night. No big deal 'cause I can't sleep worth shit."

Buddy fondled the cigar in his shirt pocket. He wanted to light up, but the Camaro smelled so goddamned clean.

Robbie read his mind.

"Go ahead," he said. "It's a on a lease. I'm getting a Lexus next month."

●

Augustus chases Jack Daniel's shots with frigid beer. Mary keeps pace. Under the table, she rests her hand on his thigh. The Black Chimney has a crowd. Most of the townies are snacking on crocks of chili. Hank Williams Jr. booms from the juke. Off in the corner four young women stop shooting pool to dance with each other. Augustus is watching those four. Their laughter is loud. Sweet smiles and golden skin. Long hair.

Mary slips two of her hot bony fingers inside his belt. Her knee presses. She's trying to be seductive. He ignores her.

The bartender and waitress are local kids home from college for the summer. They mostly help out on the weekends, but with Margot in the hospital and Buddy not around, they're working hard. Augustus motions for the waitress to come over.

"You need refills?" She clears away their bottles.

"Sure, honey, and two shots of Jack. Say, where's Buddy tonight? I wanted to ask him something."

"He's out of town for a couple of days. He'll be back this weekend. You want me to give him a message if he calls?"

"No, no. It's not important. Where'd you say he went?"

"I didn't. He never told us. Buddy's weird secretive about private stuff." She towels away the moisture rings on the table. Switches their overflowing ashtray for a clean one.

Mary says, "Maybe he's got himself a woman."

"Two shots and two beers, right?" the waitress asks.

"And bring me a bowl of that homemade chili, darlin'." Augustus puts a hand on her arm.

Mary prods him. Her hand travels the inseam of his jeans. She thinks she's making progress. Smoke leaks through her dim, jumbled teeth.

Augustus tries not to look at her.

*

They exited at Cicero. Down to Lake Street, where they turned. East again. Cruising under the El tracks, riding a flow of trash.

94

Rat heaven. Robbie said they were going to one of the strip clubs. X-ray's. Buddy remembered it, remembered Robbie's pocketful of lavender business cards. The silhouette of a dancer wearing the kind of hat nurses hadn't worn since the sixties. The logo showed her bones glowing Halloween bright. At the bottom of the card were the words: *X-ray's, See what you've been missing.*

X-ray's was on the West Side. Not far enough out to be in K-town where all the streets started with K and ended in despair. Gangbanger-controlled wasteland. Suburban junkies drove their SUVs in to score smack then hop back on the Ike. Back to home-sweet-white-home. The club was located close enough to the Loop to attract a business crowd. After dark, the neighborhood streets were scoured of legitimate life-forms. But here in the summer sunshine, Buddy saw kids, old ladies, youngbloods on the stoops drinking from sacks.

"You sure it's safe here?"

Robbie said, "Not a problem."

They pulled into an alley behind a squat cube of a building. Pea green bricks and a flat roof. The windows bricked-in, too. Except for the brass knuckles in his pocket, Buddy was unarmed. His sawed-off had stayed back in the Caddy. He got out. Broken glass crunched under his shoes. His eyes sucked in everything.

"Shut the door and let me park. This place is okay," his brother said.

Buddy slammed his door, and Robbie shoehorned the Camaro into a slot between a chain-link fence and the side of the building. Dill weed grew through fissures in the alley's broken concrete. Buddy could smell it. A crow flapped out of a

Dumpster, what looked like a slice of roast beef dangling from its feet. The bird landed on a telephone pole, cawed.

"Snug fit, but nobody's gonna sideswipe me."

Robbie told him he owned ten percent of X-ray's. He bought in a year ago. Making book in the rear offices launched his profits off the charts. He was earning triple what Buddy cleared at the Chimney. Robbie needed three keys to open the back door. Over the door was a sign. RESPECT OUR NEIGHBORS, LEAVE QUIETLY.

They walked into a blast of blues guitar trying hard to fake Tuesday lunchtime into Saturday midnight.

No windows and the air-conditioning gave the club an underground vibe. Buddy watched Robbie shove the door; its bottom scraping over buckled concrete. Once they were inside, Robbie jerked the door free. He took thirty seconds to relock while Buddy's eyes adjusted to the dark.

They stepped over a threshold into a surprisingly wide, spacious, almost breezy room. Emerald tile covered the floor. The bar was shaped like a horseshoe. It capped the end of an elevated stage that divided the big room in half. Every spare inch of wall was mirrored. They even had mirrors screwed into the ceiling above the dancers. If you weren't seeing enough, then you could look up. Nobody was sitting at the bar. But the swivel seats on either side of the catwalk were filled. Buddy never understood why guys hung out in strip clubs. He thought it was like watching somebody grilling a steak, then going home listening to your stomach growl.

A huge black man was pouring drinks. He wasn't tall, but

his arms–jutting out of a sleeveless T-shirt–were bigger than Buddy's legs. The guy had cornrows, tats running up and down his muscles. Japanese calligraphy. Buddy wasn't interested in finding out what they said.

Three brass poles. Three naked dancers. A redhead, a brunette, and a blonde.

"Neapolitan hour," Robbie said, above the thumping bass notes.

A few heads glanced up at the brothers. Buddy followed Robbie down a hallway where a lit golden arrow pointed to the restrooms. There was an office door. And its twin facing it across the hall. The men's room at the end of the hall had no door, just a turn so the patrons could piss in a trough without offending their modesty.

Robbie maneuvered himself behind a wooden teacher's desk. He squeezed into his computer chair. Indoor-outdoor carpeting crunched under the wheels. A bamboo torch lamp was plugged into a surge protector next to the computer on the desk. Buddy took a seat in one of two brown plaid chairs on his side of the desk. Apparently, they got their furnishings from Goodwill. The office had an odor. Somewhere between a barbershop and a locker room. Robbie picked up his phone while he clacked two fresh pencils against the edge of an open drawer. He punched in a number and sat down.

An old Mosler safe loomed over Robbie's shoulder. He tucked the phone under his jaw and reached into the drawer. His hands came up twisting the cap off a bottle of Wild Turkey. He poured bourbon into two plastic cups. Pushed the far cup to his brother.

Then the Turkey went back into the drawer with the pencils. Robbie hung up the phone, propped his sandaled feet on the desk. He sipped and exhaled.

"There are worse ways to ruin a liver."

Buddy nodded and drank. "Who you calling?"

Robbie shook his head, waved the question away. "Business."

For the first time, Buddy noticed how far his brother's close-cropped hairline had receded and that his beard was mostly gray. The backs of his hands were veined like a septuagenarian's. *We're getting to be the old men on the block, Rob. Where'd all the time go?*

Buddy said, "Tell me. What's this complicated stuff you called about?"

Robbie stood up, went to the file cabinet in the corner, and flipped through a rack of folders. He picked out one of the folders and shuffled through a pack of 8×10 glossies.

Robbie selected a photo, laid it in front of his brother.

"That's her," he said.

The girl wore nothing but a snakeskin thong and sweat. Buddy wouldn't have recognized her. But she was the right age. Red hair and freckles. *Melissa Teagles.*

"What are you trying to say here, Robbie?"

"She's the one who got killed in Gunnar."

"I figured that out."

"She danced at X-ray's."

"Yeah. So what?" Here was the link Buddy had been looking for. But Melissa working at X-ray's was coming at him from left field. He needed to fit it into a framework he could understand. Having Robbie hand it to him was too easy. He wanted Robbie to help him get to the core of his Chicago problems. Now it looked like Robbie lived at that core. Buddy slid the photo back across the desk.

Robbie looked surprised. "I thought that'd be important."

"Small world Robbie. I don't think it means anything. Her folks said she was in college. So somebody's lying. Big deal." Buddy finished his bourbon. Something in the air made him want to gag.

"She did go to college. To DePaul."

"Nice Catholic girl."

"She *was* nice. A good dancer, too. She had lots of fans."

"I'm sure. So why's she working here? Why's she shaking her ass in the faces of guys she wouldn't talk to at the corner bar?"

"Why do any of these girls do it?" Robbie rubbed two fingers against the ball of his thumb. "She needed the money. For school."

"What's this got to do with me?"

"Well . . . Red knew her." Robbie was looking at the photo, not putting it away.

"How's that?" Buddy felt the bourbon firing in his gut, threatening to come back up. His vision skewed. The odor in the room finally clicked in his brain. It was the same cheap aftershave Red splashed on the back of his neck. "Red's got something to do with X-ray's? Some interest?"

Robbie let out a nervous laugh, brushed his palm over the fuzz on his skull. "Yeah, about ninety-percent interest." His words hit Buddy like hollow points, exploding through his chest. "He's my partner."

5

Black worms.

Mary is skinny-dipping, and Augustus thinks her wet hair looks like a crown of black worms. He sits on the gnarled roots of a riverside tree. He's smoking weed packed in a small briar pipe. Sharp smoke trickles from his nostrils. The bowl of the pipe has an octagonal rim and a scarab etched on its underside. Burning leaves make the beetle feel warm. Augustus imagines the roots forming his chair are the desiccated talons of a dinosaur he has slain. Then he decides they're not dinosaur bones but ancient dragon bones. He choked the dragon with potent magic.

He mouths words, "I am the Nameless Dragonkiller, and she is Princess Blackworms." He hears Mary splashing, sees her dunk under the gliding current and stand up. She's in waist-high water. She kneels down so the water can bubble over her shoulders.

Mary has shed her shoes and socks, left them on a grass mound in a pile with her jeans and blouse. She waded in wearing her bra and panties. She strips underwater and tosses her soaked garments up on a rock.

A scratch of smoke tells her where Augustus is on the river-bank.

"Come swimming," she says.

Mary can't see what Augustus is doing under the tree. A rough fin flutters against her thigh, swims away. She touches the tiny welt raised on her skin. Then Augustus lumbers out of the gloom, naked as a bear. The moon bleaches his bulk. His matted body hair shines like greasy fur. His head hunches forward. He's chewing his mustache lip. Augustus paces. Mary smells a wave of his boozy, musky sweat.

"It's not too cold." She swims around, lazy frog kicks, to show she's comfortable.

Augustus steps into the river. Something like sleep is in his eyes. Mary paddles over. She intertwines her legs through his. Her stubbly calves chafe against him. He paws at her breasts unenthusiastically. She cuddles closer. Underwater, she toys with him. He pulls back, releases her, and twists away. Mary wants Augustus to loosen up. She's afraid he's too stoned, the river's too cold for him to get hard. She scissors her legs around his hips and crosses her ankles to lock him in. She tightens her grip. Augustus feels her sex grinding into him. She rakes her nails down his sloped back.

He breaks free of her hold. He slogs his way to the bank.

"Where are you going, Gus?"

Mud coats Augustus' legs. Mary watches his stony leg mus-cles pump as he marches out of sight, uphill past the tree where he undressed, in the direction of his parked truck. He combs wet fingers through his hair. His head swings side to side.

"You can't leave me here." Mary charges through the current, chooses a poor angle, and tumbles sideways. The flow carries her downriver ten yards. She barks her shin on a rock, but she gains her balance and stands again, coughing murky water.

"Get back here, you bastard!"

Augustus says, "Hold your horses, Princess. Got to get something from the truck."

Mary swims, is ready to kiss and make up. "I hope you're bringing me a drink!"

•

Buddy sat there wishing he had more whiskey in his cup. "You bring me into a place owned by a guy who put money on the street to have me whacked?"

"Calm down."

"Robbie, where's your brain at?"

"Nothing's going to happen."

"I'm glad you're so fucking sure."

Robbie adjusted the Mosler's tumblers, opened it, and brought out a .22 revolver. Without a word, he reached back inside for a box of ammo and a metal cylinder—a tube silencer. It made a skirling sound as Robbie married it to the revolver.

Robbie said, "You want to cap him? This piece is colder than an Eskimo cemetery. Stolen from the factory. Serial number is filed. Double-erased with acid. Red sends his boys to clip some dude, this is how they do it. Don't leave prints on the bullets. Take them out and wipe them. Use your handkerchief when you reload. Got it?"

"Wait a minute."

"Why?" Robbie's face flushed pink. He clenched his teeth.

The office lighting accentuated his cropped silver hair, the whiteness of his scalp. The .22 in his hand looked like a squirt gun. "He killed her to frame you. Can't you see it?" He thumped the silencer against his wide-open palm.

For the first time, Buddy witnessed his brother's potential for violence. Where was the little fat kid who cried every day at school for a year? The one who was afraid of nuns because he thought they could read his mind? The star wrestler who told Buddy he had nightmares about breaking his opponents' necks?

"Don't you think we're going too fast here?" Buddy asked.

Robbie shrugged.

"Let's take a minute, okay? Think this through."

"You're the man, Earl. Got to do him before he does you."

•

Inside a satin pillowcase: gold clip-on earrings encrusted with rhinestones and a matching brooch, a woman's fancy Sunday hat made entirely of speckled feathers, a dusty fox boa, and matching wedding bands. The year engraved in the rings is 1950, with no day or month inscribed. They are cheap and thin and greenish. They feel weightless.

Augustus drops the pillowcase near his pipe and clothes. He chooses an item. The brooch. Hides it nestled in his palm. He belts his hunting knife to his thigh. Eases into the river.

I am the Nameless Dragonkiller.

The Nameless. The Many-Named. Dragonkiller, Boarhunter, Moonslave.

Augustus nods, affirming each name as he recites it. He raises his arms. He turns in the water, consecrating the site according to his laws.

Dragonkiller. Boarhunter. Moonslave.

He sees Mary's head, just her head, above the water. Her hair is slick. Her face is long and pointed. Her eyes bulge, her tongue lolls as she bleats at him.

Soon they are kissing. He breaks the kiss. Slides his fingers into her wet mouth.

The goat is screaming.

Goatskinner quiets her.

•

Robbie had to be paying a hefty cut to Red for the right to work. Buddy knew that much. His brother needed protection from competitors, collection muscle when it was necessary. These were things Red could provide. Buddy wondered if Red's cut was deep enough that Robbie might be hurting, working like a dog and getting thrown nothing but scraps. Maybe Red had him twisted up in a business relationship and Robbie couldn't find a way out. Maybe putting a gun in Buddy's hand *was* his way out.

"Let's get out of here, grab some dinner," Buddy said.

"What about Red?"

"He's not going anywhere." Buddy smiled. The whole thing started to feel like a setup. But this was Robbie sitting across from him. This was his brother, his *blood.* "C'mon, you must know someplace where we can get a steak and a bottle of wine."

"Sure, I know places." Robbie put away the gun and shut the safe. He swiped his wrist across his forehead.

"You want to check the hallway and make sure it's clear?" Buddy said.

"Uh, yeah, I'd better." Robbie moved heavy, like he still carried the extra weight. He slipped out the door.

Something solid thudded into the wall and shook the door. Buddy reached the safe, tried the handle. No luck turning it. The door opened a few inches. Then it slammed shut. Robbie on the other side was talking fast but Buddy couldn't make out words.

A fist pounded three times on the wall. It was Robbie warning him.

Buddy remembered how Robbie opened the safe without twirling through a sequence of numbers. Robbie was lazy and had the tumbler just set off the number that would release the handle. Buddy tried the digits nearest to the right. The handle didn't budge. He went left with the same result. Back right, but he was afraid he'd gone too far. When the handle turned, it was like hitting triple bars.

He picked up the silenced .22 and tipped the desk forward just as the door burst inward, loosened from its frame. Three men bunched together. Robbie was the one falling backward and bleeding.

Buddy steadied his wrist on the desk. He fired once into the drop ceiling. The shot came out muffled, but the players knew the sound. Bar music kept the club from clearing out.

Buddy recognized Red. More hollow in the cheeks, deader in the eyes, and still dressed like a Nashville fiddler–Red had probably never been south of Joliet in his life. The other guy was the black bartender. He had a Colt King Cobra in his hand, squeezing so the tendons jumped like baby snakes.

"Red, I'll drop you both if I have to," Buddy said.

Red showed his empty palms.

The bartender pointed his Cobra at Buddy's head.

"Tell him, Red. Or you go down." Buddy aimed squarely at Red's chest.

"Back off, Zo. Do what he says."

"Okay," Buddy said. "Lay the piece on the floor. Step back. And do it real slow."

Zo bent. Put the Colt down on the indoor-outdoor. Robbie stopped thumbing blood from his nose long enough to snatch it from the floor. Then he crossed in front of the desk, and whipped the Colt's butt into Zo's cheekbone.

Zo didn't sway or make a sound. Buddy guessed Robbie was paying him back for the broken nose, but he hadn't expected Robbie's move. Any more pressure from Buddy's trigger finger, and Robbie would have walked into a bullet.

Robbie stepped back. He avoided making any eye contact with Red.

Buddy rose from his crouch. He remembered that Red used to wear a straight razor on a shoelace around his neck.

"Red, toss your razor in the wastebasket."

The mother-of-pearl handle shimmered in an arc to the trash. A soft rap as it disappeared beneath shredded papers.

"You have the office bugged?" Buddy asked.

"What do you think?"

"I think your partnership with my brother is over. Robbie, you'd better settle up."

Robbie filled a drawstring sack with cash he unloaded from inside the Mosler. He said, "There's not much here. Real money is in his office. He's got a floor safe."

"You know the combination?" Buddy asked.

Robbie shook his head.

"Red?"

"Fuck you, man."

Buddy shot him.

Red buckled. Buddy saw past his paling face to the white bone nudging between two knuckles of Red's ruined left hand. Blood gushing onto Red's pointy boots. Zo held steady, but fear was flicking in his droopy eyes.

Red spit three numbers at the wall. He knelt as the pain crushed him.

Robbie went to collect the money.

"You trying to set me up for something?" Buddy asked. "Huh? Kill Melissa, then attack my waitress." Buddy flashed on Melissa's hand in the bundle. "You're a real mess, Red. That fist of yours hurting?"

Red said, "I don't know what you're talking about."

"That right?" Buddy's thoughts splintered in fifty directions. One splinter lodged behind his eyes. What if Red was telling the truth?

"Christ, it took me five minutes to figure out whose voice I was hearing on the goddamned wire." Red looked up at him, and Buddy saw nothing. No recognition. No lie trying desperately to hide. Red was many things, but clever wasn't one of them. Buddy wondered if Robbie was wrong.

What if Red had nothing to do with what was happening in Gunnar? If he were orchestrating this mayhem, he'd gloat. He would rub Buddy's face in the sickness of it. Instead, he was kneeling on the carpet trying not to faint.

"Robbie was talking about whacking me. I'm supposed to let that slide?" Red asked, his voice going thin.

Buddy thought about it.

Red's blood trickled off his fingers. The door opened. Robbie walked in with the sack on his shoulder. It was heavy now. Difficult to manage.

Red whispered, "The thing with my brother is history. But you walk out of here with my money . . . I'm telling you, you're fucked. No matter what reason you think you got."

"Take your own advice, Red. Let this drop." Buddy turned to his brother. "Get the car out front. Wait for me."

Robbie disappeared into the hall.

"Big mistake." Red's voice was empty.

"We'll see."

Buddy found a roll of electrician's tape in the desk, told Zo to secure Red's ankles and wrists. Then he ordered Zo to get down on his belly. Buddy bound his wrists, used up the tape doing it. But it wasn't going to be enough to stop him. Buddy finished the roll, stood up, and kicked Zo hard in the temple. The bartender groaned, went slack.

Buddy saw Red flinch.

Red was still watching him, lying there, curled up in a ball, in a puddle of his own blood, as Buddy walked right out the door.

●

"Get your mother a club soda."

"I don't want a soda."

"You heard me. Now, go."

Augustus follows his Pop's orders. He's learned that's the best way, the safest way to live in their home. His mother knows it, too, but tonight she's arguing. *In a mood* is what his Pop calls it when she doesn't follow along. Augustus drags a kitchen chair over in front of the sink. He climbs to reach the cabinets above, where they keep the tall cocktail glasses. Highball glasses. He sees the rocks glasses and the shot glasses. Pop taught him the names. Standing on the chair, he's tall like Pop, and he imagines one day when he won't need a chair to stand on. There's a double window above the sink, looking out directly at the boat dock. Pop's sitting in a lawn chair, facing the lake. He's got a line out. His ultralight rod is wedged between the wooden dock slats. Pop didn't change out of his work clothes. Augustus could smell the animals on him. His mother is dressed up for a dinner party. A green gown with silver threads slashed across the skirt. Bright crystal earrings. She had had her hair done. The windows are open to allow a breeze, and Augustus can hear their arguing. Pop says he's not going to dinner at the Samuelsons'.

"Go by yourself," he says, recasting his line, "I can't stomach an evening of Don Samuelson's asinine conversation."

"You know very well I can't go alone."

"Then don't go."

"We said we'd be there."

"No, *you* said we'd be there. And *you* can still go if it's so important."

"It's not important."

"Then go back in the house and wash that shit out of your hair, scrub the paint off your face. You can fry up dinner after I catch it."

Augustus hears his mother and knows she is crying. It is not an unfamiliar sound. He watches Pop shift in his lawn chair. The sunlight catches the bent aluminum frame and fires a brief star. It reminds Augustus of the sparkling chrome bumpers on Pop's new Buick. He climbs down and fills his mother's glass with ice cubes. On the liquor cart, he can't find club soda. None in the fridge either. He unscrews the cap on a half bottle of tonic water and no gas escapes. He pours the cold, flat liquid over the ice. He notices a word on the label and wonders what *quinine* is. That's a good question for Pop. *I'll get his mind off the argument,* Augustus thinks.

The screen door bangs. Augustus walks quickly but is also careful not to spill the soda. The horizon looks, to Augustus, like a Creamsicle turned sideways and melting. Rain sprinkles lightly across the lake, dimpling the water's surface, but on their dock his parents are dry under a floral canopy. Cool breezes riffle around them. He slows when he sees Mother's face. She is leaning in close to Pop's ear. Her lips are drawn back tight over her teeth and she speaks rough language in a voice Augustus does not recognize. Her chin quivers, but her words are flying fast. Wet bugs landing in Pop's ear. He fidgets. One of her hands, the nails peach and glossy, claws into Pop's shoulder and digs down to hold him still.

A flask of Puerto Rican rum slips from its place, tucked between the blue webbing of the lawn chair, and thunks on the boards under Pop's seat. Pop bends forward to retrieve it. He sweeps his hand through the shadow underneath himself and finds the bottle. Mother attempts to knock it from his grasp. She misses, strikes Pop's wrist. He rises. Mother is screaming at him, using names Augustus hears the older boys use in school. Swear words. Pop swings his hand, the one gripping the bottle, gently at his side. Mother is backing up on the dock.

"Stop it!" Augustus yells at them.

Mother turns and stares at him, open-mouthed. Her face is sweating, red, and splotchy. She returns her gaze to her husband and is about to speak again when he hits her in the mouth with the rum bottle. He steps forward and puts his weight into the blow. Her head snaps back and she sits down hard on the dock. She lies back. Pop straddles her fallen body and hits her with the bottle, a glass pile driver dropping repeatedly on her head. The bottle breaks. But Pop keeps hitting.

Augustus is frozen on the grass.

Pop stands up straight. A string of saliva dangles from his lower lip. He snaps it with his fingers. Wipes his hand on his pants. His shirtfront is speckled with blood. He steps over her leg, wedges one of his shoes under her hipbone, and kicks her into the shallow water beside the dock. She flips, going over the edge. One leg cartwheels high and awkward over the other, the brown toes of her pantyhose showing because her shoes came off during the beating. There is a loud splash. The water is not deep enough for her to float, and she settles on her side in the sand. Her mouth and nose are underwater. The rain has stopped and the water surface is smooth.

Pop reels in a bluegill that has taken down his plastic bobber. He removes the hook, having some difficulty because the fish has been on the line for a while and the bait's been swallowed. He measures the bluegill against the width of his palm. He tosses the fish into a wire basket that hangs at the end of the dock. Pop is ignoring him. But Augustus has not moved.

"Take a good look at her if you want."

Pop's voice makes the hair prickle on Augustus' neck. The handprint bruises on his back sting as if they were fresh. He is dizzy. Pop is going to kill him.

"I've got to make a telephone call, Son. Take this chance to say good-bye to your mother. Don't touch anything until I get back."

Pop passes, and Augustus smells the rum.

Pop says, "That's what you'll get if you don't learn to listen to me."

He pauses at the screen door. He clicks open his Zippo and touches the flame to the tip of a Pall Mall. His smoke hangs like a ghost. He disappears into the unlighted house.

The sun has set. Twilight dwindles on the far shore.

The boy wants to look, feels guilty, and creeps across the dock boards, never taking his wide-eyed stare from her resting place. The disturbed sand has settled. Her dress billows. The subtle currents have turned her in an unnatural position, balanced still on her side but rolling slightly onto her back. She is suspended mid-roll by the water and her body's buoyancy in death. The top of her pinned hairdo is the only part of her not submerged. A plump black stone props the back of her head. She is reachable, sunk in inches of lake water.

Augustus sees, in the quickly darkening water, the gap where her front teeth once were. One of her eyes is mashed shut, but the other watches him. He pulls back. He leans much closer. The eye bulges, is magnified by the water, its iris reflects blue, and the pupil appears soft around the edges like a hole punched through a tin can. Augustus' image in the water grows like a stain as he looms over her, getting nearer. A startled crayfish, not looking or moving in the manner of a living creature but resembling a crude toy, fashioned from sewn-together leather scraps and jerked by a string through the water, stops between her breasts and investigates the sequins affixed to her buttons.

Augustus hears Pop's booming voice speaking in his deep, controlled office tone.

"Well, I'm sorry to call you with such short notice, but Marian's sick and we won't be able to make it."

Augustus pictures the stern features of Pop's face softening as they do when he deals with business matters. Pop makes a joke to Mr. Samuelson about female problems.

"I'll tell her, and I'm sure she'll be feeling better tomorrow. Okay, good-bye, I'll be seeing you, Don."

Augustus is intent on listening, but he can't turn away from the sight below him. When Pop speaks again, he is suddenly at Augustus' side.

"Now go to bed. Take a couple of slices of bread up to your bedroom, if you're hungry. I'll allow you to eat there tonight. Don't make a mess. I've got to straighten things out here."

Augustus empties his mind. He tries to show Pop a face void of expression, judgment, or worries. Pop has to trust him; Augustus needs him. Pop glances over Augustus' shoulder at his murdered wife. Father and son walk back up to the house together.

the other watches him. He pulls back. He leans much closer. The eye bulges, is magnified by the water, its iris reflects blue, and the pupil appears soft around the edges like a hole punched through a tin can. Augustus' image in the water grows like a stain as he looms over her, getting nearer. A startled crayfish, not looking or moving in the manner of a living creature but resembling a crude toy, fashioned from sewn-together leather scraps and jerked by a string through the water, stops between her breasts and investigates the sequins affixed to her buttons.

Augustus hears Pop's booming voice speaking in his deep, controlled office tone.

"Well, I'm sorry to call you with such short notice, but Marian's sick and we won't be able to make it."

Augustus pictures the stern features of Pop's face softening as they do when he deals with business matters. Pop makes a joke to Mr. Samuelson about female problems.

"I'll tell her, and I'm sure she'll be feeling better tomorrow. Okay, good-bye, I'll be seeing you, Don."

Augustus is intent on listening, but he can't turn away from the sight below him. When Pop speaks again, he is suddenly at Augustus' side.

"Now go to bed. Take a couple of slices of bread up to your bedroom, if you're hungry. I'll allow you to eat there tonight. Don't make a mess. I've got to straighten things out here."

Augustus empties his mind. He tries to show Pop a face void of expression, judgment, or worries. Pop has to trust him; Augustus needs him. Pop glances over Augustus' shoulder at his murdered wife. Father and son walk back up to the house together.

Quietly, Pop says, "Lord, she looks bad."

The boy doesn't reply.

Pop locks the bedroom door behind him, and Augustus can hear the opening and closing of drawers in the other bedroom. Their house is modest and neat. A third bedroom is vacant, filled with cardboard boxes, old patient files that Pop is storing becaus his office in town is too small. Pop is a veterinarian. People c him Doc. He went through school on scholarships, and th what Augustus will have to do, even though there's enc money to send him to college when the time comes. Pop him that studying and hard work are best learned early. N loaders in this family. Augustus scores the highest mark fourth-grade class. Kids don't like him.

After Pop exits the house, Augustus peers through hi window. He crawls across the hardwood floor of Inside a shoebox at the bottom of his closet, he binoculars. He is forbidden to touch them; their usu a high shelf in the den. But weeks earlier, he stole th he likes to watch the moon. If Pop found out he t

Mother can't protect him anymore.

He unsnaps the hard-shelled case, loops th head, and presses his eyes to the twin scopes. H

Pop stands in the shallows. Lake water wick Augustus can't make out the sounds. Can't ri dow. So it is a silent movie he follows with h

Pop is working hard. He halts to clear Then, without warning, he gazes up at th glasses turn silver with the moon's glow.

Augustus ducks down. Fears he's bee

Quietly, Pop says, "Lord, she looks bad."

The boy doesn't reply.

Pop locks the bedroom door behind him, and Augustus can hear the opening and closing of drawers in the other bedroom. Their house is modest and neat. A third bedroom is vacant, filled with cardboard boxes, old patient files that Pop is storing because his office in town is too small. Pop is a veterinarian. People call him Doc. He went through school on scholarships, and that's what Augustus will have to do, even though there's enough money to send him to college when the time comes. Pop tells him that studying and hard work are best learned early. No freeloaders in this family. Augustus scores the highest marks in his fourth-grade class. Kids don't like him.

After Pop exits the house, Augustus peers through his upstairs window. He crawls across the hardwood floor of his room. Inside a shoebox at the bottom of his closet, he finds Pop's binoculars. He is forbidden to touch them; their usual place is on a high shelf in the den. But weeks earlier, he stole them. At night, he likes to watch the moon. If Pop found out he took them . . .

Mother can't protect him anymore.

He unsnaps the hard-shelled case, loops the strap over his head, and presses his eyes to the twin scopes. He has to watch.

Pop stands in the shallows. Lake water wicks up his pant legs. Augustus can't make out the sounds. Can't risk opening his window. So it is a silent movie he follows with his eyes.

Pop is working hard. He halts to clear his throat and spit. Then, without warning, he gazes up at the house, and his eyeglasses turn silver with the moon's glow.

Augustus ducks down. Fears he's been seen. Creeps up again.

Pop strips the body and dresses it again in everyday clothes. He has to force Mother's wet arms into her favorite pink windbreaker. The Bodines own one of only a half-dozen homes on Big Hatchet Lake. The shore is black, and Pop doesn't worry about witnesses.

But I'm a witness, Augustus thinks. He could tell the sheriff's police the whole story and put Pop in jail, get him the gas chamber. But Pop's too smart. He'd make things come out so that Augustus would be blamed, or at least he'd have people convinced his son was a liar. For now, Augustus just wants to watch and remember.

Pop is lean but bone strong. His belt bites into a belly that's hard and shiny and almost hairless. Augustus sees it in the mornings when Pop shaves.

Mother gets crammed in the bow of their boat. Pop starts the motor and rides out toward the center of Big Hatchet. Augustus is ice-cold with fright, thinking that Pop is abandoning him, escaping. But the boat angles—a curve in the foam—until it's pointing back at the shore. To a spot only slightly northeast from where it started.

Pop guns the motor and rams into a massive hump of rocks the locals know to steer clear around—unless you're anchoring nearby and trying to pick up some walleye. He dumps the body headfirst onto the far side of the hump. The boat's lodged in tight and nosing upward. The prop pin's broken, and the motor smoke is gray in the black sky. Pop lowers himself into the water. He locates the sandbar forming a horseshoe just beyond the rocks. Seconds later, he's kicking up splashes, the lake no deeper

than his ankles. He begins his walk home. The accident is set less than fifty yards from the Bodine's dock.

Pop picks his way along the pitched and cluttered shoreline.

Augustus hides the binoculars and climbs into bed.

Marian went for a boat ride to get some fresh air. He urged her not to go, Pop says, told her it was foolish, but, *damn-it-to-hell*, he should've gone with her or insisted she stay put. It was all his fault. He reminded her to run the lights and, *forgodsake dear*, he recalled saying, *please go slow.* He showed friends her heart pills, *the tiny bottle she forgot,* he said, shaking the keepsake of his loss like a baby rattle. She must've felt one of her attacks coming on, panicked, and drove the boat up on those brutal rocks.

It threw her. He would gesture with a sweep of his hand. She was rushing to get home, and he was already sleeping. When he woke up to the coughing motor, smelled it burning out there . . . Pop would point now, wherever he was telling his story and say, "I just knew something bad had happened." He was all broken up inside.

"My fault, my fault."

No, don't do this to yourself, Doc. You couldn't have known. Remember, you have to be strong for your son.

Pop would nod to show he understood. But words failed him when he thought about his poor, motherless boy.

6

Buddy drove five miles over the limit, watching the configurations of headlights in his rearview mirror. Robbie slept in the Caddy's backseat. They had switched cars at O'Hare, leaving Robbie's Camaro in the long-term parking lot. If Red tracked them to the airport, he would assume the brothers had caught a flight out of town. He'd make a guess, thinking they would cross a few borders for security. But Buddy was heading back to Gunnar, and it wouldn't take long for Red to find him there.

Let him come, Buddy thought. *We'll fight, and win or lose in my backyard.*

Robbie didn't want to chance going to his apartment to pack. Their only stop was at a bank, where Robbie emptied his safety deposit box. His savings, plus the cash they'd stolen from Red, which Robbie's quick count put at a hundred grand and change, would finance a comfortable trip to the other side of the world. Buddy wasn't going anywhere. Robbie knew only one way to get by, and that was bookmaking. Anywhere in the country, if he started bringing in real money, Red would track him down. Besides that, Robbie was a hometown boy. Getting him to pull up stakes was a pure fantasy.

Buddy turned off the highway every twenty miles or so, checking for a tail. He reached under the passenger seat and felt the pistol grip of the sawed-off. At close range the load of double-aught shot would cut a man in half. *But you had better not miss,* he told himself.

Buddy wondered what his life would have been if he'd lived straight. Those thoughts led nowhere. They didn't lead to Margot. He'd gotten to her by taking his own crooked path. He knew he could continue keeping his past a secret from her. Fold up the facts and bury them deep. But where did that leave him down the road? One day they'd fold *him* up, put him in a box, and throw dirt on it. He'd lie in the ground forever with his bundle of lies. If she pulled through this, then he'd tell her about the way he had lived, the choices and the mistakes. Let her decide if he was worth anything.

Buddy drafted behind a speeding tanker hauling kerosene.

Stars salted the sky. The moon reflected on the Caddy's waxed hood. Trees were missing from the landscape. Farmers' fields lay planted on both sides of the highway. Buddy could smell the crops when he slowed for the exit ramps. Along a monotonous stretch of blacktop, he opened his window. Robbie woke up, shifted, and dozed again. Nervous sweat had dried into their clothes. The breeze whistled around inside the Caddy and chased away the stale air surrounding two middle-aged men.

Buddy reached for the radio knobs, tuned in a small college station playing classic jazz. The signal was weak, but he left it there. Slow music. The song faded. The hiss of a cymbal lingered and faded too. A kid's voice came on. He had a good set of pipes. Buddy pictured him holed up in a dinky studio, nursing his coffee and a cigarette. All his friends asleep. He was doing something he loved and it came through. He introduced the next song, praising the fullness of tone achieved by a trumpeter long dead and largely forgotten. The record popped, caught a scratch, cleaned up in time for the first bars. Another ballad from another time, a time when it was okay to be sad and alone and not looking for a quick cure. Buddy pictured Margot in her hospital bed. In a few hours, the skim-milk light of dawn would spill into the room. But she wouldn't be awake to see it.

They passed outside the range of the signal. Static broke in, and Buddy rotated the dial until he found a weather report. He switched the radio off, and the dashboard dimmed. The green face of the speedometer lit the Roman numerals on his wristwatch. They would arrive at the cabin by one A.M.

The next time Buddy exited, he pulled up to the pumps of a twenty-four-hour gas station. He filled the tank, took out his money clip, and tapped the rear window. Robbie frowned and tried to focus one eye while squeezing the other shut against the exploding glare of lights.

"You want coffee?" Buddy said through the glass.

A yawn. "Sure."

"Cream and sugar?"

"Two creams, three sugars. And, hey, if they got 'em, buy me a Hershey bar with almonds."

Buddy nodded. Three strides nearer the mini-market, Buddy heard a car door open behind him. He turned.

"One of those little packs of cheese and crackers, too, if they got 'em," Robbie called out. His face was haggard and puffy.

Buddy waved to show he'd understood.

"If they look fresh, pick out some doughnuts. Jellies or frosted," Robbie said.

Buddy nodded.

The clerk had a magenta rash on his neck. His Adam's apple convulsed as he swallowed the dregs of a blueberry slush. He did a double take when Buddy stepped toward the cash register. Put his hands in the air. His ass backing up, knocking over a Skoal dispenser.

"Whatever, dude, take it all."

Buddy closed his eyes, realized he'd forgotten about the .22 stuck in his belt.

•

Augustus hears the news from a girl selling soft-serve ice cream. Rumors. She's talking to her girlfriend after dealing out cones to a group of toddlers that her friend baby-sits at a nursery school. The children assemble in a straggly line and hold sticky hands. Lost napkins blow across the gravel. Augustus buys a butter-scotch sundae.

Margot is awake.

The pale gold topping adheres to his spoon, and Augustus licks the edge. The frozen treat sparks a headache. Mild pain, sweet and cold and soon passing.

Shaded, under a red vinyl umbrella that leans askew in the hole of a telephone cable spool, he listens for details.

The girls' talk turns to boys.

Augustus pitches his topping-smeared dish into a garbage can teeming with honeybees. A bee lands on his lips. He dusts it

away, strolls the length of the parking lot, and gets into his truck.

The children move off in a V, like ducks. Augustus doesn't approve of their pastel shirts, sunny untrimmed hair, and chunky shoes. He hates how both sexes are dressed alike. A person can't tell boys from girls. The unisex tots wave good-bye to the ice-cream girl.

*

Maybe it was because the Caddy was confessional dark and Robbie was in the backseat not having to look at his brother's face. Maybe Robbie just needed to let go of some of the guilt.

"Hey, Earl."

"Uh-huh."

"Look, I'm sorry about last time. When I was in Gunnar, you know, passing out my cards. It was stupid."

"Forget it."

"No, listen. I think I'm partly responsible for this. Nykki, she had a card. That's how she found out about X-ray's. She had one of my cards."

"Who's Nykki?"

"Oh, I mean Melissa. Nykki was the name she used when she danced."

"Melissa was Nykki?"

"Yeah." Robbie turned over. "She was nice, you know? A decent person."

Buddy heard him gulping air like he was going to cry. But he didn't. As far as Buddy could tell, Robbie went back to sleep.

•

Augustus is counting windows.

Third floor, fourth window from the left. A vase filled with pink carnations on the sill. He hears a siren. An ambulance lurches around the corner and accelerates to the EMERGENCY sign. Paramedics bounce a woman on a stretcher up the concrete skirt, triggering the automatic doors. The woman is dazed, tousled, but she is speaking to the female paramedic. Both women are in their late twenties, brunettes. The patient looks familiar, a party girl, and most likely an overdose victim.

I know you. Augustus thinks. *Yes, Amanda.*

Augustus waits, smelling oil dripping from his engine. Thunder rumbles in the distance, though the sky above is blue. On the wind, the damp odor of rain comes. He smokes and watches. The male paramedic sips a can of orange soda. The brunette stares at the first falling raindrops. A wind gust shakes the trees and sprays loose dirt into the air. Bottlecap droplets clap the hot cement. Summer storm. Through the sudden sheeting rain, Augustus reaches the emergency room doors. He asks the intake coordinator about Amanda.

"Amanda Austin?"

"Yes. It's an overdose."

"Are you a member of the patient's family?"

"A good friend. I'm here to help until her family arrives. They might not come because of the circumstances. You know, because it was from drugs. They're not supportive, haven't been in the past. They're her problem, if you ask me."

"Well . . ."

"The *paramedic?* He told me to follow them here in my car. He said I could go in with her."

A hesitation. Her eyes survey the busy waiting room. She decides.

"Room Six, through these doors past the nurses' station." Then she calls out, "Next." A sweaty woman, wearing a cropped Black Sabbath tank top and shooting glasses, makes her way to the counter. Sunburn blisters her shoulders.

The security buzzer hums and Augustus is in. He waltzes past the nurses, past Amanda doped on her stretcher, down the hall to the elevators. Arrow up. He lights it. The door retracts, he steps forward, punches three. He's lifted away.

Going smoothly, slick as can be, until the battleship floor nurse turns the hose on his plans.

"She's gone for tests. You can't wait here. Let me see, yes, she won't be back for an hour at least. Where's your pass?"

"Pass?"

"You must have registered downstairs. Did you do that, sir? I'll call down to the Visitors' Desk and ask them if you left your pass on the counter. Can I have your name? Sir? Can I please have your . . ."

He takes the stairway, bursts out a fire door, setting off the alarm. The hospital wails. The rain has stopped, but everything outside is soaked and dripping. Augustus worries about a security guard checking the exits. The downpour releases smells trapped in the soil. He can taste corpses as he walks through rainbow puddles to his truck. Pulling slowly out of the lot, he hears an inner voice.

What are you telling them, Goat? Better not be talking about me. I'm coming for you.

Because you're mine.

•

Robbie was restless. He'd slept too long. Sleep had been a stranger since Buddy plucked Nykki's hand from a Wisconsin river. Robbie pushed himself off the cot and kicked aside Buddy's sleeping bag. It smelled from wood smoke and gun oil. The rural silence got to him. A glance into the storm outside did nothing to soothe his nerves. His bleary eyes mimed ghostly in the window glass. He moved away. Located the chain that worked the light over the sink. Under the weak bulb, Robbie fried grits, Canadian bacon, and eggs in a skillet.

Buddy woke up. Night and morning passed while he tossed on the mattress, dreaming. *Margot lying in the weeds at the river's edge, and he was too weak and too slow—his gun hand moved in syrup—he couldn't stop what was happening. A bear carried her off into the woods, claws like knives clicking on the rocks. Face like a man's but covered in fur. Black snout drizzling blood.* He rolled out of bed. Stuffed his feet into old brown slippers.

Robbie had one of the cigars from Vic in his mouth. He was attempting to light it off the stove's electric coils.

"Need a match?" Buddy asked.

"That would help."

Buddy pointed to the cupboard. A box of lucifers. Robbie fired one with his thumbnail. He puffed, waved the flame out, and filled his corner with smoke. On the stovetop, the match smoldered. Buddy sat in a wooden rocker that made his butt go numb. He stood, stretched, and wandered into the bathroom to throw cold water on his face. He soaped his chin and shaved. Brushed his teeth. The well water tasted like sulfur and iron. Buddy spit into the drain. Went back to the kitchen.

The coffee machine gurgled and leaked into the pot.

Buddy said, "I've got to go to town to buy us groceries, then swing by the hospital and check on Margot. You want to come along?"

"Out here, you're the boss." Robbie talked around the cigar.

Buddy nodded. "Hang around the cabin. I'll leave the sawed-off just in case. The Cobra is under the bed. I'll take the .22."

Robbie unlatched the backdoor. "Hey, look," he said. "The sun's out again."

●

"Open your eyes."

Margot did.

"Do you understand me?"

"Yes." Her voice, dry and scraped, was digging itself out of a grave.

Someone stood next to her bed.

A doctor. Dr. Genesee.

She had talked to her mother during the night. Asked her simple questions. *Where's Duncan? What happened? When can I go home?*

Dr. Genesee said, "You have a visitor. Would you like a visitor right now?"

Buddy leaned forward and did his best to appear cheerful.

Margot's eyes made a slow unsteady sweep from Genesee to the vase of carnations to the pale wall. Then her eyes closed. Stayed closed. Genesee shook his head and Buddy started to leave. Her thin hand lifted and dropped to the sheet top.

"Hi, Buddy."

"Oh, hey, welcome back."

"What's wrong with you?"

Buddy shifted his weight.

"Your arm." She swallowed, nodded. "Is broken?"

Buddy touched his sling. "No. I'm doing okay." *God,* he thought, *she looks like hell.* "Doc says you're doing fine. I told him she's . . . I told him you're a strong person."

"Tell my mom I can't go to practice because I hit my head."

"I can do that." Buddy looked at Genesee.

Genesee waved him off. "She just coming out of it," the doctor said. "Nothing to worry about."

"You'll have to play one of the other girls," Margot said.

"Then that's what I'll do."

"Bye."

"Okay, bye."

Margot pointed at him. "Don't forget about practice."

"You rest. I'll play the other girls."

"And tell my mom."

"Yes, and I'll tell your mom."

•

Beetles crawl over one another to eat. Shells click and mouth parts champ. With his eyes shut, Augustus enjoys listening to them here in the coolness of his cellar. Rude creatures thrive without sunlight. He toes the bones with his work boot. On a particle-board bookcase, a Coleman lantern burns. His notebook lies open. He uncaps his marker and writes.

How marvelous it is to observe Nature. I am her instrument. I am active in my town, my river, and my woods. I deliver signs unto the People. They know of me, yet know not me. But I am changing. New growth has begun. I am made strange. I will follow where my Nature leads.

•

The town isn't talking about Margot anymore. There's a headless body washed up on an oxbow getting all the attention. TV vans zoom into Gunnar. Locals are stunned at the developing news.

A shocking discovery: two skeletons buried practically on top of each other a quarter mile downriver from the oxbow crime scene. A birdwatcher lacing his boot notices, in a pocket of silky mud, the lumps of a human spine.

There is digging. When the State Police detectives find the third leg, they slow the excavation and contemplate driving in a backhoe to unearth the entire slope. But they are misguided. It is not a grave. Dead bodies went into the water. These two were dropped together. A rain-soaked three A.M. and something moved on the wet black bridge, alone. The river was foaming with pearls. Where the water went, the bodies did too. An unspectacular springtime flood left them on higher ground.

Media people are checking into motels and filling the diners by lunchtime. Nationwide coverage. The buzz says a serial murderer stalks along the Skin River.

Melissa Teagles, the decapitated woman, and two unidentified skeletons.

Sheriff Rafferty catches a shitstorm when he refuses to call a press conference. He sends an unspoken message to get out of town and let the lawmen solve the crimes. The cameras capture it perfectly: he's in way over his head.

"Bozo the Cop," Augustus says. He picks a strawberry seed from his teeth, drops the toothpick on his plate. Townies sit at the counter. Reporters prefer booths.

The waitress fetches cheeseburgers and Cokes ordered by the gang of four from Channel 9.

Rafferty strides past the window. The reporters leave their booth and trail him down the sidewalk. They shout questions.

Augustus shakes his head. He tells Laurie the waitress, "I feel a little bit sorry for poor Rafferty."

"You think he won't find this maniac?"

"He's no maniac. And I bet he gets away with it."

"What makes you so sure?"

"Evil generally knows where to hide."

The waitress nods, thinks, *that's sad but probably true.*

•

Buddy was lying awake, thinking about Margot. Genesee said that if she continued to show improvement, he'd send her home from the hospital in a couple of days. Buddy wondered if she'd want to come back to the apartment, back to the Chimney. He rolled over, felt the sutures in his shoulder pulling. During the night, Red had slithered into his dreams, where he sat on the fender of a Trans Am cleaning dirt from under his fingernails. Lester was in the front seat, a syringe between his teeth, tapping his arm, looking for a vein.

Buddy promised himself, no matter what was going to happen, he had to keep Margot out of harm's way.

He heard a metallic ping as his clock radio switched itself on.

●

Augustus sews the skin and hides his stitch. A shot of Jack passes his lips, and he brushes the hair clean. With his thumbnail, he scrapes a dried trickle of glue from the left eyeball. He rubs a soft cloth between the antlers and appraises his handiwork. *This buck looks better restored than he did the afternoon the hunter bagged him.*

It's been a week since they found her body.

From the radio comes the announcement of a name: *Mary O'Connor.*

●

Since Buddy returned to managing the Chimney, Robbie had taken over one corner of the cabin near the TV so he could watch his games. He punched up the volume. Boy began pacing from the TV stand to an invisible spot under the window. Robbie rose from the cot to let him outside.

He saw headlights turning off. Their white afterglow swimming before his eyes.

"Buddy, we've got company."

Buddy looked up from a jumble of tackle he was sorting, a

burr of rusty hooks and monofilament line. He wore bifocals. "What? Turn the damn television down. I can't hear you."

Robbie said, "There's a fucking car down at the bottom of the driveway. Headlights just went out."

Buddy snatched the sawed-off from next to the woodstove. He cocked the hammers and flattened himself beside the door.

"Tell me what you see. Keep low, goddamnit."

"Maybe somebody's walking this way. Too dark to see."

"Okay, I'm going out. I'll come at him from the side of the house." Buddy pointed with the shotgun. "He still on the move?"

Robbie nodded. "Left side of the driveway."

"I'll shoot across the porch if he comes up. Cut his legs out. You hear the sawed-off, take my path around the side. If they're firing back, then head for the river. Follow the water to town. Don't wait for me."

"Got it."

"Take the money and the Cobra. If you get caught, dump everything."

Robbie slid down the wall, duck-walked underneath the window, and went into Buddy's bedroom. Buddy headed outside.

Boy chased after him.

Going through the shrubs planted against the cabin, Buddy reached the porch and nosed the shotgun between the lowest porch rails.

Boy bounded past him, snapping his jaws like some backwoods hound.

The blast.

Boy's tail dropped, his good ear flattened, and a whimper replaced the growl in his throat. He scooted under the porch.

Robbie called out, "Buddy, you okay?"

"I almost shot the fucking dog."

"Anybody out there?"

"Not now." Buddy's eyes were still flashing. He spun around. But it was only darkness and trees and a scared dog.

Robbie opened the front door and hit the floodlight. His silhouette dwarfed the cabin behind him.

A voice from the woods, "Hey, Bud, is that you?"

Buddy had the shotgun up again. Robbie dropped from sight.

"What you shootin' at, man?" The voice was coming closer.

Buddy saw nothing. He had one barrel left. Wanted the target on top of him before he pulled the trigger again.

"He's in the trees," Robbie whispered.

"Stay there. Let me get my shot." Buddy jammed the sawed-off against his hip. His eyes were still picking out ghosts from the blast.

"Don't level me, okay, I'm coming out," the voice said.

Not ten feet away. And not coming up from the road where Robbie said he saw the car. But behind him, the opposite direction. Up from the river.

A breakaway shadow ambled into the light. Buddy spun on it.

"Ho, ho. Easy does it," the shadow said.

"Augustus?"

"Last time I checked." The big man had his hands in his pockets. He wore a sleeveless camouflage shirt and a black calfskin vest with long fringe. His jeans were muddied. He rocked on his heels, smiled. He was lighting a joint in the corner of his mouth. He waved out the match like a white flag.

Buddy heard his brother shifting on the porch, the thunk of

something heavy he was dragging along the boards. A loud creak said he was about to move hard.

Buddy had no time to call him off.

Robbie launched a firewood log the size of a cinder block. It soared high, over Augustus' head, and landed on the ground.

"Jeez, you boys are wired. I gotta get a taste of what you're holding," Augustus laughed. Coughed. He bent forward and slapped his knees. There was something forced about his behavior. Buddy wrote it off to the homegrown cigarette.

"Sorry. We're paranoid. Me and my brother." Buddy pointed and said, "That's him chucking stumps." He wiped his forehead with the back of his hand, watching the knuckles come away as wet as if he'd dipped them in a rain barrel.

"Nah, don't apologize. Paranoia's good. Especially in your case."

"Why's that?"

"Lemme say this, okay? Keep your eyes on Rafferty. Man has got it in for you. He's been bringing up your name in some pretty suspect circles. Seein' if you're dirty. There're folks running with those crowds who'd say anything about anybody if it got them a get-out-of-jail-free card."

"Is that right?"

"Watch your back, man. Keep your powder dry and all that crap." Augustus sucked in, and blew a cloud of smoke thick enough to set off alarms. His pupils were as big as thumbholes. He swayed.

"Thanks for the heads-up," Buddy said.

But Augustus was out of sight.

Shadow merged with shadows. The woods swallowed him

whole, then spit out a glint of steel earring turning in the moon-light.

The brothers could hear the murmur of a soft chuckle and a low voice talking to itself until it dropped away and all that was left was river music.

The sound of water running over rock.

7

Margot slapped the flyswatter on the weathered board.

Got him. One transparent wing stuck up from the bloody blot. She wiped it with a paper towel. The flyswatter rested across her lap. With hooded eyes, she went back to rocking. She watched another fly, swirling. The afternoon crawled an inch. Bands of sunlight heated the outer edges of the porch. A pitcher of iced tea sweated marbles, brewing in the sunniest corner. She had just washed her hair again. Her blossomy sundress smelled like the soap roses in her suitcase.

The stink of pigs traveled on the breeze. Their pen was built as close to the house as some people dug swimming pools. If she turned her head, out of the wind, she could watch an orange tomcat hunting mice along the foundation of the barn. He peeked into holes where the mortar had been eaten away.

Beyond the barn were stables. Horses. But she was in no shape to ride. Her task was to remember, and she couldn't.

Her bruises were turning ocher and brown. But the monster's handprints were lasting. She wondered if they'd be permanent. If she'd have to explain them to people, like tattoos. She developed a habit of inspecting herself, unscrewing the shade from her night table lamp and tipping it so the bare bulb warmed her skin. She would stand there naked in the otherwise dark room. Her fresh nightgown fanned out on the end of the bed. She would pass the light over her wounds. Looking for changes. Fading.

For Duncan, she would get better. Emotionally, she was doing everything she could to keep from blowing apart. She had to keep her son safe. Had to keep her family together. *Why did that suddenly seem so impossible?*

The bruises were giant fuzzy moths. Drawn to the light source, they spread their ripped velvet wings. She sensed a constant pressure coming from them. Wished they'd fly.

A broad-shouldered man stepped out of the barn. He leaned on a pitchfork while his jaw worked a piece of maple taffy. His red overalls were covered in pig manure. He pulled another taffy from his pocket and shot the wrapper at the tomcat. The tom spooked. The man glanced up at the farmhouse.

Margot kept silent.

From behind her, a soft voice said, "Are you cool enough, honey?"

"I'm comfortable."

"Would you like some of my lotion?"

Margot stopped scratching the purple spot above her elbow. "No thank you."

"All right, dear. Your mother's trying to put Duncan down for his nap."

"Tell her to wait. I've done enough sitting for one day."

"Whatever you think is best."

Margot left the rocker, and her aunt called past her to the

man loitering by the barn. Uncle Bill stabbed his pitchfork into the ground. He hobbled across the yard. Before coming inside, he bent for the tea pitcher. He hugged the warm glass, teabags sloshing, against his chest.

Margot went to her son.

•

They identified the body by matching prints to a DUI arrest. Rafferty had his men searching the riverbanks for Mary O'Connor's head, though he was convinced the killer took it for a trophy. He couldn't scrub the smell of her from his hands or forget the sight of detectives standing around him in a circle, wearing handkerchiefs folded into triangles over their noses and mouths. His undigested breakfast messed the front of his shirt, and he bent double over the stained water lapping at his rubber boots. Where he stepped clouds of sand puffed into miniature Hiroshimas. Scattered snails floated in the lethargic grassy oxbow. Bulrushes grew high. The naked body had come to rest on a sandbar.

Insects had found her first.

Preliminary reports from the medical examiner noted bite marks on her breasts, thighs, and buttocks. A pattern of the killer's teeth would be difficult to obtain because each bite had been sliced across in several directions. Multiple superficial stab wounds were concentrated on the upper torso. Upward and downward thrusts entered the victim from numerous angles, indicating that her killer had switched the weapon from hand to hand during one phase of the attack. Two potentially lethal wounds were apparent: one severed her aorta and the other punctured her heart. The weapon was probably a sturdy hunting knife, the kind you could find on display in every discount sporting goods department.

O'Connor was left-handed. The killer had wrenched her stronger arm from its socket. It was not clear if the decapitation occurred postmortem or if it was the cause of death. Taken as a whole, the murder and mutilation pointed to a suspect who possessed considerable physical strength and ambidexterity, as well as a general knowledge of anatomy and practical skill with a blade.

A six-inch lock of black hair had been cut from Mary's now missing head and woven between her fingers. It confirmed Rafferty's worst fears. Add this signature to the Teagles case, throw in the two skeletons—well, it didn't take the FBI to figure out what the evidence said. They had a serial killer trolling the quiet streets of Gunnar.

Rafferty cursed. Except for dealing with the tribal bullshit, his job had been easy, an office other men envied.

Autumn weather was probably less than a month away. Merchants always had hopes for a lingering summer. The sheriff's ulcer fried in his stomach like it was leaking battery acid. He munched Zantac. Sleep dwindled. He turned his clock to the wall.

The night after finding O'Connor, Rafferty filled a glass with cold milk and went into the yard to drink it. He stood next to the Weber grill in his underwear. Stomped morning dew from a chaise longue and sat. He owned all the land for a half-mile around his house.

Observing his fifth sunrise of the week, Rafferty decided his future. He set a seasonal deadline. If he didn't have the killer in his jail by the first snow, a real snow announcing winter, then he'd walk away from the job. He'd come to hate the long, tough, dark part of the year. The prospect of meat-locker cold and being shut in with his failure made it simple. Rafferty would take his family and his pride to Pensacola.

But he still had some time to turn things around. *Hell,* he thought, *it shouldn't be all that hard to find what was needed.* To Rafferty, that was simple, too. Bayes giving them Melissa's hand, practically saying *Look what I did, fellas.* Then he attacks his own waitress. Both a stupid move and a bold one. Now the simple answer wasn't always so simple to prove. But Rafferty told himself that he *knew* Bayes did it, knew it as if he'd stood there in the woods watching the blood fly.

●

Out on the redwood glider, Robbie smoked his way to the bottom of Buddy's cigar box. His nostrils burned. Frogs were singing in the dampness while Robbie contemplated a wedge of the night sky glittering through the treetops. He pushed off with his heels and sawed the glider back and forth, making the dry hinges cry for a squirt of oil. Boy sprawled across the top stair. His paws twitched, lively with dreams.

Inside the cabin, a bottle neck clinked against a heavy glass.

Robbie abandoned the glider and tried to jog up the driveway with a stogie between his teeth. *I thought I saw lights. I'm sorry.* He ran a little faster. Ran from the answering silence. *But there was somebody out there, even if he didn't have a car. That hopped-up Grizzly Adams taking a walk in woods so thick you could poke your eye out seven times just bending over to tie your shoe.* Robbie ran until the cigar glowed cherry bright. Something about that guy in the woods nagged at him.

Under a low-slung branch sprouting jackknife fronds, Robbie started coughing. He saw stars. Then his mind showed him a vision of Nykki. She emerged from a fog and paraded into view. Her hair was wet and sleek as feathers. She wasn't dressed for dancing. Fresh from a shower in the X-ray's dressing room, she was wearing jeans and a denim shirt. She had her backpack, her college books. She was heading off to the library to study for an English midterm. She put on her glasses and complained about how the smoke in the club irritated her contact lenses. His eyes followed her. Robbie's knowledge of Nykki, a woman so sweet in nature, so kind, who could transform herself into a sensual being, was thrilling. Robbie thought that, in another life, this would be the woman he'd marry. But in this life, he asked her if she had time for a cup of coffee and a raisin Danish.

Robbie coughed again to clear his head. Her unreal image melted away. Sick of the cigar and his thoughts, he hunted the side yard for a place to sleep. When his fingers discovered the hammock, he crawled in. The pouch sagged, almost touching the grass.

Light bled into the forest, suffusing the lakeside with bottle ambers and greens. It seeped along the tree trunks and dappled the vast canopy of leaves with gold. Underneath, coy salamanders raced for the shade.

•

After a night like the last, Buddy's brain started in a slower gear. He was thirsty but not enough to raise himself from the bed.

Warm sunlight touched the bedposts, and he kicked his legs free from the sheet. Tried to will himself back to sleep.

He saw the painted bay as he steered his fishing boat to the sea. Calm waters in the distance. Spray cooled his lips. He imagined himself alone on the damp deck. The horizon before him empty and impossibly white.

●

Outskirts of Gunnar. A midnight blue Ford Bronco hugs the blacktop. Climbs and dips. The hills pass. Windows open to let the smoke out. Smells of nearby water, scrub pine, and burning truck exhaust swirl inside. On the roadside, farms in various stages of dying give way to gas stations and burger joints. Bait shops and motels take over the landscape close to the town. Some of the motel owners hang faded wooden signs advertising AIR-CONDITIONING AND FREE IN-ROOM TV.

There's a train trestle painted with graffiti. The two-lane scoops down under. Any farther is the town limits. Banana yellow letters are spray-painted on the trestle supports. Across rusted beams, the words: INJUN KILLER. Higher up, but not hard to see, a drippy green: HOLLY BLOWS ME. The one driving says, "Junior, don't forget *her* number." The other man in the truck laughs.

Lower, off in the corner and hidden by a tree, too small to read from a speeding vehicle, WELCOME ALL GOATS is written in crumbling bronze. GUNNAR SUCKS in baby blue.

"Smokestack." A thick finger points to the horizon, the Black Chimney.

"Yeah, let's turn around. Pick a motel. Get settled."

The Bronco pulls into the Breezy Rock parking lot. What Marcy Johns notices first from the motel office is the black man. Then she sees the white guy's cast, stark against an unbuttoned cuff of orange silk. It looks likes he's carrying an enormous mushroom.

•

Margot moving beneath him, her teeth clenched, the muscles in her pretty face knotting softly. Slickness between their bodies. A scratchy Pendleton blanket under them, underneath her. Night above them like colored glass. A kerosene lantern sputtered. He looked down, saw fine gingery hairs on her stomach. Lower, a smear of shadow and movement.

Her fingers laced behind his head. Wet, white teeth parting. He dropped his shoulders. An oily pivot of her hips loosened something in him. Her mouth opened to scream. But he'd taped it shut. Taped her eyes too. She pushed him out. Blood, thick as honey, covered his torso.

Buddy was suddenly awake.

Rolling over, alone, he found a wet spot on his hip for the first time in a decade. A flaring of arthritis began to work an ice pick into his neck. Guilt, on a bad switch, flickered inside him. He left the bed, cold-showered, and put on fresh underwear. Then went into the living room where his brother slept.

Robbie wasn't there. Car in the drive so Buddy guessed he'd gone for a walk.

He came back to the bedroom and paused at the window long enough to inspect his reflection and drag a comb through his hair. He looked though the drawers, found a clean pair of jeans and a blue cotton shirt.

Robbie banged through the door.

"What is it?" Buddy asked.

"That guy last night who came up from the river?"

"Augustus."

"I've seen him before, Earl. Last night I wasn't so sure. But the more I'm thinking about it . . . it's the same guy."

"Where was it you saw him?"

"At X-ray's. That guy was at X-ray's."

●

"Look, I'm no informer."

"You're just somebody who knows something."

"It's been bugging me."

"I can imagine."

"I consider him a friend. And let's get this straight from the get-go, I don't think he's guilty." At least forty pairs of eyes were watching them. Silent witnesses.

"Go on."

"It was damn strange, that's all."

"Strange doesn't mean guilty. You shouldn't feel bad about talking to me. We need all the help we can get."

"I know. Well, it's that he asked me this question."

"What question?"

"He asked me how long a body would last on ice. *In a tub of ice* were his exact words as I recall."

"A human body?"

"Yes."

"This conversation was before Melissa Teagles was kidnapped?"

"Yes, it was. Day or two before she went missing."

Sheriff Rafferty looked away from the man's face. He jotted a few notes on his pad, underlined the word *Bayes*. The man rose to refill his cup without offering the coffeepot to his guest. Rafferty studied the fish, the deer heads, and the bear with its terrible mouth frozen open. The plastic tongue fixed between real teeth. The room smelled strongly of paint thinner.

"Why do you think he asked you?"

"Because of my special knowledge. The work I do here in my shop everyday."

Rafferty nodded. "I'll need you to come to the office and make an official statement. To sign off on what you've told me here today, Mr. Bodine."

"I don't want this talk we had getting back to him. I think the man is innocent."

"We will keep it private unless it becomes a matter for the court."

"Oh, let's hope it never goes that far."

*

Buddy sat across from his brother, listening.

Robbie said, "He was motioning like, you know, with a bill in his hand, and when Nykki gets close to him . . . that guy . . . Augustus, he says something to her. And she gets angry and kind of weepy at the same time. Goes running off the stage. She almost quit over it."

"What did he say?"

"She wouldn't tell me." Robbie was nodding his head. "But I'm pretty sure it was something about knowing her. I mean he's from Gunnar. She's from Gunnar. And the one thing Nykki worried about was that her parents might find out she was … dancing at a place like X-ray's."

"You're sure it was him."

"No question."

Buddy was thinking, *Robbie and his little lavender cards.* Buddy had invited Robbie up to Gunnar for the reopening of the Black Chimney. Robbie was feeling good, drinking too much, and he started handing out cards for X-ray's. "Show the card and get in for a free show," he was saying to anyone who'd listen. Buddy had pulled him into the Chimney's kitchen.

"What the fuck are you doing?"

"Let go. What's the matter if I drum up some business?"

"What's the matter is I'm trying to keep a low profile. I don't need people associating me with a strip club in Chicago."

"What, I'm somebody to be ashamed of?"

"No. That's not it." Buddy released Robbie's arm. *"How you figure anybody from up here is gonna travel all the way to Chicago just to go to X-ray's?"*

"Guys might be there anyway. On business."

"Robbie, no cards." He took the stack from Robbie's hand. *"My place is a family bar and grill. Don't piss on it."*

The next morning Robbie left without saying good-bye. Cleaning up the bar that afternoon, Buddy found more cards stuck in the corners of the men's room mirrors. Since then, he hadn't opened any of Robbie's letters. Had only talked to him, reluctantly, on the phone.

Buddy got up and went into his bedroom. He opened a drawer. He came to the table and dropped the letter in front of Robbie.

"Did you send me this?"

Robbie stared at his fingernails.

"Robbie." Buddy touched his brother's shoulder. "Why would you do that?"

"You shut me out."

"I had reasons."

"Yeah, well, you're not the only person on the planet with reasons for what you do." Robbie's lip was trembling. "I thought Red . . . I thought he was the one that did Nykki. I needed help."

"You were . . . seeing her? Something like that?"

"No, no. She had a boyfriend here, in Gunnar. Kyle. She was in love with Kyle."

"The two of you never . . ."

"We used to go out for breakfast after the club closed. Only thing we ever shared was pancakes."

Buddy watched Robbie trying to hold it together.

"Hey, Rob, it's okay."

"She was . . . good to be around."

Buddy said, "Don't we all wish for somebody like that?"

As he uttered those words, he thought about Margot inviting him up to her apartment the night of the attack. Her eyes were shining, softened yet bright like sea glass. They held the promise of all she could offer to a man on the downward slope of mid-life, one who had lived brutally, dangerously and, at times, with no hope. Then he saw the slouching outline of

Augustus sitting on the riverside, eager to snatch that promise away.

The hand on his brother's shoulder closed into a fist.

●

This afternoon they're peeping on a couple groping in the back-seat of a blue Cavalier. Augustus detects the ruffled edge of an invaded bra. Urgent caresses and two faces mashed together, slumping against the passenger's door. The lovers squeeze closer. Augustus focuses where their bodies meet. He makes a kind of contact. Augustus concentrates on the woman's face. He tries to read the shade of lust in her expression. Comparisons will be made. He looks for *the look*. Like a swimmer she turns for a breath, to the window and the second glass of the binocular lens. Finally, a judgment can be handed down. She's not one. Augustus is bored. He drops the binoculars into a cardboard box filled with newspapers.

"Lou says he thinks you killed those women."

"Fat Lou or Lou the Swede?"

Kurt holds up a long knobby finger. He's keeping in a big hit of pot. His eyes close, and then with the cloud come words, "The Swede."

"He's sore at me for dogging him in front of Geraldine at Maxie's birthday party."

Kurt says, "You were goofing off."

"But the Swede's a touchy fucker."

"Nobody listens to him."

Kurt goes up between the seats and pops an Allman Brothers

bootleg into the cassette player, cranks it. Bass chords rumble the side panels. Behind tinted windows, the Chevy van's interior is permanent evening. Outside, the body paint is custom two-tone, beige over brown. Kurt sprayed the whole thing himself. For soundproofing, he glued shag carpeting to the floor, ceiling, and walls. He bought it dirt-cheap. The pile is the color of grape juice. On humid days, it gaps where Kurt didn't spread enough glue.

Hauling groceries a couple of weeks ago, he broke a jar of dill pickles; a trace odor of vinegar and garlic lingers. Still, he's proud. Kurt thinks the van is perfect for lounging or napping when he takes breaks at the hospital. He keeps a hand-wound alarm clock on the dash so he doesn't oversleep.

For several stretches, the van has served as his home. Not really so bad, Kurt tells people. His transportation certainly beats his apartment for price and versatility. He can sell pot or stolen pills in relative privacy, and for kicks he and Augustus can surveil the local petting goats. That's what Augustus calls them. The women they spy on. *Petting goats.* In the back of the van, the seats are beanbag chairs and velveteen pillows. The largest pillow shows the silver head of a wolf and a full moon. Dusty dreamcatchers hang from suction cups on the rear doors. Under a hidden trapdoor, there's a loaded .410 pump shotgun and a brick of weed. The marijuana is full of stems and seeds. They sampled it earlier, snipping a corner and rolling two jumbo joints.

Kurt closes the hole and retapes the brick with a continuous overlapping strip. Augustus likes to complain about the free dope he smokes. Kurt's learned to let it go. Letting things go is his expertise.

"This last batch of shit you grew is very bitter."

"Uh-huh."

Killing time in a parking lot. Wood chips under the tires and a long view of the river before their eyes, the occupants of the two Chevys have the place to themselves. The reason for the lot is a boat rental. An old man is snoring in the hut where he manages a cashbox and a short dog of peach schnapps. In the van they're waiting for a kid from the high school coming to buy Kurt's pot. The kid's safe. Kurt's been supplying him for three years. Today he's running late. Nothing unusual in that. If he showed up on time, then Kurt might be worried. This delay is typical. There's no rush.

"Where're my glasses?" Kurt asks.

Augustus points to the newspapers.

Soft crush of shifting Styrofoam kernels as Kurt kneels on a beanbag. He resumes watching. Augustus lolls his head against the wolf print. He says, "That goat's nothing special."

"Hey, she's not bad. Leave the lady alone."

"Do you think I could've killed those goats?"

"Sure you *could have* killed them. But you didn't. You and me, we're just guys that like to watch. Why would you kill some choice petting goats like Teagles and Mary O? We must've spent hours following those two. I mean, if you were killing all the best goats, then we wouldn't have anything fun to do."

Augustus studies the dumb smile. "Where's this kid of yours? I wanted to do a little cruising."

"Give him till the end of this song. Kid's reliable."

Augustus cracks a smile of his own. Kurt is his only real friend. Loyal and supportive. Never a threat. If he knew the truth, Kurt would probably volunteer to be his partner. So it is without reason that Augustus takes his friend's life. The bayonet is loose in the sleeve of his army jacket. He lets his arm drop, and the blade slips into his hand. He takes a two-handed grip and strikes. Stabs low. He lifts the bayonet upward, taking Kurt off his knees and into the air. He works the metal to the breastbone, withdraws. He steps back quickly to avoid the gushing blood. There's not enough room. Kurt doesn't scream but shivers as if he's been covered by a gust of snow. Kurt crumples, slouches over, and dies.

Augustus pats his friend's knee.

A final shudder passes through Kurt's body. Nerves, not life. Augustus lays his head on Kurt's chest, listening for heartbeats. He knows better. The blood pool shines.

"Pal, you should've steered clear of me." He shuts Kurt's eyes and turns him over, facedown onto the wolf pillow. "No pleasure in this life."

Augustus bows his head. "I miss you already, man."

He opens the van doors. He takes his bayonet, slips it up his sleeve, and walks over to the rental hut. The old man nods with his chin against his chest. A radio plays church music under his chair. Augustus raps the butt of the bayonet against the counter.

"Alright, you don't need to knock my brains in." The man never looks up. He rubs his eyes. "Need a boat and motor, or only a boat?" His tongue pokes out to wet his pencil. He tears a receipt in half, tries again, and separates the next receipt slowly along the perforation.

"Two boats."

The old man looks now, leans forward through the cut-away window, elbows anchored to the counter. "Why two?"

"I've got a friend."

"Hmph. Twenty-four dollars. Cash only."

Augustus peels five bills and hands them over. The man stares at the money.

"What's that shit on there? Looks like . . ."

"Are you renting boats or asking questions?"

"I got a right to refuse any customer. And you're filthier than the sewer under a slaughterhouse. What have you been into, son?"

"I'm going to be into your asshole with this bayonet, old-timer. Now give me two pairs of oars. I'll turn over the boats myself. You won't have to leave your outhouse."

Augustus taps the man's shirt buttons with the tip of the knife.

The old man says, "I'm a fool, nothin' but an old dummy runnin' his mouth off. Oars are under the tarp next to the steps goin' down to the launch. Take what you need. You don't pay, neither."

"Now do I look like a thief?"

"I didn't say that. It's more a courtesy."

"You take the money, old-timer. Don't shit your pants."

"Okay."

"I'm going to get my friend."

The old man is searching with a blind hand for his peach schnapps. Augustus marches to the van and slings Kurt over his shoulder. His drab jacket turns crimson. Walking back, he notices the old-timer ducking behind his chair.

"I'll beach the boats downriver."

The old man waits for the smell of blood to leave his nose.

A last sip for courage, then he runs to the pay phone on the edge of the lot. He calls the sheriff's station. Sucks the dregs of his bottle.

The deputies arrive. He shows them where two boats are missing. His mouth is dry and he stoops to drink from a spigot that cranes up from the gravel by the launch. He splashes water into his face, guzzles, and spits into the river rock. He grasps the cold pipe in both hands as if it were his only possession in the world.

The deputies gawk downstream, weapons drawn.

8

Augustus dumps Kurt's body overboard. Kurt sinks, his arms outflung, airplaning into the current. Augustus watches the body bank left, dive. The last sight of Kurt is the soles of his sneakers in the murky water. They disappear.

Augustus winds the anchor rope he's been using to tow the other boat. He transfers into the clean boat. He strips to the waist and tosses his soiled clothing into the water. Augustus rinses himself. His muscles shake as he tips the first boat and allows the river to fill it. The weight of the water pulls the aluminum shell from his grip. Sunk to the oarlocks, the rowboat will soon submerge.

Augustus paddles, begins the next phase of his escape.

•

Buddy called Margot. Now he was driving out to the farm to pick her up. He passed an old Ford, the man behind the wheel wearing a straw hat.

Buddy's mind flashed to a memory of his parents' car. He saw the silver hood and frost built up on the windshield. Ma and Dad dressed for a night on the town. Dad scraped the frost with a red-bristled brush. He swept tiny icy curls off the glass–trying not to rub his suit against the fenders. Ma, in her fox stole, fussed with her hairdo in a side mirror. She touched up her lipstick.

That was the last time Buddy saw them alive. He wasn't sure if the memory was real or something he dreamed.

The local newspaper ran a picture of the crash. The Ford showed up gray against a background of fallen snow. The railroad tracks were a pair of heavy black lines leading to, and then away from, the wreckage. Sand mounded beside the tracks could've been mistaken for snow, but the snowy patches were whiter. The frozen ground lay mostly bare. Inside the Ford, shadows masked the bodies. Years later, sitting at a microfiche machine in the UW library, he recognized those shadows for what they were: his parents' blood.

Margot smiled at him weakly when he pulled up. She still looked groggy. Black-eyed Susans patterned her sundress. Her hair was the prettiest he'd ever seen it. Pinned back around her oval face, and her wistful down-turned smile lingering.

She got in. But she didn't kiss him.

See what you lost? He said to himself. *See what you've never had?*

He told her his brother was visiting. Then he went ahead and asked if she recalled anything from that night at the Chimney, the attack.

"I don't remember."

"Because of the ether," he said.

"I can still taste it."

Buddy's eyes flicked from the road to a grove of fir trees as they whistled by.

"Could it have been Tommy?"

"No," she said. "Not Tommy."

"What about Augustus?"

She sat there, staring at the grain in the dashboard.

"Maybe." She shrugged. "You were there too. You saw him."

"Not his face. But he was about the right size to be Tommy or Augustus."

"Tommy wouldn't. Because of Duncan, and . . . it wasn't him."

"Okay."

Margot sighed and tucked the sundress under her thighs. "Could you take me to my apartment? I need some things."

"Sure. But I think Robbie's cooking us dinner."

"Oh."

"We can stop at my place and say hi. Then go right out again."

"I don't want to be rude to your brother."

"He'll understand."

*

Robbie stood in front of the Weber grill on Buddy's porch. He had a big fork in one hand, a cut lemon in the other.

They opened the Caddy doors and smelled chicken and oregano. Charcoal lighter fluid and smoke.

"Good timing," Robbie said.

Margot waved. Buddy climbed onto the porch and talked to his brother.

"Okay, no problem," Robbie said. "It's ready now. Let me get some foil and I'll wrap this up. You can eat later. Or whatever."

Margot sat on the Caddy's bumper. She knew she wasn't handling it right, but she didn't feel up to being social. Maybe tomorrow. Maybe never. She thought about Augustus, his bushy beard, and his eyes that stayed on you too long. *Oh God,* she thought, *it could be him.*

Buddy tapped her on the shoulder and she jumped.

"Sorry," he said.

"Not your fault."

"Look, Robbie wants to go for a drive. He's been stir crazy. So is it okay if he drops us off? We only have the one car."

"Fine with me."

"Thanks. I'll tell him."

•

To anyone on the shore, the rowboat appears empty. When he rises to breathe, he spouts water. The river is the driver. Augustus merely steers. In his ears, the Skin plays music. Augustus wonders: *Do you want me?* If the river answers, he'll suck the dirty brown water and welcome annihilation. But the Skin won't answer. So he swims, drifts, swims. He guides the rowboat in the current. He has no fear of the deputies waiting downstream. They've seen the boat by now, but their shouting doesn't reach him. The flood of water is a flood of power.

"Here it comes," Sherry says.

"Carl, please get a bead on it, in case he jumps up." Rafferty turns to the deputy who steadies his rifle on the open cruiser door. "Dammit, you need a better angle than that. Climb on the hood."

"There's nobody in the boat."

"Hold on."

Rookie deputy John Harper wades in the Skin to his armpits. He wants to catch the rowboat as it passes. Rafferty yells to him.

"Careful, John, it's coming right to you. Watch it, watch it."

Harper plants his feet in the mud so he won't be swept down-river. Deputy Sherry is standing on the hood of his cruiser now, aiming his rifle into the empty boat. Rafferty radios back to his men at the boat rental.

"We only got one boat here. Your guy sure the suspect took two? Over."

"Yessir, that's correct. The suspect put two boats in the water."

"Does the witness know if the suspect fled *in the same boat* with the victim?"

"He was hiding at that point, sir. Over."

"Stay where you are. This boat we got might be a decoy. Suspect might be heading upstream or he might be back on land. Be alert, boys." Rafferty leans against the cruiser where Deputy Sherry peers through his riflescope. But it doesn't take a scope to see what's happening in front of them.

Sherry says, "It's clear. He must've gotten out." Ten feet and closing between the boat and the outstretched arms of Harper.

"Grab it, John." Rafferty tries to will the boat in. He wants Buddy Bayes flattened against the hull.

Deputy Harper hears his boss as he grips the rowboat, putting his shoulder into the bow to stop its progress. He feels a hard bump against his stomach. Later, he tells his wife the blow might've been a kick. The rear of the boat comes around in the current. Harper hauls it to the bank where he's helped from the water by one of the other deputies.

"How come there's no blood?" Harper asks. "Witness said the guy was a mess."

Harper's gasping, holding his side.

The boat is clean.

Sherry hops down from the cruiser. He and Rafferty stare at its emptiness. Sherry balances the rifle butt on his hip and removes his sunglasses.

Rafferty says, "This can't be the boat." He points a finger at the rookie. "Harper, you don't go anywhere. Wait and see if anything else floats by. Carl and I are going to cover the ground between here and the boat rental on foot. Fiedler, you call Anderson and Putee and ask them to make sure they review the witness' description."

Deputy Walt Fiedler lopes over to his vehicle and fumbles with the radio.

Sherry says, "Last report we heard the suspect is a white male in his late thirties, approximately six-foot-six and weighing two-seventy-five or more. He has a beard and he's covered in blood. Chief, that doesn't sound like Bayes."

Rafferty reacts. "Putee said the witness smells like a distillery. Maybe when he sobers up we'll get a new story."

"Anderson said he's ninety-nine percent sure that the van belongs to Kurt Walinski. You know him. We had a tip he's been dealing homegrown on a local level. He fits the description of the victim. And–"

Rafferty cuts Sherry off. "What?"

"Kurt hangs around with that big taxidermist, Bodine. Guy did the work on the northern I caught in June. That was right after Melissa Teagles disappeared. He's a creep, lives alone. Looks like he could be our boy. Shit, he might've had her in the house when I dropped my fish off."

Rafferty thinks about Augustus coming to him with his so-called suspicions. But that direction of thought is too untidy. He shakes his head. "Bayes did it. I'm sticking with him until somebody proves me wrong. This investigation is mine, my ass on the line, okay, so keep your bullshit theory to yourself."

Sherry is steaming.

"Let's get going," Rafferty says. "You take point."

Rafferty and Sherry enter the woods. Fiedler says he's going to take a ride, check the nearby roads.

Harper's shirt itches as it dries on his back. He straps his gun on. He pulls the shirt away from his skin. He scans the river. Far downstream, a swimmer appears, climbing up on the opposite bank.

The swimmer turns and waves.

Harper sees a tall man. Thick all over. His naked torso glistens with black hair. He wears camouflage pants. The tall man–Harper wonders if it's Bodine–continues to wave in slow motion, as if he's still underwater. *You can't touch me,* the wave says.

Harper shouts and draws his weapon. The man heads for the trees. Harper, out of range, fires a warning. The gunshot calls the two lawmen from their hunt upriver. Rafferty and Sherry race along the trail. They see Harper on their side of the Skin.

But they're all too far away.

Through lazy green willows, the figure retreats, and by layers, like a diver fathoming an emerald sea, he becomes obscure, a simple shadow, then he is gone.

●

Red wanted some beer. He tore a fifty from the roll in his pocket and dropped it on Zo's bed.

"Try not to get lost," he said.

"Like Little Red Riding Hood," Zo said, sitting up, rubbing his abs.

"She wasn't lost."

"What?"

"She was at Grandma's house, right? Not lost."

"But she got the wolf, either way."

"You mean the wolf got her?"

"Same thing," Zo said. He found the keys.

"Be glad you're a wolf, Zo."

"Why you say that?"

❈

Robbie dropped them off in the tavern's rear lot. Boy jumped from the backseat to scatter sparrows pecking at the gravel. Buddy and Margot entered through the kitchen. Boy squeezing through the door before it closed.

There was a good-sized crowd in the bar. Buddy ducked into the walk-in cooler to pick out a bottle of Chardonnay. Margot waited with the dog in the stairwell.

They walked up together. She unlocked the door, the troll swinging below her fingers as she turned her key. Buddy tried to forget the last time he was there.

Margot switched on the air-conditioner, turned it to HIGH COLD. Buddy fixed their plates. She found a book of matches and lit two candles. Boy sniffed at the carpeting, head low and gliding inches from the floor. He found the bathroom and flopped down on the tiles. Buddy opened a drawer. Moved silverware aside. The wine bottle dripped a bracelet on the counter.

"You have a corkscrew?"

"Here." She passed him the keys, and he unfolded the corkscrew from the Swiss Army knife. He popped the cork. She set two wineglasses next to the bottle.

"Only a half-glass for me. I'm walking around lightheaded as it is."

Buddy poured.

The chicken tasted delicious. Margot was surprised by her hunger.

"I think it would be a good idea for you to go away. Just for a while. Until this all clears up," Buddy said.

Margot swallowed. She pushed her plate away. "What about Augustus?"

"I'll take care of him."

"What's that supposed to mean? Look, I'm not positive he's the one."

"If he is, then Robbie and I can deal with him. We're not going to discuss . . . he's a problem we can solve. Leave it at that."

"And I'm not part of this?"

"No, you're not." Buddy shook his head. "There are other things, Chicago things, that we're going to clean up, too. You wouldn't be safe."

"This is crazy." Margot got up and went into the other room. She sat down. "Why wouldn't I be safe if I'm . . . why wouldn't I be safe with you?"

"Because, to some people, I'm already as good as dead."

"Maybe, I'm dead too."

Buddy winced.

"Margot." He came around to stand in front of her. "You don't really know me."

"Why not?"

"Nobody knows me."

"Not even Robbie."

"That's different. He's my brother."

"And what am I?" she said. The blood rising in her cheeks as her voice lost its force. Her eyes broke away, found the sunset smoldering in the window. "What do you want me to be?"

Buddy sat on the sofa.

Margot curled into him. She touched his mouth with her fingertips.

He told her everything.

She never said a word. She drank her wine. When the wine was gone, she held the empty wineglass in her palms, pressed to her chest.

He went on and on. The room fell into darkness around them. The only sound was Buddy's voice, breaking its silence.

●

Zo's thinking.

In the Bronco he's got the volume jacked and the bass is thumpity thump thump so he can feel it in his skull. The windshield vibrating like it's an earthquake.

Alright, alright, you send me out. Be your errand boy. Go get you refreshments. That's cool. Back at home every time you need to turn hard with some asshole, it's my name gets called. But Zo gets paid. Don't forget that all y'all. Zo makes his dollar being hard for a white dude. Zo breaks bones sucks out the marrow, spits gold. So who's stupid, fool?

Zo checks the rearview. Two empty shotgun racks. The pieces are back in the motel with Red. Mossberg 590A1s. Heavy-duty patrol weapons. Expanded capacity. Nine shots before you reload.

He sees a lighted storefront. Wigg's Grocery and Liquors. Cases of beer stacked high in the windows. Zo parks, leaves the machine running. He walks slow, sees himself in the glass. Smooth all over, like stone.

●

Robbie circled down Main Street again. He didn't know how Buddy did it. The town was so small, so dead. He passed antique shops, bait shops, and fudge shops. Six months up here in the north and he'd have a drinking problem. Maybe that's why the Chimney stayed afloat. He made three right turns and started the parade all over.

Robbie couldn't believe it.

Zo holding a gas can in one hand, a case of Miller in the other, and, as always, totally self-absorbed. Zo starred in his own movie. Robbie eyed him, covered half his face with his fingers. He watched as Zo packed the Bronco and slammed the tailgate. The light changed. Robbie pulled away. He hooked the Caddy around into a KFC drive-thru.

So they're here. The shit has hit the almighty fan.

Zo merged into traffic. Robbie gunned it, cut out of line, and dropped in two cars back. The Bronco didn't go far. Zo took the turn too sharply, scraped Red's muffler on broken asphalt. He coasted, braked, killed the engine.

Room Nineteen. Breezy Point Motel.

The motel was shaped like an L. Office in the corner, Nineteen was second from the end on the long side. Robbie parked on the dead end of the short side, nothing next to him but cinderblock painted teal. He flipped off his headlights, shrank into his seat.

Call Buddy.

But wasn't that what he always did since they were kids? Running to Buddy whenever he got into a jam. And wasn't it his own weakness that dragged Red out from under his rock and put him in Gunnar?

Robbie fingered the trigger guard on the sawed-off.

He wasn't about to go in there and commit cold-blooded murder.

But he wasn't leaving, either. He thought about Red's money sitting in the Caddy's trunk, where they put it when they left the cabin. It made Robbie happy. Nice change watching Red wriggling on the pointy end of the stick.

Sit tight, he told himself. He had his cell phone and knew the Chimney number by heart. If things got hairy, he could warn Buddy.

Zo bringing in the brew. Didn't that make it look like they were shutting down for the evening? Resting up for their big day.

All he had to do was stay awake. Come up on their asses when they decided to bolt. Ring Buddy and tell him, for a change, he played it cool, played it right.

*

Buddy didn't remember falling asleep, but here he was in the morning light–still inside Margot's apartment. He saw the wineglasses on the carpet, the empty bottle. The blanket folded under his chin.

Margot was breathing deeply, asleep at his side.

●

Augustus wakes not quite outdoors, sheltered from the sun, reclining on an unfamiliar couch. His pants have dried, but his pockets are full of sand. He flexes his balled fist. His big knuckles are raw. He remembers the way Kurt split open. It was no dream. He escaped the sheriff's men, walked around the woods in no particular direction but away from the river.

Now he can hear helicopters.

A voice in the back of his neck guided him.

They're looking for you, the voice said. It was his father's voice talking, yet it had been altered in a way he couldn't quite name. The words ring holy. But another blackout has clouded his mind.

Where am I?

Answers blur just out of reach. He can see his body with clarity, the couch too, but beyond that ... he is so sleepy ...

Screens.

A cross-breeze caresses him. He looks around, lies back. A screened-in porch. He recognizes it. He dreads this place. He needs to leave immediately, but rather than trying to stand he turns his face to the couch, buries his nose in the corner, in the crack where zippers run along seams. He wants to wake up anywhere else, to be dead.

Augustus sighs. He's overcome with the smell, taste, and total presence of a horrible stench. The stink is old. It's in the material so deep only burning will destroy it.

Vomited spiced rum and pineapple juice.

He heaves but nothing comes.

The front door opens and a cool black cane whips down on his shins.

Pain trips his circuits, sending him into another blackout, and through the blackout slickly to the other side, tumbling backward. Backward into himself.

Oily with fear, his body is too slow to protect itself from an assault. He is exposed. Powerless. A collision occurs between memories and the deformed fantasies he's created to escape. Augustus revisits the time where he was reborn. Welcome to the first cogs in the beginning cycle. The mighty black cycle where black is not simply a color or a mood but a deadly gaping wound kept from closing. Where he returns and returns. Exploring. Augustus can touch his dead mother's face. The shock never wears off. *This happened.* Then he is in the kennel. His father is a robot wearing a green surgeon's gown, a floating mask, and rubber gloves. *This happened to me.*

His mother went first. But he never told.

This happened.

Because he was next.

This happened to me.

9

He's in the last cage, and it's padlocked. Today there's a dog in there with him: a medium-sized mutt, short hair the color of peanuts, except where a splash of kidney brown paints two egg-shaped spots on her chest. She's still a puppy really, and she licks his face until he pushes her away. She sleeps against his out-stretched legs.

Augustus sits on the bare concrete. The cold floor smells of dog piss and Pine-Sol. Augustus bends his knees and leans against the cage. His shins are lumpy with contusions. The wire fencing digs into his soft, flabby back. He's become a fat boy, the second fattest in his grade at school. Next year he'll graduate to Gunnar High.

Luckily, the kennel is noisy. In the quiet he can always hear playground laughter and insults shot like spitballs from the last row of his homeroom. Sometimes at night, in his bed before falling to sleep, he prays for tornadoes to rip apart his town. Killing everyone.

Pop's shoes come scuffling down the hallway. A pause, and the lock to the kennel door pings open. Augustus pretends he is sleeping, head nodding into his ample chest. He is aware of the dog's breathing. It quickens.

"Do you have an answer for me?" Pop talks through a surgical mask. The blood from someone's pet has smeared a feathery pattern on his gown. Sweat makes Pop's glasses slide to the tip of his nose. But he doesn't lift a finger to push them into place. They seem to defy gravity and overhang his face. He gazes downward into the cage where his son pretends to awaken.

Augustus rubs his eyes. He imagines he is a Death Row prisoner and Pop is the executioner arriving to escort him to the gas chamber. But he has no time for fantasies. He needs an answer. Yet every answer Augustus can think of might send his father into a rage.

"I don't know." He hears the feebleness of his response.

Headshake. The mask obliterates both mouth and chin. Pop's brow furrows.

"I'm sorry and I won't . . ." Augustus begins again. He blanks. A simple apology is never good enough.

"Well, then, I guess you need to sit there until you think of something." Pop motions as if he is intending to leave for the night. His hand, gloved in opaque rubber, descends to the light switch, and suddenly it is dark in the kennel. A hound in the next stall lifts his head.

"No, please. I *have* been thinking." Lights on again. Pop advances and lingers just beyond the wire. "I guess I've got no reason why I drew those pictures."

Pop sighs deeply. Air blows out the paper sides of the mask.

"Son, how am I supposed to retain an ounce of my pride when your teacher feels compelled to call me, during a busy work day I remind you, to inform me that my precious offspring is scribbling dirty pictures of ladies' private parts in the margins of his schoolbooks? What words can I possibly offer on your behalf? None. I am put in a most awkward position."

Pop shows the contaminated scalpel he's been concealing between his thumb and palm. He holds it overhead, an electric blue threat in the halo of naked lamplight. Augustus' eyes widen. With his other hand, Pop strikes the cage wall and caves it inward. Taking hold of his son's hair, he yanks Augustus' face tight against the cage. The unclean blade chimes along the wire. Augustus cries out. The dog cowers over the drain.

"Because of *you* I am made to look ridiculous! It is unimaginable that I should be brought so low by *a child*. People are talking, Augustus. Oh, yes. They're saying, *Dr. Bodine has to account for his flesh-and-blood, for the disgusting actions of his perverted pig-boy.* You can bet your little teacher, whose tits and twat decorate your algebra lessons, is in the teachers' lounge right this very minute showing your artwork to the entire faculty. And how can I erase what everyone has already seen?"

Augustus says, "But I'm the one, I'm the one who drew them. Not you."

Pop releases his hair and pockets the blade.

"If you act like an animal, then you can stay penned up like one."

"I won't."

"Promise."

"I swear."

"Tomorrow you will go to school and tell them you *copied*

those pictures after viewing similar obscenities in an older boy's notebook."

"Yes."

"If they ask for a name, tell them you're not a tattler. Accept whatever punishment they assign you."

Augustus agrees.

Pop finds the key to the padlock. He lets his son out and shoos the dog away from the cage door. For a moment father and son face each other squarely. In another year, Augustus will surpass his father's height.

Pop withdraws. His gloves come off with a pair of smacking sounds. He tears away the paper covering half his face and throws the gloves and mask into a trash bin. Outside of the cage, Augustus tucks the ends of his shirt into his trousers. Pop closes in, smiles.

"Son, you're growing fat like a woman." He reaches out and pinches one of Augustus' nipples. The boy winces but doesn't attempt to break free.

His father laughs. "Better watch out some football player doesn't make you his sweetheart next year."

Red-faced, Augustus collects his book bag, turns to go.

"Nobody wants this dog," Pop states the fact offhandedly, over his shoulder, but knowing not a word is missed.

Augustus stops in the doorway. He asks, "She sick?"

"Wormy and a little wild, but nothing else is wrong with her." Pop washes up at the sink where they shampoo the animals. Under the flow of hot water, the pumice soap lathers mint green, and the vigorous scrubbing leaves his hands and forearms pink. He shuts off the faucet and dries himself with brown paper towels pulled from the wall dispenser. "You can have her." He reads his son's expression perfectly. "Put her in the water if you want to. It'll save me the trouble. There's a potato sack and a brick by the door here. Don't let anyone see you on the path. Throw her out to the middle so she doesn't end up washing right back up on shore like that other one–the spaniel bitch from last Fourth of July."

"I'll do it right."

"Anybody finds her up here, she'll be your last."

Augustus watches the dog pace from barrier to barrier in her cell. "I think she's too big for a potato sack."

"Son, I can fit your lard ass into that sack quicker than you can eat a Hershey bar. Would you like to see me do it?"

"No, sir."

"Okay then. Now get going. I'll be having my dinner at Marsh's Supper Club tonight. Be asleep when I get home." Pop pulled open the cage and tossed a rope leash to his son.

Augustus knelt. "Let's go, Peanut. Let's go."

●

Bony, chilly knuckles rap against his cheek. Augustus opens his eyes to the vision of his father's ravaged face. The years of living alone and the alcohol have etched a mask of the miserable soul within. Pop uses a cane to support a ruined knee. A screw threads the joint, but the muscles beneath his pant leg are atrophied. The leg would not seem strange connected to a corpse.

"What are you doing on my porch?" He slaps his son's thick jowls. "Thought you were some shitfaced kid trespassing on my property." He laughs. The sound he makes is like a pair of dusty bricks clapped together three times.

Since he retired a decade ago, Pop has had limited interaction with people. After the pet hospital was gone, his health's decline came on swiftly. Now he was in ruins.

The worst of his vices bloomed in privacy. Smoke and drink and a paid girl to knock around on Saturday night. Teeth lost in the sink. Blood caked on his pillowcase and undershorts. Weight dropping. He's a renter of this shack, and he eats monotonous dinners of canned pork and beans. For meals, he pulls his chair up to the wooden tomato box where he cooks on a hot plate and eats. The short cord from the underside of the plate leads into a brown-slitted socket. He owns a single spoon.

Worried the liquor money will run out before he dies, he's become a miser, cutting his own hair bent over a terra cotta birdbath in the yard. He talks to himself. Sentences flowing nonstop, overrunning each other, and no one to interrupt. Days pass and he sees no reason to bathe. If the weather's hot, he'll dip into a cast-iron tub of rusty well water. But he gets cold so fast when he's wet. During those hot evenings he's willing to burn enough electricity to spin a fan in the bedroom window. He sleeps where he falls. At night, stubby white candles light his cluttered lodge.

Smells like church, he has noticed, feeling no peace at the thought.

Dawn has greeted him with pillows of ceiling smoke. He fought the little fires by refilling a salad bowl he carried back and forth from the kitchen sink. Once he turned a garden hose on the velvet easy chair—erupted, as it was, in gorgeous flames. He's caught himself with two or three Pall Malls going at the same time, noticing the forgotten cigarettes and first guessing he had visitors. Always thinking they were of the unwelcome variety: kids breaking in to steal his bottles...cops, ghosts...or his son, Augustus.

Pop doesn't remember, but the last time Augustus checked the old man's savings account there were one hundred and fourteen thousand dollars there.

"I'm leaving." Augustus tries to stand, but a shower of golden fireworks stops him. He grips the edge of the couch for balance, to keep from pitching forward.

"You don't have to go. Have a drink at least." Pop leans on his cane.

"I really need to be on my way."

"Are you ill?"

Augustus has to laugh.

"How's business? How's the house?"

Augustus notices a front tooth missing from his father's smile. "Everything is just fine, Pop. I'm going now."

"Won't you have a drink with me?" Pop asks.

Augustus finds his legs. He moves for the screen door and the two stairs down to the dirt path. "The sheriff is coming."

"Who?"

Augustus opens the door with a sound like nails being ripped from warped wood.

"I said that the sheriff is after me."

"Sheriff Oltendorf?"

"Oltendorf's dead."

"So he is." Pop caresses the smooth hook of the cane. His memories these days are tied in bundles. Untying this particular bundle, he finds a question. "Is all this trouble about your mother?"

Augustus staggers through the doorway. He tramples weeds. Pop hurls obscenities like darts into his back. Augustus penetrates the living warmth of the woods. He will seek out the weapons he's hidden. He will look for his carved mark: a pyramid of six crosses stacked one above two on a base of three, notched in the smooth bark of a white birch. All the time he is imagining his knives staked in the soil. Those in leather sheaths and scabbards; others that fold, and quickly, with a flick of the wrist, snap open again, their inner mechanisms clicking as the blades lock in.

The back of his neck is speaking to him. Telling him what's important.

His power is becoming manifest.

10

Augustus arms himself. On his knees, he digs for treasure. Glinting blades. In the hole with his knives, he rediscovers a memento. As a kindness to himself, he has planted items of sentimental value in special, protected places. Finding one of them is like receiving a gift. His spirit lifts.

A folded square of butcher paper. No bigger than a teabag. Augustus works loose the knotted kitchen twine holding the package together. The prize spills into his palm. It slightly resembles a pearl. It is a human tooth, a canine. She was *Number One*. He can't recall her face exactly. Plain girl. Fine brown hair combed away from her face, a high forehead, and the scent of baby powder on her skin. They went to the same college in Iowa. He dropped out soon after. He was never a suspect.

Augustus searches his dirty forearm for the tiny white oval. But the scar has long since vanished into his flesh. She bit him. Drew blood. It was the little push he needed. He sees himself as he was then: oafish, shy, attracting the stares of dorm mates as the hallway conversations dropped off a cliff whenever he opened his door or made the turn from the top of the staircase.

Always apart.

He had thought college would be a clean slate. Augustus had won a partial academic scholarship to Milton College and had worked full-time for three years after high school. He swept floors and cleaned the locker-room toilets in a paper mill. Over the summers, he guided fishermen.

Pop had a first cousin, Ida, who lived with her family a few miles from the college, near the Nebraska border. They were farmers. During his only dinner with them, the first week of classes, Ida kept staring across the table. Her four children were in grade school and well behaved. They ate and went to their chores. Augustus' crew cut itched, but he resisted the urge to scratch behind his ears. Ida poured coffee for the adults. Then her husband excused himself and they were a pair. A pleasant breeze swam through the house. Augustus sipped his coffee. Ida brushed crumbs off the hand-sewn tablecloth. She had a question she wanted to ask but she was afraid. She tried easier questions instead. *Are you excited? Do you know what subjects you'll pursue? Yes, and I don't know, well, maybe biology. I like animals. Oh. Just like your father. That'll make him proud.*

After the meal, Ida was anxious to return Augustus to his dorm. She gave him a jar of raspberry preserves. She waved from her porch as the pickup rolled through pockets of shade to the road. Her husband drove the twenty minutes in silence, letting Augustus off in front of the freshman dormitory. As Augustus climbed down from the cab, Ida's husband—Dale was his name—extended his hand. "Young man, you play your cards right, you'll get more pussy here than you ever dreamed." He was smiling.

Pop had allowed Augustus to go into the world. But what Augustus found beyond Gunnar was more of the same. Other people were alien. Their words, their interactions, the essential scenes of their lives passed in front of Augustus. It was as if they conducted themselves behind a thick pane of aquarium glass. They breathed a foreign element. They were another species. He couldn't play his cards right. He didn't even know the aliens' game.

Augustus and Number One attended the same Introduction to Western Philosophy class. He sat in the back row of the auditorium where his companions were trying to sleep or shake off their hangovers. She always took the same seat: second row, third chair in from the left. She arrived five minutes before the bell, habitually. Always quiet and alone. She reviewed the assigned pages of the text until the professor started his lecture. She wrote down what the professor said in her notebook. She used pencils. After Philosophy, she crossed the campus to the library. Again, she had her favorite spot: a desk on the fourth floor in an abandoned zone of the building. Volumes of Italian literature filled the shelves down the long aisle over her shoulder. There was a drinking fountain jutting from the wall to her right. She would stay for close to two hours. The window she looked out faced the brown brick wall of a building housing a few small classrooms and the offices of the Math and Physical Sciences professors. She would leave promptly for the afternoon session of Spanish II. Augustus could not follow, but he learned to recognize her strangely accented voice through the floor of the unlocked janitor's closet directly above the Romance Languages department. He studied her for half a semester before making his approach.

She would eat lunch in the busier of the two cafeterias. She must have been hungry when the Spanish discussion groups finally broke, because she never bothered to drop off her books. She lived away from the heart of the campus. Her dorm was on the edge of the track field.

Augustus watched and hated. He wondered how long it would take for her virtue to be sacrificed.

It was a Saturday night. She sat at a round café-style table in the Richter Student Union. The place was empty. Most students were relaxing or out at parties, drinking. She was copying her notes onto index cards. Augustus walked up to the deli concession and bought a bag of barbecued potato chips. The student working the counter had the odor of marijuana wafting from his bushy red beard. He rang up the chips and disappeared into the mop room for another toke. Augustus proceeded to her table.

"Studying for the midterm?"

She looked up at him, blinked, and narrowed her hazel eyes. Augustus snagged a chair from nearby. He could see she didn't recognize him from class. He tore into the corner of the bag with his teeth. He held it out to her.

"Uh, no thanks."

"Werner's Intro to Philosophy, right? You always sit in front. Writing down everything he says. Don't worry about the test. You'll ace it. Questions come straight from the lectures." He offered his hand. "My name's Gus Bodine. I sit in the back."

She shook his hand. Told him her name.

They discussed how much Professor Werner expected on the essay questions. She wanted to know the topic Augustus had chosen for the paper due at the semester's final.

Augustus hadn't given it much thought. "'Isolation and the Progress of the Human Soul,'" he said.

She seemed impressed.

They talked about their hometowns. She came from Minnesota, up north, near the Boundary Waters. Her dad operated a repair shop, fixing appliances, lawn mowers, and anything else a customer could fit through the door. Her mom had given birth to twins last summer. They kept her hopping. More girls.

Augustus soaked her story in. He bought her a cup of tea. "You look like a tea person," he said. And she admitted she was. He asked if she felt lonely sometimes. Homesick. She nodded. Augustus told her he missed his folks. She understood.

The Union was closing. She gathered her notes and cards. Zipped her bag. He asked permission to walk with her back to the dorm. "Sure," she said, "but I'm all the way over in Macaulay."

It was a nice night for walking.

Augustus ended up strangling her, bashing her head into the stone arch of a culvert. He had a knife in his boot, and he used it afterward. He wanted to save her body, to keep it a while. But that was impossible.

He left her remains in the dry creek bed under the culvert. Choosing his souvenir was easy. Then the voice in his neck told him, *Go, you've been here too long already.* Crossing the football field at dawn, he paused to wipe his bloody hands on the dew-drenched grass.

Augustus cuts himself accidentally. His thumb slips back and forth along one of the sharpened steel weapons in his lap. His hand cups blood. The trance breaks. He lays the offending knife aside and examines his wound. Not deep. There is no pain, but a stinging sensation in his thumb. He massages the tooth between his wet fingers and enjoys the evil, greasy way it slides against his skin. Augustus is touching her. With his other hand he pushes the mound of dirt back into the hole.

•

The deputy knocks on the windshield with his nightstick

Robbie startles, sits up straight behind the steering wheel. There's a cruiser blocking him in.

"Rise and shine."

Robbie shoves the sawed-off under the seat with his heels.

"Sorry, officer. I got car trouble. Must've dozed off."

"More comfortable in the motel. You got a license?"

"I do."

Robbie went for his wallet. He looked past the cop to see if Red's truck was still parked at the other end of the lot. It was.

"Here you go."

"Chicago? What're you doing in Gunnar, Mr. Bayes?"

"Visiting my brother. The car overheated."

"Why didn't you call him?"

"He's not home. I thought he might end up here."

"At Breezy's? That's awful strange if he lives in town, ain't it?"

"He was with a woman. Said he might bring her here. But they never showed."

"Hmph." The cop said, "You stay in the vehicle. I'm gonna run your information. It'll take a minute." He started for the cruiser, then turned back. "Is your brother the guy that runs the Black Chimney?"

"Uh-huh. If the car starts, I'll just go there."

"Hold tight. You need a tow, I can call a truck."

"Thanks."

Robbie sat there swearing softly. *Goddamn cruiser parked outside Red's room. Perfect.*

●

Buddy was down in the tavern when he heard the buzzer. The .22 was in his hand, bouncing lightly against his thigh, as he spread the blinds and saw Robbie standing there, red-faced. He opened the door. A cruiser pulled away from the lot.

"What's going on?"

"Fucking cops. This Fiedler, he follows me all the way to your door. I mean, shit, man, he's got nothing better to do this morning?"

"Robbie, where were you? I'm phoning the cabin since six."

●

Buddy cleared everybody out of the Chimney. He hung a sign on the door that said there might be a possible gas leak and they were closed until further notice. Margot called Uncle Bill to come and pick her up.

"Buddy, why can't you tell the sheriff?" she asked.

"I don't see the use in that."

"But you'll call if Red shows up."

"I don't want Red hanging over me the rest of my life. He's got to be dealt with."

"You're going to get yourselves killed."

"He won't try and hit us in the daytime. He doesn't know I

closed the tavern. We have to wait and see what happens. Next twenty-four hours, he should show."

Robbie poked his head into the office. "Margot, your uncle's here."

She nodded, then under her breath said, *"Wait and see."*

"You have to trust me that I know what I'm doing with Red. Listen, if by tomorrow morning, nothing happens? Then okay. We'll call up Rafferty and let him sort it out."

Margot took two steps and paused in the doorway. "Tomorrow's bullshit."

11

Augustus sees the deputy's cruiser parked in his driveway. He sneaks up to the rear fender and, crouching, reaches underneath the car. The exhaust pipe's hot. Augustus raises his head to peek over the trunk.

Now where was that deputy?

Augustus begins a slow perimeter walk. *Has the deputy gone inside to investigate? Is he alone?* Augustus times his steps with gusts of wind so his movement and sounds might go unnoticed by anyone in the house. He wonders how the deputy will react if he discovers the house's secrets. Augustus would be happy to hear him scream.

Halfway around the house, Augustus spots the deputy–the same one who'd brought him the pike–still outside, looking into a kitchen window.

Even at this distance, Augustus can see the sweat running through the deputy's crew cut. *What was his name again?* It was a girl and a drink too. *Margarita, Ginger Brandy, Shirley Temple. Cherry Something. Not cherry. Sherry.* That was it. *Deputy Carl Sherry, at your service, ma'am.* He'd been Margot's lover. Augustus had watched them park on one of the old logging roads. Sherry took her bent over a fat, rain-softened stump. He'd been in uniform, his gun belt around his ankles, boots digging in. Augustus noticed the dirty soles of Margot's naked feet. Sherry looked around, massaging his jaw as if he took a solid punch but won the fight. Margot helped him buckle his pants.

Sherry tries the window, but it won't budge. Nailed to the casement.

Augustus drops to the earth. The butt of the knife slips from his sweaty fingers.

He rolls, gets it back in hand.

Then he slides on his belly, keeping low, plowing through the uncut grass and breathing through his teeth, more like something born underground than a man. He watches Sherry pulling on the screen, the cellar doors. Finding everything locked.

Augustus creeps along.

Stops.

He is motionless as a man can be. He does not blink.

Sherry turns. He puts on his sunglasses. The sunset glare reflects fireballs where his eyes should be. He is stepping off the porch—considering the effort needed to obtain a search warrant—as the ground below him erupts into human form.

●

Augustus retrieves the magnetized Hide-A-Key from the propane tank hunkered beside the house. He takes out two keys. Opens the back door. He brings Carl Sherry inside. Augustus takes away the deputy's service revolver and his radio. He lays them on the drain board by the sink. He turns on the water, washes up. Augustus leaves the deputy alone while he changes into fresh clothes. He dresses in a vinyl rain suit. Although he is naked under the suit, he's perspiring. He walks into his shop to get his tools. He goes into his bedroom and puts on the record *Bing & Satchmo.* The speakers hiss and pop. He adjusts the volume, and music begins.

Back in the kitchen, he deposits his tools in a pile next to the gun and radio. Sherry has rolled under the table, but he is quiet. Augustus opens the cabinets under the sink. He finds what he is looking for: a spray bottle of Glass Plus and a roll of paper towels. He leaves the deputy again, this time heading for the living room.

Augustus draws aside the curtains in the front window. The sun has begun to set. He switches on a lamp and spritzes cleaner across the glass. Crosby's voice coaxes him into humming along as he washes the window. He steps back to inspect his work. Mountains of blazing orange clouds fill the horizon. He goes outside to wash the other side of the glass. When he is through, ten minutes have passed and night has begun to fall.

He pushes the furniture against the walls so there is some space to work. He gathers all the lamps in the house and removes their shades. He groups them on the floor, centered in the window, in the middle of the room. He plugs the lamps into a power strip.

The room is intensely bright.

In the kitchen, Sherry has remained under the table but now is lying on his side with his back pressed to the wall. Augustus, barefoot, is careful not to slip. He picks up his Black & Decker electric drill and a pack of six extra-large storage hooks. The hooks are made of stainless steel. Except for the threaded screw tips, they're soft-coated in green rubber. Returning to the living room, he drills six holes in the window's upper casement. The flinty smell of the Black & Decker's motor fill his nostrils. The falling sawdust makes him sneeze.

He blows his nose in the curtains. Then he screws in the hooks. There's about a foot of space between each of them. They're all facing inward. When he has finished, the record needs turning.

Satchmo spins on the flipside. Augustus enters the kitchen once more. He puts his darning needle and a spool of 50 pound test fishing line in one of the rain suit's large pockets. All that's left is the heavy lifting.

He attempts several different grips without success.

The suit is slick inside and out. Augustus decides it's easiest to carry him by the neck. He nearly trips over a lamp cord on his way to the window.

Augustus rests on the window seat. He doubles the fishing line for strength, threads the thick needle, and plunges it deep into Sherry's shoulder muscle. Loop, knot, and cut. He repeats this procedure on the other side of the spine. When he pulls up, the skin bunches but doesn't tear. He hangs the torso from the two middle hooks. Sherry is crooked left, and Augustus straightens him.

"Drip, drop, it's the deputy cop."

Augustus wipes his hands on the sofa. He tries to position Sherry's head so he's looking out the window, where they'll see him when they walk up to the door, but he can't keep him from slumping forward. Augustus goes into the yard to collect the limbs. He strings them on the remaining hooks.

Arm, leg, torso, leg, arm.

"Oh, well," he says in defeat after one final attempt to position the dead man's head.

Augustus quits, strips off the rain suit and, standing in his bedroom again, he dresses in street clothes. He climbs the ladder in
his bedroom closet. The attic trapdoor swings upward. Augustus
balances his feet on the top rung and reaches for the box. He lifts
it, tucks it under his arm as he descends. There's a cocktail table
in the living room, and Augustus sets the box down. Made of
cherry and lacquered to a liquid sheen, the box is large enough
to hold fifty black spiral notebooks.

A stuffed goat's head adorns the box lid. A gold-plated penta-
gram designed under it. The goat has stubby horns, black and
white hair, and two large, cloudy green marbles for eyes. Augustus removes the top notebook, and turns over the pages until he
comes to a blank sheet near the end. He tears it loose. Then,
using a felt-tip pen taken from a pouch of six inside the box, he
tries to write. No words come. He taps his pen against the edge
of the table, puts it down. He returns the notebook to the box
where it rejoins its forty-nine brothers. Augustus can't concentrate. With the back of his knuckles, he strokes the goat's
bearded chin. He picks up the pen and his hand seems to move
involuntarily, of its own free will, putting ink on the page in
strokes. The words do not register with the writer. He sees himself as a bystander. His hand is an instrument. When the message finishes, the pen drops from his hand. Augustus reads the
transcription. These are the words of the voice in his neck
speaking for him.

WELCOME A display window is what I have entended here
Gentlemen Please excus the croodeness of it but I was
RUSHED Pardon the mess in the kitchen Surely you can

apreciate As servants of the people you must know the preshure of time TIME Time and expectations I too am a SERVANT Please toure the house at your leizure I've done what I could to eliminate the SMELL But in certain instants I believe it actually INTENSIFIES the encounter The ANIMAL within us stirs No room is off limits Don't miss THE CELLAR I asure you it alone is worthe the price of admision Photos are permited My showing here shared for the first time with the public is the acumulation of years of searching and good old-fashioned hard work LOOK in the Goatshead Box. The journals contaned there may give you valuuable insite to the pieces you will see exhibited about my humbel lodging For YEARS I have lived a DOUBLE LIFE The creative part of me is very very old and I have lived before sew many lives inside my head collected together like DUST Forever I was torchured SUFFERING confined in the shell of a drunkard and consumett failure my sadnesse required repairs and disguises I AM SO MUCH MORE I am a RESURRECTED SOUL My pieces SPEAK for themselves I hope they will be etched or likewise SCORCHED into your memorees I hope you can come away from this EXPERIENCE changed men Lastly I hope you never can quite drive me from the darkliest corners of your minds Here's a promise—STAY WITH ME and I will stay with you ALWAYS

Augustus the GOATskinner

Augustus drives Sherry's cruiser in the direction of the Black Chimney. He takes a detour onto Ketchel Road, finds the turnaround, drives through the gravel and follows the grassy lane. He turns off the engine and rolls to the water's edge. Sherry's service revolver is on the passenger seat. A pump shotgun is locked in a rack perpendicular to the passenger-side dashboard. Augustus has the key for it on Sherry's ring. He leaves the keys and the guns. He'll make do with the Bowie.

It's time for walking.

Augustus breathes deeply and touches his ribs. He feels a strange twist in between the bones. Once he believed he was growing antlers inside his chest. Or perhaps horns. Now he is convinced a whole animal has taken shape. When they are ready to kill him, his soul will be transferred into the animal. He'll tear his way out of this body and run for the woods. He can't decide what the animal is, and he's waiting to be surprised on the day it happens.

The spot where Buddy fishes in the morning. Augustus stands on the rocks. He looks around. He *feels something*. An energy. Forces. He watched Buddy fishing sometimes. Augustus watched all of Gunnar. Just ahead, at the sandy beach, he watched Melissa Teagles and Kyle Harkin. That very day the little goat would die.

But he wasn't going to the sandy beach tonight. He walked through the bushes.

●

The phone was ringing. Buddy picked it up. No caller. It rang again, and he caught it quick, mid-ring. In his ear he heard the disconnect, then a dial tone. And then the line went dead. He jabbed at the receiver. No sound.

"Robbie," Buddy called out from his office, "I think they're here. Somebody just cut the phone line."

"Terrific."

*

Margot had talked herself into and out of calling Carl Sherry–laying the whole story out for him–a dozen times. But wouldn't that be betraying Buddy at the moment he committed to trusting her?

She wanted to say that Buddy was innocent. Rafferty was wrong to suspect him. And men from Chicago were in Gunnar planning to kill Buddy. It was Augustus who attacked her at the Chimney. Augustus Bodine. She started to see it. The horrible event coming back to her and making her retch. Augustus and his big flabby arms, his unclean clothes, and his animal stink.

She made her decision. She pulled on her old softball sweatshirt, with its hood and deep pockets, and she piled into her rustbucket Escort. Drove away from the farm. She wasn't going to the Chimney.

Buddy's cabin. She'd drive to the cabin and leave him a note.

She'd write that the past was just that: *past*. It was behind him. And she wanted to be in his future, to at least make an attempt to be a part of it.

She rolled down her window and felt the air turning cool now that the sun had set.

Margot was careful. Red and Zo could be at the cabin.

But Buddy's road is quiet. The cabin is dark. There are no cars, no people. She drives to the dead end and backs out. She turns the Escort a hundred and eighty degrees, makes another pass.

Red was looking for Buddy and Robbie. They weren't here. But they'd be easy enough to find. In Buddy's driveway, she cranks the handbrake, lets the motor idle. She's got pen and paper. She writes what she's been thinking. Then her door's open and she's kneeling on the porch, sliding the folded note under Buddy's door.

"You've bounced back nicely."

She doesn't have to see his face. It's Augustus. He must've been hiding in the woods. Hiding and waiting for Buddy. But he got her instead. She didn't want to see his joy. She reaches in the dark under the Weber grill. But there's no fork, no weapon. Her hand seizes the squeeze bottle of charcoal lighter fluid. She stuffs it into her pocket.

"You know, Carl wants to talk to you. I just left him. Parked down over on Ketchel. He wanted to talk to Buddy, too. He's, ah, discovered some strong evidence related to these attacks."

She knows he's lying. But she can't run and she can't fight him here. If she screams, he'll be on her in a second. She knows he has a knife. Knows she'll be dead and he'll be gone before anyone comes to help.

She stands. Pulls the hood over her head because if she has to look at him she might just die right there. And she didn't plan on doing that.

She says, "Okay. Let's go."

He raises his arm so she can pass.

●

Under the moon, river at my feet, and I will have the Wounded Goat. Augustus feels the antlers stir against his ribs. The Bowie comes alive and rubs his hip. He pets it.

Not now. But soon, very soon.

•

Margot's ankle trips on a root. She's falling. Her hand flies up for support, slaps bark, the hard, round trunk of a tree. Stiff-arm and she's falling the other way. Augustus bumps against her from behind. He envelops her. His arms come around to keep them from going down together. She's queasy. His smell: hair tonic, sweat, and stale breath. A hard shape in the pocket. The knife. Another smell, this one like iron.

"I'm fine." She pushes on.

"Keep to your left," he says. "Do you see the moon in the water?"

•

"Check the kitchen door."

"Sure thing."

"Remember, no lights but your flash."

Robbie flipped his flashlight on.

"Stay away from the windows. Keep the blinds shut. I'm leaving the lot lit up for us. But there's a full moon, too."

A bullet shattered glass. Robbie turned sideways and took a half step backward as if he'd just walked into an invisible wall. His flashlight beam swept yellow along the ceiling in a crazy arc and then changed abruptly to a lower angle, shining at Buddy crouched in his office, the jolt coming as Robbie let the lamp fall from his hand. The light continued to roll over the uneven boards in the direction Robbie gently kicked it, toward the bar.

"Get on the floor!" Buddy had the .22, but Robbie was blocking the window.

Robbie stumbled to a round table. He sat down in one of the mismatched wooden chairs and let the sawed-off drop between his knees. The sound of multiple gunshots and breaking glass echoed from the parking lot as they knocked out the floodlights. Buckshot tore off chunks of wood and spit them on the roof. Lead pellets ticked in the gutters. The brothers were submerged together in the dark.

But the moon was up. As long as they could see out, they'd have an edge inside the Chimney. If they could hold on, bunker down through the initial assault. The whole thing could be over in five minutes. *Shots this close to town,* Buddy thought, *the closest neighbors were probably already dialing 911.* Through the splintered blinds, moonlight landed like a blue flannel blanket on Robbie's shoulders. Buddy couldn't tell if the rocking motion he saw was an effect of the light. His brother put his head down on the table.

Holes appeared in the walls. The sounds were coming so fast, the blasts so loud and constant they were merged into one sound, like heavy surf crashing over the tavern. Leather hands punched the ruined glass still hanging in the windows. Fire barked from the discharging shotguns. More buckshot and deer slugs. Barrels probing into the tavern. A pause, then orange flashes and pieces of furniture, bottles, wallboards exploding across the barroom. The stench of burnt plastic. Five seconds of quiet. Water flooded through the windows. Not water.

Gasoline.

Robbie said, "They shot me."

"Where's my *money?*" Red's voice shouting from somewhere in the lot. "You shitty pigfuckers didn't think I was coming. Now you know better. Throw the bag out the front door. *Hey, Bayes!* One minute till the pig roast."

Buddy's ears were ringing.

"Robbie, get down out of that chair."

Robbie picked his head up off the table and stretched his arm out to Buddy, keeping his face turned away.

His index finger was gone and his thumb was just hanging there, on a string.

Buddy said, "Get over here."

Robbie stood up. Buddy saw the entrance wound. Low in the center of his brother's gut. Blood burping out fast. Above the wound, a flap of skin was pulled away like a turned-out pocket. Robbie's feet were slipping on his own blood.

"I'm on fire."

"Try to make it to me."

Robbie fell facedown in the gasoline. He tried to get up and couldn't.

"Oh, man, I don't want to die. Earl, I'm hurt bad." He was gasping now, and his elbows were sliding.

"I'm coming." Buddy crawled over to his brother. The stitched-up knife wound in Buddy's shoulder made carrying Robbie impossible. He locked his left arm under Robbie's right and dragged him into a corner. Then Buddy went back for the sawed-off.

"It's in my legs or something. *Jesus.* Don't let me die, Earl. I'm burning up. Tell the girl to call an ambulance."

Buddy pulled off his own shirt, folded it, and pressed down on the wound.

Robbie rolled his head from side to side. "Where's the girl?"

"The girl's gone. She's okay."

A long pause. Then Robbie said, "Nykki got out?"

His shoulders slacked. A look of puzzlement came over his face. His mouth formed a soft *O.*

Buddy blew into Robbie's lips and tasted gasoline. Out of the corner of his eye, he saw a tongue of fire, rising and falling.

Mizel stood in the doorway. A crowbar and gas-soaked rags made the torch he held up over his head. He was squinting. He couldn't find Buddy in the shadows.

"Your minute's up."

Red threw the crowbar. The revolving wheel of fire skidded on the wooden floor.

The moon traced Red out. Buddy leveled the sawed-off. Then the wood lit.

12

The flow of silky black water, smelling cool and rank, breezes past.

The mosquitoes are finding her. Margot slaps her naked legs. She can feel bites on her neck. *Blood like sugar. They're eating me alive.* She sees clouds of mosquitoes like suspended smoke beside the river. The clouds change shape. Ghosts, their gray forms bend over the water, looking in. She wanted light. Light against the dark water, the night, the heavy man lumbering behind her.

She forces herself not to look back. The river is there for distraction. Some animal swims away, its triangular head bobbing in the current. The water is not black or silver but a constant switching of the two. Her eyes close. Temples pounding. Everything in her recedes, and she has a second of pure clarity and calm.

The adrenaline is hitting her hard and fast. Her ears fill with river noise.

Eyes open, down on her naked knees, fallen. Augustus, wordless, breathing through his open mouth. He stops behind her. Her bruised and scraped skin rubs against the angular, jutted stone. She stands. Looks up. Watches a meteor shower that isn't happening. Feels his breath on her cheek.

●

The fire scurried along the floor. It ran for the exits where the gasoline soaked the boards. It climbed onto Robbie's chest and sat there. Orange tail switching, the heat of it made Buddy pull away. A wall of smooth logs met his back. His angle toward Red cut off, no sight of him in the doorway. His dead brother on fire. The tavern filled with smoke.

They were waiting for him outside.

Buddy crawled to the giant mouth of the fireplace. When he stood, it was chest-high. He leaned the sawed-off against the stone hearth and plunged his hands into the cool ashes, pulling out the burnt chunks of firewood until he could grab hold of the andirons. He fought to drag the iron log supports away from the hearth. The andirons inched forward and bumped against the stones. Roar from behind and a sudden blast of great heat. Buddy tried to squeeze past but could not. Over his shoulder he saw the vinyl booths engulfed in green-edged flames. A purple devil emerged from the pinball machine, wagging its head. Fumes and no air to breathe, just smoke under Buddy's chin. He closed his eyes and changed his grip. Pulling. Something gave between the iron and stone, and Buddy hauled the andirons out. With his foot, he shoved them under one of the tables.

Clearing a space for himself inside the hearth, Buddy bought some temporary protection from the fire. He retrieved the sawed-off. The smoke was deadly in the room. Head and shoulders back inside the chimney, Buddy could taste the outside air.

He filled his lungs and coughed. He filled them again more slowly and wiped the sooty tears from his eyes. Buddy's right arm was tingling. He could feel a stinging in his shoulder where the knife wound had spread apart and started bleeding like it was fresh. He wouldn't be able to use his right arm to climb. He took off his boots and socks.

Buddy found a toehold and stuffed himself into the chimney. The first ten feet were easy. An instinct to survive pushed him into the hole, making it seem like a good idea. Knees to chest. He had the sawed-off jammed sideways through his belt at the small of his back. He reached up with his left arm. Fingers searching for an edge of brick, a crack, a lump of excess mortar. When his fingers found purchase, he dug in. Then he moved up—left leg, right, left, right—one at a time, pulling himself higher with the arm that worked, making his legs take the heaviest burden of his weight. The balls of his feet wedged into the corners, pinning him in place. He shimmied with his spine grinding against the bricks. His ass slung low, belly jamming his lungs and making it harder to breathe. Below him, they were at it with the shotguns again. Murdering smoke. The inside of the chimney was rectangular. If it had been round, he would've already been dead.

Smoke slipped between his knees, up his groin and torso, past his face, and higher into the narrowing, black-bricked throat of the chimney.

●

"You want to rest?" Augustus asks.

But she's walking. Wearing him down so when she runs, she

has a chance. His footfalls land at her heels. If she stops, he'll be on top of her. She is not about to go slow. Margot sprints ahead ten yards.

"Stick close to the water." His voice is loud.

She finally looks at him over her shoulder.

He sees fear painted over her pretty face.

His eyes are spider holes, so she watches his teeth through the beard, sees his lips pulling back, not in a smile, and as he gains ground Margot hears his growing effort. *Keep him moving.* She thinks about running now. Impossible in the dense woods, but here along the river it would be easier.

Her foot senses an abrupt change of ground. There's a gully cut through the path. She can't judge how deep or wide across. She needs to stop. Augustus is so close she can feel his body heat.

He says, "My truck. And Carl. I'm just a little farther upriver."

Margot can't see any truck. She palms her keys, opens the corkscrew on her Swiss Army knife, but Augustus doesn't touch her. He points out a log and then the gap in the weeds where the path continues on the other side. Three inches of water flows through a muddy channel. She thinks, *I need to hurt him before I run.*

●

"That's Carl, sir, it sure is. I can see his badge. Somebody's pinned it to his nose."

"Any movement?"

"No way. He's dead. His arms and legs are cut off and there's some wire . . ."

"In the house, Harper! Any movement in the house?"

"Uh, nothing I can make out from here."

"Where's Fiedler?"

"Walt got sick. Threw up all over. He's . . . I'm not sure where he is."

"Anderson and Putee?"

"They went around back."

"Okay, tell Fiedler to get his ass in gear and help you watch the front door. Bob and Arnie should keep covering the back. Tell them to drive their cruiser *and Sherry's* through the side yard and park with the high-beams pointed at the house. Anybody comes out, don't hesitate to shoot. I'm on my way. Nobody goes in till I get there, that clear?"

"Yessir."

"Five minutes, boys. I'll be there in five."

"Sir?"

"What is it, Harper?"

"Carl's cruiser isn't here."

●

The space got tighter.

Buddy had no idea if he was close to the chimney's opening or not. He reached up and touched smooth brick walls. There was heat in the chimney now, building under him. The smoke was everywhere. Tears wet his cheeks. He couldn't open his eyes. He choked. Lost his sense of orientation. Should he keep climbing or slide down for another run at it? Could he get a better angle? Had he been moving at all? Buddy forced one eye open. A watery view of nothing. The eye shut involuntarily. His hand knocked down layers of soot. Flakes of carbon fell into his mouth. He tried to pull his head away but there was nowhere to go. Knowing he might not be able to take another breath, he reached up again and held the filthy air in his lungs until it turned to fire.

The tavern started to rumble. He could feel a tremor in the chimney. He attempted to turn himself, to ease the pressure on his wounded shoulder, and he ended up slipping down a foot. Buddy inhaled. What filled the chimney was poison, and it crushed his chest. He willed his legs to push off the walls. His good arm swam upward.

A ledge. He gripped it. Buddy hauled himself through the gray swells and over the rim of the chimney and he held on, coughing, breathing–head and shoulders out of the rising smoke, arms dangling, spittle blowing under his chin.

•

Margot knows it's coming when he mentions the moon again.

"Would you look at that? How'd you like to live there? You could, you know. Lots of ladies living on the moon these days. Living higher than ever. Not low like a goat. Trash eaters."

A scattering of white gravel appears on the trail. Crooked line of crumbs on the forest ground.

"I'm thinking of a number," he says. "Can you guess it?"

Shush of wild grasses. Augustus breathes deeply through his nose. His tongue pokes out from between his lips as if he can taste the air.

Margot doesn't know what say. But Augustus isn't waiting for her answer.

"Of course you can't. There's no porthole cut into my brain so people can look around. No God, no Great Spirit bullshit. No one can see what we do here. Only animals. Heaven's empty. You want God, don't look up, honey, look behind you."

Ahead, she sees Carl's cruiser parked at the river's edge. She runs for it.

●

Buddy clung to the bricks. He waited for his vision to return. Waited for the gun blast that would take off the top of his head. The one he'd never hear if it came.

●

They checked and rechecked the rooms on the first floor. Then Rafferty sent two deputies upstairs while two waited outside. Rafferty shouted commands from the kitchen. Since the house had no lighting in the ceilings, and all the lamps were arranged behind Sherry's body hanging in the front window, the lawmen used their flashlights. White cones played jerkily on tea-stained floral wallpaper, pine floors, and fifty-year-old furniture. Underfoot, the staircase moaned. Screws in the railing were loose. Toward the front of the house, they saw a bathroom with a claw-footed tub and a porcelain pedestal sink. The HOT/COLD taps were little iron clubs. A rust-streaked toilet gurgled in the corner. Beneath them was a checkerboard of black and white tiles. You could smell mold.

The other end of the hallway showed three shut doors. One revealed an office, used for storage, crowded with stacks of cardboard boxes. Everywhere, a cloth of dust.

Each deputy took a bedroom.

The darkness in the bedrooms covered their eyes like gloved hands. Rafferty's voice kept yelling out questions from downstairs. It was no way to be conducting a search.

Deputy Walt Fiedler opened a closet door. An exhalation of naphthalene and mildew. In went his light. A red-and-blue bathrobe mended with green thread at the cuffs. Hat boxes stacked on a high shelf, next to Christmas sweaters. Purses. Dresses obscured in plastic sleeves. A raincoat. Fox fur stole. Brown-and-orange mackinaw. Thin leather belts of various colors, including pink, on a hanger. Women's shoes propped along a wire rack on the floor.

Victims' belongings? Walt wondered.

He turned to the quilted bedspread, the lace curtains in the window, and on the dresser a statuette of a lady watering roses. He let his beam wash under the bed.

●

The cruiser's empty and locked. Inside on the seat are Carl's keys and gun. Margot whirls around.

"Carl!"

Augustus' boots crunch gravel. He's talking quietly. To her or to himself, she can't tell. Margot slides past the cruiser's front bumper, putting the car between them. She tries the passenger door and when it doesn't open, she pounds her elbow against the window. Carl let her fire his sidearm on the range over at Cullerton's Guns 'N More. *If she could just get her hands on that weapon.*

Augustus kicks his side of the cruiser. The sound of it booms and the car rocks.

"Carl! Somebody help me!" Then, looking at Augustus over the cruiser's roof, she says, "Stay away!"

His boot launches white stones in her direction. "You salty little bitch. I hope your Carl can roll awful fast 'cause I chopped him up pretty good."

Margot steals a glance at Ketchel Road. The yellow double line curving into a downhill chute through a stand of jack pines. *I can outrun him.* Sidestepping. Her fingers graze the cruiser's tail lamps. But she doesn't move farther.

"Now where you gonna go?"

He has the knife twinkling in his fist as he gestures to the roadway. He's closing.

"Get back!"

"Nobody's watching."

"Why are you doing this?"

"I like it."

"Leave me alone."

"I don't think so."

Hard head fake to the road, and she changes direction. His footing on the gravel is lost. He's on his back as she races down the path they had come up from the river. Her feet punch the earth.

The moon's a descending skull. She pulls the blood in waves through his chest. The creature growing inside him flips against his heart. Through his nose he draws the sweet night air and the goat smell of the woman. He rolls on his stomach. The moon drops so close he feels her coolness above him, then lower, pressing on his cheek like a cave wall. Augustus wants to be crushed. The back of his neck and the creature inside him speak.

Up, up. The moon pulls his blood, raises his head. But he can't look.

Up, my slave, up.

●

Smoke leaked through the shingles but there was no fire on the roof. Not yet. Buddy wiped his eyes. He held the shotgun against his thigh. Buddy got a leg up over the bricks. The wind swirled the smoke into a funnel. Buddy found the climbing rungs and went down through the haze.

Buddy heard a sound like bacon grease crackling on a hot griddle. One of the power lines, severed by a gun blast, spit honey-colored sparks. The shotgun was tight in his right hand as his left grabbed the chimney for balance. He trained his eyes on the parking lot. A diseased cork elm loomed above the tavern. Ashes floated upward through its withered boughs—a reverse snow. Buddy jumped up and snagged a branch, cracked the dry wood, and stripped off the dead brown leaves.

He used the branch's point to pass the cut power line to the edge of the roof and then off.

"I got him! He's up top."

Buddy saw the muzzle flashes and ducked. Hollow-points whizzed through the smoke-filled air. He cradled the shotgun and crawled, sticking his head over the edge of the roof to look into Margot's burning apartment. The hallway subfloor and floor had burned through, and he could see the exposed, blackened joists and flames mounting from below. The whole tavern could collapse. Buddy picked his head up and saw balled-up gas rags, landing on the roof. He could see Zo, too. The apricot glow of the tavern trembled over him. Zo, laughing and lighting up more rags. Pitching them to the rooftop with the barrel end of his shotgun.

Zo's eyes met Buddy's. He panicked and struggled to shoulder his Mossberg.

Buddy's sawed-off bucked once, twice.

●

Fiedler first thought it was a round bowl with a lid. Painted glossy black with yellow dots and numbers. He put down his flashlight to reach under the bed with both hands. But there was no lid. It was one solid piece and heavier than it looked. He guessed it was a good-sized stone, smooth on the side facing him and covered with holes on the side touching his fingers. In the dark, he placed the stone on the bed and picked up his light.

●

He put him on the ground.

Zo's big chest absorbed the double load of buckshot. His heels danced Irish over the gravel.

The rags on the roof raged. Buddy found the extra shells in his pocket. He reloaded. His fingers were slippery. His right hand tingled. A yellow hand of flame reached up through the chimney and waved. There'd be no going back down into the tavern. His right arm was useless. Swordlike pain slicing into his shoulder and neck. He crabbed to the edge for a look at the back lot.

Where was Red?

In the firelight, impossible things looked real. Shadows thrashed and broke apart, turned into a dog. Buddy saw Boy trot onto the gravel. His ruby-fired eyes, searching.

Buddy turned away. He had to get off the burning tavern.

•

Rafferty was two steps from the bottom of the cellar stairs when the smell of formaldehyde floated up from the dampness, and he was transported to Mr. Pomeroy's biology class. *Old Crusty Face Pomeroy, an ancient memory if ever there was one; I haven't thought about him in twenty-five years. Everyone stood in line with their wax-coated pans while Crusty Face dipped his blue rubber glove into a barrel to serve up the fetal pigs. What a hellacious stink. And I cut out the heart of my little guy and dropped it down the front of Francine Bellows' blouse so she would go nuts and we'd see her bra.*

Rafferty gagged on bile and whipped the brightness of his Maglite through the crowded cellar. He saw a row of tall, padlocked metal cabinets, a cheap bookcase, and a sledgehammer lying on top of the bookcase. The farthest wall was partially demolished and showed through to layers of exposed dirt. Hunks of concrete had been heaved up from the floor, and the rubble from the broken wall lay in a pyramid beside the last cabinet. Forty-pound bags of lye were stacked next to the hole in the floor where a hump of freshly turned soil seemed to be an obvious grave.

Taking up the rest of the floor, sprinkled as it was–liberally, with sawdust–four aluminum tubs sat covered with sheets of plywood. Cinder blocks weighted the plywood in place. A heap of dirty laundry had been piled at the foot of the stairs, blocking Rafferty's way. He claimed the bottom step and kicked at the mound of threadbare, stiffened socks and gray underwear, stirring up a sour vinegary odor to rival the formaldehyde. Directly opposite the stairs, a finger painting of a stick-figured man and a procession of women ran diagonally up the wall. The man was three times the size of the women. He wore a crown. Above the painting were words:

Midnight Meat Sale!

Lumpy dark bronze paint. Rafferty was right to think it was dried blood. Below the message was a like-colored smear. Rafferty squinted without moving from his step. The smear was really more of a scribble. Thinner, more faint, but they were letters. Rafferty bent forward but he couldn't read them. Fiedler started shouting from the bedroom. *Incompetent shithead. Fire his lard ass once this is over.* Rafferty tried to step over the pile of dirty clothes but it was too big. He kicked it down some, sending shirts and a pair of overalls into the corner. The reek was beyond foul. Rafferty shone his light into ratty Fruit-of-the-Looms and a white beach towel with its price tag still intact. Rafferty put his foot on the towel and leaned toward the vague marks. As he transferred his weight downward, the words became distinct:

Come closer.

The laundry flew up as if it were infested with ghosts. The loud snap Rafferty heard was his pelvis cracking. A sudden grip on him was so jarring it knocked his shoes off. His Maglite tumbled between the tubs, and so he had to learn about his situation in a blackout. He did not scream. He felt no pain; or rather the pain was so great that his body had spared his brain for a moment.

This much was certain: Rafferty could not move. An arc of heat crossed him at the waist, front and back, but the heat vanished and unbearable cold replaced it as if he were being crushed between two ice blocks. His arms were soaking wet. It never registered that this wetness was his blood. The apparatus holding him would not give him the relief of falling.

Rafferty slid his palm along the curve of the bear trap. Triangular teeth as big as toast points. The pain was approaching like a speeding train, but he would not be there when it arrived. His last thought swirled as consciousness drained away. *It can't be too bad because I'm still standing.*

•

It was a matter of patience.

Bayes couldn't stay up there forever. The place was a goddamned tinderbox. *Didn't these hicks have a Volunteer Fire Department?* Red tried to get a bead on the mutt with his SIG .45. He hesitated, fearing he'd give away his position in the tree line.

Zo was on the ground, dead. *Sonofabitch Bayes was nails, man, you had to give him that. Nails. And lucky, too.* Red crouched and watched the rooftop. His face was hot, tight-skinned. Felt like he had a sunburn. *Like standing too close to a fucking furnace.* He draped his leather coat over his hand to hide the white cast. He wore a tangerine silk shirt with yellow piping and pearly buttons.

Sweat rolled out of his hairline and into the gullies of his neck. He thought about hiking through the woods back to the motel. *Bayes is gonna get burned extra crispy. So what am I even here for?* Red scrambled deeper into the trees, found a thick one to stand behind. He holstered the SIG pistol under his arm. He'd tossed the Mossberg when he'd run out of shells. The SIG was more accurate at this distance from the tavern. He patted his pockets for the keys to the truck. But he hadn't been driving because of his hand. Zo had the keys. Red wasn't about to run into the open and spend time going through a dead man's pockets.

●

Margot couldn't believe what she was seeing.

His arms are spread wide. The path is blocked in both directions by his span.

How did he get ahead of her?

"Because I know the woods. I am the Moonslave. She shows me a way."

Augustus backhands Margot across the face. She hits the ledge. He steps on the back of her head. Her lip bleeds. A tooth is gone, and she hears a crunching in her nose. The pressure lets up. He catches her arm and twists. Margot digs a hand into the pocket of her sweatshirt.

She slashes with the corkscrew. Neck and face. Strokes it deep, four times five six times, on the forearm clutching her close. Under his ear, she jabs with all her strength. The screw point finds the hard line of his jaw. He squeaks. Her attacking arm strikes and recoils, avoids his grip.

Augustus shoves her down onto the ledge.

Margot has the squeeze bottle of charcoal lighter fluid, the matches. Her hands are sticky with his blood. Her stomach curls. The matchbook tumbles away through her fingers.

Augustus is humming. He picks at the hole in his neck. Spits blood. He prods the wounds with his fingertips, checking himself. His face is messed up, and she got him good on the arm. When he makes a fist, there's a little geyser south of the elbow. Stooping, he seizes Margot by her shoulders. Turns her around to face the water. She puts her hands behind her head and, for a second, he considers the possibility of the gun. But she's squirting fluid in his eyes, on his flesh, into his wide-open mouth.

Like oil, the feel of it. Like gasoline, the taste.

It stings. A terrific swarm of stinging. *How cruel of her to do this to me.* His eyes cloud over. She drives her heel onto his instep.

He falls. On top of her, on the rock ledge, he pitches himself forward. She's his cushion. The wind's knocked from her chest. He feels it go at once.

He hugs Margot tighter and struggles to stand with her. The Wounded Goat brushes her fingers on the ledge, plucks something from its surface. He rises. They rise together.

●

I have brought Hell to him, Red thought. Buddy's tavern groaned and from inside flashed its gold like a street hood. Rippling sheets of superheated air cooked the lot. Trees caught fire and the ring of destruction grew. *Hello, Smokey, we got a goddamned forest fire.* He fired the SIG at the roof antenna. *Keeping you honest, Buddy. I hope you left your keys in the Caddy or I got a long walk.* Red broke from the tree line. The cast banged against his thigh, caused him to wince and swear, but he high-stepped his pointy boots and kept going. He made it to the Caddy. Driver's door was locked. He busted the window with a swipe of the SIG. A locked door, of course, meant no keys. Red squinted through the windshield.

The tavern's skeleton burned. He had to put the SIG on the seat. *One-handed bullshit.* Case XX pocketknife open in his nimble fingers, and *always working in the goddamned dark,* Red stripped the wires. His criminal heart was high. Mayhem, killing, and stealing—the rush had more throttle than coke and this shit was tougher to quit. The engine turned over. *I feel fucking good! Like this hunk of junk was my first ever, like I busted my cherry and I got a gallon of strawberry wine and a pair of sister sluts waiting for me to hurry come home.* Red shifted into gear and rolled up alongside the tavern. He held the switch to lower the passenger window. When it slid down, he jammed his foot on the brake, and leaned across the plush seat. Red emptied the SIG into the flaming rooftop.

Well, Angel of Mercy, what have we here? Buddy's faithful companion?

Red blinked and gunned the motor. The dog never stirred. Smoke smudged its face black as a crow. Red aimed to run it down. But the dog jogged up to the driver's door and just stood there, staring at him.

I've got to high-tail it, he thought. Red had no bullets and he might have been just as low on luck. But it didn't feel that way. It felt all aces and somebody else was buying the whiskey. Red had to laugh out loud. He looked at the case knife but left it on the dashboard. Red took the razor from around his neck. The pearly handle was sweaty and warm from his chest. The blade, once exposed, was white-blue action. He poked his head out of the driver's side with his cast resting on the steering wheel. Then he ducked in and opened his door.

The dog stayed.

Outside the car, Red moved quicker now, crouching beside the dog.

"Come, Boy. Come."

Red stood up fast.

He was trying to get back into the Caddy when, from above, a hail of buckshot as deadly as God's right hand cut him in two.

Buddy jumped down from the elm.

•

Scratch, scratch.

Night, yes, and his foggy pain-filled eyes. *But look!* The Wounded Goat has her hands working like she's deaf and talking. *But she will never, never, never escape him the way she shakes and he's holding her so very close.* He tells her what she won't do.

Scratch, scratch, scratch.

"You must have a real itch, goat."

Scratch-pop. Margot touches the flaming matchbook to his hair, beard, collar.

Of course! Gods are born in fire!

He drops Margot. The goat is on her back, kicking him.

13

Deputy Walter Fiedler had been shouting about the stone that turned out to be a human skull he'd pulled from under a bed in the Bodine residence. The decorated cranium (and leg bones found later in a highboy drawer) proved to be the remains of a missing real estate agent, Leslie Jean Habersham, from Winter Park, Colorado. Skeletal evidence recovered from the "guest bedroom" alone linked Bodine to nine murdered women.

Rookie Deputy John Harper discovered the now infamous "Attic Mannequins." Then he quit his job with the sheriff's police to manage a chain of paint stores in the Wausau area. DNA samples taken from the dried skins of the mannequins connected Bodine to at least fourteen other female victims. None of the sheriff's officers at the scene responded to the multiple calls that evening reporting gunshots and a fire at the Black Chimney tavern. The men said they were consumed with the task of freeing their sheriff, Glen Rafferty III, from an antique grizzly bear trap in the Bodine cellar. Sheriff Rafferty bled to death before he could be removed from the site of the so-called "Goatskinner's House of Horrors."

The local fire department was admittedly "seriously delayed" in its arrival at the Black Chimney blaze because it had been called out to a house fire where two elderly sisters were trapped in a second-floor closet. No one was hurt, though the sisters' home was destroyed. The cause of the fire was later traced to a tea cozy left on a lit burner of the kitchen stove.

Trick-or-treaters claimed to have encountered the Goatskinner in the woods on Halloween.

Robed in furs, disguised under a pile of wet moldering leaves, he grabbed at them. His face was worse than a rubber mask because pieces were flaking off; shiny black scabs, and white scabs too, peeling, detaching with singed facial hair still on them. A tangled wisp of gray hairs emerged from the base of his skull. On his scorched head, where so few hairs survived, they resembled a newborn's fuzz. His beard whiskers clumped in brown knots on his throat. Nothing was left of his chin except a loose pouch of skin.

Hunched, he windmilled his arms but missed even the smallest child, a preschooler wearing a pumpkin costume stuffed with balls of newspaper. The girls and boys screamed. Augustus stumbled forward and flopped onto his stomach. The frightened group of children made their escape down a path crisscrossed with fallen logs.

Augustus went down, crunching leaves as he fell. Small heads turned and fixed their panicked eyes on him. He coughed and spat thick yellow curds. His breath rattled. A spasm seized him. He bucked in his fur jacket. Had to swallow a clot of mucus to clear his windpipe. His breathing settled into a jagged, wet rhythm.

This creature was not constructed with makeup and road-kill pelts.

He had a hole beside his nose. The socket above it gaped. A ridge of cheek under his eye was just bone. It showed white. His smell was evil. A laugh came from him but changed somewhere in his chest. He was puking on the ground, lifting his head between heaves to check if they were still watching. While the children fled to the highway, he covered his vomit carefully with dirt.

The children said his exposed skin swelled with blisters, some already broken into pale, running sores. "Probably pus," said Joel Watkiss, a boy who'd been there. He recounted the gruesome adventure to his classmates in the school cafeteria. The girls at his table made faces. A boy in a green turtleneck pressed his lips tight and ripped a lewd farting sound.

"Augustus popping a blister!" he shouted. Joel laughed. But he was twisting his fingers as he remembered how his mother had to throw out his underwear from that Halloween night because he peed through it.

An earlier report from September had a thirteen-year-old boy swearing he shot Augustus with a pellet rifle one Sunday at dusk. The day was unseasonably warm, and, that evening, copper clouds lit the west. Augustus was squatting by the riverside. He was eating a live bluegill he had scavenged from a little girl's fishing line. Sue Ann Macklin, a tomboy at the age of six, had been flipping her cane-pole for sunfish. Her face was rosy, and she looked cherubic. Augustus surprised her near the place where he cut off Mary O'Connor's head. Hiding in the shallows near the bank, he scooped up the bluegill as soon as she had it on the grass. He began to chew at the fish. To Sue Ann it looked like she'd dragged up a monster from the river's deep.

Cal, the girl's older brother, was shooting at squirrels farther up the hillside. He said, "I put two in his back. The Goatskinner hollered and crashed into the woods downstream." He showed the deputies blood spattered on the dogwood bushes and a big drop still wet on a square stone. The grass was mashed down and branches bent far inward. Cal produced the fish with a bite-shape missing from the belly. Sue Ann waited in the backseat of a cruiser. A fat deputy with a blond mustache tried to soothe her, offering a paper cup of cocoa too warm for her to hold. She avoided touching his pudgy hands and said, "No, thank you." He spilled the cup outside the cruiser's open door. Sue Ann watched the liquid chocolate steam up through fallen leaves. The deputies concluded the whole thing was a hoax. They confiscated Cal's gun, drove the Macklin children home, and warned their parents to keep a better watch over them.

Cal went back and dug up the bloody stone as a souvenir.

The Goatskinner wasn't alive anymore. He couldn't hurt you.

Margot saw him, too.

In the hour before dinnertime, mid-week mid-October, standing in the woods behind the ruins of the Black Chimney, he steadied himself against a tree trunk and gazed at her. She froze, unable to turn away. Like two wooden totems, one carved to instill fear and the other to depict it, they exchanged stares.

Sundown highlighted his pink, melted face. He wore a greasy feather pasted over his scalp. He appeared as a dead thing in need of burial. Margot raised her fist, and his figure, stepping backward, dissolved into orange leaves and blowing shadows.

Buddy wanted to believe Augustus was gone from this world. To be sure, he knew they needed a body. Remains don't simply vanish. Decomposition takes time. Augustus had learned the lesson of how hard it was to cast off your dead.

Fury surrounded his departure. A woman took charge of him. Augustus found himself bleeding, with his shirt soaked in charcoal lighter fluid. Recognition of the smell and the whoosh of exploding fumes hit him at the same time.

Augustus sought his talisman. He staggered into the boiling Skin River. Went under fast, hissing danger.

Everyone seemed convinced that his wounds were mortal, or that he drowned in the same water where he had delivered his victims. The irony of his exit wasn't wasted. But for two solid days State Police divers worked the Skin's stained water from where Augustus entered and south to the river mouth in Dark Cloud, then fanning outward along the lake's sandy flats. They came up with nothing.

Was he still down in the river?

Buddy pictured Augustus' bloated face locked in a green-toothed grin. *If Augustus had surrendered to the pull of the current as the facts suggested, then why hadn't he floated up like so many drunken boaters with their pitiful flies unzipped?* His decomposing body somehow stayed under, caught, some said, in a vortex tumbling at the bottom.

First week of November, volunteers helped the sheriff's deputies drag Dark Cloud Lake end to end. The water went down fifty, fifty-five feet. Skim ice already covered the shallowest bays. The shoreline trees were picked clean of colors. Their bald, witchy limbs clawed the air so fiercely even the crows seemed afraid to alight on the branches for too long. Boats headed for open water and currents. They used depth finders and mean-looking grapple hooks. But the atmosphere was no longer one of pressing need.

Many of the volunteers took the opportunity to do a little late-season fishing, some outfitted in puffy, winter-camouflage hunting suits with their hoods pulled over and drawstrings cinched to form gloomy, steaming snouts. Others sported khaki outerwear and knitted caps. The standouts wore glow-bright orange. Each man had sacrificed his Saturday. They tugged off their gloves to rebait hooks and light cigarettes. The less prac-ticed were betrayed by their flaring, wind-chapped hands. Those not fishing lounged across their boat cushions or talked about the Packers.

A north wind was throwing cold scissors across the water.

There were whoops of excitement when Dusty Sinclair hooked an old crib and nearly took a header into the frigid chop. After the lunch break, it rained off and on, killing conversations. Fritz Haupt and his brother Georg had to be towed in after they busted their Merc's propeller against an unmapped rock hump. Clouds changed from slate to iron, the wind picked up a couple of knots, and waves were whitecapping at three feet. A few boats quit. A larger number stuck close to the public boat launch, where the base of operations was a heated tent with free coffee, peanut butter cookies, and a kettle of homemade venison stew. In a steady rain turning to snow, the new sheriff called off the search because of darkness. He thanked the men for a good effort in tough conditions. Not a lucky day for catching the Goatskinner.

The town created explanations. Hypotheses spun off in the pattern of fish stories. The more subtle attempts were almost plausible. He might be clogged in a trench with a river's worth of sticks, or lost among the used Christmas trees fishermen bundled and tossed out in the bays for springtime crappie. He was bulky enough that he could've wedged tight under a rock ledge, and body gases corked him in. Or he might've simply broken the surface on a remote stretch of the shoreline and gone unnoticed. Privately, the birds would be eating the lake's leftovers.

Hope of his discovery cooled with the temperatures. The winter ice would build around him. Canadian snowstorms were coming from the north to bury Gunnar as they always did. People returned to familiar worries. The spring thaw would flush Augustus and clean the town of his presence. *Wait till next year* was the attitude expressed.

Buddy thought the unspeakable: *Augustus the Goatskinner was alive.*

14

Following the fire, Buddy spent two nights in the county jail while the authorities tried to sort things out. He called his lawyer, Hugan Alvarez, in Chicago. Hugan knew people in Madison. A bail bondsman named Sam Big Bear picked up Hugan at the airport. They met up with another lawyer, Estrella Ramos-Hirshbeck, who handled the court appearance. Freed and at home sipping a much-needed Glenfiddich, Buddy told his story to Hugan and Estrella. The lawyers sounded confident.

"What they'll hear about is a businessman under siege from Chicago thugs. This businessman loses his business, loses a brother. But he's able to save his own life. No cops come to help him. No fire trucks, no ambulance. It's a tragedy. The prosecutor will have a hard time convincing people otherwise. He's got his hands full with this serial killer whose body hasn't turned up. You'll walk." Hugan lit a Kool off the one burning in his hand.

"You'll have to talk with the FBI first thing in the morning." Estrella had her shoes off. She poured herself a second scotch, neat. The cabin was drafty, but Estrella wasn't the complaining type. She asked Buddy where the wood was. A cold front had blown in overnight, dropping the temperature thirty degrees. It was raining and windy: instant autumn. Using iron tongs, she fed a log into the wood stove. It wouldn't take long to warm the small space where Buddy lived.

"We'll both go with you." Hugan loosened his tie. Buddy nodded. Hugan was one of the reasons he'd never been convicted of a crime. The man was sharp, connected, and impossible to shame. "Your lady friend has her own representation. But again, self-defense is obvious given the circumstances. FBI agents questioned her again today. Formalities. The Big Law and the local law are pissing on trees to mark their territory. We've got media crawling everywhere. The lady is going to be fine. You, too. Give it a week, this'll pass."

"I agree with Hugan," Estrella said. "But the situation is, shall we say, complex? They're covering their asses, making sure no bad guys walk away. For them it's not a happy resolution. They've got a dismembered deputy and a sheriff in a beartrap, a serial killer, and a house full of remains. Across town there're three dead and a burned-down bar. What they see is nobody in handcuffs. No perp walk for the cameras. It looks very much like failure on the part of law enforcement. The PR on this is a nightmare. So now we get thoroughness, we get a slow, careful inspection of the people still on the scene."

Buddy said, "I'm holding up. I've been through interrogations before. I'm not going to run at the mouth. But I've never had to talk to the Feds. That's got me worried."

"They want to make sure you and Bodine weren't a team. Remember the Hillside Stranglers?" Hugan asked. "Two Italian cousins killed a slew of women in California. It was in the late '70s. What were their names? Started with *B*."

"Bianchi and Buono," Estrella said.

"Right, Bianchi and Buono. Well, Hillside Stranglers the Sequel, that's what's got them worried. Strictly tabloid fodder. You're safe." Buddy watched Hugan open a window because the wood stove had him sweating rings.

"Cross your fingers and hope they find his body," Estrella said. She stretched out on the sofa and closed her eyes.

Buddy took Hugan outside to ask him a question.

•

The lawyers were right. In a week's time, everyone went home: the feds, the forensics teams, the reporters, the photographers, and the whole curious crowd. Margot went to her uncle's farm, Robbie to the family plot at St. Joe's, hearses drove through Gunnar carrying Red and Zo.

Genesee said Buddy's arm would come back if he just let himself heal. The insurance check for the fire was "in process." Buddy had nothing to do. So he took long walks with Boy and tried to empty his mind. He made a point of avoiding the river. One month became two. If anyone had asked, it would have been hard for him to explain what he did all day long. Just lived.

Margot called to say she was moving to San Diego. She had a cousin there.

"Can we get together before I fly out?" she asked.

They made a date.

•

Buddy knew it was time to leave town when, on a freezing Tuesday night, he caught himself timing the armored cars as they left the War Dance Indian casino.

The next day he packed his few possessions and rented a U-haul truck. He put a FOR SALE sign in the Caddy's window, parked it in front of Vic's service station. He would have hit the road except Genesee had invited him to Thanksgiving dinner and wouldn't take any excuses. And Margot was coming over in the morning so they could tell each other good-bye. Buddy wasn't looking forward to it. He wanted to slip away, but he owed her more than that.

So on Thanksgiving morning they took a last walk, and they followed the river. Took it north, farther than Buddy had ever ventured before. He passed the bridge where he found Melissa Teagles' hand. Light snow dusted down from the sky. There were fourteen inches of week-old accumulation on the ground. They didn't stop.

Up the hill were the Black Chimney ruins, and here was where Augustus went into the Skin *twice*. Buddy brushed wet snow off Margot's shoulders. He avoided her eyes. His head stayed low, fixed on the path. He checked the .22 in his jacket pocket. He pulled the brim of his cap snug.

"The little girl saw him about here," Margot said.

The spot where sad, drunken Mary O'Connor died.

Buddy thought he heard drums. Chippewas practicing for a powwow. The tribal center was on the other side of the river, over the rise. He strained to see their flagpole above the trees, but visibility was poor. He saw birches. Wisconsin snow falling like lace. But the wind was the right direction to carry a sound from there. Drums muffled by snowfall on the ground. They walked on, and soon the drums and snow ceased. The path showed heavy use. Around the bend it turned into a rut. Footprints in the snow. Lots of prints, from boots and shoes, and even a set of bare feet. Beer cans scattered like forgotten toys along the bank. Neon sizzled in the cold morning.

BEER GAS BAIT

The first item was the real draw today. People without families or people whose families wouldn't miss them at the holiday table were getting an early start. The crowd packed the riverside Glowworm Saloon. Buddy asked Margot if she wanted to go in and warm up. He'd buy shots of ginger schnapps.

"It'll be mostly college-age kids," Margot said, "They'll be looking forward to football and getting buzzed. I don't want to be around that today."

Buddy nodded.

Papier-mâché turkeys were stationed on the deck rails. A pilgrim taped to the storm door had a cardboard beer stein raised in his hand. They trudged past the signpost. Awash in neon from the sign, the frozen snow looked sugary and pink.

•

Buddy paused at the boat rental to light a cigar. He thought, *Here's the place Augustus killed Walinski and rowed off in two boats. Dumped the body and sank one, let the other drift downstream.*

A ragged rip of blue sky showed itself for a moment before the clouds converged and the snow came swirling again. The sun was a frosty lemon brushstroke set high in the east. *We're walking through his past. Every connection he made to this snaking brown flow of river.*

Margot was quiet. Her arm looped through Buddy's, and he could feel her strength. She wasn't smiling but seemed determined to make their last hour together a relaxing one.

Buddy broke the silence. "I'm leaving town, too."

"Where are you going?"

"Not sure. Thought I'd start in New Mexico, then decide."

"Out West?"

"Not California, though. I want to see wide spaces, you know?"

"The frontier."

"What's left of it, maybe." Buddy shook his head. "I don't know. Haven't been there yet."

The Skin widened. Quarter-mile shore to shore. On their side of the river, a clearing emerged. There were shacks grouped in camps. Twenty or thirty clustered in fours or fives around fire pits. Here and there, spaced out from the rest, a string of lone structures stood separate. The solitary shelters were perhaps a little more battered, leaning harder, windswept, many of them falling in on themselves. Hunters would pull the plywood on the slapped-together sheds. Go inside to thaw their toes and empty thermoses of coffee. A few of the shelters were ice shanties with no floors. Only meant to block the wind and snow, their walls were screwed onto sled runners. Fishermen would drag them out over the lakes with snowmobiles or ATVs when the ice was thick enough. Sit and fish through holes.

An elbow bend of exposed sand appeared, and Buddy pointed to deer prints where at least two animals had come to drink.

"Spooky out here with no one around," he said. *Augustus could be hiding in any of those Northwoods phone booths. More than likely dead, frozen solid if he made it this far, going this long with no medical attention for his injuries, no food, no proper clothes.*

The snow stopped. But the light from above was being sucked away and the color drained with it. So they walked inside a pencil drawing. The gray of the river was indistinguishable from the gray bark, the low ceiling of clouds, the mud, sand, and the puddles of water trying not to freeze. Buddy held up Margot's hand and saw red fingers.

"You cold?"

"Not bad. Let's go a little farther," she said.

On the opposite shore, a score of willows had fallen backward from the river's edge. Their upturned stumps showed cabled root work, both intricate and horribly wild.

Dead trees, he told himself. *That's all they are, Bud.*

He smoked the cigar down to a nub, and then crushed the butt under his heel. *Time to turn around and go home. Shower, change clothes, go eat some turkey and cranberries. Drink Genesee's twenty-year-old scotch, join him and his pointer for a lap around the Doc's fields. Boy could scare a pheasant or two.*

They walked. Prairie grasses had cropped up to his right. Stalks poked through the fallen snow. Ahead, a real estate agent's placard, framed in metal and pronged into the earth, vibrated dully in the wind.

Margot said, "I wonder whose land is for sale?"

Six cottages. A tiny chapel. Tire swing hanging straight down and the tire's hollow was full of snow. A pair of teeter-totters, their wooden seats cut in the shape of peanuts, sat on an oval of hard-packed yellow sand. Buddy pulled down on the high end of the nearest plank, heard the fulcrum squeak, and balanced the toe of his boot on the seat's handlebar.

"Do you know what this place is?"

"No." Margot turned full circle. "I haven't been up this way in years."

Together, they read the answer. The writing was blue and thick-lettered, upside-down because it was painted on the hull of an overturned canoe: HIS Word Bible Camp. Margot wanted a closer look.

The cottages were neat, gray, four-person boxes topped with snow. Outer lines trimmed in periwinkle, the same paint as the letters on the canoe. She used her sleeve to rub a circle on the glass of the first cottage's window. Plain white curtains tied back with blue ribbons. Two sets of bunk beds, kitchenette, toilet and a shower stall. Pegs on the wall for summer jackets. The door wouldn't budge.

Buddy turned his back on the cottage. *Something's wrong with that chapel.*

The chapel was an A-frame, an older building with a faded paint job the color of cigar ash. Giant peeling white cross varnished on the facade. Glistening wet black roof.

No snow. No snow on the roof because it had melted. *Somebody's forgotten to shut the heat off, that's all. Or they're still coming here to preach on Sundays. Keeping the church toasty so the congregation doesn't stay home under the blankets.*

Buddy discovered a cluster of strawberry-red piss holes drilled in a snowbank between the cottages and the church house. *Could be some dog with a sick bladder. Don't get too worked up.*

"You want to see if the chapel's open?" she said.

"I think we should get back."

"Oh, c'mon. I'm not going to make you get married."

Inside the chapel, the wooden walls were dark and heavy as if the structure had been cobbled together from an older church's dismantled pews. They went in the unlocked back door. Entered what seemed to be a small chamber behind the pulpit. The altar was visible through a second open doorway. This preacher's room, Buddy guessed that's what it was, had a mirror, a sink, and–he thought it oddly out of place in a house of worship–a stovetop range. There was a chair and a child's school desk. On top of the desk were a can opener and a collection of cans with their lids removed. Cherry pie filling, asparagus spears, peaches, stewed tomatoes, corn, lima beans, Hawaiian fruit cocktail.

Under the desk was a cardboard box. In green permanent marker, a child's scrawl: HELP THE HOMELESS. A dozen more dusty cans stacked at the bottom. Margot noticed a second box, pushed into the far corner of the little room, labeled by the same childish hand. She pulled it out. It once held a Kenmore washing machine, but now it was a depository for hand-me-down clothing.

Buddy went to the stovetop. Soup pot filled with snow waited on the front burner. He twisted a knob on the range. Blue flames. *So the propane tank isn't dry.* That explained the heat too. He could feel it radiating from the chapel. They stepped into the stifling air bath. Buddy thought instantly of his tavern, of Robbie and the destruction boiling around him. Gray light filtered through high, narrow windows. Dust motes danced in the steeple.

The heat was on full blast. Very warm inside these thick walls where people prayed. Swampy. Like the reptile house at the zoo. It stunk nearly as bad. Goddamn ripe.

He saw Margot go rigid. She waved him closer.

I hope it's just his body and no one else's. Buddy put his handkerchief over his nose. He took the .22 out, backed the safety off. His eyes swept the empty rows. Hymnbooks aligned on the benches. Shadows packed close and kneeling on the floor like penitent sinners.

Augustus is asleep in the last pew. Awakened, he sits up.

Someone's pulled a tube out of Buddy and is blowing cold air into his arteries.

Crisco smeared all over his burnt face, Augustus' one good eye rolls, then it fixes on Margot, the eyeball quivering like a separate life-form inhabiting his red skull. He stands. His left hand carries a large hunting knife.

"Hold it. Drop the knife," Buddy says.

Augustus is wearing a woman's large-sized silver parka, gray jogging sweats, and red wool mittens with snowmen stitched across the knuckles. The jacket hangs on him because he's skeletal, wasted. His exposed torso is a blue ladder of bones. He can barely lift his arm, but he does. He motions toward the preacher's room.

"The Good Lord provides." He croaks with laughter. "I live on snow and peaches."

Buddy raises the pistol. Aims it at Augustus' head.

A red mitten moves, carefully, probing between rib bones.

"Drop the knife!"

"Wait! Wait, let me show you something. I want the goat to see." Quick, merciless thrusts. Using the knife tip to open a door-way. With the last of his strength, Augustus cuts triumphantly into his own chest.

15

Buddy's coffee was cold and he was finished talking. Hugan shuffled papers into his briefcase. The two FBI agents were tired. They had all they needed from this man they didn't like or trust. But he didn't matter to them anymore. The older agent, *the royal asshole,* as Buddy would later remember him, rose from his chair and whistled.

"I'll tell you what, Bud, that Bodine was a sight. One look at his face would clear your sinuses for a week." Special Agent Wes Tolander laughed at his own joke and adjusted the belt holding up his slacks.

Buddy made no comment or eye contact. *Don't encourage him* had been Hugan's advice. He stared at the agent's scrimshaw belt buckle: a silhouette of a stag's head in profile.

"I guess you're more man than I am. Because I would've taken that shot in the church. But maybe you'd already met your quota of killing for the year?"

The other FBI agent, a black guy, Roderick Coakley, pursed his lips and said nothing.

Buddy thought, *Coakley must hate the royal asshole more than we do.*

Tolander spoke to Hugan as if, now that they had their answers, Buddy was only worthy of receiving wisecracks. "Get him out of here, counselor."

Hugan cupped his hand on Buddy's upper arm and steered him to the door.

"Hey, Bud," Tolander said. "See if you can make it all the way to the parking lot without committing a felony."

Buddy's boots stopped. He decided he *did* have something more to say to Special Agent Tolander.

Hugan's hand squeezed. The squeeze said: *Take it. You know how to do that. In a minute it'll be over. We'll drive away and leave this prick in the rearview mirror.*

Buddy listened to what his lawyer said.

●

Margot and Duncan were in the air now. Buddy imagined their plane flying over a desert.

He'd left this thing for the last because he wasn't sure he wanted to do it at all. He drove back to his cabin. The unmarked gravel road, the private driveways, and his place popping up before the dead end. He aimed the U-Haul straight between the railroad ties. Backing up would be a bitch-and-a-half when he was through. But he would go slow and make it work. He stopped at the cabin's front door. Didn't bother going in. The place was emptied, locked, no longer home. Buddy hadn't decided if he'd sell or rent it out.

He told Boy to stay in the front seat, that he'd be back in a minute. Then he opened the truck's sliding rear door to get the pole. Red's moneybag was back there, stuffed inside an oversized nylon duffle along with Robbie's savings. Buddy shoved it aside, grabbed the pole, and shut the door. He started down the trail to the river mouth.

He heard water. The clump of birches waited like a friend. Buddy brushed past. He marched out to the big square boulder. It was too cold for anybody to be out there fishing, but Buddy looked around just to be sure. Satisfied, he got down on his knees. His eyes followed a deep fissure in the rock and marked where the fissure opened to the width of his hand. He inserted his hand in the crevice to take a measurement. Six times his palm slid back along the widening crack. The sun had warmed the top of the rock some, but inside the crack it was ice-cold. Six palm widths from the spot where his hand first fit was about right, Buddy guessed. Close enough to start fishing. He grabbed the pole. It wasn't a fishing pole but a gaff wedded to a broomstick. There was a cheap plastic flashlight strapped to the hooking end with electrician's tape. Buddy snapped the light on and lowered the pole into the rock.

It didn't take him long. First he felt the chain sliding at the bottom of the crack. He swept the gaff steadily along until he caught one of the links. Then he pulled up his homemade safety deposit box: a PVC pipe, capped at both ends, an eyebolt superglued to one of the caps, and the chain welded to the bolt.

Buddy reached into his pocket and took out the melted gold chain Tolander had given to him at the interview. It was Robbie's. The coroner had snipped it off his scorched corpse. They didn't need it for evidence because nobody was going to trial for the bloodbath at the tavern.

Buddy unscrewed the chainless cap and tilted the pipe. The emerald necklace spilled into his cupped palm.

And then a leather zippered pouch.

He tugged at the tab and the row of metal teeth unfastened. *The second necklace. The one Lester and Red never knew about. The one nobody knew about.*

Buddy had a dead smile on his face. The Egyptian was holding more than they had dreamed. Not pearls or emeralds this time, but diamonds. Buddy never knew where they came from, what rich guy got ripped off, or why the fence was carrying them. They were like magic. *A pipe dream come true, and I'm the one with the pipe.*

Three-quarters of a million dollars looked small and brilliant in the wintry sunlight.

Buddy added the emerald necklace and Robbie's necklace to the pouch. He was standing, leaning on the broomstick. He put the pouch inside his pocket. The cap screwed back onto the pipe with a couple twists.

That day in the cabin with the lawyers, he had asked Hugan to step outside to answer a question. Now he had the name and phone number of a fence in Santa Fe.

Buddy wrapped the chain around the pipe and tossed it into the river.

•

You see a neatly made bunk. A small writing table and a wooden chair complete the room. There are back issues of *Field & Stream* and *National Geographic* stacked on the table. Sketches of bears lie spread out between the stack and a box of pastel crayons. The treatment team suggested giving him a notebook. He keeps it in the table's shallow drawer. The pages have remained blank.

He had missed the spring and summer, never so much as taking a glance outside the wire-hatched windows. But he is finally gaining weight. The infections have cleared his system. They sewed up his chest. Naked, he is a human scarecrow. Dr. Sather gave him an eye patch and a wig to aid the rebuilding of his "self-esteem." One week until the trial starts, and he is to wear this disguise in court.

Today he received a letter telling him his father is dead.

Some might miss it, but if you look out his window—there in the distance, easy to mistake for a dark blue, glinting slab of asphalt—you can see a river. He doesn't know the name, where it comes from, or where it goes. But he casts his eye on it a hundred times a day.

Most nights the river disappears. Not always. Tonight it is a grounded star.

Goatskinner dangles his hands between the window's iron rods. He hears the med cart being pushed along the corridor. After the trial, they will take him to another, far worse place. For now, he enjoys the October air flowing through his fingers.

Chilly water.

ALLEGIANT

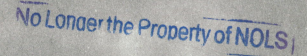

"You'll be up all night with **DIVERGENT**, a brainy thrill-ride of a novel."

—BOOKPAGE

"The imaginative action and glimpses of a sprawling conspiracy are serious attention-grabbers, and the portrait of a shattered, derelict, overgrown, and abandoned Chicago is evocative as ever."

—HOLLYWOODCRUSH.MTV.COM

"Author Roth tells the riveting and complex story of a teenage girl forced to choose between her routinized, selfless family and the adventurous, unrestrained future she longs for. A memorable, unpredictable journey from which it is nearly impossible to turn away."

—PUBLISHERS WEEKLY (STARRED REVIEW)

"With brisk pacing and lavish flights of imagination, **DIVERGENT** clearly has thrills, but it also movingly explores a more common adolescent anxiety—the painful realization that coming into one's own sometimes means leaving family behind, both ideologically and physically."

—NEW YORK TIMES BOOK REVIEW

"Nonstop, adrenaline-heavy action. Packed with stunning twists and devastating betrayals."

—BCCB

"**DIVERGENT** is really an extended metaphor about the trials of modern adolescence: constantly having to take tests that sort and rank you among your peers, facing separation from your family, agonizing about where you fit in, and deciding when (or whether) to reveal the ways you may diverge from the group."

—WALL STREET JOURNAL

"This gritty, paranoid world is built with careful details and intriguing scope. The plot clips along at an addictive pace, with steady jolts of brutal violence and swoony romance. Fans snared by the ratcheting suspense will be unable to resist speculating on their own factional allegiance."

—KIRKUS REVIEWS

"Roth knows how to write. The novel's love story, intricate plot, and unforgettable setting work in concert to deliver a novel that will rivet fans of the first book."

—PUBLISHERS WEEKLY

"In this addictive sequel to the acclaimed
DIVERGENT, a bleak postapocalyptic Chicago
collapses into all-out civil war.
Another spectacular cliff-hanger."

"**INSURGENT** explores several critical themes,
including the importance of family
and the crippling power of grief at its loss."

"Roth's plotting is intelligent and complex.
Dangers, suspicion, and tension lurk around every
corner, and the chemistry between Tris and Tobias
remains heart-poundingly real. . . . This final
installment will capture and hold attention until
the divisive final battle has been waged."

"The tragic conclusion, although shocking, is
thematically consistent; the bittersweet epilogue
offers a poignant hope."

Also by Veronica Roth

DIVERGENT

INSURGENT

FOUR: A DIVERGENT COLLECTION

ALLEGIANT

VERONICA ROTH

KATHERINE TEGEN BOOKS
An Imprint of HarperCollins Publishers

Library of Congress Control Number: 2013941315

ISBN 978-0-06-242008-4

Typography by Joel Tippie

16 17 18 19 20   PC/RRDH   10 9 8 7 6 5 4 3 2 1

❖

Revised edition, 2016

To Jo,
who guides and steadies me

Every question that can be answered must be
answered or at least engaged.
Illogical thought processes must be
challenged when they arise.
Wrong answers must be corrected.
Correct answers must be affirmed.

—From the Erudite faction manifesto

CHAPTER
ONE

TRIS

I PACE IN our cell in Erudite headquarters, her words echoing in my mind: *My name will be Edith Prior, and there is much I am happy to forget.*

"So you've *never* seen her before? Not even in pictures?" Christina says, her wounded leg propped up on a pillow. She was shot during our desperate attempt to reveal the Edith Prior video to our city. At the time we had no idea what it would say, or that it would shatter the foundation we stand on, the factions, our identities. "Is she a grandmother or an aunt or something?"

"I told you, no," I say, turning when I reach the wall. "Prior is—was—my father's name, so it would have to be on his side of the family. But Edith is an Abnegation name,

1

and my father's relatives must have been Erudite, so . . ."

"So she must be older," Cara says, leaning her head against the wall. From this angle she looks just like her brother, Will, my friend, the one I shot. Then she straightens, and the ghost of him is gone. "A few generations back. An ancestor."

"Ancestor." The word feels old inside me, like crumbling brick. I touch one wall of the cell as I turn around. The panel is cold and white.

My ancestor, and this is the inheritance she passed to me: freedom from the factions, and the knowledge that my Divergent identity is more important than I could have known. My existence is a signal that we need to leave this city and offer our help to whoever is outside it.

"I want to know," Cara says, running her hand over her face. "I need to know how long we've been here. Would you stop pacing for *one minute*?"

I stop in the middle of the cell and raise my eyebrows at her.

"Sorry," she mumbles.

"It's okay," Christina says. "We've been in here way too long."

It's been days since Evelyn mastered the chaos in the lobby of Erudite headquarters with a few short commands and had all the prisoners hustled away to cells on the third floor. A factionless woman came to doctor our wounds and distribute painkillers, and we've eaten and showered several times, but no one has told us what's going on outside. No matter how forcefully I've asked them.

"I thought Tobias would come by now," I say, dropping to the edge of my cot. "Where *is* he?"

"Maybe he's still angry that you lied to him and went behind his back to work with his father," Cara says.

I glare at her.

"Four wouldn't be that petty," Christina says, either to chastise Cara or to reassure me, I'm not sure. "Something's probably going on that's keeping him away. He told you to trust him."

In the chaos, when everyone was shouting and the factionless were trying to push us toward the staircase, I curled my fingers in the hem of his shirt so I wouldn't lose him. He took my wrists in his hands and pushed me away, and those were the words he said. *Trust me. Go where they tell you.*

"I'm trying," I say, and it's true. I'm trying to trust him. But every part of me, every fiber and every nerve, is straining toward freedom, not just from this cell but from the prison of the city beyond it.

I need to see what's outside the fence.

CHAPTER
TWO

TOBIAS

I CAN'T WALK these hallways without remembering the days
I spent as a prisoner here, barefoot, pain pulsing inside
me every time I moved. And with that memory is another
one, one of waiting for Beatrice Prior to go to her death, of
my fists against the door, of her legs slung across Peter's
arms when he told me she was just drugged.

I hate this place.

It isn't as clean as it was when it was the Erudite compound; now it is ravaged by war, bullet holes in the walls
and the broken glass of shattered lightbulbs everywhere.
I walk over dirty footprints and beneath flickering lights
to her cell and I am admitted without question, because I
bear the factionless symbol—an empty circle—on a black

band around my arm and Evelyn's features on my face. Tobias Eaton was a shameful name, and now it is a powerful one.

Tris crouches on the ground inside, shoulder to shoulder with Christina and diagonal from Cara. My Tris should look pale and small—she *is* pale and small, after all—but instead the room is full of her.

Her round eyes find mine and she is on her feet, her arms wound tightly around my waist and her face against my chest.

I squeeze her shoulder with one hand and run my other hand over her hair, still surprised when her hair stops above her neck instead of below it. I was happy when she cut it, because it was hair for a warrior and not a girl, and I knew that was what she would need.

"How'd you get in?" she says in her low, clear voice.

"I'm Tobias Eaton," I say, and she laughs.

"Right. I keep forgetting." She pulls away just far enough to look at me. There is a wavering expression in her eyes, like she is a heap of leaves about to be scattered by the wind. "What's happening? What took you so long?"

She sounds desperate, pleading. For all the horrible memories this place carries for me, it carries more for her, the walk to her execution, her brother's betrayal, the fear serum. I have to get her out.

Cara looks up with interest. I feel uncomfortable, like I have shifted in my skin and it doesn't quite fit anymore. I hate having an audience.

"Evelyn has the city under lockdown," I say. "No one goes a step in any direction without her say-so. A few days ago she gave a speech about uniting against our oppressors, the people outside."

"Oppressors?" Christina says. She takes a vial from her pocket and dumps the contents into her mouth—painkillers for the bullet wound in her leg, I assume.

I slide my hands into my pockets. "Evelyn—and a lot of people, actually—think we shouldn't leave the city just to help a bunch of people who shoved us in here so they could use us later. They want to try to heal the city and solve our own problems instead of leaving to solve other people's. I'm paraphrasing, of course," I say. "I suspect that opinion is very convenient for my mother, because as long as we're all contained, she's in charge. The second we leave, she loses her hold."

"Great." Tris rolls her eyes. "Of course she would choose the most selfish route possible."

"She has a point." Christina wraps her fingers around the vial. "I'm not saying I don't want to leave the city and see what's out there, but we've got enough going on here. How are we supposed to help a bunch of people we've never met?"

Tris considers this, chewing on the inside of her cheek. "I don't know," she admits.

My watch reads three o'clock. I've been here too long—long enough to make Evelyn suspicious. I told her I came to break things off with Tris, that it wouldn't take much time. I'm not sure she believed me.

I say, "Listen, I mostly came to warn you—they're starting the trials for all the prisoners. They're going to put you all under truth serum, and if it works, you'll be convicted as traitors. I think we would all like to avoid that."

"Convicted as *traitors*?" Tris scowls. "How is revealing the truth to our entire city an act of betrayal?"

"It was an act of defiance against your leaders," I say. "Evelyn and her followers don't want to leave the city. They won't thank you for showing that video."

"They're just like Jeanine!" She makes a fitful gesture, like she wants to hit something but there's nothing available. "Ready to do anything to stifle the truth, and for what? To be kings of their tiny little world? It's ridiculous."

I don't want to say so, but part of me agrees with my mother. I don't owe the people outside this city anything, whether I am Divergent or not. I'm not sure I want to offer myself to them to solve humanity's problems, whatever that means.

But I do want to leave, in the desperate way that an

animal wants to escape a trap. Wild and rabid. Ready to gnaw through bone.

"Be that as it may," I say carefully, "if the truth serum works on you, you will be convicted."

"*If* it works?" says Cara, narrowing her eyes.

"Divergent," Tris says to her, pointing at her own head. "Remember?"

"That's fascinating." Cara tucks a stray hair back into the knot just above her neck. "But atypical. In my experience, most Divergent can't resist the truth serum. I wonder why you can."

"You and every other Erudite who ever stuck a needle in me," Tris snaps.

"Can we focus, please? I would like to avoid having to break you out of prison," I say. Suddenly desperate for comfort, I reach for Tris's hand, and she brings her fingers up to meet mine. We are not people who touch each other carelessly; every point of contact between us feels important, a rush of energy and relief.

"All right, all right," she says, gently now. "What did you have in mind?"

"I'll get Evelyn to let you testify first, of the three of you," I say. "All you have to do is come up with a lie that will exonerate both Christina and Cara, and then tell it under truth serum."

"What kind of lie would do that?"

"I thought I would leave that to you," I say. "Since you're the better liar."

I know as I'm saying the words that they hit a sore spot in both of us. She lied to me so many times. She promised me she wouldn't go to her death in the Erudite compound when Jeanine demanded the sacrifice of a Divergent, and then she did it anyway. She told me she would stay home during the Erudite attack, and then I found her in Erudite headquarters, working with my father. I understand why she did all those things, but that doesn't mean we aren't still broken.

"Yeah." She looks at her shoes. "Okay, I'll think of something."

I set my hand on her arm. "I'll talk to Evelyn about your trial. I'll try to make it soon."

"Thank you."

I feel the urge, familiar now, to wrench myself from my body and speak directly into her mind. It is the same urge, I realize, that makes me want to kiss her every time I see her, because even a sliver of distance between us is infuriating. Our fingers, loosely woven a moment ago, now clutch together, her palm tacky with moisture, mine rough in places where I have grabbed too many handles on too many moving trains. Now she looks pale and small, but her eyes make me think of wide-open skies that I have never actually seen, only dreamed of.

"If you're going to kiss, do me a favor and tell me so I can look away," says Christina.

"We are," Tris says. And we do.

I touch her cheek to slow the kiss down, holding her mouth on mine so I can feel every place where our lips touch and every place where they pull away. I savor the air we share in the second afterward and the slip of her nose across mine. I think of something to say, but it is too intimate, so I swallow it. A moment later I decide I don't care.

"I wish we were alone," I say as I back out of the cell.

She smiles. "I almost always wish that."

As I shut the door, I see Christina pretending to vomit, and Cara laughing, and Tris's hands hanging at her sides.

CHAPTER THREE

"I THINK YOU'RE all idiots." My hands are curled in my lap like a sleeping child's. My body is heavy with truth serum. Sweat collects on my eyelids. "You should be thanking me, not questioning me."

"We should thank you for defying the instructions of your faction leaders? Thank you for trying to prevent one of your faction leaders from killing Jeanine Matthews? You behaved like a traitor." Evelyn Johnson spits the word like a snake. We are in the conference room in Erudite headquarters, where the trials have been taking place. I have now been a prisoner for at least a week.

I see Tobias, half-hidden in the shadows behind his mother. He has kept his eyes averted since I sat in the chair and they cut the strip of plastic binding my wrists together. For just for a moment, his eyes touch mine, and I know it's time to start lying.

It's easier now that I know I can do it. As easy as pushing the weight of the truth serum aside in my mind.

"I am not a traitor," I say. "At the time I believed that Marcus was working under Dauntless-factionless orders. Since I couldn't join the fight as a soldier, I was happy to help with something else."

"Why couldn't you be a soldier?" Fluorescent light glows behind Evelyn's hair. I can't see her face, and I can't focus on anything for more than a second before the truth serum threatens to pull me down again.

"Because." I bite my lip, as if trying to stop the words from rushing out. I don't know when I became so good at acting, but I guess it's not that different from lying, which I have always had a talent for. "Because I couldn't hold a gun, okay? Not after shooting . . . him. My friend Will. I couldn't hold a gun without panicking."

Evelyn's eyes pinch tighter. I suspect that even in the softest parts of her, there is no sympathy for me.

"So Marcus told you he was working under my orders," she says, "and even knowing what you do about his rather tense relationship with both the Dauntless and the factionless, you believed him?"

"Yes."

"I can see why you didn't choose Erudite." She laughs.

My cheeks tingle. I would like to slap her, as I'm sure many of the people in this room would, though they wouldn't dare to admit it. Evelyn has us all trapped in the city, controlled by armed factionless patrolling the streets. She knows that whoever holds the guns holds the power. And with Jeanine Matthews dead, there is no one left to challenge her for it.

From one tyrant to another. That is the world we know, now.

"Why didn't you tell anyone about this?" she says.

"I didn't want to have to admit to any weakness," I say. "And I didn't want Four to know I was working with his father. I knew he wouldn't like it." I feel new words rising in my throat, prompted by the truth serum. "I brought you the truth about our city and the reason we are in it. If you aren't thanking me for it, you should at least *do* something about it instead of sitting here on this mess you made, pretending it's a throne!"

Evelyn's mocking smile twists like she has just tasted something unpleasant. She leans in close to my face, and I see for the first time how old she is; I see the lines that frame her eyes and mouth, and the unhealthy pallor she wears from years of eating far too little. Still, she is handsome like her son. Near-starvation could not take that.

"I am doing something about it. I am making a new world," she says, and her voice gets even quieter, so that I can barely hear her. "I was Abnegation. I have known the truth far longer than you have, Beatrice Prior. I don't know how you're getting away with this, but I promise you, you will not have a place in my new world, especially not with my son."

I smile a little. I shouldn't, but it's harder to suppress gestures and expressions than words, with this weight in my veins. She believes that Tobias belongs to her now. She doesn't know the truth, that he belongs to himself.

Evelyn straightens, folding her arms.

"The truth serum has revealed that while you may be a fool, you are no traitor. This interrogation is over. You may leave."

"What about my friends?" I say sluggishly. "Christina, Cara. They didn't do anything wrong either."

"We will deal with them soon," Evelyn says.

I stand, though I'm weak and dizzy from the serum. The room is packed with people, shoulder to shoulder, and I can't find the exit for a few long seconds, until someone takes my arm, a boy with warm brown skin and a wide smile—Uriah. He guides me to the door. Everyone starts talking.

Uriah leads me down the hallway to the elevator bank. The elevator doors spring open when he touches the button, and I follow him in, still not steady on my feet. When the doors close, I say, "You don't think the part about the mess and the throne was too much?"

"No. She expects you to be hotheaded. She might have been suspicious if you hadn't been."

I feel like everything inside me is vibrating with energy, in anticipation of what is to come. I am free. We're going to find a way out of the city. No more waiting, pacing a cell, demanding answers that I won't get from the guards.

The guards did tell me a few things about the new factionless order this morning. Former faction members are required to move closer to Erudite headquarters and mix, no more than four members of a particular faction in each dwelling. We have to mix our clothing, too. I was given a yellow Amity shirt and black Candor pants earlier as a result of that particular edict.

"All right, we're this way. . . ." Uriah leads me out of the elevator. This floor of Erudite headquarters is all glass, even the walls. Sunlight refracts through it and casts slivers of rainbows across the floor. I shield my eyes with one hand and follow Uriah to a long, narrow room with beds on either side. Next to each bed is a glass cabinet for clothes and books, and a small table.

"It used to be the Erudite initiate dormitory," Uriah says. "I reserved beds for Christina and Cara already."

Sitting on a bed near the door are three girls in red shirts—Amity girls, I would guess—and on the left side of the room, an older woman lies on one of the beds, her spectacles dangling from one ear—possibly one of the Erudite. I know I should try to stop putting people in factions when I see them, but it's an old habit, hard to break.

Uriah falls on one of the beds in the back corner. I sit on the one next to his, glad to be free and at rest, finally.

"Zeke says it sometimes takes a little while for the factionless to process exonerations, so they should be out later," Uriah says.

For a moment I feel relieved that everyone I care about will be out of prison by tonight. But then I remember that Caleb is still there, because he was a well-known lackey of Jeanine Matthews, and the factionless will never exonerate him. But just how far they will go to destroy the mark Jeanine Matthews left on this city, I don't know.

I don't care, I think. But even as I think it, I know it's a lie. He's still my brother.

"Good," I say. "Thanks, Uriah."

He nods, and leans his head against the wall to prop it up.

"How are you?" I say. "I mean . . . Lynn . . ."

Uriah had been friends with Lynn and Marlene as long as I'd known them, and now both of them are dead. I feel like I might be able to understand—after all, I've lost two friends too, Al to the pressures of initiation and Will to the attack simulation and my own hasty actions. But I don't want to pretend that our suffering is the same. For one thing, Uriah knew his friends better than I did.

"I don't want to talk about it." Uriah shakes his head. "Or think about it. I just want to keep moving."

"Okay. I understand. Just . . . let me know if you need . . ."

"Yeah." He smiles at me and gets up. "You're okay here, right? I told my mom I'd visit tonight, so I have to go soon. Oh—almost forgot to tell you—Four said he wants to meet you later."

I pull up straighter. "Really? When? Where?"

"A little after ten, at Millennium Park. On the lawn." He smirks. "Don't get too excited, your head will explode."

CHAPTER FOUR

TOBIAS

MY MOTHER ALWAYS sits on the edges of things—chairs, ledges, tables—as if she suspects she will have to flee in an instant. This time it's Jeanine's old desk in Erudite headquarters that she sits on the edge of, her toes balanced on the floor and the cloudy light of the city glowing behind her. She is a woman of muscle twisted around bone.

"I think we have to talk about your loyalty," she says, but she doesn't sound like she's accusing me of something, she just sounds tired. For a moment she seems so worn that I feel like I can see right through her, but then she straightens, and the feeling is gone.

"Ultimately, it was you who helped Tris and got that video released," she says. "No one else knows that, but *I* know it."

"Listen." I lean forward to prop my elbows on my knees. "I didn't know what was in that file. I trusted Tris's judgment more than my own. That's all that happened."

I thought telling Evelyn that I broke up with Tris would make it easier for my mother to trust me, and I was right—she has been warmer, more open, ever since I told that lie.

"And now that you've seen the footage?" Evelyn says. "What do you think now? Do you think we should leave the city?"

I know what she wants me to say—that I see no reason to join the outside world—but I'm not a good liar, so instead I select a part of the truth.

"I'm afraid of it," I say. "I'm not sure it's smart to leave the city knowing the dangers that might be out there."

She considers me for a moment, biting the inside of her cheek. I learned that habit from her—I used to chew my skin raw as I waited for my father to come home, unsure which version of him I would encounter, the one the Abnegation trusted and revered, or the one whose hands struck me.

I run my tongue along the bite scars and swallow the memory like it's bile.

She slides off the desk and moves to the window. "I've been receiving disturbing reports of a rebel organization among us." She looks up, raising an eyebrow. "People always organize into groups. That's a fact of our existence. I just didn't expect it to happen this quickly."

"What kind of organization?"

"The kind that wants to leave the city," she says. "They released some kind of manifesto this morning. They call themselves the Allegiant." When she sees my confused look, she adds, "Because they're *allied* with the original purpose of our city, see?"

"The original purpose—you mean, what was in the Edith Prior video? That we should send people outside when the city has a large Divergent population?"

"That, yes. But also living in factions. The Allegiant claim that we're meant to be in factions because we've been in them since the beginning." She shakes her head. "Some people will always fear change. But we can't indulge them."

With the factions dismantled, part of me has felt like a man released from a long imprisonment. I don't have to evaluate whether every thought I have or choice I make fits into a narrow ideology. I don't want the factions back.

But Evelyn hasn't liberated us like she thinks—she's just made us all factionless. She's afraid of what we would choose, if we were given actual freedom. And that means that no matter what I believe about the factions, I'm relieved that someone, somewhere, is defying her.

I arrange my face into an empty expression, but my heart is beating faster than before. I have had to be careful, to stay in Evelyn's good graces. It's easy for me to lie to everyone else, but it's more difficult to lie to her, the only person who knew all the secrets of our Abnegation house, the violence contained within its walls.

"What are you going to do about them?" I say.

"I am going to get them under control, what else?"

The word "control" makes me sit up straight, as rigid as the chair beneath me. In this city, "control" means needles and serums and seeing without seeing; it means simulations, like the one that almost made me kill Tris, or the one that made the Dauntless into an army.

"With simulations?" I say slowly.

She scowls. "Of course not! I am not Jeanine Matthews!"

Her flare of anger sets me off. I say, "Don't forget that I barely know you, Evelyn."

She winces at the reminder. "Then let me tell you that I will never resort to simulations to get my way. Death would be better."

It's possible that death is what she will use—killing people would certainly keep them quiet, stifle their revolution before it begins. Whoever the Allegiant are, they need to be warned, and quickly.

"I can find out who they are," I say.

"I'm sure that you can. Why else would I have told you about them?"

There are plenty of reasons she would tell me. To test me. To catch me. To feed me false information. I know what my mother is—she is someone for whom the end of a thing justifies the means of getting there, the same as my father, and the same, sometimes, as me.

"I'll do it, then. I'll find them."

I rise, and her fingers, brittle as branches, close around my arm. "Thank you."

I force myself to look at her. Her eyes are close above her nose, which is hooked at the end, like my own. Her skin is a middling color, darker than mine. For a moment I see her in Abnegation gray, her thick hair bound back with a dozen pins, sitting across the dinner table from me. I see her crouched in front of me, fixing my mismatched shirt buttons before I go to school, and standing at the window, watching the uniform street for my father's car, her hands clasped—no, clenched, her tan knuckles white with tension. We were united in fear then, and now that she isn't afraid anymore, part of me wants to see what it would be like to unite with her in strength.

I feel an ache, like I betrayed her, the woman who used to be my only ally, and I turn away before I can take it all back and apologize.

I leave Erudite headquarters amid a crowd of people, my eyes confused, hunting for faction colors automatically when there are none left. I am wearing a gray shirt, blue jeans, black shoes—new clothes, but beneath them, my Dauntless tattoos. It is impossible to erase my choices. Especially these.

CHAPTER FIVE

TRIS

I SET MY watch alarm for ten o'clock and fall asleep right away, without even shifting to a comfortable position. A few hours later the beeps don't wake me, but the frustrated shout of someone across the room does. I turn off the alarm, run my fingers through my hair, and half walk, half jog to one of the emergency staircases. The exit at the bottom will let me out in the alley, where I probably won't be stopped.

Once I'm outside, the cool air wakes me up. I pull my sleeves down over my fingers to keep them warm. Summer is finally ending. There are a few people milling around the entrance to Erudite headquarters, but none of them notices me creeping across Michigan Avenue. There are some advantages to being small.

I see Tobias standing in the middle of the lawn, wearing mixed faction colors—a gray T-shirt, blue jeans, and a black sweatshirt with a hood, representing all the factions my aptitude test told me I was qualified for. A backpack rests against his feet.

"How did I do?" I say when I'm close enough for him to hear me.

"Very well," he says. "Evelyn still hates you, but Christina and Cara have been released without questioning."

"Good." I smile.

He pinches the front of my shirt, right over my stomach, and tugs me toward him, kissing me softly.

"Come on," he says as he pulls away. "I have a plan for this evening."

"Oh, really?"

"Yes, well, I realized that we've never been on an actual date."

"Chaos and destruction do tend to take away a person's dating possibilities."

"I would like to experience this 'date' phenomenon." He walks backward, toward the mammoth metal structure at the other end of the lawn, and I follow him. "Before you, I only went on group dates, and they were usually a disaster. They always ended up with Zeke making out with whatever girl he intended to make out with, and me sitting in awkward silence with some girl that I had somehow offended in some way early on."

"You're not very nice," I say, grinning.

"You're one to talk."

"Hey, I could be nice if I tried."

"Hmm." He taps his chin. "Say something nice, then."

"You're very good-looking."

He smiles, his teeth a flash in the dark. "I like this 'nice' thing."

We reach the end of the lawn. The metal structure is larger and stranger up close than it was from far away. It's really a stage, and arcing above it are massive metal plates that curl in different directions, like an exploded aluminum can. We walk around one of the plates on the right side to the back of the stage, which rises at an angle from the ground. There, metal beams support the plates from behind. Tobias secures his backpack on his shoulders and grabs one of the beams. Climbing.

"This feels familiar," I say. One of the first things we did together was scale the Ferris wheel, but that time it was me, not him, who compelled us to climb higher.

I push up my sleeves and follow him. My shoulder is still sore from the bullet wound, but it is mostly healed. Still, I bear most of my weight with my left arm and try to push with my feet whenever possible. I look down at the tangle of bars beneath me and beyond them, the ground, and laugh.

Tobias climbs to a spot where two metal plates meet in a V, leaving enough room for two people to sit. He scoots back, wedging himself between the two plates, and reaches for my waist to help me when I get close enough. I don't really need the help, but I don't say so—I am too busy enjoying his hands on me.

He takes a blanket out of his backpack and covers us with it, then produces two plastic cups.

"Would you like a clear head or a fuzzy one?" he says, peering into the bag.

"Um . . ." I tilt my head. "Clear. I think we have some things to talk about, right?"

"Yes."

He takes out a small bottle with clear, bubbling liquid in it, and as he twists open the cap, says, "I stole it from the Erudite kitchens. Apparently it's delicious."

He pours some in each cup, and I take a sip. Whatever it is, it's sweet as syrup and lemon-flavored and makes me cringe a little. My second sip is better.

"Things to talk about," he says.

"Right."

"Well . . ." Tobias frowns into his cup. "Okay, so I understand why you worked with Marcus, and why you felt like you couldn't tell me. But . . ."

"But you're angry," I say. "Because I lied to you. On several occasions."

He nods, not looking at me. "It's not even the Marcus thing. It's further back than that. I don't know if you can understand what it was like to wake up alone, and know that you had gone"—*to your death*, is what I suspect he wants to say, but he can't even say the words—"to Erudite headquarters."

"No, I probably can't." I take another sip, turning the sugary drink over in my mouth before swallowing. "Listen, I . . . I used to think about giving my life for things, but I didn't understand what 'giving your life' really was until it was right there, about to be taken from me."

I look up at him, and finally, he looks back at me.

"I know now," I say. "I know I want to live. I know I want to be honest with you. But . . . but I can't do that, I won't do it, if you won't trust me, or if you talk to me in that condescending way you sometimes do—"

"Condescending?" he says. "You were doing ridiculous, risky things—"

"Yeah," I say. "And do you really think it helped to talk to me like I was a child who didn't know any better?"

"What else was I supposed to do?" he demands. "You wouldn't see reason!"

"Maybe reason wasn't what I needed!" I sit forward, not able to pretend I am relaxed anymore. "I felt like I was being eaten alive by guilt, and what I needed was your patience and your kindness, not for you to *yell* at me. Oh, and for you to constantly keep your plans from me like I couldn't possibly handle—"

"I didn't want to burden you more than you already were."

"So do you think I'm a strong person, or not?" I scowl at him. "Because you seem to think I can take it when you're scolding me, but you don't think I can handle anything else? What does that mean?"

"Of course I think you're a strong person." He shakes his head. "I just . . . I'm not used to telling people things. I'm used to handling things on my own."

"I'm reliable," I say. "You can trust me. And you can let me be the judge of what I can handle."

"Okay," he says, nodding. "But no more lies. Not ever."

"Okay."

I feel stiff and squeezed, like my body was just forced into something too small for it. But that's not how I want the conversation to end, so I reach for his hand.

"I'm sorry I lied to you," I say. "I really am."

"Well," he says. "I didn't mean to make you feel like I didn't respect you."

We stay there for a while, our hands clasped. I lean back against the metal plate. Above me, the sky is blank and dark, the moon shielded by clouds. I find a star ahead of us, as the clouds shift, but it seems to be the only one.

When I tilt my head back, though, I can see the line of buildings along Michigan Avenue, like a row of sentries keeping watch over us.

I am quiet until the stiff, squeezed feeling leaves me. In its place I now feel relief. It isn't usually that easy for me to let go of anger, but the past few weeks have been strange for both of us, and I am happy to release the feelings I have been holding on to, the anger and the fear that he hates me and the guilt from working with his father behind his back.

"This stuff is kind of gross," he says, draining his cup and setting it down.

"Yes, it is," I say, staring at what remains in mine. I drink it in one gulp, wincing as the bubbles burn my throat. "I don't know what the Erudite are always bragging about. Dauntless cake is much better."

"I wonder what the Abnegation treat would have been, if they had one."

"Stale bread."

He laughs. "Plain oatmeal."

"Milk."

"Sometimes I think I believe everything they taught us," he says. "But obviously not, since I'm sitting here holding your hand right now without having married you first."

"What do the Dauntless teach about . . . that?" I say, nodding to our hands.

"What do the Dauntless teach, hmm." He smirks. "Do whatever you want, but use protection, is what they teach."

I raise my eyebrows. Suddenly my face feels warm.

"I think I'd like to find a middle ground for myself," he says. "To find that place between what I want and what I think is wise."

"That sounds good." I pause. "But what do you want?"

I think I know the answer, but I want to hear him say it.

"Hmm." He grins, and leans forward onto his knees. He presses his hands to the metal plate, framing my head with his arms, and kisses me, slowly, on my mouth, under my jaw, right above my collarbone. I stay still, nervous about doing anything, in case it's stupid or he doesn't like it. But then I feel like a statue, like I am not really here at all, and so I touch his waist, hesitantly.

Then his lips are on mine again, and he pulls his shirt out from under my hands so that I am touching his bare skin. I come to life, pressing closer, my hands creeping up his back, sliding over his shoulders. His breaths come faster and so do mine, and I taste the lemon-syrup-fizz we just drank and I smell the wind on his skin and all I want is more, more.

I push his shirt up. A moment ago I was cold, but I don't think either of us is cold now. His arm wraps around my waist, strong and certain, and his free hand tangles in my hair and I slow down, drinking it in—the smoothness of his skin, marked up and down with black ink, and the insistence of the kiss, and the cool air wrapped around us both.

I relax, and I no longer feel like some kind of Divergent soldier, defying serums and government leaders alike. I feel softer, lighter, and like it is okay to laugh a little as his fingertips brush over my hips and the small of my back, or to sigh into his ear when he pulls me against him, burying his face in the side of my neck so that he can kiss me there. I feel like myself, strong and weak at once—allowed, at least for a little while, to be both.

I don't know how long it is before we get cold again, and huddle under the blanket together.

"It's getting more difficult to be wise," he says, laughing into my ear.

I smile at him. "I think that's how it's supposed to be."

CHAPTER SIX

TOBIAS

SOMETHING IS BREWING.

I can feel it as I walk the cafeteria line with my tray, and see it in the huddled heads of a group of factionless as they lean over their oatmeal. Whatever is about to happen will happen soon.

Yesterday when I left Evelyn's office I lingered in the hallway to eavesdrop on her next meeting. Before she closed the door, I heard her say something about a demonstration. The question that is itching at the back of my mind is: Why didn't she tell me?

She must not trust me. That means I'm not doing as good a job as her pretend right-hand man as I think I am.

I sit down with the same breakfast as everyone else: a

bowl of oatmeal with a sprinkle of brown sugar on it, and a mug of coffee. I watch the group of factionless as I spoon it into my mouth without tasting it. One of them—a girl, maybe fourteen—keeps flicking her eyes toward the clock.

I'm halfway done with breakfast when I hear the shouts. The nervy factionless girl jolts from her seat as if stuck with a live wire, and they all start toward the door. I am right behind them, elbowing my way past slow-movers through the lobby of Erudite headquarters, where the portrait of Jeanine Matthews still lies in shreds on the floor.

A group of factionless has already gathered outside, in the middle of Michigan Avenue. A layer of pale clouds covers the sun, making the daylight hazy and dull. I hear someone shout, "Death to the factions!" and others pick up the phrase, turning it into a chant, until it fills my ears, *Death to the factions, death to the factions.* I see their fists in the air, like excitable Dauntless, but without the Dauntless joy. Their faces are twisted with rage.

I push toward the middle of the group, and then I see what they're all gathered around: The huge, man-sized faction bowls from the Choosing Ceremony are turned on their sides, their contents spilling across the road, coals and glass and stone and earth and water all mingling together.

I remember slicing into my palm to add my blood to the

coals, my first act of defiance against my father. I remember the surge of power inside me, and the rush of relief. Escape. These bowls were my escape.

Edward stands among them, shards of glass ground to dust beneath his heel, a sledgehammer held above his head. He brings it down on one of the overturned bowls, forcing a dent into the metal. Coal dust rises into the air.

I have to stop myself from running at him. He can't destroy it, not that bowl, not the Choosing Ceremony, not the symbol of my triumph. Those things should not be destroyed.

The crowd is swelling, not just with factionless wearing black armbands with empty white circles on them, but with people from every former faction, their arms bare. An Erudite man—his faction still indicated by his neatly parted hair—bursts free of the crowd just as Edward is pulling back the sledgehammer for another swing. He wraps his soft, ink-smudged hands around the handle, just above Edward's, and they push into each other, teeth gritted.

I see a blond head across the crowd—Tris, wearing a loose blue shirt without sleeves, showing the edges of the faction tattoos on her shoulders. She tries to run to Edward and the Erudite man, but Christina stops her with both hands.

The Erudite man's face turns purple. Edward is taller

and stronger than he is. He has no chance; he's a fool for trying. Edward rips the sledgehammer handle from the Erudite man's hands and swings again. But he's off balance, dizzy with rage—the sledgehammer hits the Erudite man in the shoulder at full force, metal cracking bone.

For a moment all I hear is the Erudite man's screams. It's like everyone is taking a breath.

Then the crowd explodes into a frenzy, everyone running toward the bowls, toward Edward, toward the Erudite man. They collide with one another and then with me, shoulders and elbows and heads hitting me over and over again.

I don't know where to run: to the Erudite man, to Edward, to Tris? I can't think; I can't breathe. The crowd carries me toward Edward, and I grab his arm.

"Let go!" I shout over the noise. His single bright eye fixes on me, and he bares his teeth, trying to wrench himself away.

I bring my knee up, into his side. He stumbles back, losing his grip on the sledgehammer. I hold it close to my leg and start toward Tris.

She is somewhere in front of me, struggling toward the Erudite man. I watch as a woman's elbow hits her in the cheek, sending her reeling backward. Christina shoves the woman away.

Then a gun goes off. Once, twice. Three times.

The crowd scatters, everyone running in terror from the threat of bullets, and I try to see who, if anyone, was shot, but the rush of bodies is too intense. I can barely see anything.

Tris and Christina crouch next to the Erudite man with the shattered shoulder. His face is bloody and his clothes are dirty with footprints. His combed Erudite hair is tousled. He isn't moving.

A few feet away from him, Edward lies in a pool of his own blood. The bullet hit him in the gut. There are other people on the ground too, people I don't recognize, people who got trampled or shot. I suspect the bullets were meant for Edward and Edward alone—the others were just bystanders.

I look around wildly but I don't see the shooter. Whoever it was seems to have dissolved into the crowd.

I drop the sledgehammer next to the dented bowl and kneel beside Edward, Abnegation stones digging into my kneecaps. His remaining eye moves back and forth beneath his eyelid—he's alive, for now.

"We have to get him to the hospital," I say to whoever is listening. Almost everyone is gone.

I look over my shoulder at Tris and the Erudite man, who hasn't moved. "Is he . . . ?"

Her fingers are on his throat, taking his pulse, and her eyes are wide and empty. She shakes her head. No, he is not alive. I didn't think he was.

I close my eyes. The faction bowls are printed on my eyelids, tipped on their sides, their contents in a pile on the street. The symbols of our old way of life, destroyed—a man dead, others injured—and for what?

For nothing. For Evelyn's empty, narrow vision: a city where factions are wrenched away from people against their will.

She wanted us to have more than five choices. Now we have none.

I know for sure, then, that I can't be her ally, and I never could have.

"We have to go," Tris says, and I know she's not talking about leaving Michigan Avenue or taking Edward to the hospital; she's talking about the city.

"We have to go," I repeat.

+ + +

The makeshift hospital at Erudite headquarters smells like chemicals, almost gritty in my nose. I close my eyes as I wait for Evelyn.

I'm so angry I don't even want to sit here, I just want to pack up my things and leave. She must have planned that demonstration, or she wouldn't have known about it the day before, and she must have known that it would get out of control, with tensions running as high as they are. But she did it anyway. Making a big statement about the factions was more important to her than safety or the potential loss of lives. I don't know why that surprises me.

I hear the elevator doors slide open, and her voice: "Tobias!"

She rushes toward me and seizes my hands, which are sticky with blood. Her dark eyes are wide with fear as she says, "Are you hurt?"

She's worried about me. The thought is a little pinprick of heat inside me—she must love me, to worry about me. She must still be capable of love.

"The blood is Edward's. I helped carry him here."

"How is he?" she says.

I shake my head. "Dead."

I don't know how else to say it.

She shrinks back, releasing my hands, and sits on one of the waiting room chairs. My mother embraced Edward after he defected from Dauntless. She must have taught him to be a warrior again, after the loss of his eye and his faction and his footing. I never knew they were so close, but I can see it now, in the gleam of tears in her eyes and the trembling of her fingers. It's the most emotion I've seen her show since I was a child, since my father slammed her into our living room walls.

I press the memory away as if stuffing it into a drawer that is too small for it.

"I'm sorry," I say. I don't know if I really mean it or if I'm just saying it so she still thinks I'm on her side. Then I add tentatively, "Why didn't you tell me about the demonstration?"

She shakes her head. "I didn't know about it."

She's lying. I know. I decide to let her. In order to stay on her good side, I have to avoid conflict with her. Or maybe I just don't want to press the issue with Edward's death looming over both of us. Sometimes it's hard for me to tell where strategy ends and sympathy for her begins.

"Oh." I scratch behind my ear. "You can go in and see him, if you want."

"No." She seems far away. "I know what bodies look like." Drifting further.

"Maybe I should go."

"Stay," she says. She touches the empty chair between us. "Please."

I take the seat beside her, and though I tell myself that I am just an undercover agent obeying his supposed leader, I feel like I am a son comforting his grieving mother.

We sit with our shoulders touching, our breaths falling into the same rhythm, and we don't say a word.

CHAPTER
SEVEN

CHRISTINA TURNS A black stone over and over in her hand as we walk. It takes me a few seconds to realize that it's actually a piece of coal, from the Dauntless Choosing Ceremony bowl.

"I didn't really want to bring this up, but I can't stop thinking about it," she says. "That of the ten transfer initiates we started with, only six are still alive."

Ahead of us is the Hancock building, and beyond it, Lake Shore Drive, the lazy strip of pavement that I once flew over like a bird. We walk the cracked sidewalk side by side, our clothes smeared with Edward's blood, now dry.

It hasn't hit me yet: that Edward, by far the most talented transfer initiate we had, the boy whose blood I cleaned off the dormitory floor, is dead. He's dead now.

"And of the nice ones," I say, "it's just you, me, and . . . Myra, probably."

I haven't seen Myra since she left the Dauntless compound with Edward, right after his eye was claimed by a butter knife. I know they broke up not long after that, but I never found out where she went. I don't think I ever exchanged more than a few words with her anyway.

A set of doors to the Hancock building are already open, dangling from their hinges. Uriah said that he would come here early to turn on the generator, and sure enough, when I touch my finger to the elevator button, it glows through my fingernail.

"Have you been here before?" I say as we walk into the elevator.

"No," Christina says. "Not inside, I mean. I didn't get to go zip lining, remember?"

"Right." I lean against the wall. "You should try to go before we leave."

"Yeah." She's wearing red lipstick. It reminds me of the way candy stains children's skin if they eat it too sloppily. "Sometimes I get where Evelyn's coming from. So many awful things have happened, sometimes it feels like a good idea to stay here and just . . . try to clean up this mess before we get ourselves involved in another." She smiles a little. "But of course, I'm not going to do that," she adds. "I'm not even sure why. Curiosity, I guess."

"Have you talked to your parents about it?"

Sometimes I forget that Christina isn't like me, with no family loyalty to tie her to one place anymore. She has a mother and a little sister, both former Candor.

"They have to look after my sister," she says. "They don't know if it's safe out there; they don't want to risk her."

"But they would be okay with you leaving?"

"They were okay with me joining another faction. They'll be okay with this, too," she says. She looks down at her shoes. "They just want me to live an honest life, you know? And I can't do that here. I just know that I can't."

The elevator doors open, and the wind hits us immediately, still warm but woven with threads of winter cold. I hear voices coming from the roof, and I climb the ladder to get to them. It bounces with each of my footsteps, but Christina holds it steady for me until I reach the top.

Uriah and Zeke are there, throwing pebbles off the roof and listening for the clatter when they hit the windows. Uriah tries to bump Zeke's elbow before he throws, to mess him up, but Zeke is too quick for him.

"Hey," they say in unison when they spot Christina and me.

"Wait, are you guys related or something?" Christina

says, grinning. They both laugh, but Uriah looks a little dazed, like he's not quite connected to this moment or this place. I guess losing someone the way he lost Marlene can do that to a person, though that's not what it did to me.

There are no slings on the roof for the zip line, and that's not why we came. I don't know why the others did, but I wanted to be up high—I wanted to see as far as I could. But all the land west of where I am is black, like it's draped in a dark blanket. For a moment I think I can make out a glimmer of light on the horizon, but the next it's gone, just a trick of the eyes.

The others are quiet too. I wonder if we're all thinking the same thing.

"What do you think's out there?" Uriah finally says.

Zeke just shrugs, but Christina ventures a guess. "What if it's just more of the same? Just . . . more crumbling city, more factions, more of everything?"

"Can't be," Uriah says, shaking his head. "There has to be something *else*."

"Or there's nothing," Zeke suggests. "Those people who put us all in here, they could just be dead. Everything could be empty."

I shiver. I had never thought of that before, but he's right—we don't know what's happened out there since they put us in here, or how many generations have lived and died since they did. We could be the last people left.

"It doesn't matter," I say, more sternly than I mean to. "It doesn't matter what's out there, we have to see it for ourselves. And then we'll deal with it once we have."

We stand there for a long time. I follow the bumpy edges of buildings with my eyes until all the lit windows smear into a line. Then Uriah asks Christina about the riot, and our still, silent moment passes as if carried away by the wind.

+ + +

The next day, Evelyn stands among the pieces of Jeanine Matthews's portrait in the Erudite headquarters lobby and announces a new set of rules. Former faction members and factionless alike are gathered in the space and spilling out into the street to hear what our new leader has to say, and factionless soldiers line the walls, their fingers poised over the triggers of their guns. Keeping us under control.

"Yesterday's events made it clear that we are no longer able to trust each other," she says. She looks ashen and exhausted. "We will be introducing more structure into everyone's lives until our situation is more stable. The first of these measures is a curfew: Everyone is required to return to their assigned living spaces at nine o'clock at night. They will not leave those spaces until eight o'clock the next morning. Guards will be patrolling the streets at all hours to keep us safe."

I snort and try to cover it up with a cough. Christina elbows me in the side and touches her finger to her lips. I don't know why she cares—it's not like Evelyn can hear me from all the way at the front of the room.

Tori, former leader of Dauntless, ousted by Evelyn herself, stands a few feet away from me, her arms crossed. Her mouth twitches into a sneer.

"It's also time to prepare for our new, factionless way of life. Starting today, everyone will begin to learn the jobs the factionless have done for as long as we can remember. We will then *all* do those jobs on a rotation schedule, in addition to the other duties that have traditionally been performed by the factions." Evelyn smiles without really smiling. I don't know how she does it. "We will all contribute equally to our new city, as it should be. The factions have divided us, but now we will be united. Now, and forever."

All around me the factionless cheer. I just feel uneasy. I don't disagree with her, exactly, but the same faction members who rose up against Edward yesterday won't remain quiet after this, either. Evelyn's hold on this city is not as strong as she might like.

+ + +

I don't want to wrestle with the crowds after Evelyn's announcement, so I weave through the hallways until I find one of the staircases in the back, the one we climbed to reach Jeanine's laboratory not too long ago. The steps were crowded with bodies then. Now they are clean and cool, like nothing ever happened here.

As I walk past the fourth floor, I hear a yell, and some scuffling sounds. I open the door to a cluster of people—young, younger than I am, and all sporting factionless armbands—gathered around a young man on the ground.

Not just a young man—a Candor, dressed in black and white from head to toe.

I run toward them, and when I see a tall factionless girl draw back her foot to kick again, I shout, "Hey!"

No use—the kick hits the Candor boy in the side, and he groans, twisting away from it.

"Hey!" I yell again, and this time the girl turns. She's much taller than I am—a good six inches, in fact—but I'm only angry, not afraid.

"Back up," I say. "Back away from him."

"He's in violation of the dress code. I'm well within my rights, and I don't take orders from faction lovers," she says, her eyes on the ink creeping over my collarbone.

"Becks," the factionless boy beside her says. "That's the Prior video girl."

The others look impressed, but the girl just sneers. "So?"

"So," I say, "I had to hurt a lot of people to get through Dauntless initiation, and I'll do it to you, too, if I have to."

I unzip my blue sweatshirt and toss it at the Candor boy, who looks at me from the ground, blood streaming from his eyebrow. He pushes himself up, still holding his side with one hand, and pulls the sweatshirt around his shoulders like a blanket.

"There," I say. "Now he's not violating the dress code."

The girl tests the situation in her mind, evaluating whether she wants to fight me or not. I can practically hear what she's thinking—I'm small, so I'm an easy target, but I'm Dauntless, so I'm not that easy to beat. Maybe she knows that I've killed people, or maybe she just doesn't want to get into trouble, but she's losing her nerve; I can tell by the uncertain set of her mouth.

"You'd better watch your back," she says.

"I guarantee you that I don't need to," I say. "Now get out of here."

I stay just long enough to see them scatter, then keep walking. The Candor boy calls, "Wait! Your sweatshirt!"

"Keep it!" I call back.

I turn a corner that I think will take me to another staircase, but I end up in another blank hallway, just like the last one I was in. I think I hear footsteps behind me, and I spin around, ready to fight the factionless girl off, but there's no one there.

I must be getting paranoid.

I open one of the doors off the main corridor, hoping to find a window so I can reorient myself, but I find only a ransacked laboratory, beakers and test tubes scattered across each counter. Torn pieces of paper litter the floor, and I'm bending to pick one up when the lights shut off.

I lunge toward the door. A hand grabs my arm and drags me to the side. Someone shoves a sack over my head while someone else pushes me against the wall. I thrash against them, struggling with the fabric covering my face, and all I can think is, *Not again not again not again.* I twist one arm free and punch, hitting someone in a shoulder or a chin, I can't tell.

"Hey!" a voice says. "That *hurt!*"

"We're sorry for frightening you, Tris," another voice says, "but anonymity is integral to our operation. We mean you no harm."

"Let *go* of me, then!" I say, almost growling. All the hands holding me to the wall fall away.

"Who are you?" I demand.

"We are the Allegiant," the voice replies. "And we are many, yet we are no one. . . ."

I can't help it: I laugh. Maybe it's the shock—or the fear, my pounding heart slowing by the second, my hands shaking with relief.

The voice continues, "We have heard that you are not loyal to Evelyn Johnson and her factionless lackeys."

"This is ridiculous."

"Not as ridiculous as trusting someone with your identity when you don't have to."

I try to see through the fibers of whatever is over my head, but they are too dense and it is too dark. I try to relax against the wall, but it's difficult without my vision to orient me. I crush the side of a beaker under my shoe.

"No, I'm not loyal to her," I say. "Why does that matter?"

"Because it means you want to leave," the voice says. I feel a prickle of excitement. "We want to ask you for a favor, Tris Prior. We're going to have a meeting tomorrow night, at midnight. We want you to bring your Dauntless friends."

"Okay," I say. "Let me ask you this: If I'm going to see who you are tomorrow, why is it so important to keep this thing over my head today?"

This seems to temporarily stump whoever I'm talking to.

"A day contains many dangers," the voice says. "We'll see you tomorrow, at midnight, in the place where you made your confession."

All at once, the door swings open, blowing the sack against my cheeks, and I hear running footsteps down the hallway. By the time I'm able to pull the sack from my head, the corridor is silent. I look down at it—it's a dark-blue pillowcase with the words "Faction before blood" painted on it.

Whoever they are, they certainly have a flair for the dramatic.

The place where you made your confession.

There's only one place that could be: Candor headquarters, where I succumbed to the truth serum.

+ + +

When I finally make it back to the dormitory that evening, I find a note from Tobias tucked under the glass of water on my bedside table.

> *VI—*
>
> > *Your brother's trial will be tomorrow morning, and it will be private. I can't go or I'll raise suspicion, but I'll get you the verdict as soon as possible. Then we can make some kind of plan.*
> >
> > *No matter what, this will be over soon.*
>
> *—IV*

CHAPTER EIGHT

TRIS

IT'S NINE O'CLOCK. They could be deciding Caleb's verdict right now, as I tie my shoes, as I straighten my sheets for the fourth time today. I put my hands through my hair. The factionless only make trials private when they feel the verdict is obvious, and Caleb was Jeanine's right-hand man before she was killed.

I shouldn't worry about his verdict. It's already decided. All of Jeanine's closest associates will be executed.

Why do you care? I ask myself. *He betrayed you. He didn't try to stop your execution.*

I don't care. I do care. I don't know.

"Hey, Tris," Christina says, rapping her knuckles against the door frame. Uriah lurks behind her. He still smiles all the time, but now his smiles look like they're made of water, about to drip down his face.

"You had some news?" she says.

I check the room again, though I already know it's empty. Everyone is at breakfast, as required by our schedules. I asked Uriah and Christina to skip a meal so that I could tell them something. My stomach is already rumbling.

"Yeah," I say.

They sit on the bed across from mine, and I tell them about getting cornered in one of the Erudite laboratories the night before, about the pillowcase and the Allegiant and the meeting.

"I'm surprised all you did was punch one of them," Uriah says.

"Well, I was outnumbered," I say, feeling defensive. It wasn't very Dauntless of me to just trust them immediately, but these are strange times. And I'm not sure how Dauntless I really am, anyway, now that the factions are gone.

I feel a strange little ache at the thought, right in the middle of my chest. Some things are hard to let go of.

"So what do you think they want?" Christina says. "Just to leave the city?"

"It sounds that way, but I don't know," I say.

"How do we know they're not Evelyn's people, trying to trick us into betraying her?"

"I don't know that, either," I say. "But it's going to be impossible to get out of the city without someone's help, and I'm not just going to stay here, learning how to drive buses and going to bed when I'm told to."

Christina gives Uriah a worried look.

"Hey," I say. "You don't have to come, but I need to get out of here. I need to know who Edith Prior was, and who's waiting for us outside the fence, if anyone. I don't know why, but I need to."

I take a deep breath. I'm not sure where that swell of desperation came from, but now that I've acknowledged it, it's impossible to ignore, like a living thing has awakened from a long sleep inside me. It writhes in my stomach and throat. I need to leave. I need the truth.

For once, the weak smile playing over Uriah's lips is gone. "So do I," he says.

"Okay," Christina says. Her dark eyes are still troubled, but she shrugs. "So we go to the meeting."

"Good. Can one of you tell Tobias? I'm supposed to be keeping my distance, since we're 'broken up,'" I say. "Let's meet in the alley at eleven thirty."

"I'll tell him. I think I'm in his group today," Uriah says. "Learning about the factories. I can't *wait*." He smirks.

"Can I tell Zeke, too? Or is he not trustworthy enough?"

"Go ahead. Just make sure he doesn't spread it around."

I check my watch again. Nine fifteen. Caleb's verdict has to be decided by now; it's almost time for everyone to go learn their factionless jobs. I feel like the slightest thing could make me jump right out of my skin. My knee bounces of its own volition.

Christina puts her hand on my shoulder, but she doesn't ask me about it, and I'm grateful. I don't know what I would say.

+ + +

Christina and I weave a complicated path through Erudite headquarters on our way to the back staircase, avoiding patrolling factionless. I pull my sleeve down over my wrist. I drew a map on my arm before I left—I know how to get to Candor headquarters from here, but I don't know the side streets that will keep us away from prying factionless eyes.

Uriah waits for us just outside the door. He wears all black, but I can see a hint of Abnegation gray peeking over the collar of his sweatshirt. It's strange to see my Dauntless friends in Abnegation colors, as if they've been with me my entire life. Sometimes it feels that way anyway.

"I told Four and Zeke, but they're going to meet us there," Uriah says. "Let's go."

We run in a pack down the alley toward Monroe Street. I resist the urge to wince at each of our loud footsteps. It's more important to be quick than silent at this point, anyway. We turn onto Monroe, and I check behind us for factionless patrols. I see dark shapes moving closer to Michigan Avenue, but they disappear behind the row of buildings without stopping.

"Where's Cara?" I whisper to Christina, when we're on State Street and far enough away from Erudite headquarters that it's safe to talk.

"I don't know, I don't think she got an invitation," Christina says. "Which is really bizarre. I know she wants to—"

"Shh!" Uriah says. "Next turn?"

I use my watch light to see the words written on my arm. "Randolph Street!"

We settle into a rhythm, our shoes slapping on the pavement, our breaths pulsing almost in unison. Despite the burn in my muscles, it feels good to run.

My legs ache by the time we reach the bridge, but then I see the Merciless Mart across the marshy river, abandoned and unlit, and I smile through the pain. My pace slows when I am across the bridge, and Uriah slings an arm across my shoulders.

"And now," he says, "we get to walk up a million flights of stairs."

"Maybe they turned the elevators on?"

"Not a chance." He shakes his head. "I bet Evelyn's monitoring all the electricity usage—it's the best way to figure out if people are meeting in secret."

I sigh. I may like to run, but I hate climbing stairs.

+ + +

When we finally reach the top of the stairs, our chests heaving, it is five minutes to midnight. The others go ahead while I catch my breath near the elevator bank. Uriah was right—there isn't a single light on that I can see, apart from the exit signs. It is in their blue glow that I see Tobias emerge from the interrogation room up ahead.

Since our date I have spoken to him only in covert messages. I have to resist the urge to throw myself at him and brush my fingers over the curl of his lip and the crease in his cheek when he smiles and the hard line of his eyebrow and jaw. But it's two minutes to midnight. We don't have any time.

He wraps his arms around me and holds me tight for a few seconds. His breaths tickle my ear, and I close my eyes, letting myself finally relax. He smells like wind and sweat and soap, like Tobias and like safety.

"Should we go in?" he says. "Whoever they are, they're probably prompt."

"Yes." My legs are trembling from overexertion—I can't imagine going down the stairs and running back to Erudite headquarters later. "Did you find out about Caleb?"

He winces. "Maybe we should talk about that later."

That's all the answer I need.

"They're going to execute him, aren't they," I say softly.

He nods, and takes my hand. I don't know how to feel. I try not to feel anything.

Together we walk into the room where Tobias and I were once interrogated under the influence of truth serum. *The place where you made your confession.*

A circle of lit candles is arranged on the floor over one of the Candor scales set into the tile. There is a mix of familiar and unfamiliar faces in the room: Susan and Robert stand together, talking; Peter is alone on the side of the room, his arms crossed; Uriah and Zeke are with Tori and a few other Dauntless; Christina is with her mother and sister; and in a corner are two nervous-looking Erudite. New outfits can't erase the divisions between us; they are ingrained.

Christina beckons to me. "This is my mom, Stephanie,"

she says, indicating a woman with gray streaks in her dark curly hair. "And my sister, Rose. Mom, Rose, this is my friend Tris, and my initiation instructor, Four."

"Obviously," Stephanie says. "We saw their interrogations several weeks ago, Christina."

"I know that, I was just being *polite*—"

"Politeness is deception in—"

"Yeah, yeah, I know." Christina rolls her eyes.

Her mother and sister, I notice, look at each other with something like wariness or anger or both. Then her sister turns to me and says, "So you killed Christina's boyfriend."

Her words create a cold feeling inside me, like a streak of ice divides one side of my body from the other. I want to answer, to defend myself, but I can't find the words.

"Rose!" Christina says, scowling at her. At my side, Tobias straightens, his muscles tensing. Ready for a fight, as always.

"I just thought we would air everything out," Rose says. "It wastes less time."

"And you wonder why I left our faction," Christina says. "Being honest doesn't mean you say whatever you want, whenever you want. It means that what you choose to say is true."

"A lie of omission is still a lie."

"You want the truth? I'm uncomfortable and don't want to be here right now. I'll see you guys later." She takes my arm and walks Tobias and me away from her family, shaking her head the whole time. "Sorry about that. They're not really the forgiving type."

"It's fine," I say, though it's not.

I thought that when I received Christina's forgiveness, the hard part of Will's death would be over. But when you kill someone you love, the hard part is never over. It just gets easier to distract yourself from what you've done.

My watch reads twelve o'clock. A door across the room opens, and in walk two lean silhouettes. The first is Johanna Reyes, former spokesperson of Amity, identifiable by the scar that crosses her face and the hint of yellow peeking out from under her black jacket. The second is another woman, but I can't see her face, just that she is wearing blue.

I feel a spike of terror. She looks almost like . . . Jeanine.
No, I saw her die. Jeanine is dead.

The woman comes closer. She is statuesque and blond, like Jeanine. A pair of glasses dangles from her front pocket, and her hair is in a braid. An Erudite from head to foot, but not Jeanine Matthews.

Cara.

Cara and Johanna are the leaders of the Allegiant?

"Hello," Cara says, and all conversation stops. She

smiles, but on her the expression looks compulsory, like she's just adhering to a social convention. "We aren't supposed to be here, so I'm going to keep this meeting short. Some of you—Zeke, Tori—have been helping us for the past few days."

I stare at Zeke. *Zeke* has been helping Cara? I guess I forgot that he was once a Dauntless spy. Which is probably when he proved his loyalty to Cara—he had some kind of friendship with her before she left Erudite headquarters not long ago.

He looks at me, wiggles his eyebrows, and grins.

Johanna continues, "Some of you are here because we want to ask for your help. All of you are here because you don't trust Evelyn Johnson to determine the fate of this city."

Cara touches her palms together in front of her. "We believe in following the guidance of the city's founders, which has been expressed in two ways: the formation of the factions, and the Divergent mission expressed by Edith Prior, to send people outside the fence to help whoever is out there once we have a large Divergent population. We believe that even if we have not reached that Divergent population size, the situation in our city has become dire enough to send people outside the fence anyway.

"In accordance with the intentions of our city's founders, we have two goals: to overthrow Evelyn and the factionless so that we can reestablish the factions, and to send some of our number outside the city to see what's out there. Johanna will be heading up the former effort, and I will be heading up the latter, which is what we will mostly be focusing on tonight." She presses a loose strand of hair back into her braid. "Not many of us will be able to go, because a crowd that large would draw too much attention. Evelyn won't let us leave without a fight, so I thought it would be best to recruit people who I know to be experienced with surviving danger."

I glance at Tobias. We certainly are experienced with danger.

"Christina, Tris, Tobias, Tori, Zeke, and Peter are my selections," Cara says. "You have all proven your skills to me in one way or another, and it's for that reason that I'd like to ask you to come with me outside the city. You are under no obligation to agree, of course."

"*Peter?*" I demand, without thinking. I can't imagine what Peter could have done to "prove his skills" to Cara.

"He kept the Erudite from killing you," Cara says mildly. "Who do you think provided him with the technology to fake your death?"

I raise my eyebrows. I had never thought about it before—too much happened after my failed execution for me to dwell on the details of my rescue. But of course, Cara was the only well-known defector from Erudite at that time, the only person Peter would have known to ask for help. Who else could have helped him? Who else would have known how?

I don't raise another objection. I don't want to leave this city with Peter, but I'm too desperate to leave to make a fuss about it.

"That's a lot of Dauntless," a girl at the side of the room says, looking skeptical. She has thick eyebrows that don't stop growing in the middle, and pale skin. When she turns her head, I see black ink right behind her ear. A Dauntless transfer to Erudite, no doubt.

"True," Cara says. "But what we need right now are people with the skills to get out of the city unscathed, and I think Dauntless training makes them highly qualified for that task."

"I'm sorry, but I don't think I can go," Zeke says. "I couldn't leave Shauna here. Not after her sister just . . . well, you know."

"I'll go," Uriah says, his hand popping up. "I'm Dauntless. I'm a good shot. And I provide much-needed eye candy."

I laugh. Cara does not seem to be amused, but she nods. "Thank you."

"Cara, you'll need to get out of the city fast," the Dauntless-turned-Erudite girl says. "Which means you should get someone to operate the trains."

"Good point," Cara says. "Does anyone here know how to drive a train?"

"Oh. I do," the girl says. "Was that not implied?"

The pieces of the plan come together. Johanna suggests we take Amity trucks from the end of the railroad tracks out of the city, and she volunteers to supply them to us. Robert offers to help her. Stephanie and Rose volunteer to monitor Evelyn's movements in the hours before the escape, and to report any unusual behavior to the Amity compound by two-way radio. The Dauntless who came with Tori offer to find weapons for us. The Erudite girl prods at any weaknesses she sees, and so does Cara, and soon they are all shored up, like we have just built a secure structure.

There is only one question left. Cara asks it:

"When should we go?"

And I volunteer an answer:

"Tomorrow night."

CHAPTER NINE

TOBIAS

THE NIGHT AIR slips into my lungs, and I feel like it is one of my last breaths. Tomorrow I will leave this place and seek another.

Uriah, Zeke, and Christina start toward Erudite headquarters, and I hold Tris's hand to keep her back.

"Wait," I say. "Let's go somewhere."

"Go somewhere? But . . ."

"Just for a little while." I tug her toward the corner of the building. At night I can almost see what the water looked like when it filled the empty canal, dark and patterned with moonlit ripples. "You're with me, remember? They're not going to arrest you."

A twitch at the corner of her mouth—almost a smile.

Around the corner, she leans against the wall and I stand in front of her, the river at my back. She's wearing something dark around her eyes to make their color stand out, bright and striking.

"I don't know what to do." She presses her hands to her face, curling her fingers into her hair. "About Caleb, I mean."

"You don't?"

She moves one hand aside to look at me.

"Tris." I set my hands on the wall on either side of her face and lean into them. "You don't want him to die. I know you don't."

"The thing is . . ." She closes her eyes. "I'm so . . . *angry*. I try not to think about him because when I do I just want to . . ."

"I know. God, I know." My entire life I've daydreamed about killing Marcus. Once I even decided how I would do it—with a knife, so I could feel the warmth leave him, so I could be close enough to watch the light leave his eyes. Making that decision frightened me as much as his violence ever did.

"My parents would want me to save him, though." Her eyes open and lift to the sky. "They would say it's selfish to let someone die just because they wronged you. Forgive, forgive, forgive."

"This isn't about what they want, Tris."

"Yes, it is!" She presses away from the wall. "It's always about what they want. Because he belongs to them more than he belongs to me. And I want to make them proud of me. It's all I want."

Her pale eyes are steady on mine, determined. I have never had parents who set good examples, parents whose expectations were worth living up to, but she did. I can see them within her, the courage and the beauty they pressed into her like a handprint.

I touch her cheek, sliding my fingers into her hair. "I'll get him out."

"What?"

"I'll get him out of his cell. Tomorrow, before we leave." I nod. "I'll do it."

"Really? Are you sure?"

"Of course I'm sure."

"I . . ." She frowns up at me. "Thank you. You're . . . amazing."

"Don't say that. You haven't found out about my ulterior motives yet." I grin. "You see, I didn't bring you here to talk to you about Caleb, actually."

"Oh?"

I set my hands on her hips and push her gently back against the wall. She looks up at me, her eyes clear and eager. I lean in close enough to taste her breaths, but pull back when she leans in, teasing.

She hooks her fingers in my belt loops and pulls me against her, so I have to catch myself on my forearms. She tries to kiss me but I tilt my head to dodge her, kissing just under her ear, then along her jaw to her throat. Her skin is soft and tastes like salt, like a night run.

"Do me a favor," she whispers into my ear, "and never have pure motives again."

She puts her hands on me, touching all the places I am marked, down my back and over my sides. Her fingertips slip under the waistband of my jeans and hold me against her. I breathe against the side of her neck, unable to move.

Finally we kiss, and it is a relief. She sighs, and I feel a wicked smile creep across my face.

I lift her up, letting the wall bear most of her weight, and her legs drape around my waist. She laughs into another kiss, and I feel strong, but so does she, her fingers stern around my arms. The night air slips into my lungs, and I feel like it is one of my first breaths.

CHAPTER
TEN

TOBIAS

THE BROKEN BUILDINGS in the Dauntless sector look like doorways to other worlds. Ahead of me I see the Pire piercing the sky.

The pulse in my fingertips marks the passing seconds. The air still feels rich in my lungs, though summer is drawing to a close. I used to run all the time and fight all the time because I cared about muscles. Now my feet have saved me too often, and I can't separate running and fighting from what they are: a way to escape danger, a way to stay alive.

When I reach the building, I pace before the entrance to catch my breath. Above me, panes of glass reflect light in every direction. Somewhere up there is the chair I sat in while I was running the attack simulation, and a smear of Tris's father's blood on the wall. Somewhere up there, Tris's voice pierced the simulation I was under, and I felt her hand on my chest, drawing me back to reality.

I open the door to the fear landscape room and flip open the small black box that was in my back pocket to see the syringes inside. This is the box I have always used, padded around the needles; it is a sign of something sick inside me, or something brave.

I position the needle over my throat and close my eyes as I press down on the plunger. The black box clatters to the ground, but by the time I open my eyes, it has disappeared.

I stand on the roof of the Hancock building, near the zip line where the Dauntless flirt with death. The clouds are black with rain, and the wind fills my mouth when I open it to breathe. To my right, the zip line snaps, the wire cord whipping back and shattering the windows below me.

My vision tightens around the roof edge, trapping it in the center of a pinhole. I can hear my own exhales despite the whistling wind. I force myself to walk to the edge. The rain pounds against my shoulders and head, dragging me toward the ground. I tip my weight forward just a little and fall, my jaw clamped around my screams, muffled and suffocated by my own fear.

After I land, I don't have a second to rest before the walls close in around me, the wood slamming into my spine, and then my head, and then my legs. Claustrophobia. I pull my arms in to my chest, close my eyes, and try not to panic.

I think of Eric in his fear landscape, willing his terror into submission with deep breathing and logic. And Tris, conjuring weapons out of thin air to attack her worst nightmares. But I am not Eric, and I am not Tris. What am I? What do *I* need, to overcome my fears?

I know the answer, of course I do: I need to deny them the power to control me. I need to know that I am stronger than they are.

I breathe in and slam my palms against the walls to my left and right. The box creaks, and then breaks, the boards crashing to the concrete floor. I stand above them in the dark.

Amar, my initiation instructor, taught us that our fear landscapes were always in flux, shifting with our moods and changing with the little whispers of our nightmares. Mine was always the same, until a few weeks ago. Until I proved to myself that I could overpower my father. Until I discovered someone I was terrified to lose.

I don't know what I will see next.

I wait for a long time without anything changing. The room is still dark, the floor still cold and hard, my heart still beating faster than normal. I look down to check my watch and discover that it's on the wrong hand—I usually wear mine on my left, not my right, and my watchband isn't gray, it's black.

Then I notice bristly hairs on my fingers that weren't there before. The calluses on my knuckles are gone. I look down, and I am wearing gray slacks and a gray shirt; I am thicker around the middle and thinner through the shoulders.

I lift my eyes to a mirror that now stands in front of me. The face staring back at mine is Marcus's.

He winks at me, and I feel the muscles around my eye contracting as he does, though I didn't tell them to. Without warning, his—my—*our* arms jerk toward the glass and reach into it, closing around the neck of my reflection. But then the mirror disappears, and my—his—*our* hands are around our own throat, dark patches creeping into the edge of our vision. We sink to the ground, and the grip is as tight as iron.

I can't think. I can't think of a way out of this one.

By instinct, I scream. The sound vibrates against my hands. I picture those hands as mine really are, large with slender fingers and calloused knuckles from hours at the punching bag. I imagine my reflection as water running over Marcus's skin, replacing every piece of him with a piece of me. I remake myself in my own image.

I am kneeling on the concrete, gasping for air.

My hands tremble, and I run my fingers over my neck, my shoulders, my arms. Just to make sure.

I told Tris, on the train to meet Evelyn a few weeks ago, that Marcus was still in my fear landscape, but that he had changed. I spent a long time thinking about it; it crowded my thoughts every night before I slept and clamored for attention every time I woke. I was still afraid of him, I knew, but in a different way—I was no longer a child, afraid of the threat my terrifying father posed to my safety. I was a man, afraid of the threat he posed to my character, to my future, to my identity.

But even that fear, I know, does not compare to the one that comes next. Even though I know it's coming, I want to open a vein and drain the serum from my body rather than see it again.

A pool of light appears on the concrete in front of me. A hand, the fingers bent into a claw, reaches into the light, followed by another hand, and then a head, with stringy blond hair. The woman coughs and drags herself into the circle of light, inch by inch. I try to move toward her, to help her, but I am frozen.

The woman turns her face toward the light, and I see that she is Tris. Blood spills over her lips and curls around her chin. Her bloodshot eyes find mine, and she wheezes, "Help."

She coughs red onto the floor, and I throw myself toward her, somehow knowing that if I don't get to her soon, the light will leave her eyes. Hands wrap around my arms and shoulders and chest, forming a cage of flesh and bone, but I keep straining toward her. I claw at the hands holding me, but I only end up scratching myself.

I shout her name, and she coughs again, this time more blood. She screams for help, and I scream for her, and I don't hear anything, I don't feel anything, but my heartbeat, but my own terror.

She drops to the ground, tensionless, and her eyes roll back into her head. It's too late.

The darkness lifts. The lights return. Graffiti covers the walls of the fear landscape room, and across from me are the mirror-windows to the observation room, and in the corners are the cameras that record each session, all where they're supposed to be. My neck and back are covered in sweat. I wipe my face with the hem of my shirt and walk to the opposite door, leaving my black box with its syringe and needle behind.

I don't need to relive my fears anymore. All I need to do now is try to overcome them.

I know from experience that confidence alone can get a person into a forbidden place. Like the cells on the third floor of Erudite headquarters.

Not here, though, apparently. A factionless man stops me with the end of his gun before I reach the door, and I am nervous, choking.

"Where you going?"

I put my hand on his gun and push it away from my arm. "Don't point that thing at me. I'm here on Evelyn's orders. I'm going to see a prisoner."

"I didn't hear about any after-hours visits today."

I drop my voice low, so he feels like he's hearing a secret. "That's because she didn't want it on the record."

"Chuck!" someone calls out from the stairs above us. It's Therese. She makes a waving motion as she walks down. "Let him through. He's fine."

I nod to Therese and keep moving. The debris in the hallway has been swept clean, but the broken lightbulbs haven't been replaced, so I walk through stretches of darkness, like patches of bruises, on my way to the right cell.

When I reach the north corridor, I don't go straight to the cell, but rather to the woman who stands at the end. She is middle-aged, with eyes that droop at the edges and a mouth held in a pucker. She looks like everything exhausts her, including me.

"Hi," I say. "My name is Tobias Eaton. I'm here to collect a prisoner, on orders from Evelyn Johnson."

Her expression doesn't change when she hears my name, so for a few seconds I'm sure I'll have to knock her unconscious to get what I want. She takes a piece of crumpled paper from her pocket and flattens it against her left palm. On it is a list of prisoners' names and their corresponding room numbers.

"Name?" she says.

"Caleb Prior. 308A."

"You're Evelyn's son, right?"

"Yeah. I mean . . . yes." She doesn't seem like the kind of person who likes the word "yeah."

She leads me to a blank metal door with 308A on it—I wonder what it was used for when our city didn't require so many cells. She types in the code, and the door springs open.

"I guess I'm supposed to pretend I don't see what you're about to do?" she says.

She must think I'm here to kill him. I decide to let her.

"Yes," I say.

"Do me a favor and put in a good word for me with Evelyn. I don't want so many night shifts. The name's Drea."

"You got it."

She gathers the paper into her fist and shoves it back into her pocket as she walks away. I keep my hand on the door handle until she reaches her post again and turns to the side so she isn't facing me. It seems like she's done this a few times before. I wonder how many people have disappeared from these cells at Evelyn's command.

I walk in. Caleb Prior sits at a metal desk, bent over a book, his hair piled on one side of his head.

"What do you want?" he says.

"I hate to break this to you—" I pause. I decided a few hours ago how I wanted to handle this—I want to teach Caleb a lesson. And it will involve a few lies. "You know, actually, I kind of don't hate it. Your execution's been moved up a few weeks. To tonight."

That gets his attention. He twists in his chair and stares at me, his eyes wild and wide, like prey faced with a predator.

"Is that a joke?"

"I'm really bad at telling jokes."

"No." He shakes his head. "No, I have a few weeks, it's not *tonight*, no—"

"If you shut up, I'll give you an hour to adjust to this new information. If you don't shut up, I'll knock you out and shoot you in the alley outside before you wake up. Make your choice now."

Seeing an Erudite process something is like watching the inside of a watch, the gears all turning, shifting, adjusting, working together to form a particular function, which in this case is to make sense of his imminent demise.

Caleb's eyes shift to the open door behind me, and he seizes the chair, turning and swinging it into my body. The legs hit me, hard, which slows me down just enough to let him slip by.

I follow him into the hallway, my arms burning from where the chair hit me. I am faster than he is—I slam into his back and he hits the floor face-first, without bracing himself. With my knee against his back, I pull his wrists together and squeeze them into a plastic loop. He groans, and when I pull him to his feet, his nose is bright with blood.

Drea's eyes touch mine for just a moment, then move away.

I drag him down the hallway, not the way I came, but another way, toward an emergency exit. We walk down a flight of narrow stairs where the echo of our footsteps layers over itself, dissonant and hollow. Once I'm at the bottom, I knock on the exit door.

Zeke opens it, a stupid grin on his face.

"No trouble with the guard?"

"No."

"I figured Drea would be easy to get by. She doesn't care about anything."

"It sounded like she had looked the other way before."

"That doesn't surprise me. Is this Prior?"

"In the flesh."

"Why's he bleeding?"

"Because he's an idiot."

Zeke offers me a black jacket with a factionless symbol stitched into the collar. "I didn't know that idiocy caused people to just start spontaneously bleeding from the nose."

I wrap the jacket around Caleb's shoulders and fasten one of the buttons over his chest. He avoids my eyes.

"I think it's a new phenomenon," I say. "The alley's clear?"

"Made sure of it." Zeke holds out his gun, handle first. "Careful, it's loaded. Now it would be great if you would hit me so I'm more convincing when I tell the factionless you stole it from me."

"You want me to hit you?"

"Oh, like you've never wanted to. Just do it, Four."

I do like to hit people—I like the explosion of power and energy, and the feeling that I am untouchable because I can hurt people. But I hate that part of myself, because it is the part of me that is the most broken.

Zeke braces himself and I curl my hand into a fist.

"Do it fast, you pansycake," he says.

I decide to aim for the jaw, which is too strong to break but will still show a good bruise. I swing, hitting him right where I mean to. Zeke groans, clutching his face with both hands. Pain shoots up my arm, and I shake my hand out.

"Great." Zeke spits at the side of the building. "Well, I guess that's it."

"Guess so."

"I probably won't be seeing you again, will I? I mean, I know the others might come back, but you . . ." He trails off, but picks up the thought again a moment later. "Just seems like you'll be happy to leave it behind, that's all."

"Yeah, you're probably right." I look at my shoes. "You sure you won't come?"

"Can't. Shauna can't wheel around where you guys are going, and it's not like I'm gonna leave her, you know?" He touches his jaw, lightly, testing the skin. "Make sure Uri doesn't drink too much, okay?"

"Yeah," I say.

"No, I mean it," he says, and his voice dips down the way it always does when he's being serious, for once. "Promise you'll look out for him?"

It's always been clear to me, since I met them, that Zeke

and Uriah were closer than most brothers. They lost their father when they were young, and I suspect Zeke began to walk the line between parent and sibling after that. I can't imagine what it feels like for Zeke to watch him leave the city now, especially as broken by grief as Uriah is by Marlene's death.

"I promise," I say.

I know I should leave, but I have to stay in this moment for a little while, feeling its significance. Zeke was one of the first friends I made in Dauntless, after I survived initiation. Then he worked in the control room with me, watching the cameras and writing stupid programs that spelled out words on the screen or played guessing games with numbers. He never asked me for my real name, or why a first-ranked initiate ended up in security and instruction instead of leadership. He demanded nothing from me.

"Let's just hug already," he says.

Keeping one hand firm on Caleb's arm, I wrap my free arm around Zeke, and he does the same.

When we break apart, I pull Caleb down the alley, and can't resist calling back, "I'll miss you."

"You too, sweetie!"

He grins, and his teeth are white in the twilight. They are the last thing I see of him before I have to turn and set out at a trot for the train.

"You're going somewhere," says Caleb, between breaths. "You and some others."

"Yeah."

"Is my sister going?"

The question awakes inside me an animal rage that won't be satisfied by sharp words or insults. It will only be satisfied by smacking his ear hard with the flat of my hand. He winces and hunches his shoulders, preparing for a second strike.

I wonder if that's what I looked like when my father did it to me.

"She is not your sister," I say. "You betrayed her. You tortured her. You took away the only family she had left. And because . . . what? Because you wanted to keep Jeanine's secrets, wanted to stay in the city, safe and sound? You are a coward."

"I am not a coward!" Caleb says. "I knew if—"

"Let's go back to the arrangement where you keep your mouth closed."

"Fine," he says. "Where are you taking me, anyway? You can kill me just as well here, can't you?"

I pause. A shape moves along the sidewalk behind us, slippery in my periphery. I twist and hold up my gun, but the shape disappears into the yawn of an alley.

I keep walking, pulling Caleb with me, listening for footsteps behind me. We scatter broken glass with our shoes. I watch the dark buildings and the street signs, dangling from their hinges like late-clinging leaves in autumn. Then I reach the station where we'll catch the train, and lead Caleb up a flight of metal steps to the platform.

I see the train coming from a long way off, making its last journey through the city. Once, the trains were a force of nature to me, something that continued along their path regardless of what we did inside the city limits, something pulsing and alive and powerful. Now I have met the men and women who operate them, and some of that mystery is gone, but what they mean to me will never be gone—my first act as a Dauntless was to jump on one, and every day afterward they were the source of my freedom, they gave me the power to move within this world when I had once felt so trapped in the Abnegation sector, in the house that was a prison to me.

When it comes closer, I cut the tie around Caleb's wrists with a pocketknife and keep a firm hold on his arm.

"You know how to do this, right?" I say. "Get in the last car."

He unbuttons the jacket and drops it on the ground. "Yeah."

Starting at one end of the platform, we run together along the worn boards, keeping pace with the open door. He doesn't reach for the handle, so I push him toward it. He stumbles, then grabs it and pulls himself into the last car. I am running out of space—the platform is ending—I seize the handle and swing myself in, my muscles absorbing the pull forward.

Tris stands inside the car, wearing a small, crooked smile. Her black jacket is zipped up to her throat, framing her face in darkness. She grabs my collar and pulls me in for a kiss. As she pulls away, she says, "I always loved watching you do that."

I grin.

"Is this what you had planned?" Caleb demands from behind me. "For her to be here when you kill me? That's—"

"*Kill* him?" Tris asks me, not looking at her brother.

"Yeah, I let him think he was being taken to his execution," I say, loud enough that he can hear. "You know, sort of like he did to you in Erudite headquarters."

"I . . . it isn't true?" His face, lit by the moon, is slack with shock. I notice that his shirt's buttons are in the wrong buttonholes.

"No," I say. "I just saved your life, actually."

He starts to say something, and I interrupt him. "Might not want to thank me just yet. We're taking you with us. Outside the fence."

Outside the fence—the place he once tried so hard to avoid that he turned on his own sister. It seems a more fitting punishment than death, anyway. Death is so quick, so certain. Where we're going now, nothing is certain.

He looks frightened, but not as frightened as I thought he would be. I feel like I understand, then, the way he ranks things in his mind: his life, first; his comfort in a world of his own making, second; and somewhere after that, the lives of the people he is supposed to love. He is the sort of despicable person who has no understanding of how despicable he is, and my badgering him with insults won't change that; nothing will. Rather than angry, I just feel heavy, useless.

I don't want to think about him anymore. I take Tris's hand and lead her to the other side of the car, so we can watch the city disappear behind us. We stand side by side in the open doorway, each of us holding one of the handles. The buildings create a dark, jagged pattern on the sky.

"We were followed," I say.

"We'll be careful," she answers.

"Where are the others?"

"In the first few cars," she says. "I thought we should be alone. Or as alone as we can get."

She smiles at me. These are our last moments in the city. Of course we should spend them alone.

"I'm really going to miss this place," she says.

"Really?" I say. "My thoughts are more like, 'Good riddance.'"

"There's *nothing* you'll miss? No good memories?" She elbows me.

"Fine." I smile. "There are a few."

"Any that don't involve me?" she says. "That sounds self-centered. You know what I mean."

"Sure, I guess," I say, shrugging. "I mean, I got to have a different life in Dauntless, a different name. I got to be Four, thanks to my initiation instructor. He gave me the name."

"Really?" She tilts her head. "Why haven't I met him?"

"Because he's dead. He was Divergent." I shrug again, but I don't feel casual about it. Amar was the first person who noticed that I was Divergent, and he helped me to hide it. But he couldn't hide his own Divergence, and that killed him.

She touches my arm, lightly, but doesn't say anything. I shift, uncomfortable.

"See?" I say. "Too many bad memories here. I'm ready to leave."

I feel empty, not because of sadness, but because of relief, all the tension flowing out of me. Evelyn is in that city, and Marcus, and all the grief and nightmares and bad memories, and the factions that kept me trapped inside one version of myself. I squeeze Tris's hand.

"Look," I say, pointing at a distant cluster of buildings. "There's the Abnegation sector."

She smiles, but her eyes are glassy, like a dormant part of her is fighting its way out and spilling over. The train hisses over the rails, a tear drops down Tris's cheek, and the city disappears into the darkness.

CHAPTER ELEVEN

TRIS

THE TRAIN SLOWS down when we get closer to the fence, a signal from the driver that we should get off soon. Tobias and I sit in the doorway of the car as it moves lazily over the tracks. He puts his arm around me and touches his nose to my hair, taking a breath. I look at him, at the collarbone peeking out from the neck of his T-shirt, at the faint curl of his lip, and I feel something heating up inside me.

"What are you thinking about?" he says into my ear, softly.

I jerk to attention. I look at him all the time, but not always like *that*—I feel like he just caught me doing something embarrassing. "Nothing! Why?"

"No reason." He pulls me closer to his side, and I rest my head on his shoulder, taking deep breaths of the cool air. It still smells like summer, like grass baking in the heat of the sun.

"It looks like we're getting close to the fence," I say.

I can tell because the buildings are disappearing, leaving just fields, dotted with the rhythmic glow of lightning bugs. Behind me, Caleb sits near the other door, hugging his knees. His eyes find mine at just the wrong moment, and I want to scream into the darkest parts of him so he can finally hear me, finally understand what he did to me, but instead I just hold his stare until he can't take it anymore and he looks away.

I stand, using the handle to steady me, and Tobias and Caleb do the same. At first Caleb tries to stand behind us, but Tobias pushes him forward, right up to the edge of the car.

"You first. On my mark!" he says. "And . . . go!"

He gives Caleb a push, just enough to get him off the car floor, and my brother disappears. Tobias goes next, leaving me alone in the train car.

It's stupid to miss a thing when there are so many people to miss instead, but I miss this train already, and all the others that carried me through the city, *my* city, after I was brave enough to ride them. I brush my fingers over the car wall, just once, and then jump. The train is moving so slowly that I overcompensate with my landing, too used to running off the momentum, and I fall. The dry grass scrapes my palms and I push myself to my feet, searching the darkness for Tobias and Caleb.

Before I find them, I hear Christina. "Tris!"

She and Uriah come toward me. He is holding a flashlight, and he looks far more alert than he did this afternoon, which is a good sign. Behind them are more lights, more voices.

"Did your brother make it?" Uriah says.

"Yeah." Finally I see Tobias, his hand gripping Caleb's arm, coming toward us.

"Not sure why an Erudite like you can't get it through his head," Tobias is saying, "but you aren't going to be able to outrun me."

"He's right," says Uriah. "Four's fast. Not as fast as me, but definitely faster than a Nose like you."

Christina laughs. "A what?"

"Nose." Uriah touches the side of his nose. "It's a play on words. 'Knows' with a 'K,' knowledge, Erudite . . . get it? It's like Stiff."

"The Dauntless have the weirdest slang. Pansycake, Nose . . . is there a term for the Candor?"

"Of course." Uriah grins. "Jerks."

Christina shoves Uriah, hard, making him drop the flashlight. Tobias, laughing, leads us to the rest of the group, standing a few feet away. Tori waves her flashlight in the air to get everyone's attention, then says, "All right, Johanna and the trucks will be about a ten-minute walk from here, so let's get going. And if I hear a word from anyone, I will beat you senseless. We're not out yet."

We move closer together like sections of a tightened shoelace. Tori walks a few feet in front of us, and from the back, in the dark, she reminds me of Evelyn, her limbs lean and wiry, her shoulders back, so sure of herself it's almost frightening. By the light of the flashlights I can just make out the tattoo of a hawk on the back of her neck, the first thing I spoke to her about when she administered my aptitude test. She told me it was a symbol of a fear she had overcome, a fear of the dark. I wonder if that fear still creeps up on her now, though she worked so hard to face it—I wonder if fears ever really go away, or if they just lose their power over us.

She moves farther away from us by the minute, her pace more like a jog than a walk. She is eager to leave, to escape this place where her brother was murdered and she rose to prominence only to be thwarted by a factionless woman who wasn't supposed to be alive.

She is so far ahead that when the shots go off, I only see

her flashlight fall, not her body.

"Split up!" Tobias's voice roars over the sound of our cries, our chaos. "Run!"

I search in the dark for his hand, but I don't find it. I grab the gun Uriah gave me before we left and hold it out from my body, ignoring the way my throat tightens at the feel of it. I can't run into the night. I need light. I sprint in the direction of Tori's body—of her fallen flashlight.

I hear but do not hear the gunshots, and the shouting, and the running footsteps. I hear but do not hear my heartbeat. I crouch next to the shaft of light she dropped and pick up the flashlight, intending to just grab it and keep running, but in its glow I see her face. It shines with sweat, and her eyes roll beneath her eyelids, like she is searching for something but is too tired to find it.

One of the bullets found her stomach, and the other found her chest. There is no way she will recover from this. I may be angry with her for fighting me in Jeanine's laboratory, but she's still Tori, the woman who guarded the secret of my Divergence. My throat tightens as I remember following her into the aptitude test room, my eyes on her hawk tattoo.

Her eyes shift in my direction and focus on me. Her eyebrows furrow, but she doesn't speak.

I shift the flashlight into the crook of my thumb and

reach for her hand to squeeze her sweaty fingers.

I hear someone approaching, and I aim flashlight and gun in the same direction. The beam hits a woman wearing a factionless armband, with a gun pointed at my head. I fire, clenching my teeth so hard they squeak.

The bullet hits the woman in the stomach and she screams, firing blindly into the night.

I look back down at Tori, and her eyes are closed, her body still. Pointing my flashlight at the ground, I sprint away from her and from the woman I just shot. My legs ache and my lungs burn. I don't know where I'm going, if I'm running into danger or away from it, but I keep running as long as I can.

Finally I see a light in the distance. At first I think it's another flashlight, but as I draw closer I realize it is larger and steadier than a flashlight—it's a headlight. I hear an engine, and crouch in the tall grass to hide, switching my flashlight off and keeping my gun ready. The truck slows, and I hear a voice:

"Tori?"

It sounds like Christina. The truck is red and rusted, an Amity vehicle. I straighten, pointing the light at myself so she'll see me. The truck stops a few feet ahead of me, and Christina leaps out of the passenger seat, throwing her arms around me. I replay it in my mind to make it real,

Tori's body falling, the factionless woman's hands covering her stomach. It doesn't work. It doesn't feel real.

"Thank God," Christina says. "Get in. We're going to find Tori."

"Tori's dead," I say plainly, and the word "dead" makes it real for me. I wipe tears from my cheeks with the heels of my hands and struggle to control my shuddering breaths. "I—I shot the woman who killed her."

"What?" Johanna sounds frantic. She leans over from the driver's seat. "What did you say?"

"Tori's gone," I say. "I saw it happen."

Johanna's expression is shrouded by her hair. She presses her next breath out.

"Well, let's find the others, then."

I get into the truck. The engine roars as Johanna presses the gas pedal, and we bump over the grass in search of the others.

"Did you see any of them?" I say.

"A few. Cara, Uriah." Johanna shakes her head. "No one else."

I wrap my hand around the door handle and squeeze. If I had tried harder to find Tobias . . . if I hadn't stopped for Tori . . .

What if Tobias didn't make it?

"I'm sure they're all right," Johanna says. "That boy of

yours knows how to take care of himself."

I nod, without conviction. Tobias can take care of himself, but in an attack, surviving is an accident. It doesn't take skill to stand in a place where no bullets find you, or to fire into the dark and hit a man you didn't see. It is all luck, or providence, depending on what you believe. And I don't know—have never known—exactly what I believe.

He's all right he's all right he's all right.

Tobias is all right.

My hands tremble, and Christina squeezes my knee. Johanna steers us toward the rendezvous point, where she saw Uriah and Cara. I watch the speedometer needle climb, then hold steady at seventy-five. We jostle one another in the cab, thrown this way and that way by the uneven ground.

"There!" Christina points. There is a cluster of lights ahead of us, some just pinpricks, like flashlights, and others round, like headlights.

We pull up close, and I see him. Tobias sits on the hood of the other truck, his arm soaked with blood. Cara stands in front of him with a first aid kit. Caleb and Peter sit on the grass a few feet away. Before Johanna has stopped the truck completely, I open the door and get out, running toward him. Tobias stands up, ignoring Cara's orders to stay put, and we collide, his uninjured arm wrapping around my back and lifting me off my feet. His back is wet with sweat, and when he kisses me, he tastes like salt.

All the knots of tension inside me come apart at once. I feel, just for a moment, like I am remade, like I am brand-new.

He's all right. We're out of the city. He's all right.

CHAPTER
TWELVE

TOBIAS

MY ARM THROBS like a second heartbeat from the bullet graze. Tris's knuckles brush mine as she lifts her hand to point at something on our right: a series of long, low buildings lit by blue emergency lamps.

"What are those?" Tris says.

"The other greenhouses," Johanna says. "They don't require much manpower, but we grow and raise things in large quantities there—animals, raw material for fabric, wheat, and so on."

Their panes glow in the starlight, obscuring the treasures I imagine to be inside them, small plants with berries dangling from their branches, rows of potato plants buried in the earth.

"You don't show them to visitors," I say. "We never saw them."

"Amity keeps a number of secrets," Johanna says, and she sounds proud.

The road ahead of us is long and straight, marked with cracks and swollen patches. Alongside it are gnarled trees, broken lampposts, old power lines. Every so often, there is an isolated square of sidewalk with weeds forcing their way through the concrete, or a pile of rotting wood, a collapsed dwelling.

The more time I spend thinking about this landscape that every Dauntless patrol was told was normal, the more I see an old city rising up around me, the buildings lower than the ones we left behind, but just as numerous. An old city that was transformed into empty land for the Amity to farm. In other words, an old city that was razed, burned to cinders, and crushed into the ground, even the roads disappearing, the earth left to run wild over the wreckage.

I put my hand out the window, and the wind wraps around my fingers like locks of hair. When I was very young, my mother pretended she could shape things from the wind, and she would give them to me to use, like hammers and nails, or swords, or roller skates. It was a game we played in the evenings, on the front lawn, before Marcus got home. It took away our dread.

In the bed of the truck, behind us, are Caleb, Christina,

and Uriah. Christina and Uriah sit close enough for their shoulders to touch, but they are looking in opposite directions, more like strangers than friends. Just behind us is another truck, driven by Robert, which carries Cara and Peter. Tori was supposed to be with them. The thought makes me feel hollow, empty. She administered my aptitude test. She made me think, for the first time, that I could leave Abnegation—that I had to. I feel like I owe her something, and she died before I could give it to her.

"This is it," Johanna says. "The outer limit of the Dauntless patrols."

No fence or wall marks the divide between the Amity compound and the outer world, but I remember monitoring the Dauntless patrols from the control room, making sure they didn't go farther than the limit, which is marked by a series of signs with Xs on them. The patrols were structured so that the trucks would run out of gas if they went too far, a delicate system of checks and balances that preserved our safety and theirs—and, I now realize, the secret the Abnegation kept.

"Have they ever gone past the limit?" says Tris.

"A few times," says Johanna. "It was our responsibility to deal with that situation when it came up."

Tris gives her a look, and she shrugs.

"Every faction has a serum," Johanna says. "The Dauntless serum gives hallucinated realities, Candor's

gives the truth, Amity's gives peace, Erudite's gives death—"
At this, Tris visibly shudders, but Johanna continues as if it
didn't happen. "And Abnegation's resets memory."

"Resets *memory*?"

"Like Amanda Ritter's memory," I say. "She said, 'There
are many things I am happy to forget,' remember?"

"Yes, exactly," says Johanna. "The Amity are charged
with administering the Abnegation serum to anyone who
goes out past the limit, just enough to make them forget
the experience. I'm sure some of them have slipped past
us, but not many."

We are silent then. I turn the information over and over
in my mind. There is something deeply wrong with taking
a person's memories—even though I know it was necessary to keep our city safe for as long as it needed to be, I
feel it in the pit of my stomach. Take a person's memories,
and you change who they are.

Swelling inside me is the feeling that I am about to jump
out of my own skin, because the farther we get outside the
outer limit of the Dauntless patrols, the closer we get to
seeing what lies outside the only world I've ever known.
I am terrified and thrilled and confused and a hundred
different things at once.

I see something up ahead of us, in the light of early
morning, and grab Tris's hand.

"Look," I say.

CHAPTER THIRTEEN

TRIS

THE WORLD BEYOND ours is full of roads and dark buildings and collapsing power lines.

There is no life in it, as far as I can see; no movement, no sound but the wind and my own footsteps.

It's like the landscape is an interrupted sentence, one side dangling in the air, unfinished, and the other, a completely different subject. On our side of that sentence is empty land, grass and stretches of road. On the other side are two concrete walls with half a dozen sets of train tracks between them. Up ahead, there is a concrete bridge built across the walls, and framing the tracks are buildings, wood and brick and glass, their windows dark, trees growing around them, so wild their branches have grown together.

A sign on the right says 90.

"What do we do now?" Uriah asks.

"We follow the tracks," I say, but quietly, so only I hear it.

+ + +

We get out of the trucks at the divide between our world and theirs—whoever "they" are. Robert and Johanna say a brief good-bye, turn the trucks around, and drive back into the city. I watch them go. I can't imagine coming this far and then turning back, but I guess there are things they have to do in the city. Johanna still has an Allegiant rebellion to organize.

The rest of us—me, Tobias, Caleb, Peter, Christina, Uriah, and Cara—set out with our meager possessions along the railroad tracks.

The tracks are not like the ones in the city. They are polished and sleek, and instead of boards running perpendicular to their path, there are sheets of textured metal. Up ahead I see one of the trains that runs along them, abandoned near the wall. It is metal-plated on the top and front, like a mirror, with tinted windows all along the side. When we draw closer, I see rows of benches inside it with maroon cushions on them. People must not jump on and off these trains.

Tobias walks behind me on one of the rails, his arms held out from his sides to maintain his balance. The others are spread out over the tracks, Peter and Caleb near one wall, Cara near the other. No one talks much, except to point out something new, a sign or a building or a hint of what this world was like, when there were people in it.

The concrete walls alone hold my attention—they are covered with strange pictures of people with skin so smooth they hardly look like people anymore, or color-ful bottles with shampoo or conditioner or vitamins or unfamiliar substances inside them, words I don't under-stand, "vodka" and "Coca-Cola" and "energy drink." The colors and shapes and words and pictures are so garish, so abundant, that they are mesmerizing.

"Tris." Tobias puts his hand on my shoulder, and I stop. He tilts his head and says, "Do you hear that?"

I hear footsteps and the quiet voices of our compan-ions. I hear my own breaths, and his. But running beneath them is a quiet rumble, inconsistent in its intensity. It sounds like an engine.

"Everyone stop!" I shout.

To my surprise, everyone does, even Peter, and we gather together in the center of the tracks. I see Peter draw his gun and hold it up, and I do the same, both hands joined together to steady it, remembering the ease with which I used to lift it. That ease is gone now.

Something appears around the bend up ahead. A black truck, but larger than any truck I've ever seen, large enough to hold more than a dozen people in its covered bed.

I shudder.

The truck bumps over the tracks and comes to a stop twenty feet away from us. I can see the man driving it—he has dark skin and long hair that is in a knot at the back of his head.

"God," Tobias says, and his hands tighten around his own gun.

A woman gets out of the front seat. She looks to be around Johanna's age, her skin patterned with dense freckles and her hair so dark it's almost black. She hops to the ground and puts up both hands, so we can see that she isn't armed.

"Hello," she says, and smiles nervously. "My name is Zoe. This is Amar."

She jerks her head to the side to indicate the driver, who has gotten out of the truck too.

"Amar is dead," Tobias says.

"No, I'm not. Come on, Four," Amar says.

Tobias's face is tight with fear. I don't blame him. It's not every day you see someone you care about come back from the dead.

The faces of all the people I've lost flash into my mind. Lynn. Marlene. Will. Al.

My father. My mother.

What if they're still alive, like Amar? What if the curtain that separates us is not death but a chain-link fence and some land?

I can't stop myself from hoping, foolish as it is.

"We work for the same organization that founded your city," Zoe says as she glares at Amar. "The same organization Edith Prior came from. And . . ."

She reaches into her pocket and takes out a partially crumpled photograph. She holds it out, and then her eyes find mine in the crowd of people and guns.

"I think you should look at this, Tris," she says. "I'll step forward and leave it on the ground, then back up. All right?"

She knows my name. My throat tightens with fear. *How* does she know my name? And not just my name—my nickname, the name I chose when I joined Dauntless?

"All right," I say, but my voice is hoarse, so the words barely escape.

Zoe steps forward, sets the photograph down on the train tracks, then moves back to her original position. I leave the safety of our numbers and crouch near the photograph, watching her the whole time. Then I back up, photograph in hand.

It shows a row of people in front of a chain-link fence, their arms slung across one another's shoulders and backs. I see a child version of Zoe, recognizable by her freckles, and a few people I don't recognize. I am about to ask her what the point of me looking at this picture is when I recognize the young woman with dull blond hair, tied back, and a wide smile.

My mother. What is my mother doing next to these people?

Something—grief, pain, longing—squeezes my chest.

"There is a lot to explain," Zoe says. "But this isn't really the best place to do it. We'd like to take you to our headquarters. It's a short drive from here."

Still holding up his gun, Tobias touches my wrist with his free hand, guiding the photograph closer to his face. "That's your mother?" he asks me.

"It's *Mom*?" Caleb says. He pushes past Tobias to see the picture over my shoulder.

"Yes," I say to both of them.

"Think we should trust them?" Tobias says to me in a low voice.

Zoe doesn't look like a liar, and she doesn't sound like one either. And if she knows who I am, and knew how to find us here, it's probably because she has some form of access to the city, which means she is probably telling the truth about being with the group that Edith Prior came from. And then there's Amar, who is watching every movement Tobias makes.

"We came out here because we wanted to find these people," I say. "We have to trust someone, don't we? Or else we're just walking around in a wasteland, possibly starving to death."

Tobias releases my wrist and lowers his gun. I do the same. The others follow suit slowly, with Christina putting hers down last.

"Wherever we go, we have to be free to leave at any time," Christina says. "Okay?"

Zoe places her hand on her chest, right over her heart. "You have my word."

I hope, for all our sakes, that her word is worth having.

CHAPTER
FOURTEEN

TOBIAS

I STAND ON the edge of the truck bed, holding the structure that supports the cloth cover. I want this new reality to be a simulation that I could manipulate if I could only make sense of it. But it's not, and I can't make sense of it.

Amar is alive.

"Adapt!" was one of his favorite commands during my initiation. Sometimes he yelled it so often that I would dream it; it woke me like an alarm clock, requiring more of me than I could provide. *Adapt.* Adapt faster, adapt better, adapt to things that no man should have to.

Like this: leaving a wholly formed world and discovering another one.

Or this: discovering that your dead friend is actually alive and driving the truck you're riding in.

Tris sits behind me, on the bench that wraps around the truck bed, the creased photo in her hands. Her fingers hover over her mother's face, almost touching it but not quite. Christina sits on one side of her, and Caleb is on the other. She must be letting him stay just to see the photograph; her entire body recoils from him, pressing into Christina's side.

"That's your mom?" Christina says.

Tris and Caleb both nod.

"She's so young there. Pretty, too," Christina adds.

"Yes she is. Was, I mean."

I expect Tris to sound sad as she replies, like she's aching at the memory of her mother's fading beauty. Instead her voice is nervous, her lips pursed in anticipation. I hope that she isn't brewing false hope.

"Let me see it," Caleb says, stretching his hand out to his sister.

Silently, and without really looking at him, she passes him the photograph.

I turn back to the world we are driving away from—the end of the train tracks. The huge expanses of field. And in the distance, the Hub, barely visible in the haze that covers the city's skyline. It's a strange feeling, seeing it from this place, like I can still touch it if I stretch my hand far enough, though I have traveled so far away from it.

Peter moves toward the edge of the truck bed next to

me, holding the canvas to steady himself. The train tracks curve away from us now, and I can't see the fields anymore. The walls on either side of us gradually disappear as the land flattens out, and I see buildings everywhere, some small, like the Abnegation houses, and some wide, like city buildings turned on their sides.

Trees, overgrown and huge, grow beyond the cement fixtures intended to keep them enclosed, their roots sprawling over the pavement. Perched on the edge of one rooftop is a row of black birds like the ones tattooed on Tris's collarbone. As the truck passes, they squawk and scatter into the air.

This is a wild world.

Just like that, it is too much for me to bear, and I have to back up and sit on one of the benches. I cradle my head in my hands, keeping my eyes shut so I can't take in any new information. I feel Tris's strong arm across my back, pulling me sideways into her narrow frame. My hands are numb.

"Just focus on what's right here, right now," Cara says from across the truck. "Like how the truck is moving. It'll help."

I try it. I think about how hard the bench is beneath me and how the truck always vibrates, even on flat ground, buzzing in my bones. I detect its tiny movements left and right, forward and back, and absorb each bounce as it rolls over the rails. I focus until everything goes dark around us, and I don't feel the passage of time or the panic of discovery, I feel only our movement over the earth.

"You should probably look around now," Tris says, and she sounds weak.

Christina and Uriah stand where I stood, peering around the edge of the canvas wall. I look over their shoulders to see what we're driving toward. There is a tall fence stretching wide across the landscape, which looks empty compared to the densely packed buildings I saw before I sat down. The fence has vertical black bars with pointed ends that bend outward, as if to skewer anyone who might try to climb over it.

A few feet past it is another fence, this one chain-link, like the one around the city, with barbed wire looped over the top. I hear a loud buzz coming from the second fence, an electric charge. People walk the space between them, carrying guns that look a little like our paintball guns, but far more lethal, powerful pieces of machinery.

A sign on the first fence reads BUREAU OF GENETIC WELFARE.

I hear Amar's voice, speaking to the armed guards, but I don't know what he's saying. A gate in the first fence opens to admit us, and then a gate in the second. Beyond the two fences is . . . order.

As far as I can see, there are low buildings separated by trimmed grass and fledgling trees. The roads that connect them are well maintained and well marked, with arrows pointing to various destinations: GREENHOUSES, straight ahead; SECURITY OUTPOST, left; OFFICERS' RESIDENCES, right; COMPOUND MAIN, straight ahead.

I get up and lean around the truck to see the compound, half my body hanging over the road. The Bureau of Genetic Welfare isn't tall, but it's still huge, wider than I can see, a mammoth of glass and steel and concrete. Behind the compound are a few tall towers with bulges at the top—I don't know why, but I think of the control room when I see them, and wonder if that's what they are.

Aside from the guards between the fences, there are few people outside. Those who are stop to watch us, but we drive away so quickly I don't see their expressions.

The truck stops before a set of double doors, and Peter is the first to jump down. The rest of us spill out on the pavement behind him, and we are shoulder to shoulder, standing so close I can hear how fast everyone is breathing. In the city we were divided by faction, by age, by history, but here all those divisions fall away. We are all we have.

"Here we go," mutters Tris, as Zoe and Amar approach.

Here we go, I say to myself.

+ + +

"Welcome to the compound," says Zoe. "This building used to be O'Hare Airport, one of the busiest airports in the country. Now it's the headquarters of the Bureau of Genetic Welfare—or just the Bureau, as we call it around here. It's an agency of the United States government."

I feel my face going slack. I know all the words she's saying—except I'm not sure what an "airport" or "united states" is—but they don't make sense to me all together. I'm not the only one who looks confused—Peter raises both eyebrows as if asking a question.

"Sorry," she says. "I keep forgetting how little you all know."

"I believe it's *your* fault if we don't know anything, not ours," Peter points out.

"I should rephrase." Zoe smiles gently. "I keep forgetting how little information we provided you with. An airport is a hub for air travel, and—"

"*Air* travel?" says Christina, incredulous.

"One of the technological developments that wasn't necessary for us to know about when we were inside the city was air travel," says Amar. "It's safe, fast, and amazing."

"Wow," says Tris.

She looks excited. I, however, think of speeding

through the air, high above the compound, and feel like I might throw up.

"Anyway. When the experiments were first developed, the airport was converted into this compound so that we could monitor the experiments from a distance," Zoe says. "I'm going to walk you to the control room to meet David, the leader of the Bureau. You will see a lot of things you don't understand, but it may be best to get some preliminary explanations before you start asking me about them. So take note of the things you want to learn more about, and feel free to ask me or Amar later."

She starts toward the entrance, and the doors part for her, pulled open by two armed guards who smile in greeting as she passes them. The contrast between the friendly greeting and the weapons propped against their shoulders is almost humorous. The guns are huge, and I wonder how they feel to shoot, if you can feel the deadly power in them just by curling your finger around the trigger.

Cool air rushes over my face as I walk into the compound. Windows arch high above my head, letting in pale light, but that is the most appealing part about the place—the tile floor is dull with dirt and age, and the walls are gray and blank. Ahead of us is a sea of people and machinery, with a sign over it that says SECURITY CHECK-POINT. I don't understand why they need so much security if they're already protected by two layers of fence, one of which is electrified, and a few layers of guards, but this is not my world to question.

No, this is not my world at all.

Tris touches my shoulder and points down the long entryway. "Look at that."

Standing at the far end of the room, outside the security checkpoint, is a huge block of stone with a glass apparatus suspended above it. It's a clear example of the things we will see here that we don't understand. I also don't understand the hunger in Tris's eyes, devouring everything around us as if it alone can sustain her. Sometimes I feel like we are the same, but sometimes, like right now, I feel the separation between our personalities like I've just run into a wall.

Christina says something to Tris, and they both grin. Everything I hear is muffled and distorted.

"Are you all right?" Cara asks me.

"Yeah," I say automatically.

"You know, it would be perfectly logical for you to be panicking right now," she says. "No need to continually insist upon your unshakable masculinity."

"My . . . what?"

She smiles, and I realize that she was joking.

All the people at the security checkpoint step aside,

forming a tunnel for us to walk through. Ahead of us, Zoe announces, "Weapons are not allowed inside this facility, but if you leave them at the security checkpoint you can pick them up as you exit, if you choose to do so. After you drop them off, we'll go through the scanners and be on our way."

"That woman is irritating," Cara says.

"What?" I say. "Why?"

"She can't separate herself from her own knowledge," she says as she draws her weapon. "She keeps saying things like they're obvious when they are not, in fact, obvious."

"You're right," I say without conviction. "That is irritating."

Ahead of me, I see Zoe putting her gun into a gray container and then walking into a scanner—it is a man-sized box with a tunnel through the middle, just wide enough for a body. I draw my own gun, which is heavy with unused bullets, and put it in the container the security guard holds out to me, where all the others' guns are.

I watch Zoe go through the scanner, then Amar, Peter, Caleb, Cara, and Christina. As I stand at the edge of it, at the walls that will squeeze my body between them, I feel the beginnings of panic again, the numb hands and the tight chest. The scanner reminds me of the wooden box that traps me in my fear landscape, squeezing my bones together.

I cannot, will not panic here.

I force my feet to move into the scanner, and stand in the middle, where all the others stood. I hear something moving in the walls on either side of me, and then there's a high-pitched beep. I shudder, and all I can see is the guard's hand, motioning me forward.

It is now okay to escape.

I stumble out of the scanner, and the air opens up around me. Cara gives me a pointed look, but doesn't say anything.

When Tris takes my hand after going through the scanner herself, I barely feel it. I remember going through my fear landscape with her, our bodies pressed together in the wooden box that enclosed us, my palm against her chest, feeling her heartbeat. It's enough to ground me in reality again.

Once Uriah is through, Zoe waves us forward again.

Beyond the security checkpoint, the facility is not as dingy as it was before. The floors are still tile, but they are polished to perfection, and there are windows everywhere. Down one long hallway I see rows of lab tables and computers, and it reminds me of Erudite headquarters, but it's brighter here, and nothing seems to be hidden.

Zoe leads us down a darker passageway on the right. As we walk past people, they stop to watch, and I feel their eyes on me like little beams of heat, making me warm from throat to cheeks.

We walk for a long time, deeper into the compound, and then Zoe stops, facing us.

Behind her is a large circle of blank screens, like moths circling a flame. People within the circle sit at low desks, typing furiously on still more screens, these ones facing out instead of in. It's a control room, but it's out in the open, and I'm not sure what they're observing here, since all the screens are dark. Clustered around the screens that face in are chairs and benches and tables, like people gather here to watch at their leisure.

A few feet in front of the control room is an older man wearing a smile and a dark blue uniform, just like all the others. When he sees us approaching, he spreads his hands as if to welcome us. David, I assume.

"This," the man says, "is what we've waited for since the very beginning."

CHAPTER FIFTEEN

TRIS

I TAKE THE photograph from my pocket. The man in front of me—David—is in it, next to my mother, his face a little smoother, his middle a little trimmer.

I cover my mother's face with my fingertip. All the hope growing inside me has withered. If my mother, or my father, or my friends were still alive, they would have been waiting by the doors for our arrival. I should have known better than to think what happened with Amar— whatever it was—could happen again.

"My name is David. As Zoe probably told you already, I am the leader of the Bureau of Genetic Welfare. I'm going to do my best to explain things," David says. "The first thing you should know is that the information Edith

Prior gave you is only partly true."

At the name "Prior" his eyes settle on me. My body shakes with anticipation—ever since I saw that video I've been desperate for answers, and I'm about to get them.

"She provided only as much information as you needed to meet the goals of our experiments," says David. "And in many cases, that meant oversimplifying, omitting, and even outright falsehood. Now that you are here, there is no need for any of those things."

"You all keep talking about 'experiments,'" Tobias says. "*What* experiments?"

"Yes, well, I was getting to that." David looks at Amar. "Where did they start when they explained it to you?"

"Doesn't matter where you start. You can't make it easier to take," Amar says, picking at his cuticles.

David considers this for a moment, then clears his throat.

"A long time ago, the United States government—"

"The united what?" Uriah asks.

"It's a country," says Amar. "A large one. It has specific borders and its own governing body, and we're in the middle of it right now. We can talk about it later. Go ahead, sir."

David presses his thumb into his palm and massages his hand, clearly disconcerted by all the interruptions.

He begins again:

"A few centuries ago, the government of this country became interested in enforcing certain desirable behaviors in its citizens. There had been studies that indicated that violent tendencies could be partially traced to a person's genes—a gene called 'the murder gene' was the first of these, but there were quite a few more, genetic predispositions toward cowardice, dishonesty, low intelligence—all the qualities, in other words, that ultimately contribute to a broken society."

We were taught that the factions were formed to solve a problem, the problem of our flawed natures. Apparently the people David is describing, whoever they were, believed in that problem too.

I know so little about genetics—just what I can see passed down from parent to child, in my face and in friends' faces. I can't imagine isolating a gene for murder, or cowardice, or dishonesty. Those things seem too nebulous to have a concrete location in a person's body. But I'm not a scientist.

"Obviously there are quite a few factors that determine personality, including a person's upbringing and experiences," David continues, "but despite the peace and prosperity that had reigned in this country for nearly a century, it seemed advantageous to our ancestors to reduce the risk of these undesirable qualities showing up in our population by correcting them. In other words, by editing humanity.

"That's how the genetic manipulation experiment was born. It takes several generations for any kind of genetic manipulation to manifest, but people were selected from the general population in large numbers, according to their backgrounds or behavior, and they were given the option to give a gift to our future generations, a genetic alteration that would make their descendants just a little bit better."

I look around at the others. Peter's mouth is puckered with disdain. Caleb is scowling. Cara's mouth has fallen open, like she is hungry for answers and intends to eat them from the air. Christina just looks skeptical, one eyebrow raised, and Tobias is staring at his shoes.

I feel like I am not hearing anything new—just the same philosophy that spawned the factions, driving people to manipulate their genes instead of separating into virtue-based groups. I understand it. On some level I even agree with it. But I don't know how it relates to us, here, now.

"But when the genetic manipulations began to take effect, the alterations had disastrous consequences. As it turns out, the attempt had resulted not in corrected genes, but in damaged ones," David says. "Take away someone's fear, or low intelligence, or dishonesty . . . and you take away their compassion. Take away someone's aggression and you take away their motivation, or their ability to assert themselves. Take away their selfishness and you take away their sense of self-preservation. If you think about it, I'm sure you know exactly what I mean."

I tick off each quality in my mind as he says it—fear, low intelligence, dishonesty, aggression, selfishness. He *is* talking about the factions. And he's right to say that every faction loses something when it gains a virtue: the Dauntless, brave but cruel; the Erudite, intelligent but vain; the Amity, peaceful but passive; the Candor, honest but inconsiderate; the Abnegation, selfless but stifling.

"Humanity has never been perfect, but the genetic alterations made it worse than it had ever been before. This manifested itself in what we call the Purity War. A civil war, waged by those with damaged genes, against the government and everyone with pure genes. The Purity War caused a level of destruction formerly unheard of on American soil, eliminating almost half of the country's population."

"The visual is up," says one of the people at a desk in the control room.

A map appears on the screen above David's head. It is an unfamiliar shape, so I'm not sure what it's supposed to represent, but it is covered with patches of pink, red, and dark-crimson lights.

"This is our country before the Purity War," David says. "And *this* is after—"

The lights start to recede, the patches shrinking like puddles of water drying in the sun. Then I realize that the red lights were people—people, disappearing, their lights going out. I stare at the screen, unable to wrap my mind around such a substantial loss.

David continues, "When the war was finally over, the people demanded a permanent solution to the genetic problem. And that is why the Bureau of Genetic Welfare was formed. Armed with all the scientific knowledge at our government's disposal, our predecessors designed experiments to restore humanity to its genetically pure state."

"They called for genetically damaged individuals to come forward so that the Bureau could alter their genes. The Bureau then placed them in secure environments to settle in for the long haul, equipped with basic versions of the serums to help them control their society. They would wait for the passage of time—for the generations to pass, for each one to produce more genetically healed humans. Or, as you currently know them . . . the Divergent."

Ever since Tori told me the word for what I am—Divergent—I have wanted to know what it means. And here is the simplest answer I have received: "Divergent" means that my genes are healed. Pure. Whole. I should feel relieved to know the real answer at last. But I just feel like something is off, itching in the back of my mind.

I thought that "Divergent" explained everything that I am and everything that I could be. Maybe I was wrong.

I am starting to feel short of breath as the revelations begin to work their way into my mind and heart, as David peels the layers of lies and secrets away. I touch my chest to feel my heartbeat, to try to steady myself.

"Your city is one of those experiments for genetic healing, and by far the most successful one, because of the behavioral modification portion. The factions, that is." David smiles at us, like it's something we should be proud of, but I am not proud. They created us, they shaped our world, they told us what to believe.

If they told us what to believe, and we didn't come to it on our own, is it still true? I press my hand harder against my chest. *Steady.*

"The factions were our predecessors' attempt to incorporate a 'nurture' element to the experiment—they discovered that mere genetic correction was not enough to change the way people behaved. A new social order, combined with the genetic modification, was determined to be the most complete solution to the behavioral problems that the genetic damage had created." David's smile fades as he looks around at all of us. I don't know what he expected—for us to smile back? He continues, "The factions were later introduced to most of our other experiments, three of which are currently active. We have gone to great lengths to protect you, observe you, and learn from you."

Cara runs her hands over her hair, as if checking for loose strands. Finding none, she says, "So when Edith Prior said we were supposed to determine the cause of Divergence and come out and help you, that was . . ."

"'Divergent' is the name we decided to give to those who have reached the desired level of genetic healing," says David. "We wanted to make sure that the leaders of your city valued them. We didn't expect the leader of Erudite to start hunting them down—or for the Abnegation to even tell her what they were—and contrary to what Edith Prior said, we never *really* intended for you to send a Divergent army out to us. We don't, after all, truly need your help. We just need your healed genes to remain intact and to be passed on to future generations."

"So what you're saying is that if we're not Divergent, we're *damaged*," Caleb says. His voice is shaking. I never thought I would see Caleb on the verge of tears because of something like this, but he is.

Steady, I tell myself again, and take another deep, slow breath.

"*Genetically* damaged, yes," says David. "However, we were surprised to discover that the behavioral modification component of our city's experiment was quite effective—up until recently, it actually helped quite a bit with the behavioral problems that made the genetic manipulation so problematic to begin with. So generally, you would not be able to tell whether a person's genes were damaged or healed from their behavior."

"I'm smart," Caleb says. "So you're saying that because my ancestors were *altered* to be smart, I, their descendant, can't be fully compassionate. I, and every other genetically damaged person, am limited by my damaged genes. And the Divergent are not."

"Well," says David, lifting a shoulder. "Think about it."

Caleb looks at me for the first time in days, and I stare back. Is that the explanation for Caleb's betrayal—his damaged genes? Like a disease that he can't heal, and can't control? It doesn't seem right.

"Genes aren't everything," Amar says. "People, even genetically damaged people, make choices. That's what matters."

I think of my father, a born Erudite, not Divergent; a man who could not help but be smart, choosing Abnegation, engaging in a lifelong struggle against his own nature, and ultimately fulfilling it. A man warring with himself, just as I war with myself.

That internal war doesn't seem like a product of genetic damage—it seems completely, purely *human*.

I look at Tobias. He is so washed out, so slouched, he looks like he might pass out. He's not alone in his reaction: Christina, Peter, Uriah, and Caleb all look stunned. Cara has the hem of her shirt pinched between her fingers, and she is moving her thumb over the fabric, frowning.

"This is a lot to process," says David.

That is an understatement.

Beside me, Christina snorts.

"And you've all been up all night," David finishes, like there was no interruption. "So I'll show you to a place where you can get some rest and food."

"Wait," I say. I think of the photograph in my pocket, and how Zoe knew my name when she gave it to me. I think of what David said, about observing us and learning from us. I think of the rows of screens, blank, right in front of me. "You said you've been observing us. How?"

Zoe purses her lips. David nods to one of the people at the desks behind him. All at once, all the screens turn on, each of them showing footage from different cameras. On the ones nearest to me, I see Dauntless headquarters. The Merciless Mart. Millennium Park. The Hancock building. The Hub.

"You've always known that the Dauntless observe the

city with security cameras," David says. "Well, we have access to those cameras too."

They've been watching us.

+ + +

I think about leaving.

We walk past the security checkpoint on our way to wherever David is taking us, and I think about walking through it again, picking up my gun, and running from this place where they've been watching me. Since I was small. My first steps, my first words, my first day of school, my first kiss.

Watching, when Peter attacked me. When my faction was put under a simulation and turned into an army. When my parents died.

What else have they seen?

The only thing that stops me from going is the photograph in my pocket. I can't leave these people before I find out how they knew my mother.

David takes us through the compound to a carpeted area with potted plants on either side. The wallpaper is old and yellowed, peeling from the corners of the walls. We follow him into a large room with high ceilings and wood floors and lights that glow orange-yellow. There are cots arranged in two straight rows, with trunks beside them for what we brought with us, and large windows with elegant curtains on the opposite end of the room. When I get closer to them, I see that they're worn and frayed at the edges.

David tells us that this part of the compound was a hotel, connected to the airport by a tunnel, and this room was once the ballroom. Again the words mean nothing to us, but he doesn't seem to notice.

"This is just a temporary dwelling, of course. Once you decide what to do, we will settle you somewhere else, whether it's in this compound or elsewhere. Zoe will ensure that you are well taken care of," he says. "I will be back tomorrow to see how you're all doing."

I look back at Tobias, who is pacing back and forth in front of the windows, gnawing on his fingernails. I never realized he had that habit. Maybe he was never distressed enough to do it before.

I could stay and try to comfort him, but I need answers about my mother, and I'm not going to wait any longer. I'm sure that Tobias, of all people, will understand. I follow David into the hallway. Just outside the room he leans against the wall and scratches the back of his neck.

"Hi," I say. "My name is Tris. I believe you knew my mother."

He jumps a little, but eventually smiles at me. I cross my arms. I feel the same way I did when Peter pulled my towel away during Dauntless initiation, to be cruel:

exposed, embarrassed, angry. Maybe it's not fair to direct all of that at David, but I can't help it. He's the leader of this compound—of the Bureau.

"Yes, of course," he says. "I recognize you."

From where? The creepy cameras that followed my every move? I pull my arms tighter across my chest.

"Right." I wait a beat, then say, "I need to know about my mother. Zoe gave me a picture of her, and you were standing right next to her in it, so I figured you could help."

"Ah," he says. "Can I see the picture?"

I take it out of my pocket and offer it to him. He smooths it down with his fingertips, and there is a strange smile on his face as he looks at it, like he's caressing it with his eyes. I shift my weight from one foot to the other—I feel like I'm intruding on a private moment.

"She took a trip back to us once," he says. "Before she settled into motherhood. That's when we took this."

"*Back* to you?" I say. "Was she one of you?"

"Yes," David says simply, like it's not a word that changes my entire world. "She came from this place. We sent her into the city when she was young to resolve a problem in the experiment."

"So she knew," I say, and my voice shakes, but I don't know why. "She *knew* about this place, and what was outside the fence."

David looks puzzled, his bushy eyebrows furrowed. "Well, of course."

The shaking moves down my arms and into my hands, and soon my entire body is shuddering, as if rejecting some kind of poison that I've swallowed, and the poison is knowledge, the knowledge of this place and its screens and all the lies I built my life on. "She knew you were *watching* us at every moment . . . watching as she *died* and my father died and everyone started killing each other! And did you send in someone to help her, to help me? No! No, all you did was take notes."

"Tris . . ."

He tries to reach for me, and I push his hand away. "Don't call me that. You shouldn't know that name. You shouldn't know anything about us."

Shivering, I walk back into the room.

+ + +

Back inside, the others have picked their beds and put their things down. It's just us in here, no intruders. I lean against the wall by the door and push my palms down the front of my pants to get the sweat off.

No one seems to be adjusting well. Peter lies facing the wall. Uriah and Christina sit side by side, having a conversation in low voices. Caleb is massaging his temples with his fingertips. Tobias is still pacing and gnawing on his fingernails. And Cara is on her own, dragging her hand over her face. For the first time since I met her, she looks upset, the Erudite armor gone.

I sit down across from her. "You don't look so good."

Her hair, usually smooth and perfect in its knot, is disheveled. She glowers at me. "That's kind of you to say."

"Sorry," I say. "I didn't mean it that way."

"I know." She sighs. "I'm . . . I'm an Erudite, you know."

I smile a little. "Yeah, I know."

"No." Cara shakes her head. "It's the only thing I am. Erudite. And now they've told me that's the result of some kind of flaw in my genetics . . . and that the factions them-selves are just a mental prison to keep us under control. Just like Evelyn Johnson and the factionless said." She pauses. "So why form the Allegiant? Why bother to come out here?"

I didn't realize how much Cara had already cleaved to the idea of being an Allegiant, loyal to the faction system, loyal to our founders. For me it was just a temporary iden-tity, powerful because it could get me out of the city. For her the attachment must have been much deeper.

"It's still good that we came out here," I say. "We found out the truth. That's not valuable to you?"

"Of course it is," Cara says softly. "But it means I need

other words for what I am."

Just after my mother died, I grabbed hold of my Divergence like it was a hand outstretched to save me. I needed that word to tell me who I was when everything else was coming apart around me. But now I'm wondering if I need it anymore, if we ever really *need* these words, "Dauntless," "Erudite," "Divergent," "Allegiant," or if we can just be friends or lovers or siblings, defined instead by the choices we make and the love and loyalty that binds us.

"Better check on him," Cara says, nodding to Tobias.

"Yeah," I say.

I cross the room and stand in front of the windows, staring at what we can see of the compound, which is just more of the same glass and steel, pavement and grass and fences. When he sees me, he stops pacing and stands next to me instead.

"You all right?" I say to him.

"Yeah." He sits on the windowsill, facing me, so we're at eye level. "I mean, no, not really. Right now I'm just thinking about how meaningless it all was. The faction system, I mean."

He rubs the back of his neck, and I wonder if he's thinking about the tattoos on his back.

"We put everything we had into it," he says. "All of us. Even if we didn't realize we were doing it."

"That's what you're thinking about?" I raise my eyebrows. "Tobias, they were *watching* us. Everything that happened, everything we did. They didn't intervene, they just invaded our privacy. Constantly."

He rubs his temple with his fingertips. "I guess. That's not what's bothering me, though."

I must give him an incredulous look without meaning to, because he shakes his head. "Tris, I worked in the Dauntless control room. There were cameras everywhere, all the time. I tried to warn you that people were watching you during your initiation, remember?"

I remember his eyes shifting to the ceiling, to the corner. His cryptic warnings, hissed between his teeth. I never realized he was warning me about cameras—it just never occurred to me before.

"It used to bother me," he says. "But I got over it a long time ago. We always thought we were on our own, and now it turns out we were right—they left us on our own. That's just the way it is."

"I guess I don't accept that," I say. "If you see someone in trouble, you should help them. Experiment or not. And . . . God." I cringe. "All the things they saw."

He smiles at me, a little.

"What?" I demand.

"I was just thinking of some of the things they saw,"

he says, putting his hand on my waist. I glare at him for a moment, but I can't sustain it, not with him grinning at me like that. Not knowing that he's trying to make me feel better. I smile a little.

I sit next to him on the windowsill, my hands wedged between my legs and the wood. "You know, the Bureau setting up the factions is not much different than what we thought happened: A long time ago, a group of people decided that the faction system would be the best way to live—or the way to get people to live the best lives they could."

He doesn't respond at first, just chews on the inside of his lip and looks at our feet, side by side on the floor. My toes brush the ground, not quite reaching it.

"That helps, actually," he says. "But there's so much that was a lie, it's hard to figure out what was true, what was real, what matters."

I take his hand, slipping my fingers between his. He touches his forehead to mine.

I catch myself thinking, *Thank God for this*, out of habit, and then I understand what he's so concerned about. What if my parents' God, their whole belief system, is just something concocted by a bunch of scientists to keep us under control? And not just their beliefs about God and whatever else is out there, but about right and wrong, about selflessness? Do all those things have to change because we know how our world was made?

I don't know.

The thought rattles me. So I kiss him—slowly, so I can feel the warmth of his mouth and the gentle pressure and his breaths as we pull away.

"Why is it," I say, "that we always find ourselves surrounded by people?"

"I don't know," he says. "Maybe because we're stupid."

I laugh, and it's laughter, not light, that casts out the darkness building within me, that reminds me I am still alive, even in this strange place where everything I've ever known is coming apart. I know some things—I know that I'm not alone, that I have friends, that I'm in love. I know where I came from. I know that I don't want to die, and for me, that's something—more than I could have said a few weeks ago.

+ + +

That night we push our cots just a little closer together, and look into each other's eyes in the moments before we fall asleep. When he finally drifts off, our fingers are twisted together in the space between the beds.

I smile a little, and let myself go too.

CHAPTER SIXTEEN

TOBIAS

THE SUN STILL hasn't completely set when we fall asleep, but I wake a few hours later, at midnight, my mind too busy for rest, swarming with thoughts and questions and doubts. Tris released me earlier, and her fingers now brush the floor. She is sprawled over the mattress, her hair covering her eyes.

I shove my feet into my shoes and walk the hallways, shoelaces slapping the carpets. I am so accustomed to the Dauntless compound that I am not used to the creak of wooden floors beneath me—I am used to the scrape and echo of stone, and the roar and pulse of water in the chasm.

A week into my initiation, Amar—worried that I was becoming increasingly isolated and obsessive—invited me to join some of the older Dauntless for a game of Dare.

For my dare, we went back to the Pit for me to get my first tattoo, the patch of Dauntless flames covering my rib cage. It was agonizing. I relished every second of it.

I reach the end of one hallway and find myself in an atrium, surrounded by the smell of wet earth. Everywhere plants and trees are suspended in water, the same way they were in the Amity greenhouses. In the center of the room is a tree in a giant water tank, lifted high above the floor so I can see the tangle of roots beneath it, strangely human, like nerves.

"You're not nearly as vigilant as you used to be," Amar says from behind me. "Followed you all the way here from the hotel lobby."

"What do you want?" I tap the tank with my knuckles, sending ripples through the water.

"I thought you might like an explanation for why I'm not dead," he says.

"I thought about it," I say. "They never let us see your body. It wouldn't be that hard to fake a death if you never show the body."

"Sounds like you've got it all figured out." Amar claps his hands together. "Well, I'll just go, then, if you're not curious. . . ."

I cross my arms.

Amar runs a hand over his black hair, tying it back with a rubber band. "They faked my death because I was

Divergent, and Jeanine had started killing the Divergent. They tried to save as many as they could before she got to them, but it was tricky, you know, because she was always a step ahead."

"Are there others?" I say.

"A few," he says.

"Any named Prior?"

Amar shakes his head. "No, Natalie Prior is actually dead, unfortunately. She was the one who helped me get out. She also helped this other guy too . . . George Wu. Know him? He's on a patrol right now, or he would have come with me to get you. His sister is still inside the city."

The name clutches at my stomach.

"Oh God," I say, and I lean into the tank wall.

"What? You know him?"

I shake my head.

I can't imagine it. There were just a few hours between Tori's death and our arrival. On a normal day, a few hours can contain long stretches of watch-checking, of empty time. But yesterday, just a few hours placed an impenetrable barrier between Tori and her brother.

"Tori is his sister," I say. "She tried to leave the city with us."

"*Tried* to," repeats Amar. "Ah. Wow. That's . . ."

Both of us are quiet for a while. George will never get to reunite with his sister, and she died thinking he had been murdered by Jeanine. There isn't anything to say—at least, not anything that's worth saying.

Now that my eyes have adjusted to the light, I can see that the plants in this room were selected for beauty, not practicality—flowers and ivy and clusters of purple or red leaves. The only flowers I've ever seen are wildflowers, or apple blossoms in the Amity orchards. These are more extravagant than those, vibrant and complex, petals folded into petals. Whatever this place is, it has not needed to be as pragmatic as our city.

"That woman who found your body," I say. "Was she just . . . lying about it?"

"People can't really be trusted to lie consistently." He quirks his eyebrows. "Never thought I would say that phrase—it's true, anyway. She was reset—her memory was altered to include me jumping off the Pire, and the body that was planted wasn't actually me. But it was too messed up for anyone to notice."

"She was reset. You mean, with the Abnegation serum."

"We call it 'memory serum,' since it doesn't technically just belong to the Abnegation, but yeah. That's the one."

I was angry with him before. I'm not really sure why. Maybe I was just angry that the world had become such a complicated place, that I have never known even a fraction of the truth about it. Or that I allowed myself to grieve for someone who was never really gone, the same way

I grieved for my mother all the years I thought she was dead. Tricking someone into grief is one of the cruelest tricks a person can play, and it's been played on me twice.

But as I look at him, my anger ebbs away, like the changing of the tide. And standing in the place of my anger is my initiation instructor and friend, alive again.

I grin.

"So you're alive," I say.

"More importantly," he says, pointing at me, "you are no longer upset about it."

He grabs my arm and pulls me into an embrace, slapping my back with one hand. I try to return his enthusiasm, but it doesn't come naturally—when we break apart, my face is hot. And judging by how he bursts into laughter, it's also bright red.

"Once a Stiff, always a Stiff," he says.

"Whatever," I say. "So do you like it here, then?"

Amar shrugs. "I don't really have a choice, but yeah, I like it fine. I work in security, obviously, since that's all I was trained to do. We'd love to have you, but you're probably too good for it."

"I haven't quite resigned myself to staying here just yet," I say. "But thanks, I guess."

"There's nowhere better out there," he says. "All the other cities—that's where most of the country lives, in these big metropolitan areas, like our city—are dirty and dangerous, unless you know the right people. Here at least there's clean water and food and safety."

I shift my weight, uncomfortable. I don't want to think about staying here, making this my home. I already feel trapped by my own disappointment. This is not what I imagined when I thought of escaping my parents and the bad memories they gave me. But I don't want to disturb the peace with Amar now that I finally feel like I have my friend back, so I just say, "I'll take that under advisement."

"Listen, there's something else you should know."

"What? More resurrections?"

"It's not exactly a resurrection if I was never dead, is it?" Amar shakes his head. "No, it's about the city. Someone heard it in the control room today—Marcus's trial is scheduled for tomorrow morning."

I knew it was coming—I knew Evelyn would save him for last, would savor every moment she spent watching him squirm under truth serum like he was her last meal. I just didn't realize that I would be able to see it, if I wanted to. I thought I was finally free of them, all of them, forever.

"Oh," is all I can say.

I still feel numb and confused when I walk back to the dormitory later and crawl back into bed. I don't know what I'll do.

CHAPTER
SEVENTEEN

TRIS

I WAKE JUST before the sun. No one else stirs in their cot—
Tobias's arm is draped over his eyes, but his shoes are now
on, like he got up and walked around in the middle of the
night. Christina's head is buried beneath her pillow. I lay
for a few minutes, finding patterns in the ceiling, then
put on my shoes and run my fingers through my hair to
flatten it.

The hallways in the compound are empty except for a
few stragglers. I assume they are just finishing the night
shift, because they are hunched over screens, their chins
propped on their hands, or slumped against broomsticks,
barely remembering to sweep. I put my hands in my
pockets and follow the signs to the entrance. I want to get

a better look at the sculpture I saw yesterday.

Whoever built this place must have loved light. There is glass in the curve of each hallway's ceiling and along each lower wall. Even now, when it is barely morning, there is plenty of light to see by.

I check my back pocket for the badge Zoe handed to me at dinner last night, and pass the security checkpoint with it in hand. Then I see the sculpture, a few hundred yards away from the doors we entered through yesterday, gloomy and massive and mysterious, like a living entity.

It is a huge slab of dark stone, square and rough, like the rocks at the bottom of the chasm. A large crack runs through the middle of it, and there are streaks of lighter rock near the edges. Suspended above the slab is a glass tank of the same dimensions, full of water. A light placed above the center of the tank shines through the water, refracting as it ripples. I hear a faint noise, a drop of water hitting the stone. It comes from a small tube running through the center of the tank. At first I think the tank is just leaking, but another drop falls, then a third, and a fourth, at the same interval. A few drops collect, and then disappear down a narrow channel in the stone. They must be intentional.

"Hello." Zoe stands on the other side of the sculpture. "I'm sorry, I was about to go to the dormitory for you, then saw you heading this way and wondered if you were lost."

"No, I'm not lost," I say. "This is where I meant to go."

"Ah." She stands beside me and crosses her arms. She is about as tall as I am, but she stands straighter, so she seems taller. "Yeah, it's pretty weird, right?"

As she talks I watch the freckles on her cheeks, dappled like sunlight through dense leaves.

"Does it mean something?"

"It's the symbol of the Bureau of Genetic Welfare," she says. "The slab of stone is the problem we're facing. The tank of water is our potential for changing that problem. And the drop of water is what we're actually able to do, at any given time."

I can't help it—I laugh. "Not very encouraging, is it?"

She smiles. "That's one way of looking at it. I prefer to look at it another way—which is that if they are persistent enough, even tiny drops of water, over time, can change the rock forever. And it will never change back."

She points to the center of the slab, where there is a small impression, like a shallow bowl carved into the stone.

"That, for example, wasn't there when they installed this thing."

I nod, and watch the next drop fall. Even though I'm wary of the Bureau and everyone in it, I can feel the quiet hope of the sculpture working its way through me. It's a practical symbol, communicating the patient attitude that has allowed the people here to stay for so long, watching and waiting. But I have to ask.

"Wouldn't it be more effective to unleash the whole tank at once?" I imagine the wave of water colliding with the rock and spilling over the tile floor, collecting around my shoes. Doing a little at once can fix something, eventually, but I feel like when you believe that something is truly a problem, you throw everything you have at it, because you just can't help yourself.

"Momentarily," she says. "But then we wouldn't have any water left to do anything else, and genetic damage isn't the kind of problem that can be solved with one big charge."

"I understand that," I say. "I'm just wondering if it's a good thing to resign yourself quite this much to small steps when you could take some big ones."

"Like what?"

I shrug. "I guess I don't really know. But it's worth thinking about."

"Fair enough."

"So . . . you said you were looking for me?" I say. "Why?"

"Oh!" Zoe touches her forehead. "It slipped my mind. David asked me to find you and take you to the labs.

There's something there that belonged to your mother."

"My mother?" My voice comes out sounding strangled and too high. She leads me away from the sculpture and toward the security checkpoint again.

"Fair warning: You might get stared at," Zoe says as we walk through the security scanner. There are more people in the hallways up ahead now than there were earlier—it must be time for them to start work. "Your face is a familiar one here. People in the Bureau watch the screens often, and for the past few months, you've been involved in a lot of interesting things. A lot of the younger people think you're downright heroic."

"Oh, good," I say, a sour taste in my mouth. "Heroism is what I was focused on. Not, you know, trying not to die."

Zoe stops. "I'm sorry. I didn't mean to make light of what you've been through."

I still feel uncomfortable with the idea that everyone has been watching us, like I need to cover myself or hide where they can't look at me anymore. But there's not much Zoe can do about it, so I don't say anything.

Most of the people walking the halls wear variations of the same uniform—it comes in dark blue or dull green, and some of them wear the jackets or jumpsuits or sweat-shirts open, revealing T-shirts of a wide variety of colors, some with pictures drawn on them.

"Do the colors of the uniforms mean anything?" I ask Zoe.

"Yes, actually. Dark blue means scientist or researcher, and green means support staff—they do maintenance, upkeep, things like that."

"So they're like the factionless."

"No," she says. "No, the dynamic is different here—everyone does what they can to support the mission. Everyone is valued and important."

She was right: People do stare at me. Most of them just look at me for a little too long, but some point, and some even say my name, like it belongs to them. It makes me feel cramped, like I can't move the way I want to.

"A lot of the support staff used to be in the experiment in Indianapolis—another city, not far from here," Zoe says. "But for them, this transition has been a little bit easier than it will be for you—Indianapolis didn't have the behavioral components of your city." She pauses. "The factions, I mean. After a few generations, when your city didn't tear itself apart and the others did, the Bureau implemented the faction components in the newer cities—Saint Louis, Detroit, and Minneapolis—using the relatively new Indianapolis experiment as a control group. The Bureau always placed experiments in the Midwest, because there's more space between urban areas here. Out east everything is closer together."

"So in Indianapolis you just . . . corrected their genes and shoved them in a city somewhere? Without factions?"

"They had a complex system of rules, but . . . yes, that's essentially what happened."

"And it didn't work very well?"

"No." She purses her lips. "Genetically damaged people who have been conditioned by suffering and are not taught to live differently, as the factions would have taught them to, are very destructive. That experiment failed quickly—within three generations. Chicago—your city—and the other cities that have factions have made it through much more than that."

Chicago. It's so strange to have a name for the place that was always just home to me. It makes the city smaller in my mind.

"So you guys have been doing this for a long time," I say.

"Quite some time, yes. The Bureau is different from most government agencies, because of the focused nature of our work and our contained, relatively remote location. We pass on knowledge and purpose to our children, instead of relying on appointments or hiring. I've been training for what I'm doing now for my entire life."

Through the abundant windows I see a strange vehicle—it's shaped like a bird, with two wing structures and a pointed nose, but it has wheels, like a car.

"Is that for air travel?" I say, pointing at it.

"Yes." She smiles. "It's an airplane. We might be able to take you up in one sometime, if it doesn't seem too *daunting* for you."

I don't react to the play on words. I can't quite forget how she recognized me on sight.

David is standing near one of the doors up ahead. He raises his hand in a wave when he sees us.

"Hello, Tris," he says. "Thank you for bringing her, Zoe."

"You're welcome, sir," Zoe says. "I'll leave you to it, then. Lots of work to do."

She smiles at me, then walks away. I don't want her to leave—now that she's gone, I'm left with David and the memory of how I yelled at him yesterday. He doesn't say anything about it, just scans his badge in the door sensor to open it.

The room beyond it is an office with no windows. A young man, maybe Tobias's age, sits at one desk, and another one, across the room, is empty. The young man looks up when we come in, taps something on his computer screen, and stands.

"Hello, sir," he says. "Can I help you?"

"Matthew. Where's your supervisor?" David says.

"He's foraging for food in the cafeteria," Matthew says.

"Well, maybe you can help me, then. I'll need Natalie Wright's file loaded on a portable screen. Can you do that?"

Wright? I think. Was that my mother's real last name?

"Of course," Matthew says, and he sits again. He types something on his computer and pulls up a series of documents that I'm not close enough to see clearly. "Okay, it just has to transfer.

"You must be Natalie's daughter, Beatrice." He props his chin on his hand and looks at me critically. His eyes are so dark they look black, and they slant a little at the edges. He does not look impressed or surprised to see me. "You don't look much like her."

"Tris," I say automatically. But I find it comforting that he doesn't know my nickname—that must mean he doesn't spend all his time staring at the screens like our lives in the city are entertainment. "And yeah, I know."

David pulls a chair over, letting it screech on the tile, and pats it.

"Sit. I'll give you a screen with all Natalie's files on it so that you and your brother can read them yourselves, but while they're loading I might as well tell you the story."

I sit on the edge of the chair, and he sits behind the desk of Matthew's supervisor, turning a half-empty coffee cup in circles on the metal.

"Let me start by saying that your mother was a fantastic discovery. We located her almost by accident inside the damaged world, and her genes were nearly perfect." David beams. "We took her out of a bad situation and brought her here. She spent several years here, but then we encountered a crisis within your city's walls, and she volunteered to be placed inside to resolve it. I'm sure you know all about that, though."

For a few seconds all I can do is blink at him. My mother came from outside this place? Where?

It hits me, again, that she walked these halls, watched the city on the screens in the control room. Had she sat in this chair? Had her feet touched these tiles? Suddenly I feel like there are invisible marks of my mother everywhere, on every wall and doorknob and pillar.

I grip the edge of the seat and try to organize my thoughts enough to ask a question.

"No, I don't know," I say. "What crisis?"

"The Erudite representative had just begun to kill the Divergent, of course," he says. "His name was Nor—Norman?"

"Norton," says Matthew. "Jeanine's predecessor. Seems he passed on the idea of killing off the Divergent to her, right before his heart attack."

"Thank you. Anyway, we sent Natalie in to investigate

the situation and to stop the deaths. We never dreamed she would be in there for so long, of course, but she was useful—we had never thought about having an insider before, and she was able to do many things that were invaluable to us. As well as building a life for herself, which obviously includes you."

I frown. "But the Divergent were still being killed when I was an initiate."

"You only know about the ones who died," David says. "Not about the ones who didn't die. Some of them are here, in this compound. I believe you met Amar earlier? He's one of them. Some of the rescued Divergent needed some distance from your experiment—it was too hard for them to watch the people they had once known and loved going about their lives, so they were trained to integrate into life outside the Bureau. But yes, she did important work, your mother."

She also told quite a few lies, and very few truths. I wonder if my father knew who she was, where she was really from. He was an Abnegation leader, after all, and as such, one of the keepers of the truth. I have a sudden, horrifying thought: What if she only married him because she was supposed to, as part of her mission in the city? What if their entire relationship was a sham?

"So she wasn't really born Dauntless," I say as I sort

through the lies that must have been.

"When she first entered the city, it was as a Dauntless, because she already had tattoos and that would have been hard to explain to the natives. She was sixteen, but we said she was fifteen so she would have some time to adjust. Our intention was for her to . . ." He lifts a shoulder. "Well, you should read her file. I can't do a sixteen-year-old perspective justice."

As if on cue, Matthew opens a desk drawer and takes out a small, flat piece of glass. He taps it with one fingertip, and an image appears on it. It's one of the documents he just had open on his computer. He offers the tablet to me. It's sturdier than I expected it to be, hard and strong.

"Don't worry, it's practically indestructible," David says. "I'm sure you want to return to your friends. Matthew, would you please walk Miss Prior back to the hotel? I have some things to take care of."

"And I don't?" Matthew says. Then he winks. "Kidding, sir. I'll take her."

"Thank you," I say to David, before he walks out.

"Of course," he says. "Let me know if you have any questions."

"Ready?" Matthew says.

He's tall, maybe the same height as Caleb, and his black hair is artfully tousled in the front, like he spent a lot of time making it look like he'd just rolled out of bed that way. Under his dark blue uniform he wears a plain black T-shirt and a black string around his throat. It shifts over his Adam's apple when he swallows.

I walk with him out of the small office and down the hallway again. The crowd that was here before has thinned. They must have settled in to work, or breakfast. There are whole lives being lived in this place, sleeping and eating and working, bearing children and raising families and dying. This is a place my mother called home, once.

"I wonder when you're going to freak out," he says. "After finding out all this stuff at once."

"I'm not going to freak out," I say, feeling defensive. *I already did,* I think, but I'm not going to admit to that.

Matthew shrugs. "I would. But fair enough."

I see a sign that says HOTEL ENTRANCE up ahead. I clutch the screen to my chest, eager to get back to the dormitory and tell Tobias about my mother.

"Listen, one of the things my supervisor and I do is genetic testing," Matthew says. "I was wondering if you and that other guy—Marcus Eaton's son?—would mind coming in so that I can test your genes."

"Why?"

"Curiosity." He shrugs. "We haven't gotten to test the genes of someone in such a late generation of the experiment before, and you and Tobias seem to be somewhat . . . odd, in your manifestations of certain things."

I raise my eyebrows.

"You, for example, have displayed extraordinary serum resistance—most of the Divergent aren't as capable of resisting serums as you are," Matthew says. "And Tobias can resist simulations, but he doesn't display some of the characteristics we've come to expect of the Divergent. I can explain in more detail later."

I hesitate, not sure if I want to see my genes, or Tobias's genes, or to compare them, like it matters. But Matthew's expression seems eager, almost childlike, and I understand curiosity.

"I'll ask him if he's up for it," I say. "But I would be willing. When?"

"This morning okay?" he says. "I can come get you in an hour or so. You can't get into the labs without me anyway."

I nod. I feel excited, suddenly, to learn more about my genes, which feels like the same thing as reading my mother's journal: I will get pieces of her back.

CHAPTER EIGHTEEN

TOBIAS

IT'S STRANGE TO see people you don't know well in the morning, with sleepy eyes and pillow creases in their cheeks; to know that Christina is cheerful in the morning, and Peter wakes up with his hair perfectly flat, but Cara communicates only through a series of grunts, inching her way, limb by limb, toward coffee.

The first thing I do is shower and change into the clothes they provided for us, which aren't much different from the clothes I am accustomed to, but all the colors are mixed together like they don't mean anything to the people here, and they probably don't. I wear a black shirt and blue jeans and try to convince myself that it feels normal, that I feel normal, that I am adapting.

My father's trial is today. I haven't decided if I'm going to watch it or not.

When I return, Tris is already fully dressed, perched on the edge of one of the cots, like she's ready to leap to her feet at any moment. Just like Evelyn.

I grab a muffin from the tray of breakfast food that someone brought us, and sit across from her. "Good morning. You were up early."

"Yeah," she says, scooting her foot forward so it's wedged between mine. "Zoe found me at that big sculpture thing this morning—David had something to show me." She picks up the glass screen resting on the cot beside her. It glows when she touches it, showing a document. "It's my mother's file. She wrote a journal—a small one, from the look of it, but still." She shifts like she's uncomfortable. "I haven't looked at it much yet."

"So," I say, "why aren't you reading it?"

"I don't know." She puts it down, and the screen turns off automatically. "I think I'm afraid of it."

Abnegation children rarely know their parents in any significant way, because Abnegation parents never reveal themselves the way other parents do when their children grow to a particular age. They keep themselves wrapped in gray cloth armor and selfless acts, convinced that to share is to be self-indulgent. This is not just a piece of

Tris's mother, recovered; it's one of the first and last honest glimpses Tris will ever get of who Natalie Prior was.

I understand, then, why she holds it like it's a magical object, something that could disappear in a moment. And why she wants to leave it undiscovered for a while, which is the same way I feel about my father's trial. It could tell her something she doesn't want to know.

I follow her eyes across the room to where Caleb sits, chewing on a bite of cereal—morosely, like a pouting child.

"Are you going to show it to him?" I say.

She doesn't respond.

"Usually I don't advocate giving him anything," I say. "But in this case . . . this doesn't really just belong to you."

"I know that," she says, a little tersely. "Of course I'll show it to him. But I think I want to be alone with it first."

I can't argue with that. Most of my life has been spent keeping information close, turning it over and over in my mind. The impulse to share anything is a new one, the impulse to hide as natural as breathing.

She sighs, then breaks a piece off the muffin in my hand. I flick her fingers as she pulls away. "Hey. There are plenty more just five feet to your right."

"Then you shouldn't be so worried about losing some of yours," she says, grinning.

"Fair enough."

She pulls me toward her by the front of my shirt and

kisses me. I slip my hand under her chin and hold her still as I kiss her back.

Then I notice that she's stealing another pinch of muffin, and I pull away, glaring at her.

"Seriously," I say. "I'll get you one from that table. It'll only take me a second."

She grins. "So, there's something I wanted to ask you. Would you be up for undergoing a little genetic test this morning?"

The phrase "a little genetic test" strikes me as an oxymoron.

"Why?" I say. Asking to see my genes feels a little like asking me to strip down.

"Well, this guy I met—Matthew is his name—works in one of the labs here, and he says they would be interested in looking at our genetic material for research," she says. "And he asked about you, specifically, because you're sort of an anomaly."

"Anomaly?"

"Apparently you display some Divergent characteristics and you don't display others," she says. "I don't know. He's just curious about it. You don't have to do it."

The air around my head feels warmer and heavier. To alleviate the discomfort I touch the back of my neck, scratching at my hairline.

Sometime in the next hour or so, Marcus and Evelyn

will be on the screens. Suddenly I know that I can't watch.

So even though I don't *really* want to let a stranger examine the puzzle pieces that make up my existence, I say, "Sure. I'll do it."

"Great," she says, and she eats another pinch of my muffin. A piece of hair falls into her eyes, and I am brushing it back before she even notices it. She covers my hand with her own, which is warm and strong, and the corners of her mouth curl into a smile.

The door opens, admitting a young man with slanted, angular eyes and black hair. I recognize him immediately as George Wu, Tori's younger brother. "Georgie" was the name she called him.

He smiles a giddy smile, and I feel the urge to back away, to put more space between me and his impending grief.

"I just got back," he says, breathless. "They told me my sister set out with you guys, and—"

Tris and I exchange a troubled look. All around us, the others are noticing George by the door and going quiet, the same kind of quiet you hear at an Abnegation funeral. Even Peter, who I would expect to crave other people's pain, looks bewildered, shifting his hands from his waist to his pockets and back again.

"And . . ." George begins again. "Why are you all looking at me like that?"

Cara steps forward, about to bear the bad news, but I can't imagine Cara sharing it well, so I get up, talking over her.

"Your sister did leave with us," I say. "But we were attacked by the factionless, and she . . . didn't make it."

There is so much that phrase doesn't say—how quick it was, and the sound of her body hitting the earth, and the chaos of everyone running into the night, stumbling over the grass. I didn't go back for her. I should have—of all the people in our party, I knew Tori best, knew how tightly her hands squeezed the tattoo needle and how her laugh sounded rough, like it had been scraped with sandpaper.

George touches the wall behind him for stability. "What?"

"She gave her life defending us," Tris says with surprising gentleness. "Without her, none of us would have made it out."

"She's . . . dead?" George says weakly. He leans his entire body into the wall, and his shoulders sag.

I see Amar in the hallway, a piece of toast in his hand and a smile quickly fading from his face. He sets the toast down on a table by the door.

"I tried to find you earlier to tell you," Amar says.

Last night Amar said George's name so casually, I didn't think they really knew each other. Apparently they do.

George's eyes turn glassy, and Amar pulls him into an embrace with one arm. George's fingers are bent at harsh angles into Amar's shirt, the knuckles white with tension. I don't hear him cry, and maybe he doesn't, maybe all he needs to do is hold on to something. I have only hazy memories of my own grief over my mother, when I thought she was dead—just the feeling that I was separate from everything around me, and this constant sensation of needing to swallow something. I don't know what it's like for other people.

Eventually, Amar leads George out of the room, and I watch them walk down the hallway side by side, talking in low voices.

+ + +

I barely remember that I agreed to participate in a genetic test until someone else appears at the door to the dormitory—a boy, or not really a boy, since he looks about as old as I am. He waves to Tris.

"Oh, that's Matthew," she says. "I guess we should get going."

She takes my hand and leads me toward the doorway. Somehow I missed her mentioning that "Matthew" wasn't a crusty old scientist. Or maybe she didn't mention it at all.

Don't be stupid, I think.

Matthew sticks out his hand. "Hi. It's nice to meet you. I'm Matthew."

"Tobias," I say, because "Four" sounds strange here, where people would never identify themselves by how many fears they have. "You too."

"So let's go to the labs, I guess," he says. "They're this way."

The compound is thick with people this morning, all dressed in green or dark blue uniforms that pool around the ankles or stop several inches above the shoe, depending on the height of the person. The compound is full of open areas that branch off the major hallways, like chambers of a heart, each marked with a letter and a number, and the people seem to be moving between them, some carrying glass devices like the one Tris brought back this morning, some empty-handed.

"What's with the numbers?" says Tris. "Just a way of labeling each area?"

"They used to be gates," says Matthew. "Meaning that each one has a door and a walkway that led to a particular airplane going to a particular destination. When they converted the airport into the compound, they ripped out all the chairs people used to wait for their flights in and replaced them with lab equipment, mostly taken from schools in the city. This area of the compound is basically a giant laboratory."

"What are they working on? I thought you were just observing the experiments," I say, watching a woman rush from one side of the hallway to the other with a screen balanced on both palms like an offering. Beams of light stretch across the polished tile, slanting through the ceiling windows. Through the windows everything looks peaceful, every blade of grass trimmed and the wild trees swaying in the distance, and it's hard to imagine that people are destroying one another out there because of "damaged genes" or living under Evelyn's strict rules in the city we left.

"Some of them are doing that. Everything that they notice in all the remaining experiments has to be recorded and analyzed, so that requires a lot of manpower. But some of them are also working on better ways to treat the genetic damage, or developing the serums for our own use instead of the experiments' use—dozens of projects. All you have to do is come up with an idea, gather a team together, and propose it to the council that runs the compound under David. They usually approve anything that isn't too risky."

"Yeah," says Tris. "Wouldn't want to take any risks."

She rolls her eyes a little.

"They have a good reason for their endeavors," Matthew says. "Before the factions were introduced, and the serums with them, the experiments all used to be under near-constant assault from within. The serums help the people in the experiment to keep things under control, especially the memory serum. Well, I guess no one's working on that right now—it's in the Weapons Lab."

"Weapons Lab." He says the words like they're fragile in his mouth. Sacred words.

"So the Bureau gave us the serums, in the beginning," Tris says.

"Yes," he says. "And then the Erudite continued to work on them, to perfect them. Including your brother. To be honest, we got some of our serum developments from them, by observing them in the control room. Only they didn't do much with the memory serum—the Abnegation serum. We did a lot more with that, since it's our greatest weapon."

"A weapon," Tris repeats.

"Well, it arms the cities against their own rebellions, for one thing—erase people's memories and there's no need to kill them; they just forget what they were fighting about. And we can also use it against rebels from the fringe, which is about an hour from here. Sometimes fringe dwellers try to raid, and the memory serum stops them without killing them."

"That's . . ." I start.

"Still kind of awful?" Matthew supplies. "Yes, it is. But the higher-ups here think of it as our life support, our breathing machine. Here we are."

I raise my eyebrows. He just spoke out against his own leaders so casually I almost missed it. I wonder if that's the kind of place this is—where dissent can be expressed in public, in the middle of a normal conversation, instead of in secret spaces, with hushed voices.

He scans his card at a heavy door on our left, and we walk down another hallway, this one narrow and lit with pale, fluorescent light. He stops at a door marked GENE THERAPY ROOM 1. Inside, a girl with light brown skin and a green jumpsuit is replacing the paper that covers the exam table.

"This is Juanita, the lab technician. Juanita, this is—"

"Yeah, I know who they are," she says, smiling. Out of the corner of my eye I see Tris stiffen, chafing against the reminder that our lives have been on camera. But she doesn't say anything about it.

The girl offers me her hand. "Matthew's supervisor is the only person who calls me Juanita. Except Matthew, apparently. I'm Nita. You'll need two tests prepared?"

Matthew nods.

"I'll get them." She opens a set of cabinets across the room and starts pulling things out. All of them are encased in plastic and paper and have white labels. The room is full of the sound of crinkling and ripping.

"How do you guys like it here so far?" she asks us.

"It's been an adjustment," I say.

"Yeah, I know what you mean." Nita smiles at me. "I came from one of the other experiments—the one in Indianapolis, the one that failed. Oh, you don't know where Indianapolis is, do you? It's not far from here. Less than an hour by plane." She pauses. "That won't mean anything to you either. You know what? It's not important."

She takes a syringe and needle from its plastic-paper wrapping, and Tris tenses.

"What's that for?" Tris says.

"It's what will enable us to read your genes," Matthew says. "Are you okay?"

"Yeah," Tris says, but she's still tense. "I just . . . don't like to be injected with strange substances."

Matthew nods. "I swear it's just going to read your genes. That's all it does. Nita can vouch for it."

Nita nods.

"Okay," Tris says. "But . . . can I do it to myself?"

"Sure," Nita says. She prepares the syringe, filling it with whatever they intend to inject us with, and offers it to Tris.

"I'll give you the simplified explanation of how this

works," Matthew says as Nita brushes Tris's arm with antiseptic. The smell is sour, and it nips at the inside of my nose.

"The fluid is packed with microcomputers. They are designed to detect specific genetic markers and transmit the data to a computer. It will take them about an hour to give me as much information as I need, though it would take them much longer to read all your genetic material, obviously."

Tris sticks the needle into her arm and presses the plunger.

Nita beckons my arm forward and drags the orange-stained gauze over my skin. The fluid in the syringe is silver-gray, like fish scales, and as it flows into me through the needle, I imagine the microscopic technology chewing through my body, reading me and analyzing me. Beside me, Tris holds a cotton ball to her pricked skin and offers me a small smile.

"What are the . . . microcomputers?" Matthew nods, and I continue. "What are they looking for, exactly?"

"Well, when our predecessors at the Bureau inserted 'corrected' genes into your ancestors, they also included a genetic tracker, which is basically something that shows us that a person has achieved genetic healing. In this case, the genetic tracker is awareness during simulations—it's something we can easily test for, which shows us if your genes are healed or not. That's one of the reasons why everyone in the city has to take the aptitude test at sixteen—if they're aware during the test, that shows us that they might have healed genes."

I add the aptitude test to a mental list of things that were once so important to me, cast aside because it was just a ruse to get these people the information or result they wanted.

I can't believe that awareness during simulations, something that made me feel powerful and unique, something Jeanine and the Erudite *killed* people for, is actually just a sign of genetic healing to these people. Like a special code word, telling them I'm in their genetically healed society.

Matthew continues, "The only problem with the genetic tracker is that being aware during simulations and resisting serums doesn't necessarily mean that a person is Divergent, it's just a strong correlation. Sometimes people will be aware during simulations or be able to resist serums even if they still have damaged genes." He shrugs. "That's why I'm interested in your genes, Tobias. I'm curious to see if you're actually Divergent, or if your simulation awareness just makes it look like you are."

Nita, who is clearing the counter, presses her lips together like she is holding words inside her mouth. I feel suddenly uneasy. There's a chance I'm not actually Divergent?

"All that's left is to sit and wait," Matthew says. "I'm going to go get breakfast. Do either of you want something to eat?"

Tris and I both shake our heads.

"I'll be back soon. Nita, keep them company, would you?"

Matthew leaves without waiting for Nita's response, and Tris sits on the examination table, the paper crinkling beneath her and tearing where her leg hangs over the edge. Nita puts her hands in her jumpsuit pockets and looks at us. Her eyes are dark, with the same sheen as a puddle of oil beneath a leaking engine. She hands me a cotton ball, and I press it to the bubble of blood inside my elbow.

"So you came from a city experiment," says Tris. "How long have you been here?"

"Since the Indianapolis experiment was disbanded, which was about eight years ago. I could have integrated into the greater population, outside the experiments, but that felt too overwhelming." Nita leans against the counter. "So I volunteered to come here. I used to be a janitor. I'm moving through the ranks, I guess."

She says it with a certain amount of bitterness. I suspect that here, as in Dauntless, there is a limit to her climb through the ranks, and she is reaching it earlier than she would like to. The same way I did, when I chose my job in the control room.

"And your city, it didn't have factions?" Tris says.

"No, it was the control group—it helped them to figure out that the factions were actually effective by comparison. It had a lot of rules, though—curfew, wake-up times, safety regulations. No weapons allowed. Stuff like that."

"What happened?" I say, and a moment later I wish I hadn't asked, because the corners of Nita's mouth turn down, like the memory hangs heavy from each side.

"Well, a few of the people inside still knew how to make weapons. They made a bomb—you know, an explosive—and set it off in the government building," she says. "Lots of people died. And after that, the Bureau decided our experiment was a failure. They erased the memories of the bombers and relocated the rest of us. I'm one of the only ones who wanted to come here."

"I'm sorry," Tris says softly. Sometimes I still forget to look for the gentler parts of her. For so long all I saw was the strength, standing out like the wiry muscles in her arms or the black ink marking her collarbone with flight.

"It's all right. It's not like you guys don't know about stuff like this," says Nita. "With what Jeanine Matthews did, and all."

"Why haven't they shut our city down?" Tris says. "The

same way they did to yours?"

"They might still shut it down," says Nita. "But I think the Chicago experiment, in particular, has been a success for so long that they'll be a little reluctant to just ditch it now. It was the first one with factions."

I take the cotton ball away from my arm. There is a tiny red dot where the needle went in, but it isn't bleeding anymore.

"I like to think I would have chosen Dauntless," says Nita. "But I don't think I would have had the stomach for it."

"You'd be surprised what you have the stomach for, when you have to," Tris says.

I feel a pang in the middle of my chest. She's right. Desperation can make a person do surprising things. We would both know.

+ + +

Matthew returns right at the hour mark, and he sits at the computer for a long time after that, his eyes flicking back and forth as he reads the screen. A few times he makes a revelatory noise, a "hmm!" or an "ah!" The longer he waits to tell us something, anything, the more tense my muscles become, until my shoulders feel like they are made of stone instead of flesh. Finally he looks up and turns the screen around so we can see what's on it.

"This program helps us to interpret the data in an understandable way. What you see here is a simplified depiction of a particular DNA sequence in Tris's genetic material," he says.

The picture on the screen is a complicated mass of lines and numbers, with certain parts selected in yellow and red. I can't make any sense of the picture beyond that—it is above my level of comprehension.

"These selections here suggest healed genes. We wouldn't see them if the genes were damaged." He taps certain parts of the screen. I don't understand what he's pointing at, but he doesn't seem to notice, caught up in his own explanation. "These selections over here indicate that the program also found the genetic tracker, the simulation awareness. The combination of healed genes and simulation awareness genes is just what I expected to see from a Divergent. Now, this is the strange part."

He touches the screen again, and the screen changes, but it remains just as confusing, a web of lines, tangled threads of numbers.

"This is the map of Tobias's genes," Matthew says. "As you can see, he has the right genetic components for simulation awareness, but he doesn't have the same 'healed' genes that Tris does."

My throat is dry, and I feel like I've been given bad news, but I still haven't entirely grasped what that bad news is.

"What does that mean?" I ask.

"It means," Matthew says, "that you are not Divergent. Your genes are still damaged, but you have a genetic anomaly that allows you to be aware during simulations anyway. You have, in other words, the appearance of a Divergent without actually being one."

I process the information slowly, piece by piece. I'm not Divergent. I'm not like Tris. I'm genetically damaged.

The word "damaged" sinks inside me like it's made of lead. I guess I always knew there was something wrong with me, but I thought it was because of my father, or my mother, and the pain they bequeathed to me like a family heirloom, handed down from generation to generation. And this means that the one good thing my father had— his Divergence—didn't reach me.

I don't look at Tris—I can't bear it. Instead I look at Nita. Her expression is hard, almost angry.

"Matthew," she says. "Don't you want to take this data to your lab to analyze?"

"Well, I was planning on discussing it with our subjects here," Matthew says.

"I don't think that's a good idea," Tris says, sharp as a blade.

Matthew says something I don't really hear; I'm listening to the thump of my heart. He taps the screen again, and the picture of my DNA disappears, so the screen is blank, just glass. He leaves, instructing us to visit his lab if we want more information, and Tris, Nita, and I stand in the room in silence.

"It's not that big a deal," Tris says firmly. "Okay?"

"You don't get to tell me it's not a big deal!" I say, louder than I mean to be.

Nita busies herself at the counter, making sure the containers there are lined up, though they haven't moved since we first came in.

"Yeah, I do!" Tris exclaims. "You're the same person you were five minutes ago and four months ago and eighteen years ago! This doesn't change anything about you."

I hear something in her words that's right, but it's hard to believe her right now.

"So you're telling me this affects nothing," I say. "The truth affects nothing."

"What truth?" she says. "These people tell you there's something wrong with your genes, and you just believe it?"

"It was right there." I gesture to the screen. "You saw it."

"I also see you," she says fiercely, her hand closing around my arm. "And I know who you are."

I shake my head. I still can't look at her, can't look at anything in particular. "I . . . need to take a walk. I'll see you later."

"Tobias, wait—"

I walk out, and some of the pressure inside me releases as soon as I'm not in that room anymore. I walk down the cramped hallway that presses against me like an exhale, and into the sunlit halls beyond it. The sky is bright blue now. I hear footsteps behind me, but they're too heavy to belong to Tris.

"Hey." Nita twists her foot, making it squeak against the tile. "No pressure, but I'd like to talk to you about all this . . . genetic-damage stuff. If you're interested, meet me here tonight at nine. And . . . no offense to your girl or anything, but you might not want to bring her."

"Why?" I say.

"She's a GP—genetically pure. So she can't understand that—well, it's hard to explain. Just trust me, okay? She's better off staying away for a little while."

"Okay."

"Okay." Nita nods. "Gotta go."

I watch her run back toward the gene therapy room, and then I keep walking. I don't know where I'm going, exactly, just that when I walk, the frenzy of information I've learned in the past day stops moving quite so fast, stops shouting quite so loud inside my head.

CHAPTER
NINETEEN

TRIS

I DON'T GO after him, because I don't know what to say.

When I found out I was Divergent, I thought of it as a secret power that no one else possessed, something that made me different, better, stronger. Now, after comparing my DNA to Tobias's on a computer screen, I realize that "Divergent" doesn't mean as much as I thought it did. It's just a word for a particular sequence in my DNA, like a word for all people with brown eyes or blond hair.

I lean my head into my hands. But these people still think it means something—they still think it means I'm healed in a way that Tobias is not. And they want me to just trust that, believe it.

Well, I don't. And I'm not sure why Tobias does—why

he's so eager to believe that he is damaged.

I don't want to think about it anymore. I leave the gene therapy room just as Nita is walking back to it.

"What did you say to him?" I say.

She's pretty. Tall but not too tall, thin but not too thin, her skin rich with color.

"I just made sure he knew where he was going," she says. "It's a confusing place."

"It certainly is." I start toward—well, I don't know where I'm going, but it's away from Nita, the pretty girl who talks to my boyfriend when I'm not there. Then again, it's not like it was a long conversation.

I spot Zoe at the end of the hallway, and she waves me toward her. She looks more relaxed now than she did earlier this morning, her forehead smooth instead of creased, her hair loose over her shoulders. She shoves her hands into the pockets of her jumpsuit.

"I just told the others," she says. "We've scheduled a plane ride in two hours for those who want to go. Are you up for it?"

Fear and excitement squirm together in my stomach, just like they did before I was strapped in on the zip line atop the Hancock building. I imagine hurtling into the air in a car with wings, the energy of the engine and the rush of wind through all the spaces in the walls and the possibility, however slight, that something will fail and I will plummet to my death.

"Yes," I say.

"We're meeting at gate B14. Follow the signs!" She flashes a smile as she leaves.

I look through the windows above me. The sky is clear and pale, the same color as my own eyes. There is a kind of inevitability in it, like it has always been waiting for me, maybe because I relish height while others fear it, or maybe because once you have seen the things that I have seen, there is only one frontier left to explore, and it is above.

+ + +

The metal stairs leading down to the pavement screech with each of my footsteps. I have to tilt my head back to look at the airplane, which is bigger than I expected it to be, and silver-white. Just below the wing is a huge cylinder with spinning blades inside it. I imagine the blades sucking me in and spitting me out the other side, and shudder a little.

"How can something that big stay in the sky?" Uriah says from behind me.

I shake my head. I don't know, and I don't want to think about it. I follow Zoe up another set of stairs, this one connected to a hole in the side of the plane. My hand shakes when I grab the railing, and I look over my shoulder one last time, to check if Tobias caught up to us. He isn't there. I haven't seen him since the genetic test.

I duck when I go through the hole, though it's taller than my head. Inside the airplane are rows and rows of seats covered in ripped, fraying blue fabric. I choose one near the front, next to a window. A metal bar pushes against my spine. It feels like a chair skeleton with barely any flesh to support it.

Cara sits behind me, and Peter and Caleb move toward the back of the plane and sit near each other, next to the window. I didn't know they were friends. It seems fitting, given how despicable they both are.

"How old is this thing?" I ask Zoe, who stands near the front.

"Pretty old," she says. "But we've completely redone the important stuff. It's a nice size for what we need."

"What do you use it for?"

"Surveillance missions, mostly. We like to keep an eye on what's happening in the fringe, in case it threatens what's happening in here." Zoe pauses. "The fringe is a large, sort of chaotic place between Chicago and the nearest government-regulated metropolitan area, Milwaukee, which is about a three-hour drive from here."

I would like to ask what exactly *is* happening in the

fringe, but Uriah and Christina sit in the seats next to me, and the moment is lost. Uriah puts an armrest down between us and leans over me to look out the window.

"If the Dauntless knew about this, everyone would be getting in line to learn how to drive it," he says. "Including me."

"No, they would be strapping themselves to the wings." Christina pokes his arm. "Don't you know your own faction?"

Uriah pokes her cheek in response, then turns back to the window again.

"Have either of you seen Tobias lately?" I say.

"No, haven't seen him," Christina says. "Everything okay?"

Before I can answer, an older woman with lines around her mouth stands in the aisle between the rows of seats and claps her hands.

"My name is Karen, and I'll be flying this plane today!" she announces. "It may seem frightening, but remember: The odds of us crashing are actually much lower than the odds of a car crash."

"So are the odds of survival if we *do* crash," Uriah mutters, but he's grinning. His dark eyes are alert, and he looks giddy, like a child. I haven't seen him this way since Marlene died. He's handsome again.

Karen disappears into the front of the plane, and Zoe

sits across the aisle from Christina, twisting around to call out instructions like "Buckle your seat belts!" and "Don't stand up until we've reached our cruising altitude!" I'm not sure what cruising altitude is, and she doesn't explain it, in true Zoe fashion. It was almost a miracle that she remembered to explain the fringe earlier.

The plane starts to move backward, and I'm surprised by how smooth it feels, like we're already floating over the ground. Then it turns and glides over the pavement, which is painted with dozens of lines and symbols. My heart beats faster the farther we go away from the compound, and then Karen's voice speaks through an intercom: "Prepare for takeoff."

I clench the armrests as the plane lurches into motion. The momentum presses me back against the skeleton chair, and the view out the window turns into a smear of color. Then I feel it—the lift, the rising of the plane, and I see the ground stretching wide beneath us, everything getting smaller by the second. My mouth hangs open and I forget to breathe.

I see the compound, shaped like the picture of a neuron I once saw in my science textbook, and the fence that surrounds it. Around it is a web of concrete roads with buildings sandwiched between them.

And then suddenly, I can't even see the roads or the buildings anymore, because there is just a sheet of gray and green and brown beneath us, and farther than I can see in any direction is land, land, land.

I don't know what I expected. To see the place where the world ends, like a giant cliff hanging in the sky?

What I didn't expect is to know that I have been a person standing in a house that I can't even see from here. That I have walked a street among hundreds—thousands—of other streets.

What I didn't expect is to feel so, so small.

"We can't fly too high or too close to the city because we don't want to draw attention, so we'll observe from a great distance. Coming up on the left side of the plane is some of the destruction caused by the Purity War, before the rebels resorted to biological warfare instead of explosives," Zoe says.

I have to blink tears from my eyes before I can see it, what looks at first to be a group of dark buildings. Upon further examination, I realize that the buildings aren't supposed to be dark—they're charred beyond recognition. Some of them are flattened. The pavement between them is broken in pieces like a cracked eggshell.

It resembles certain parts of the city, but at the same time, it doesn't. The city's destruction could have been caused by people. This had to have been caused by something else, something bigger.

"And now you'll get a brief look at Chicago!" Zoe says.

"You'll see that some of the lake was drained so that we could build the fence, but we left as much of it intact as possible."

At her words I see the two-pronged Hub as small as a toy in the distance, the jagged line of our city interrupting the sea of concrete. And beyond it, a brown expanse—the marsh—and just past that . . . blue.

Once I slid down a zip line from the Hancock building and imagined what the marsh looked like full of water, blue-gray and gleaming under the sun. And now that I can see farther than I have ever seen, I know that far beyond our city's limits, it is just like what I imagined, the lake in the distance glinting with streaks of light, marked with the texture of waves.

The plane is silent around me except for the steady roar of the engine.

"Whoa," says Uriah.

"Shh," Christina replies.

"How big is it compared to the rest of the world?" Peter says from across the plane. He sounds like he's choking on each word. "Our city, I mean. In terms of land area. What percentage?"

"Chicago takes up about two hundred twenty-seven square miles," says Zoe. "The land area of the planet is a little less than two hundred million square miles. The percentage is . . . so small as to be negligible."

She delivers the facts calmly, as if they mean nothing to her. But they hit me square in the stomach, and I feel squeezed, like something is crushing me into myself. So much space. I wonder what it's like in the places beyond ours; I wonder how people live there.

I look out the window again, taking slow, deep breaths into a body too tense to move. And as I stare out at the land, I think that this, if nothing else, is compelling evidence for my parents' God, that our world is so massive that it is completely out of our control, that we cannot possibly be as large as we feel.

So small as to be negligible.

It's strange, but there's something in that thought that makes me feel almost . . . free.

+ + +

That evening, when everyone else is at dinner, I sit on the window ledge in the dormitory and turn on the screen David gave me. My hands tremble as I open the file labeled "Journal."

The first entry reads:

> David keeps asking me to write down what I experienced. I think he expects it to be horrifying, maybe even wants it to be. I guess parts of it were, but they were bad for everyone, so it's not like I'm special.

I grew up in a single-family home in Milwaukee, Wisconsin. I never knew much about who was inside the territory outside the city (which everyone around here calls "the fringe"), just that I wasn't supposed to go there. My mom was in law enforcement; she was explosive and impossible to please. My dad was a teacher; he was pliable and supportive and useless. One day they got into it in the living room and things got out of hand, and he grabbed her and she shot him. That night she was burying his body in the backyard while I assembled a good portion of my possessions and left through the front door. I never saw her again.

Where I grew up, tragedy is all over the place. Most of my friends' parents drank themselves stupid or yelled too much or had stopped loving each other a long time ago, and that was just the way of things, no big deal. So when I left I'm sure I was just another item on a long list of awful things that had happened in our neighborhood in the past year.

I knew that if I went anyplace official, like to another city, the government types would just make me go home to my mom, and I didn't think I would ever be able to look at her without seeing the streak of blood my dad's head left on the living room carpet, so I didn't go anyplace official. I went to the fringe, where a whole bunch of people are living in a little colony made of tarp and aluminum in some of the postwar wreckage, living on scraps and burning old papers for warmth because the government can't provide, since they're spending all their resources trying to put us back together again, and have been for over a century after the war ripped us apart. Or they won't provide. I don't know.

One day I saw a grown man beating up one of the kids in the fringe, and I hit him over the head with a plank to get him to stop and he died, right there in the street. I was only thirteen. I ran. I got snatched by some guy in a van, some guy who looked like police. But he didn't take me to the side of the road to shoot me and he didn't take me to jail; he just took me to this secure area and tested my genes and told me all about the city experiments and how my genes were cleaner than other people's. He even showed me a map of my genes on a screen to prove it.

But I killed a man just like my mother did. David says it's okay because I didn't mean to, and because he was about to kill that little kid. But I'm pretty sure my mom didn't mean to kill my dad, either, so what difference does that make, meaning or not meaning to do something? Accident or on purpose, the result is the same, and that's one fewer life than there should be in the world.

That's what I experienced, I guess. And to hear David talk about it, it's like it all happened because a long, long time ago people tried to mess with human nature and ended up making it worse.

I guess that makes sense. Or I'd like it to.

My teeth dig into my lower lip. Here in the Bureau compound, people are sitting in the cafeteria right now, eating and drinking and laughing. In the city, they're probably doing the same thing. Ordinary life surrounds me, and I am alone with these revelations.

I clutch the screen to my chest. My mother was from here. This place is both my ancient and my recent history. I can feel her in the walls, in the air. I can feel her settled inside me, never to leave again. Death could not erase her; she is permanent.

The cold from the glass seeps through my shirt, and I shiver. Uriah and Christina walk through the door to the dormitory, laughing about something. Uriah's clear eyes and steady footsteps fill me with a sense of relief, and my eyes well up with tears all of a sudden. He and Christina both look alarmed, and they lean against the windows on either side of me.

"You okay?" she says.

I nod and blink the tears away. "Where have you guys been today?"

"After the plane ride we went and watched the screens in the control room for a while," Uriah says. "It's really weird to see what they're up to now that we're gone. Just more of the same—Evelyn's a jerk, so are all her lackeys, and so on—but it was like getting a news report."

"I don't think I'd like to look at those," I say. "Too . . . creepy and invasive."

Uriah shrugs. "I don't know, if they want to watch me scratch my butt or eat dinner, I feel like that says more about them than about me."

I laugh. "How often *are* you scratching your butt, exactly?"

He jostles me with his elbow.

"Not to derail the conversation from *butts*, which we can all agree is incredibly important—" Christina smiles a little. "But I'm with you, Tris. Just watching those screens made me feel awful, like I was doing something sneaky. I think I'll be staying away from now on."

She points to the screen in my lap, where the light still glows around my mother's words. "What's that?"

"As it turns out," I say, "my mother was from here. Well, she was from the world outside, but then she came here, and when she was fifteen, she was placed in Chicago as a Dauntless."

Christina says, "Your mother was from here?"

I nod. "Yeah. Insane. Even weirder, she wrote this journal and left it with them. That's what I was reading before you came in."

"Wow," Christina says softly. "That's good, right? I mean, that you get to learn more about her."

"Yeah, it's good. And no, I'm not still upset, you can stop looking at me like that." The look of concern that had been building on Uriah's face disappears.

I sigh. "I just keep thinking . . . that in some way I belong here. Like maybe this place can be home."

Christina pinches her eyebrows together.

"Maybe," she says, and I feel like she doesn't believe it, but it's nice of her to say it anyway.

"I don't know," Uriah says, and he sounds serious now. "I'm not sure anywhere will feel like home again. Not even if we went back."

Maybe that's true. Maybe we're strangers no matter where we go, whether it's to the world outside the Bureau, or here in the Bureau, or back in the experiment. Everything has changed, and it won't stop changing anytime soon.

Or maybe we'll make a home somewhere inside ourselves, to carry with us wherever we go—which is the way I carry my mother now.

Caleb walks into the dormitory. There's a stain on his shirt that looks like sauce, but he doesn't seem to notice it—he has the look in his eye that I now recognize as intellectual fascination, and for a moment I wonder what he's been reading, or watching, to make him look that way.

"Hi," he says, and he almost makes a move toward me,

but he must see my revulsion, because he stops in the middle of a step.

I cover the screen with my palm, though he can't see it from across the room, and stare at him, unable—or unwilling—to say anything in reply.

"You think you'll ever speak to me again?" he says sadly, his mouth turning down at the corners.

"If she does, I'll die of shock," Christina says coldly.

I look away. The truth is, sometimes I want to just forget about everything that's happened and return to the way we were before either of us chose a faction. Even if he was always correcting me, reminding me to be selfless, it was better than this—this feeling that I need to protect even my mother's journal from him, so that he can't poison it like he's done to everything else. I get up and slip it under my pillow.

"Come on," Uriah says to me. "Want to go with us to get some dessert?"

"You didn't already have some?"

"So what if I did?" Uriah rolls his eyes and puts his arm across my shoulders, steering me toward the door.

Together the three of us walk toward the cafeteria, leaving my brother behind.

CHAPTER
TWENTY

TOBIAS

"Wasn't sure if you would come," Nita says to me.

When she turns to lead me wherever we're going, I see that her loose shirt is low in the back, and there's a tattoo on her spine, but I can't make out what it is.

"You get tattoos too, here?" I say.

"Some people do," she says. "The one on my back is of broken glass." She pauses, the kind of pause you take when you're deciding whether or not to share something personal. "I got it because it suggests damage. It's . . . sort of a joke."

There's that word again, "damage," the one that's been sinking and surfacing, sinking and surfacing in my mind since the genetic test. If it's a joke, it's not a funny one even for Nita—she spits out the explanation like it tastes bitter to her.

We walk down one of the tiled corridors, nearly empty now at the end of a workday, and down a flight of stairs. As we descend, blue and green and purple and red lights dance over the walls, shifting between colors with each second. The tunnel at the bottom of the stairs is wide and dark, with only the strange light to guide us. The floor here is old tile, and even through my shoe soles, it feels grainy with dirt and dust.

"This part of the airport was completely redone and expanded when they first moved in here," Nita says. "For a while, after the Purity War, all the laboratories were underground, to keep them safer if they were attacked. Now it's just the support staff who goes down here."

"Is that who you want me to meet?"

She nods. "Support staff is more than just a job. Almost all of us are GDs—genetically damaged, leftovers from the failed city experiments or the descendants of other leftovers or people pulled in from the outside, like Tris's mother, except without her genetic advantage. And all of the scientists and leaders are GPs—genetically pure, descendants of people who resisted the genetic engineering movement in the first place. There are some exceptions, of course, but so few I could list them all for you if I wanted to."

I am about to ask why the division is so strict, but I can figure it out for myself. The so-called "GPs" grew up in this community, their worlds saturated by experiments and observation and learning. The "GDs" grew up in the experiments, where they only had to learn enough to survive until the next generation. The division is based on knowledge, based on qualifications—but as I learned from the factionless, a system that relies on a group of uneducated people to do its dirty work without giving them a way to rise is hardly fair.

"I think your girl's right, you know," Nita says. "Nothing has changed; now you just have a better idea of your own limitations. Every human being has limitations, even GPs."

"So there's an upward limit to . . . what? My compassion? My conscience?" I say. "That's the reassurance you have for me?"

Nita's eyes study me, carefully, and she doesn't respond.

"This is ridiculous," I say. "Why do you, or they, or anyone get to determine my limits?"

"It's just the way things are, Tobias," Nita says. "It's just genetic, nothing more."

"That's a lie," I say. "It's about more than genes, here, and you know it."

I feel like I need to leave, to turn and run back to the dormitory. The anger is boiling and churning inside me, filling me with heat, and I'm not even sure who it's for. For Nita, who has just accepted that she is somehow limited, or for whoever told her that? Maybe it's for everyone.

We reach the end of the tunnel, and she nudges a heavy wooden door open with her shoulder. Beyond it is a bustling, glowing world. The room is lit by small, bright bulbs on strings, but the strings are so densely packed that a web of yellow and white covers the ceiling. On one end of the room is a wooden counter with glowing bottles behind it, and a sea of glasses on top of it. There are tables and chairs on the left side of the room, and a group of people with musical instruments on the right side. Music fills the air, and the only sounds I recognize—from my limited experience with the Amity—are plucked guitar strings and drums.

I feel like I am standing beneath a spotlight and everyone is watching me, waiting for me to move, speak, something. For a moment it's hard to hear anything over the music and the chatter, but after a few seconds I get used to it, and I hear Nita when she says, "This way! Want a drink?"

I'm about to answer when someone runs into the room. He's short, and the T-shirt he wears hangs from his body, two sizes too large for him. He gestures for the musicians to stop playing, and they do, just long enough for him to shout, "It's verdict time!"

Half the room gets up and rushes toward the door. I give Nita a questioning look, and she frowns, creating a crease in her forehead.

"Whose verdict?" I say.

"Marcus's, no doubt," she replies.

And I'm running.

+ + +

I sprint back down the tunnel, finding the open spaces between people and pushing my way through if there are none. Nita runs at my heels, shouting for me to stop, but I can't stop. I am separate from this place and these people and my own body, and besides, I have always been a good runner.

I take the stairs three at a time, clutching the railing for balance. I don't know what I am so eager for—Marcus's conviction? His exoneration? Do I hope that Evelyn finds him guilty and executes him, or do I hope that she spares him? I can't tell. To me each outcome feels like it is made of the same substance. Everything is either Marcus's evil or Marcus's mask, Evelyn's evil or Evelyn's mask.

I don't have to remember where the control room is,

because the people in the hallway lead me to it. When I reach it, I push my way to the front of the crowd and there they are, my parents, shown on half the screens. Everyone moves away from me, whispering, except Nita, who stands beside me, catching her breath.

Someone turns up the volume, so we can all hear their voices. They crackle, distorted by the microphones, but I know my father's voice; I can hear it shift at all the right times, lift in all the right places. I can almost predict his words before he says them.

"You took your time," he says, sneering. "Savoring the moment?"

I stiffen. This is not Marcus's mask. This is not the person who the city knows as my father—the patient, calm leader of Abnegation who would never hurt anyone, least of all his own son or wife. This is the man who slid his belt out loop by loop and wrapped it around his knuckles. This is the Marcus I know best, and the sight of him, like the sight of him in my fear landscape, turns me into a child.

"Of course not, Marcus," my mother says. "You have served this city well for many years. This is not a decision I or any of my advisers have taken lightly."

Marcus is not wearing his mask, but Evelyn is wearing hers. She sounds so genuine she almost convinces me.

"I and the former representatives of the factions have

had a lot to consider. Your years of service, the loyalty you have inspired among your faction members, my lingering feelings for you as my former husband . . ."

I snort.

"I am still your husband," Marcus says. "The Abnegation do not allow divorce."

"They do in cases of spousal abuse," Evelyn replies, and I feel that same old feeling again, the hollowness and the weight. I can't believe she just admitted that in public.

But then, she now wants the people in the city to see her a certain way—not as the heartless woman who took control of their lives, but as the woman Marcus attacked with his might, the secret he hid behind a clean house and pressed gray clothing.

I know, then, what the outcome of this will be.

"She's going to kill him," I say.

"The fact remains," says Evelyn, almost sweetly, "that you have committed egregious crimes against this city. You deceived innocent children into risking their lives for your purposes. Your refusal to follow the orders of myself and Tori Wu, the former leader of Dauntless, resulted in countless deaths in the Erudite attack. You betrayed your peers by failing to do as we agreed and by failing to fight against Jeanine Matthews. You betrayed your own faction by revealing what was supposed to be a guarded secret."

"I did not—"

"I am not finished," Evelyn says. "Given your record of service to this city, we have decided on an alternate solution. You will not, unlike the other former faction representatives, be forgiven and allowed to consult on issues regarding this city. Nor will you be executed as a traitor. Instead, you will be sent outside the fence, beyond the Amity compound, and you will not be allowed to return."

Marcus looks surprised. I don't blame him.

"Congratulations," says Evelyn. "You have the privilege of beginning again."

Should I feel relieved, that my father isn't going to be executed? Angry, that I came so close to finally escaping him, but instead he'll still be in this world, still hanging over my head?

I don't know. I don't feel anything. My hands go numb, so I know I'm panicking, but I don't really feel it, not the way I normally do. I am overwhelmed with the need to be somewhere else, so I turn and leave my parents and Nita and the city where I once lived behind me.

CHAPTER
TWENTY-ONE

Tris

THEY ANNOUNCE THE attack drill in the morning, over the intercom, as we eat breakfast. The crisp, female voice instructs us to lock the door to whatever room we are in from the inside, cover the windows, and sit quietly until the alarms no longer sound. "It will take place at the top of the hour," she says.

Tobias looks worn and pale, with dark circles under his eyes. He picks at a muffin, pinching small pieces off and sometimes eating them, sometimes forgetting to.

Most of us woke up late, at ten, I suspect because there was no reason not to. When we left the city, we lost our factions, our sense of purpose. Here there is nothing to do but wait for something to happen, and far from making me feel relaxed, it makes me feel jittery and tense. I am used to having something to do, something to fight, all the time. I try to remind myself to relax.

"They took us up in a plane yesterday," I say to Tobias. "Where were you?"

"I just had to walk around. Process things." He sounds terse, irritated. "How was it?"

"Amazing, actually." I sit across from him so that our knees touch in the space between our beds. "The world is . . . a lot bigger than I thought it was."

He nods. "I probably wouldn't have enjoyed it. Heights, and all."

I don't know why, but his reaction disappoints me. I want him to say that he wishes he had been there with me, to experience it with me. Or at least to ask me what I mean when I say that it was amazing. But all he can say is that he wouldn't have liked it?

"Are you all right?" I say. "You look like you barely slept."

"Well, yesterday carried quite the revelation," he says, putting his forehead into his hand. "You can't really blame me for being upset about it."

"I mean, you can be upset about whatever you want," I say, frowning. "But from my perspective, it doesn't seem like there's much to be upset about. I know it's a shock, but as I said, you're still the same person you were yesterday and the day before, no matter what these people say about it."

He shakes his head. "I'm not talking about my genes. I'm talking about Marcus. You really have no idea, do you?" The question is accusatory, but his tone isn't. He gets up to toss his muffin in the trash.

I feel raw and frustrated. Of course I knew about Marcus. It was buzzing around the room when I woke up. But for some reason I didn't think it would upset him to know his father wasn't going to be executed. Apparently I was wrong.

It doesn't help that the alarms sound at that exact moment, preventing me from saying anything else to him. They are loud, screeching, so painful to listen to that I can barely think, let alone move. I keep one hand clamped over my ear and slide my other hand under my pillow to pick up the screen with my mother's journal on it.

Tobias locks the door and draws the curtains closed, and everyone sits on their cots. Cara wraps a pillow around her head. Peter just sits with his back against the wall, his eyes closed. I don't know where Caleb is—researching whatever made him so distant yesterday, probably—or where Christina and Uriah are—exploring the compound, maybe. Yesterday after dessert they seemed determined to discover every corner of the place. I decided to discover my mother's thoughts about it instead—she wrote several entries about her first impressions of the compound, the strange cleanliness of the place, how everyone smiled all the time, how she fell in love with the city by watching it in the control room.

I turn on the screen, hoping to distract myself from the noise.

Today I volunteered to go inside the city. David said the Divergent are dying and someone has to stop it, because that's a waste of our best genetic material. I think that's a pretty sick way to put it, but David doesn't mean it that way—he just means that if it wasn't the Divergent dying, we wouldn't intervene until a certain level of destruction, but since it's them it has to be taken care of now.

Just a few years, he said. All I have here are a few friends, no family, and I'm young enough that it will be easy to insert me—just wipe and resupply a few people's memories, and I'm in. They'll put me in Dauntless, at first, because I already have tattoos, and that would be hard to explain to the people inside the experiment. The only problem is that at my Choosing Ceremony next year I'll have to join Erudite, because that's where the killer is, and I'm not sure I'm smart enough to make it through initiation. David says it doesn't matter, he can alter my results, but that feels wrong. Even if the Bureau thinks the factions don't mean anything, that they're just a kind of behavioral modification that will help with the damage, those people believe they do, and it feels wrong to play with their system.

I've been watching them for a couple years now, so there's not much I need to know about fitting in. I bet I know the city better than they do, at this point. It's going to be difficult to send my updates—someone might notice that I'm connecting to a distant server instead of an intra-city server, so my entries will probably come less often, if at all. It will be hard to separate myself from everything I know, but maybe it will be good. Maybe it will be a fresh start.

I could really use one of those.

It's a lot to take in, but I find myself rereading the sentence: *The only problem is that at my Choosing Ceremony next year I'll have to join Erudite, because that's where the killer is.* I don't know what killer she's referring to—Jeanine Matthews's predecessor, maybe?—but more confusing even than that is that she *didn't* join Erudite.

What happened to make her join Abnegation instead?

The alarms stop, and my ears feel muffled in their absence. The others trickle out slowly, but Tobias lingers for a moment, tapping his fingers against his leg. I don't speak to him—I'm not sure I want to hear what he has to say right now, when we're both on edge.

But all he says is, "Can I kiss you?"

"Yes," I say, relieved.

He bends down and touches my cheek, then kisses me softly.

Well, he knows how to improve my mood, at least.

"I didn't think about Marcus. I should have," I say.

He shrugs. "It's over now."

I know it's not over. It's never over with Marcus; the wrongs he committed are too great. But I don't press the issue.

"More journal entries?" he says.

"Yes," I say. "Just some memories of the compound so far. But it's getting interesting."

"Good," he says. "I'll leave you with it."

He smiles a little, but I can tell he's still tired, still upset. I don't try to stop him from going. In a way, it feels like we are leaving each other to our grief, his over the loss of his Divergence and whatever hopes he had for Marcus's trial, and mine, finally, over the loss of my parents.

I tap the screen to read the next entry.

Dear David,

I raise my eyebrows. Now she's writing to David?

Dear David,
I'm sorry, but it's not going to happen the way we

planned it. I can't do it. I know you're just going to think I'm being a stupid teenager, but this is my life and if I'm going to be here for years, I have to do this my way. I'll still be able to do my job from outside of Erudite. So tomorrow, at the Choosing Ceremony, Andrew and I are going to choose Abnegation together.

I hope you're not angry. I guess even if you are, I won't hear about it.

—Natalie

I read the entry again, and again, letting the words sink in. *Andrew and I are going to choose Abnegation together.*

I smile into my hand, lean my head against the window, and let the tears fall in silence.

My parents did love each other. Enough to forsake plans and factions. Enough to defy "faction before blood." Blood before faction—no, *love* before faction, always.

I turn off the screen. I don't want to read anything that will spoil this feeling: that I am adrift in calm waters.

It's strange how, even though I should be grieving, I feel like I am actually getting back pieces of her, word by word, line by line.

CHAPTER
TWENTY-TWO

Tris

THERE ARE ONLY a dozen more entries in the file, and they don't tell me everything I want to know, though they do give me more questions. And instead of just containing her thoughts and impressions, they are all written *to* someone.

Dear David,

I thought you were more my friend than my supervisor, but I guess I was wrong.

What did you think would happen when I came in here, that I would live single and alone forever? That I wouldn't get attached to anyone? That I wouldn't make any of my own choices?

I left *everything* behind to come in here when no one else wanted to. You should be thanking me instead of accusing me of losing sight of my mission. Let's get this straight: I'm not going to forget why I'm here just because I chose Abnegation and I'm going to get married. I deserve to have a life of my own. One that *I* choose, not one that you and the Bureau choose for me. You should know all about that—you should understand why this life would appeal to me after all I've seen and been through.

Honestly, I don't really think you care that I didn't choose Erudite like I was supposed to. It sounds like you're actually just jealous. And if you want me to keep updating you, you'll apologize for doubting me. But if you don't, I won't send you any more updates, and I certainly won't leave the city to visit anymore. It's up to you.

—Natalie

I wonder if she was right about David. The thought itches at my mind. Was he really jealous of my father? Did his jealousy fade over time? I can only see their relationship from her eyes, and I'm not sure she's the most accurate source of information about it.

I can tell she's getting older in the entries, her language becoming more refined as time separates her from the fringe where she once lived, her reactions becoming more moderate. She's growing up.

I check the date on the next entry. It's a few months later, but it's not addressed to David the way some of the others have been. The tone is different too—not as familiar, more straightforward.

I tap the screen, flipping through the entries. It takes me ten taps to reach an entry that is addressed to David again. The date on the entry suggests that it came a full two years later.

> Dear David,
> I got your letter. I understand why you can't be on the receiving end of these updates anymore, and I'll respect your decision, but I'll miss you.
> I wish you every happiness.
> —Natalie

I try to flip forward, but the journal entries are over. The last document in the file is a certificate of death. The cause of death says *multiple gunshot wounds to the torso*. I rock back and forth a little, to dispel the image of her collapsing in the street from my mind. I don't want to think about her death. I want to know more about her and my father, and her and David. Anything to distract me from the way her life ended.

+ + +

It's a sign of how desperate I am for information—and action—that I go to the control room with Zoe later that morning. She talks to the manager of the control room about a meeting with David as I stare, determined, at my feet, not wanting to see what's on the screens. I feel like if I allow myself to look at them, even for a moment, I will become addicted to them, lost in the old world because I don't know how to navigate this new one.

As Zoe finishes her conversation, though, I can't keep my curiosity in check. I look at the large screen hanging over the desks. Evelyn is sitting on her bed, running her hands over something on her bedside table. I move closer to see what it is, and the woman at the desk in front of me says, "This is the Evelyn cam. We track her 24-7."

"Can you hear her?"

"Only if we turn the volume up," the woman replies. "We mostly keep the sound off, though. Hard to listen to that much chatter all day."

I nod. "What is that she's touching?"

"Some kind of sculpture, I don't know." The woman shrugs. "She stares at it a lot, though."

I recognize it from somewhere—from Tobias's room, where I slept after my almost-execution in Erudite head-quarters. It's made of blue glass, an abstract shape that looks like falling water frozen in time.

I touch my fingertips to my chin as I search my memory. He told me that Evelyn gave it to him when he was young, and instructed him to hide it from his father, who wouldn't approve of a useless-but-beautiful object, Abnegation that he was. I didn't think much of it at the time, but it must mean something to her, if she carried it all the way from the Abnegation sector to Erudite headquarters to keep on her bedside table. Maybe it was her way of rebelling against the faction system.

On the screen, Evelyn balances her chin on her hand and stares at the sculpture for a moment. Then she gets up and shakes out her hands and leaves the room.

No, I don't think the sculpture is a sign of rebellion. I think it's just a reminder of Tobias. Somehow I never realized that when Tobias charged out of the city with me, he wasn't just a rebel defying his leader—he was a son abandoning his mother. And she is grieving over it.

Is he?

Fraught with difficulty as their relationship has been, those ties never really break. They can't possibly.

Zoe touches my shoulder. "You wanted to ask me something?"

I nod and turn away from the screens. Zoe was young in the photograph where she stood next to my mother, but she was still there, so I figure she must know something. I would have asked David, but as the leader of the Bureau, he is difficult to find.

"I wanted to know about my parents," I say. "I'm reading her journal, and I guess I'm having a hard time figuring out how they even met, or why they joined Abnegation together."

Zoe nods slowly. "I'll tell you what I know. Mind walking with me to the labs? I need to leave a message with Matthew."

She holds her hands behind her back, resting them at the bottom of her spine. I am still holding the screen David gave me. It's marked all over with my fingerprints, and warm from my constant touch. I understand why Evelyn keeps touching that sculpture—it's the last piece of her son she has, just like this is the last piece of my mother that I have. I feel closer to her when it's with me.

I think that's why I can't give it to Caleb, even though he has a right to see it. I'm not sure I can let go of it yet.

"They met in a class," Zoe says. "Your father, though a very smart man, never quite got the knack of psychology, and the teacher—an Erudite, unsurprisingly—was very hard on him for it. So your mother offered to help him after school, and he told his parents he was doing some kind of school project. They did this for several weeks, and then started to meet in secret—I think one of their favorite places was the fountain south of Millennium Park. Buckingham Fountain? Right by the marsh?"

I imagine my mother and father sitting beside a fountain, under the spray of water, their feet skimming the concrete bottom. I know the fountain Zoe is referring to hasn't been operational for a long time, so the spraying water was never there, but the picture is prettier that way.

"The Choosing Ceremony was approaching, and your father was eager to leave Erudite because he saw something terrible—"

"What? What did he see?"

"Well, your father was a good friend of Jeanine Matthews," says Zoe. "He saw her performing an experiment on a factionless man in exchange for something—food, or clothing, something like that. Anyway, she was testing the fear-inducing serum that was later incorporated into Dauntless initiation—long ago, the fear simulations weren't generated by a person's individual fears, you see, just general fears like heights or spiders or something—and Norton, then the representative of Erudite, was there, letting it go on for far longer than it should have. The factionless man was never quite right again. And that was the last straw for your father."

She pauses in front of the door to the labs to open it with her ID badge. We walk into the dingy office where David gave me my mother's journal. Matthew is sitting with his nose three inches from his computer screen, his eyes narrow. He barely registers our presence when we walk in.

I feel overwhelmed by the desire to smile and cry at the same time. I sit down in a chair next to the empty desk, my hands clasped between my knees. My father was a difficult man. But he was also a good one.

"Your father wanted out of Erudite, and your mother didn't want in, no matter what her mission was—but she still wanted to be near Andrew, so they chose Abnegation together." She pauses. "This caused a rift between your mother and David, as I'm sure you saw. He eventually apologized, but said he couldn't receive updates from her anymore—I don't know why, he wouldn't say—and after that her reports were very short, very informational. Which is why they're not in that journal."

"But she was still able to carry out her mission in Abnegation."

"Yes. And she was much happier there, I think, than she would have been among the Erudite," Zoe says. "Of course, Abnegation turned out to be no better, in some ways. It seems there's no escaping the reach of genetic damage. Even the Abnegation leadership was poisoned by it."

I frown. "Are you talking about Marcus? Because he's Divergent. Genetic damage had nothing to do with it."

"A man surrounded by genetic damage cannot help but mimic it with his own behavior," Zoe says. "Matthew, David wants to set up a meeting with your supervisor to discuss one of the serum developments. Last time Alan completely forgot about it, so I was wondering if you could escort him."

"Sure," Matthew says without looking away from his computer. "I'll get him to give me a time."

"Lovely. Well, I have to go—I hope that answered your question, Tris." She smiles at me and slips out the door.

I sit hunched, with my elbows on my knees. Marcus was Divergent—genetically pure, just like me. But I don't accept that he was a bad person because he was surrounded by genetically damaged people. So was I. So was Uriah. So was my mother. But none of us lashed out at our loved ones.

"Her argument has a few holes in it, doesn't it," says Matthew. He's watching me from behind his desk, tapping his fingers on the arm of his chair.

"Yeah," I say.

"Some of the people here want to blame genetic damage for everything," he says. "It's easier for them to accept than the truth, which is that they can't know everything about people and why they act the way they do."

"Everyone has to blame something for the way the world is," I say. "For my father it was the Erudite."

"I probably shouldn't tell you that the Erudite were always my favorite, then," Matthew says, smiling a little.

"Really?" I straighten. "Why?"

"I don't know, I guess I agree with them. That if everyone would just keep learning about the world around them, they would have far fewer problems."

"I've been wary of them my whole life," I say, resting my chin on my hand. "My father hated the Erudite, so I learned to hate them too, and everything they did with their time. Only now I'm thinking he was wrong. Or just . . . biased."

"About the Erudite or about learning?"

I shrug. "Both. So many of the Erudite helped me when I didn't ask them to." Will, Fernando, Cara—all Erudite, all some of the best people I've known, however briefly. "They were so focused on making the world a better place." I shake my head. "What Jeanine did has nothing to do with a thirst for knowledge leading to a thirst for power, like my father told me, and everything to do with her being terrified of how big the world is and how powerless that made her. Maybe it was the Dauntless who had it right."

"There's an old phrase," Matthew says. "Knowledge is power. Power to do evil, like Jeanine . . . or power to do good, like what we're doing. Power itself is not evil. So knowledge itself is not evil."

"I guess I grew up suspicious of both. Power and knowledge," I say. "To the Abnegation, power should only be given to people who don't want it."

"There's something to that," Matthew says. "But maybe it's time to grow out of that suspicion."

He reaches under the desk and takes out a book. It is thick, with a worn cover and frayed edges. On it is printed HUMAN BIOLOGY.

"It's a little rudimentary, but this book helped to teach me what it is to be human," he says. "To be such a complicated, mysterious piece of biological machinery, and more amazing still, to have the capacity to analyze that machinery! That is a special thing, unprecedented in all of evolutionary history. Our ability to know about ourselves and the world is what makes us human."

He hands me the book and turns back to the computer. I look down at the worn cover and run my fingers along the edge of the pages. He makes the acquisition of knowledge feel like a secret, beautiful thing, and an ancient thing. I feel like, if I read this book, I can reach backward through all the generations of humanity to the very first one, whenever it was—that I can participate in something many times larger and older than myself.

"Thank you," I say, and it's not for the book. It's for giving something back to me, something I lost before I was able to really have it.

+ + +

The lobby of the hotel smells like candied lemon and bleach, an acrid combination that burns my nostrils when I breathe it in. I walk past a potted plant with a garish flower blossoming among its branches, and toward the dormitory that has become our temporary home here. As I walk I wipe the screen with the hem of my shirt, trying to get rid of some of my fingerprints.

Caleb is alone in the dormitory, his hair tousled and his eyes red from sleep. He blinks at me when I walk in and toss the biology book onto my bed. I feel a sickening ache in my stomach and press the screen with our mother's file against my side. *He's her son. He has a right to read her journal, just like you.*

"If you have something to say," he says, "just say it."

"Mom lived here." I blurt it out like a long-held secret, too loud and too fast. "She came from the fringe, and they brought her here, and she lived here for a couple years, then went into the city to stop the Erudite from killing the Divergent."

Caleb blinks at me. Before I lose my nerve, I hold out the screen for him to take. "Her file is here. It's not very long, but you should read it."

He gets up and closes his hand around the glass. He's so much taller than he used to be, so much taller than I am. For a few years when we were children, I was the taller one, even though I was almost a year younger. Those were some of our best years, the ones where I didn't feel like he was bigger or better or smarter or more selfless than I was.

"How long have you known this?" he says, narrowing his eyes.

"It doesn't matter." I step back. "I'm telling you now. You can keep that, by the way. I'm done with it."

He wipes the screen with his sleeve and navigates with deft fingers to our mother's first journal entry. I expect him to sit down and read it, thus ending the conversation, but instead he sighs.

"I have something to show you, too," he says. "About Edith Prior. Come on."

It's her name, not my lingering attachment to him, that draws me after him when he starts to walk away.

He leads me out of the dormitory and down the hallway and around corners to a room far away from any that I have seen in the Bureau compound. It is long and narrow, the walls covered with shelves that bear identical blue-gray books, thick and heavy as dictionaries. Between the first two rows is a long wooden table with chairs tucked beneath it. Caleb flips the light switch, and pale light fills the room, reminding me of Erudite headquarters.

"I've been spending a lot of time here," he says. "It's the

record room. They keep some of the Chicago experiment data in here."

He walks along the shelves on the right side of the room, running his fingers over the book spines. He pulls out one of the volumes and lays it flat on the table, so it spills open, its pages covered in text and pictures.

"Why don't they keep all this on computers?"

"I assume they kept these records before they developed a sophisticated security system on their network," he says without looking up. "Data never fully disappears, but paper can be destroyed forever, so you can actually get rid of it if you don't want the wrong people to get their hands on it. It's safer, sometimes, to have everything printed out."

His green eyes shift back and forth as he searches for the right place, his fingers nimble, built for turning pages. I think of how he disguised that part of himself, wedging books between his headboard and the wall in our Abnegation house, until he dropped his blood in the Erudite water on the day of our Choosing Ceremony. I should have known, then, that he was a liar, with loyalty only to himself.

I feel that sickening ache again. I can hardly stand to be in here with him, the door closing us in, nothing but the table between us.

"Ah, here." He touches his finger to a page, then spins

the book around to show me.

It looks like a copy of a contract, but it's handwritten in ink:

I, Amanda Marie Ritter, of Peoria, Illinois, give my consent to the following procedures:

- The "genetic healing" procedure, as defined by the Bureau of Genetic Welfare: "a genetic engineering procedure designed to correct the genes specified as 'damaged' on page three of this form."
- The "reset procedure," as defined by the Bureau of Genetic Welfare: "a memory-erasing procedure designed to make an experiment participant more fit for the experiment."

I declare that I have been thoroughly instructed as to the risks and benefits of these procedures by a member of the Bureau of Genetic Welfare. I understand that this means I will be given a new background and a new identity by the Bureau and inserted into the experiment in Chicago, Illinois, where I will live out the remainder of my days.

I agree to reproduce at least twice to give my corrected genes the best possible chance of survival. I understand that I will be encouraged to do this when I am reeducated after the reset procedure.

I also give my consent for my children and my children's children, etc., to continue in this experiment until such time as the Bureau of Genetic Welfare deems it to be complete. They will be instructed in the false history that I myself will be given after the reset procedure.

Signed,

Amanda Marie Ritter

Amanda Marie Ritter. She was the woman in the video, Edith Prior, my ancestor.

I look up at Caleb, whose eyes are alight with knowledge, like there's a live wire running through each of them.

Our ancestor.

I pull out one of the chairs and sit. "She was Dad's ancestor?"

He nods and sits down across from me. "Seven generations back, yes. An aunt. Her brother is the one who carried on the Prior name."

"And this is . . ."

"It's a consent form," he says. "Her consent form for joining the experiment. The endnotes say that this was just a first draft—she was one of the original experiment designers. A member of the Bureau. There were only a few Bureau members in the original experiment; most of the people in the experiment weren't working for the government."

I read the words again, trying to make sense of them. When I saw her in the video, it seemed so logical that she would become a resident of our city, that she would immerse herself in our factions, that she would volunteer to leave behind everything she left behind. But that was before I knew what life was like outside the city, and it doesn't seem as horrific as what Edith described in her message to us.

She delivered a skillful manipulation in that video, which was intended to keep us contained and dedicated to the vision of the Bureau—*the world outside the city is badly broken, and the Divergent need to come out here and heal it*. It's not quite a lie, because the people in the Bureau do believe that healed genes will fix certain things, that if we integrate into the general population and pass our genes on, the world will be a better place. But they didn't need the Divergent to march out of our city like an army to fight injustice and save everyone, as Edith suggested. I wonder if Edith Prior believed her own words, or if she just said them because she had to.

There's a photograph of her on the next page, her mouth in a firm line, wisps of brown hair hanging around her face. She must have seen something terrible, to volunteer for her memory to be erased and her entire life remade.

"Do you know why she joined?" I say.

Caleb shakes his head. "The records suggest—though they're fairly vague on this front—that people joined the experiment so their families could escape extreme poverty—the families of the subjects were offered a monthly stipend for the subject's participation, for upward of ten years. But obviously that wasn't Edith's motivation, since she worked for the Bureau. I suspect something traumatic must have happened to her, something she was determined to forget."

I frown at her photograph. I can't imagine what kind of poverty would motivate a person to forget themselves and everyone they loved so their families could get a monthly stipend. I may have lived on Abnegation bread and vegetables for most of my life, with nothing to spare, but I was never that desperate. Their situation must have been much worse than anything I saw in the city.

I can't imagine why Edith was that desperate either. Or maybe it's just that she didn't have anyone to keep her memory for.

"I was interested in the legal precedent for giving consent on behalf of one's descendants," Caleb says. "I think it's an extrapolation of giving consent for one's children under eighteen, but it seems a little odd."

"I guess we all decide our children's fates just by making our own life decisions," I say vaguely. "Would we have chosen the same factions we did if Mom and Dad hadn't chosen Abnegation?" I shrug. "I don't know. Maybe we wouldn't have felt as stifled. Maybe we would have become different people."

The thought creeps into my mind like a slithering creature—*Maybe we would have become better people. People who don't betray their own sisters.*

I stare at the table in front of me. For the past few minutes it was easy to pretend that Caleb and I were just brother and sister again. But a person can only keep reality—and anger—at bay for so long before the truth comes back again. As I raise my eyes to his, I think of looking at him in just this way, when I was still a prisoner in Erudite headquarters. I think of being too tired to fight with him anymore, or to hear his excuses; too tired to care that my brother had abandoned me.

I ask tersely, "Edith joined Erudite, didn't she? Even though she took an Abnegation name?"

"Yes!" He doesn't seem to notice my tone. "In fact, most of our ancestors were in Erudite. There were a few Abnegation outliers, and one or two Candor, but the through line is fairly consistent."

I feel cold, like I might shiver and then shatter.

"So I suppose you've used this as an excuse in your twisted mind for what you did," I say steadily. "For joining

Erudite, for being loyal to them. I mean, if you were supposed to be one of them all along, then 'faction before blood' is an acceptable thing to believe, right?"

"Tris . . ." he says, and his eyes plead with me for understanding, but I do not understand. I won't.

I stand up. "So now I know about Edith and you know about our mother. Good. Let's just leave it at that, then."

Sometimes when I look at him I feel the ache of sympathy toward him, and sometimes I feel like I want to wrap my hands around his throat. But right now I just want to escape, and pretend this never happened. I walk out of the records room, and my shoes squeak on the tile floor as I run back to the hotel. I run until I smell sweet citrus, and then I stop.

Tobias is standing in the hallway outside the dormitory. I am breathless, and I can feel my heartbeat even in my fingertips; I am overwhelmed, teeming with loss and wonder and anger and longing.

"Tris," Tobias says, his brow furrowed with concern. "Are you all right?"

I shake my head, still struggling for air, and crush him against the wall with my body, my lips finding his. For a moment he tries to push me away, but then he must decide that he doesn't care if I'm all right, doesn't care if he's all right, doesn't care. We haven't been alone together in days. Weeks. Months.

His fingers slide into my hair, and I hold on to his arms to stay steady as we press together like two blades at a stalemate. He is stronger than anyone I know, and warmer than anyone else realizes; he is a secret that I have kept, and will keep, for the rest of my life.

He leans down and kisses my throat, hard, and his hands smooth over me, securing themselves at my waist. I hook my fingers in his belt loops, my eyes closing. In that moment I know exactly what I want; I want to peel away all the layers of clothing between us, strip away everything that separates us, the past and the present and the future.

I hear footsteps and laughter at the end of the hallway, and we break apart. Someone—probably Uriah—whistles, but I barely hear it over the pulsing in my ears.

Tobias's eyes meet mine, and it's like the first time I really looked at him during my initiation, after my fear simulation; we stare too long, too intently. "Shut up," I call out to Uriah, without looking away.

Uriah and Christina walk into the dormitory, and Tobias and I follow them, like nothing happened.

CHAPTER TWENTY-THREE

TOBIAS

THAT NIGHT WHEN my head hits the pillow, heavy with thoughts, I hear something crinkle beneath my cheek. A note under my pillowcase.

> *T—*
>
> *Meet me outside the hotel entrance at eleven. I need to talk to you.*
>
> *—Nita*

I look at Tris's cot. She's sprawled on her back, and there is a piece of hair covering her nose and mouth that shifts with each exhale. I don't want to wake her, but I feel strange, going to meet a girl in the middle of the night without telling her about it. Especially now that we're trying so hard to be honest with each other.

I check my watch. It's ten to eleven.

Nita's just a friend. You can tell Tris tomorrow. It might be urgent.

I push the blankets back and shove my feet into my shoes—I sleep in my clothes these days. I pass Peter's cot, then Uriah's. The top of a flask peeks out from beneath Uriah's pillow. I pinch it between my fingers and carry it toward the door, where I slide it under the pillow on one of the empty cots. I haven't been looking after him as well as I promised Zeke I would.

Once I'm in the hallway, I tie my shoes and smooth my hair down. I stopped cutting it like the Abnegation when I wanted the Dauntless to see me as a potential leader, but I miss the ritual of the old way, the buzz of the clippers and the careful movements of my hands, knowing more by touch than by sight. When I was young, my father used to do it, in the hallway on the top floor of our Abnegation house. He was always too careless with the blade, and scraped the back of my neck, or nicked my ear. But he never complained about having to cut my hair for me. That's something, I guess.

Nita is tapping her foot. This time she wears a white short-sleeved shirt, her hair pulled back. She smiles, but it doesn't quite reach her eyes.

"You look worried," I say.

"That's because I am," she answers. "Come on, there's a place I've been wanting to show you."

She leads me down dim hallways, empty except for the occasional janitor. They all seem to know Nita—they wave at her, or smile. She puts her hands in her pockets, guiding her eyes carefully away from mine every time we happen to look at each other.

We go through a door without a security sensor to keep it locked. The room beyond it is a wide circle with a chandelier marking its center with dangling glass. The floors are polished wood, dark, and the walls, covered in sheets of bronze, gleam where the light touches them. There are names inscribed on the bronze panels, dozens of names.

Nita stands beneath the glass chandelier and holds her arms out, wide, to encompass the room in her gesture.

"These are the Chicago family trees," she says. "Your family trees."

I move closer to one of the walls and read through the names, searching for one that looks familiar. At the end, I find one: Uriah Pedrad and Ezekiel Pedrad. Next to each name is a small "DD," and there is a dot next to Uriah's name, and it looks freshly carved. Marking him as Divergent, probably.

"Do you know where mine is?" I say.

She crosses the room and touches one of the panels.

"The generations are matrilineal. That's why Jeanine's records said Tris was 'second generation'—because her mother came from outside the city. I'm not sure how Jeanine knew that, but I guess we'll never find out."

I approach the panel that bears my name with trepidation, though I'm not sure what I have to fear from seeing my name and my parents' names carved into bronze. I see a vertical line connecting Kristin Johnson to Evelyn Johnson, and a horizontal one connecting Evelyn Johnson to Marcus Eaton. Below the two names is just one: Tobias Eaton. The small letters beside my name are "AD," and there's a dot there too, though I now know I'm not actually Divergent.

"The first letter is your faction of origin," she says, "and the second is your faction of choice. They thought that keeping track of the factions would help them trace the path of the genes."

My mother's letters: "EAF." The "F" is for "factionless," I assume.

My father's letters: "AA," with a dot.

I touch the line connecting me to them, and the line connecting Evelyn to her parents, and the line connecting them to their parents, all the way back through eight generations, counting my own. This is a map of what I've always known, that I am tied to them, bound forever to this empty inheritance no matter how far I run.

"While I appreciate you showing me this," I say, and I feel sad, and tired, "I'm not sure why it had to happen in the middle of the night."

"I thought you might want to see it. And I had something I wanted to talk to you about."

"More reassurance that my limitations don't define me?" I shake my head. "No thanks, I've had enough of that."

"No," she says. "But I'm glad you said that."

She leans against the panel, covering Evelyn's name with her shoulder. I step back, not wanting to be so close to her that I can see the ring of lighter brown around her pupils.

"That conversation I had with you last night, about genetic damage . . . it was actually a test. I wanted to see how you would react to what I said about damaged genes, so I would know whether I could trust you or not," she says. "If you accepted what I said about your limitations, the answer would have been no." She slides a little closer to me, so her shoulder covers Marcus's name too. "See, I'm not really on board with being classified as 'damaged.'"

I think of the way she spat out the explanation of the tattoo of broken glass on her back like it was poison.

My heart starts to beat harder, so I can feel my pulse in

my throat. Bitterness has replaced the good humor in her voice, and her eyes have lost their warmth. I am afraid of her, afraid of what she says—and thrilled by it too, because it means I don't have to accept that I am smaller than I once believed.

"I take it you aren't on board with it either," she says.

"No. I'm not."

"There are a lot of secrets in this place," she says. "One of them is that, to them, a GD is expendable. Another is that some of us are not just going to sit back and take it."

"What do you mean, expendable?" I say.

"The crimes they have committed against people like us are serious," Nita says. "And hidden. I can show you evidence, but that will have to come later. For now, what I can tell you is that we're working against the Bureau, for good reasons, and we want you with us."

I narrow my eyes. "Why? What is it you want from me, exactly?"

"Right now I want to offer you an opportunity to see what the world is like outside the compound."

"And what you get in return is . . . ?"

"Your protection," she says. "I'm going to a dangerous place, and I can't tell anyone else from the Bureau about it. You're an outsider, which means it's safer for me to trust you, and I know you know how to defend yourself. And if you come with me, I'll show you that evidence you want to see."

She touches her heart, lightly, as if swearing on it. My skepticism is strong, but my curiosity is stronger. It's not hard for me to believe that the Bureau would do bad things, because every government I've ever known has done bad things, even the Abnegation oligarchy, of which my father was the head. And even beyond that reasonable suspicion, I have brewing inside me the desperate hope that I am not damaged, that I am worth more than the corrected genes I pass on to any children I might have.

So I decide to go along with this. For now.

"Fine," I say.

"First," she says, "before I show you anything, you have to accept that you won't be able to tell anyone—even Tris—about what you see. Are you all right with that?"

"She's trustworthy, you know." I promised Tris I wouldn't keep secrets from her anymore. I shouldn't get into situations where I'll have to do it again. "Why can't I tell her?"

"I'm not saying she isn't trustworthy. It's just that she doesn't have the skill set we need, and we don't want to put anyone at risk that we don't have to. See, the Bureau doesn't want us to organize. If we believe we're not 'damaged,' then we're saying that everything they're doing—the experiments, the genetic alterations, all of it—is a waste of time. And no one wants to hear that their life's work is a sham."

I know all about that—it's like finding out that the factions are an artificial system, designed by scientists to keep us under control for as long as possible.

She pulls away from the wall, and then she says the only thing she could possibly say to make me agree:

"If you tell her, you would be depriving her of the choice I'm giving you now. You would force her to become a coconspirator. By keeping this from her, you would be protecting her."

I run my fingers over my name, carved into the metal panel, Tobias Eaton. These are my genes, this is my mess. I don't want to pull Tris into it.

"All right," I say. "Show me."

+ + +

I watch her flashlight beam bob up and down with her footsteps. We just retrieved a bag from a mop closet down the hall—she was ready for this. She leads me deep into the underground hallways of the compound, past the place where the GDs gather, to a corridor where the electricity no longer flows. At a certain place she crouches and slides her hand along the ground until her fingers reach a latch. She hands me the flashlight and pulls back the latch, lifting a door from the tile.

"It's an escape tunnel," she says. "They dug it when they first came here, so there would always be a way to escape during an emergency."

From her bag she takes a black tube and twists off the top. It sprays sparks of light that glow red against her skin. She releases it over the doorway and it falls several feet, leaving a streak of light on my eyelids. She sits on the edge of the hole, her backpack secure around her shoulders, and drops.

I know it's just a short way down, but it feels like more with the space open beneath me. I sit, the silhouette of my shoes dark against the red sparks, and push myself forward.

"Interesting," Nita says when I land. I lift up the flashlight, and she holds the flare out in front of her as we walk down the tunnel, which is just wide enough for the two of us to walk side by side, and just tall enough for me to straighten up. It smells rich and rotten, like mold and dead air. "I forgot you were afraid of heights."

"Well, I'm not afraid of much else," I say.

"No need to get defensive!" She smiles. "I actually have always wanted to ask you about that."

I step over a puddle, the soles of my shoes gripping the gritty tunnel floor.

"Your third fear," she says. "Shooting that woman. Who was she?"

The flare goes out, so the flashlight I'm holding is our only guide through the tunnel. I shift my arm to create more space between us, not wanting to skim her arm in the dark.

"She wasn't anyone in particular," I say. "The fear was shooting her."

"You were afraid of shooting people?"

"No," I say. "I was afraid of my considerable capacity to kill."

She is silent, and so am I. That's the first time I've ever said those words out loud, and now I hear how strange they are. How many young men fear that there is a monster inside them? People are supposed to fear others, not themselves. People are supposed to aspire to become their fathers, not shudder at the thought.

"I've always wondered what would be in my fear landscape." She says it in a hushed tone, like a prayer. "Sometimes I feel like there is so much to be afraid of, and sometimes I feel like there is nothing left to fear."

I nod, though she can't see me, and we keep moving, the flashlight beam bouncing, our shoes scraping, the moldy air rushing toward us from whatever is on the other end.

+ + +

After twenty minutes of walking, we turn a corner and I smell fresh wind, cold enough to make me shudder. I turn off the flashlight, and the moonlight at the end of the tunnel guides us to our exit.

The tunnel let us out somewhere in the wasteland we drove through to get to the compound, among the crumbling buildings and overgrown trees breaking through the pavement. Parked a few feet away is an old truck, the back covered in shredded, threadbare canvas. Nita kicks one of the tires to test it, then climbs into the driver's seat. The keys already dangle from the ignition.

"Whose truck?" I say when I get into the passenger's seat.

"It belongs to the people we're going to meet. I asked them to park it here," she says.

"And who are they?"

"Friends of mine."

I don't know how she finds her way through the maze of streets before us, but she does, steering the truck around tree roots and fallen streetlights, flashing the headlights at animals that scamper at the edge of my vision.

A long-legged creature with a brown, spare body picks

its way across the street ahead of us, almost as tall as the headlights. Nita eases on the brakes so she doesn't hit it. Its ears twitch, and its dark, round eyes watch us with careful curiosity, like a child.

"Sort of beautiful, aren't they?" she says. "Before I came here I'd never seen a deer."

I nod. It is elegant, but hesitant, halting.

Nita presses the horn with her fingertips, and the deer moves out of the way. We accelerate again, then reach a wide, open road suspended across the railroad tracks I once walked down to reach the compound. I see its lights up ahead, the one bright spot in this dark wasteland.

And we are traveling northeast, away from it.

+ + +

It is a long time before I see electric light again. When I do, it is along a narrow, patchy street. The bulbs dangle from a cord strung along the old streetlights.

"We stop here." Nita jerks the wheel, pulling the truck into an alley between two brick buildings. She takes the keys from the ignition and looks at me. "Check in the glove box. I asked them to give us weapons."

I open the compartment in front of me. Sitting on top of some old wrappers are two knives.

"How are you with a knife?" she says.

The Dauntless taught initiates how to throw knives even before the changes to initiation that Max made before I joined them. I never liked it, because it seemed like a way to encourage the Dauntless flair for theatrics, rather than a useful skill.

"I'm all right," I say with a smirk. "I never thought that skill would actually be worth anything, though."

"I guess the Dauntless are good for something after all . . . *Four*," she says, smiling a little. She takes the larger of the two knives, and I take the smaller one.

I am tense, turning the handle in my fingers as we walk down the alley. Above me the windows flicker with a different kind of light—flames, from candles or lanterns. At one point, when I glance up, I see a curtain of hair and dark eye sockets staring back at me.

"People live here," I say.

"This is the very edge of the fringe," Nita says. "It's about a two-hour drive from Milwaukee, which is a metropolitan area north of here. Yeah, people live here. These days people don't venture too far away from cities, even if they want to live outside the government's influence, like the people here."

"Why do they want to live outside the government's influence?" I know what living outside the government is like, by watching the factionless. They were always hungry, always cold in the winter and hot in the summer, always struggling to survive. It's not an easy life to choose—you have to have a good reason for it.

"Because they're genetically damaged," Nita says, glancing at me. "Genetically damaged people are technically—legally—equal to genetically pure people, but only on paper, so to speak. In reality they're poorer, more likely to be convicted of crimes, less likely to be hired for good jobs . . . you name it, it's a problem, and has been since the Purity War, over a century ago. For the people who live in the fringe, it seemed more appealing to opt out of society completely rather than to try to correct the problem from within, like I intend to do."

I think of the fragment of glass tattooed on her skin. I wonder when she got it—I wonder what put that dangerous look in her eyes, what put such drama in her speech, what made her become a revolutionary.

"How do you plan on doing that?"

She sets her jaw and says, "By taking away some of the Bureau's power."

The alley opens up to a wide street. Some people prowl along the edges, but others walk right in the middle, in lurching groups, bottles swinging from their hands. Everyone I see is young—not many adults in the fringe, I guess.

I hear shouting up ahead, and glass shattering on the pavement. A crowd there stands in a circle around two punching, kicking figures.

I start toward them, but Nita grabs my arm and drags me toward one of the buildings.

"Not the time to be a hero," she says.

We approach the door to the building on the corner. A large man stands beside it, spinning a knife in his palm. When we walk up the steps, he stops the knife and tosses it into his other hand, which is gnarled with scars.

His size, his deftness with the weapon, his scarred and dusty appearance—they are all supposed to intimidate me. But his eyes are like that deer's eyes, large and wary and curious.

"We're here to see Rafi," she says. "We're from the compound."

"You can go in, but your knives stay here," the man says. His voice is higher, lighter than I expected. He could be a gentle man, maybe, if this were a different kind of place. As it is, I see that he isn't gentle, doesn't even know what that means.

Even though I myself have discarded any kind of softness as useless, I find myself thinking that something important is lost if this man has been forced to deny his own nature.

"Not a chance," Nita says.

"Nita, is that you?" says a voice from inside. It is expressive, musical. The man to whom it belongs is short, with a wide smile. He comes to the doorway. "Didn't I tell you to just let them in? Come in, come in."

"Hi, Rafi," she says, her relief obvious. "Four, this is Rafi. He's an important man in the fringe."

"Nice to meet you," Rafi says, and he beckons for us to follow him.

Inside is a large, open room lit by rows of candles and lanterns. There is wooden furniture strewn everywhere, all the tables empty but one.

A woman sits in the back of the room, and Rafi slides into the chair beside her. Though they don't look the same—she has red hair and a generous frame; his features are dark and his body, spare as wire—they have the same sort of look, like two stones hewn by the same chisel.

"Weapons on the table," Rafi says.

This time, Nita obeys, putting her knife on the edge of the table right in front of her. She sits. I do the same. Across from us, the woman surrenders a gun.

"Who's this?" the woman says, jerking her head toward me.

"This is my associate," Nita says. "Four."

"What kind of a name is 'Four'?" She doesn't ask with a

sneer, the way people have often asked me that question.

"The kind you get inside the city experiment," Nita says. "For having only four fears."

It occurs to me that she might have introduced me by that name just to have an opportunity to share where I'm from. Does it give her some kind of leverage? Does it make me more trustworthy to these people?

"Interesting." The woman taps the table with her index finger. "Well, *Four*, my name is Mary."

"Mary and Rafi lead the Midwest branch of a GD rebel group," Nita says.

"Calling it a 'group' makes us sound like old ladies playing cards," Rafi says smoothly. "We're more of an uprising. Our reach stretches across the country—there's a group for every metropolitan area that exists, and regional overseers for the Midwest, South, and East."

"Is there a West?" I say.

"Not anymore," Nita says quietly. "The terrain was too difficult to navigate and the cities too spread out for it to be sensible to live there after the war. Now it's wild country."

"So it's true what they say," Mary says, her eyes catching the light like slivers of glass as she looks at me. "The people in the city experiments really don't know what's outside."

"Of course it's true, why would they?" Nita says.

Fatigue, a weight behind my eyes, creeps up on me suddenly. I have been a part of too many uprisings in my short life. The factionless, and now this GD one, apparently.

"Not to cut the pleasantries short," Mary says, "but we shouldn't spend much time here. We can't keep people out for long before they come sniffing around."

"Right," Nita says. She looks at me. "Four, can you make sure nothing's happening outside? I need to talk to Mary and Rafi privately for a little while."

If we were alone, I would ask why I can't be here when she talks to them, or why she bothered to bring me in when I could have stood guard outside the whole time. I guess I haven't actually agreed to help her yet, and she must have wanted them to meet me for some reason. So I just get up, taking my knife with me, and walk to the door where Rafi's guard watches the street.

The fight across the street has died down. A lone figure lies on the pavement. For a moment I think it's still moving, but then I realize that's because someone is rifling through its pockets. It's not a figure—it's a body.

"Dead?" I say, and the word is just an exhale.

"Yep. If you can't defend yourself here, you won't last a night."

"Why do people come here, then?" I frown. "Why don't

they just go back to the cities?"

He's quiet for so long that I think he must not have heard my question. I watch the thief turn the dead person's pockets inside out and abandon the body, slipping into one of the nearby buildings. Finally, Rafi's guard speaks:

"Here, there's a chance that if you die, someone will care. Like Rafi, or one of the other leaders," the guard says. "In the cities, if you get killed, definitely no one will give a damn, not if you're a GD. The worst crime I've ever seen a GP get charged with for killing a GD was 'manslaughter.' Bullshit."

"Manslaughter?"

"It means the crime is deemed an accident," Rafi's smooth, lilting voice says behind me. "Or at least not as severe as, say, first-degree murder. *Officially*, of course, we're all to be treated the same, yes? But that is rarely put into practice."

He stands beside me, his arms folded. I see, when I look at him, a king surveying his own kingdom, which he believes is beautiful. I look out at the street, at the broken pavement and the limp body with its turned-out pockets and the windows flickering with firelight, and I know the beauty he sees is just freedom—freedom to be seen as a whole man instead of a damaged one.

248

I saw that freedom, once, when Evelyn beckoned to me from among the factionless, called me out of my faction to become a more complete person. But it was a lie.

"You're from Chicago?" Rafi says to me.

I nod, still looking at the dark street.

"And now that you are out? How does the world seem to you?" he says.

"Mostly the same," I say. "People are just divided by different things, fighting different wars."

Nita's footsteps creak on the floorboards inside, and when I turn she is standing right behind me, her hands buried in her pockets.

"Thanks for arranging this," Nita says, nodding to Rafi. "It's time for us to go."

We make our way down the street again, and when I turn to look at Rafi, he has his hand up, waving good-bye.

+ + +

As we walk back to the truck, I hear screams again, but this time they are the screams of a child. I walk past snuffling, whimpering sounds and think of when I was younger, crouched in my bedroom, wiping my nose on one of my sleeves. My mother used to scrub the cuffs with a sponge before throwing them in the wash. She never said anything about it.

When I get into the truck, I already feel numb to this place and its pain, and I am ready to get back to the dream of the compound, the warmth and the light and the feeling of safety.

"I'm having trouble understanding why this place is preferable to city life," I say.

"I've only been to a city that wasn't an experiment once," Nita says. "There's electricity, but it's on a ration system—each family only gets so many hours a day. Same with water. And there's a lot of crime, which is blamed on genetic damage. There are police, too, but they can only do so much."

"So the Bureau compound," I say. "It's easily the best place to live, then."

"In terms of resources, yes," Nita says. "But the same social system that exists in the cities also exists in the compound; it's just a little harder to see."

I watch the fringe disappear in the rearview mirror, distinct from the abandoned buildings around it only by that string of electric lights draped over the narrow street.

We drive past dark houses with boarded-up windows, and I try to imagine them clean and polished, as they must have been at some point in the past. They have fenced-in yards that must have once been trim and green, windows that must once have glowed in the evenings. I imagine that the lives lived here were peaceful ones, quiet ones.

"What did you come out here to talk to them about, exactly?" I say.

"I came out here to solidify our plans," Nita says. I notice, in the glow of the dashboard light, that there are a few cuts on her lower lip, like she has spent too much time biting it. "And I wanted them to meet you, to put a face on the people inside the faction experiments. Mary used to be suspicious that people like you were actually colluding with the government, which of course isn't true. Rafi, though . . . he was the first person to give me proof that the Bureau, the government, was lying to us about our history."

She pauses after she says it, like that will help me to feel the weight of it, but I don't need time or silence or space to believe her. I have been lied to by my government for my entire life.

"The Bureau talks about this golden age of humanity before the genetic manipulations in which everyone was genetically pure and everything was peaceful," Nita says. "But Rafi showed me old photographs of *war*."

I wait a beat. "So?"

"So?" Nita demands, incredulous. "If genetically pure people caused war and total devastation in the past at the same magnitude that genetically damaged people supposedly do now, then what's the basis for thinking that we need to spend so many resources and so much time working to correct genetic damage? What's the use of the experiments at all, except to convince the right people that the government is doing something to make all our lives better, even though it's not?"

The truth changes everything—isn't that why Tris was so desperate to get the Edith Prior video shown that she allied herself with my father to do it? She knew that the truth, whatever it was, would change our struggle, would shift our priorities forever. And here, now, a lie has changed the struggle, a lie has shifted priorities forever. Instead of working against the poverty or crime that have run rampant over this country, these people have chosen to work against genetic damage.

"Why? Why spend so much time and energy fighting something that isn't really a problem?" I demand, suddenly frustrated.

"Well, the people fighting it now probably fight it because they have been taught that it *is* a problem. That's another thing that Rafi showed me—examples of the propaganda the government released about genetic damage," Nita says. "But initially? I don't know. It's probably a dozen things. Prejudice against GDs? Control, maybe? Control the genetically damaged population by teaching them that there's something wrong with them, and control the genetically pure population by teaching them that they're healed and whole? These things don't happen overnight, and they don't happen for just one reason."

I lean the side of my head against the cold window and close my eyes. There is too much information buzzing in my brain to focus on any single part of it, so I give up trying and let myself drift off.

By the time we make it back through the tunnel and I find my bed, the sun is about to rise, and Tris's arm is hanging over the edge of her bed again, her fingertips brushing the floor.

I sit down across from her, for a moment watching her sleeping face and thinking of what we agreed, that night in Millennium Park: no more lies. She promised me, and I promised her. And if I don't tell her about what I heard and saw tonight, I will be going back on that promise. And for what? To protect her? For Nita, a girl I barely know?

I brush her hair away from her face, gently, so I don't wake her.

She doesn't need my protection. She's strong enough on her own.

CHAPTER
TWENTY-FOUR

TRIS

PETER IS ACROSS the room, gathering a stack of books into a pile and shoving them into a bag. He bites down on a red pen and carries the bag out of the room; I hear the books inside it smacking against his leg as he walks down the hallway. I wait until I can't hear them anymore before I turn to Christina.

"I've been trying not to ask you, but I'm giving up," I say. "What's going on with you and Uriah?"

Christina, sprawled across her cot with one long leg dangling over the edge, gives me a look.

"What? You've been spending a lot of time together," I say. "Like a lot."

It's sunny today, the light glowing through the white

curtains. I don't know how, but the dormitory smells like sleep—like laundry and shoes and night sweats and morning coffee. Some of the beds are made, and some still have rumpled sheets bunched up at the bottom or the side. Most of us came from Dauntless, but I'm struck by how different we are anyway. Different habits, different temperaments, different ways of seeing the world.

"You may not believe me, but it's not like that." Christina props herself up on her elbows. "He's grieving. We're both bored. Also, he's *Uriah*."

"So? He's good-looking."

"Good-looking, but he can't have a serious conversation to save his life." Christina shakes her head. "Don't get me wrong, I like to laugh, but I also want a relationship to mean something, you know?"

I nod. I do know—better than most people, maybe, because Tobias and I aren't really the joking type.

"Besides," she says, "not every friendship turns into a romance. I haven't tried to kiss you yet."

I laugh. "True."

"Where have *you* been lately?" Christina says. She wiggles her eyebrows. "With Four? Doing a little . . . addition? Multiplication?"

I cover my face with my hands. "That was the worst joke I've ever heard."

"Don't dodge the question."

"No 'addition' for us," I say. "Not yet, anyway. He's been a little preoccupied with the whole 'genetic damage' thing."

"Ah. *That* thing." She sits up.

"What do you think about it?" I say.

"I don't know. I guess it makes me angry." She frowns. "No one likes to be told there's something wrong with them, especially something like their genes, which they can't change."

"You think there's really something wrong with you?"

"I guess so. It's like a disease, right? They can see it in our genes. That's not really up for debate, is it?"

"I'm not saying your genes aren't different," I say. "I'm just saying that doesn't mean one set is damaged and one set isn't. The genes for blue eyes and brown eyes are different too, but are blue eyes 'damaged'? It's like they just arbitrarily decided that one kind of DNA was bad and the other was good."

"Based on the evidence that GD behavior was worse," Christina points out.

"Which could be caused by a lot of things," I retort.

"I don't know why I'm arguing with you when I'd really like for you to be right," Christina says, laughing. "But don't you think a bunch of smart people like these Bureau scientists could figure out the cause of bad behavior?"

"Sure," I say. "But I think that no matter how smart,

people usually see what they're already looking for, that's all."

"Maybe you're biased too," she says. "Because you have friends—and a boyfriend—with this genetic issue."

"Maybe." I know I'm fumbling for an explanation, one I may not really believe, but I say it anyway: "I guess I don't see a reason to believe in genetic damage. Will it make me treat other people better? No. The opposite, maybe."

And besides, I see what it's doing to Tobias, how it's making him doubt himself, and I don't understand how anything good can possibly come from it.

"You don't believe things because they make your life better, you believe them because they're true," she points out.

"But"—I speak slowly as I mull that over—"isn't looking at the result of a belief a good way of evaluating if it's true?"

"Sounds like a Stiff way of thinking." She pauses. "I guess my way is very Candor, though. God, we really can't escape factions no matter where we go, can we?"

I shrug. "Maybe it's not so important to escape them."

Tobias walks into the dormitory, looking pale and exhausted, like he always does these days. His hair is pushed up on one side from lying on his pillow, and he's still wearing what he wore yesterday. He's been sleeping in his clothes since we came to the Bureau.

Christina gets up. "Okay, I'm going to go. And leave you two . . . to *all this space*. Alone." She gestures at all the empty beds, and then winks conspicuously at me as she walks out of the dormitory.

Tobias smiles a little, but not enough to make me think he's actually happy. And instead of sitting next to me, he lingers at the foot of my bed, his fingers fumbling over the hem of his shirt.

"There's something I want to talk to you about," he says.

"Okay," I say, and I feel a spike of fear in my chest, like a jump on a heart monitor.

"I want to ask you to promise not to get mad," he says, "but . . ."

"But you know I don't make stupid promises," I say, my throat tight.

"Right." He does sit, then, in the curve of blankets left unmade on his bed. He avoids my eyes. "Nita left a note under my pillow, telling me to meet her last night. And I did."

I straighten, and I can feel an angry heat spreading through me as I picture Nita's pretty face, Nita's graceful feet, walking toward my boyfriend.

"A pretty girl asks you to meet her late at night, and you *go*?" I demand. "And then you want me not to get *mad* about it?"

"It's not about that with Nita and me. At all," he says hastily, finally looking at me. "She just wanted to show me something. She doesn't believe in genetic damage, like she led me to believe. She has a plan to take away some of the Bureau's power, to make GDs more equal. We went to the fringe."

He tells me about the underground tunnel that leads outside, and the ramshackle town in the fringe, and the conversation with Rafi and Mary. He explains the war that the government kept hidden so that no one would know that "genetically pure" people are capable of incredible violence, and the way GDs live in the metropolitan areas where the government still has real power.

As he speaks, I feel suspicion toward Nita building inside me, but I don't know where it comes from—the gut instinct I usually trust, or my jealousy. When he finishes, he looks at me expectantly, and I purse my lips, trying to decide.

"How do you know she's telling you the truth?" I say.

"I don't," he says. "She promised to show me evidence. Tonight." He takes my hand. "I'd like you to come."

"And Nita will be okay with that?"

"I don't really care." His fingers slide between mine. "If she really needs my help, she'll have to figure out how to be okay with it."

I look at our joined fingers, at the fraying cuff of his gray shirt and the worn knee of his jeans. I don't want to spend time with Nita and Tobias together, knowing that her supposed genetic damage gives her something in common with him that I will never have. But this is important to him, and I want to know if there's evidence of the Bureau's wrongdoing as much as he does.

"Okay," I say. "I'll go. But don't for a second think that I actually believe she's not interested in you for more than your genetic code."

"Well," he says. "Don't for a second think I'm interested in anyone but you."

He puts his hand on the back of my neck and draws my mouth toward his.

The kiss and his words both comfort me, but my unease doesn't completely disappear.

CHAPTER
TWENTY-FIVE

TOBIAS

TRIS AND I meet Nita in the hotel lobby after midnight, among the potted plants with their unfurling flowers, a tame wilderness. When Nita sees Tris at my side, her face tightens like she just tasted something bitter.

"You promised you wouldn't tell her," she says, pointing at me. "What happened to protecting her?"

"I changed my mind," I say.

Tris laughs, harshly. "That's what you told him, that he would be protecting me? That's a pretty skillful manipulation. Well done."

I raise my eyebrows at her. I never thought of it as a manipulation, and that scares me a little. I can usually rely on myself to see a person's ulterior motives, or to invent them in my mind, but I was so used to my desire to protect Tris, especially after almost losing her, that I didn't even think twice.

Or I was so used to lying instead of telling difficult truths that I welcomed the chance to deceive her.

"It wasn't a manipulation, it was the truth." Nita doesn't look angry anymore, just tired, her hand sliding over her face and then smoothing back her hair. She isn't defensive, which means she might be telling the truth. "You could be arrested just for knowing what you know and not reporting it. I thought it would be better to avoid that."

"Well, too late," I say. "Tris is coming. Is that a problem?"

"I would rather have both of you than neither of you, and I'm sure that's the implied ultimatum," Nita says, rolling her eyes. "Let's go."

+ + +

Tris, Nita, and I walk back through the silent, still compound to the laboratories where Nita works. None of us speaks, and I am conscious of every squeak of my shoes, every voice in the distance, every snap of every closing door. I feel like we're doing something forbidden, though technically we aren't. Not yet, anyway.

Nita stops by the door to the laboratories and scans her card. We follow her past the gene therapy room where I saw a map of my genetic code, farther into the heart of the compound than I have been yet. It's dark and grim back here, and clumps of dust dance over the floor when we walk past.

Nita pushes another door open with her shoulder, and we walk into a storage room. Dull metal drawers cover the walls, labeled with paper numbers, the ink worn off with time. In the center of the room is a lab table with a computer and a microscope, and a young man with slicked-back blond hair.

"Tobias, Tris, this is my friend Reggie," Nita says. "He's also a GD."

"Nice to meet you," Reggie says with a smile. He shakes Tris's hand, then mine, his grip firm.

"Let's show them the slides first," Nita says.

Reggie taps the computer screen and beckons us closer. "Not gonna bite."

Tris and I exchange a glance, then stand behind Reggie at the table to see the screen. Pictures start flashing on it, one after another. They're in grayscale and look grainy and distorted—they must be very old. It takes me only a few seconds to realize that they are photographs of suffering: narrow, pinched children with huge eyes, ditches full of bodies, huge mounds of burning papers.

The photographs move so fast, like book pages

fluttering in the breeze, that I get only impressions of horrors. Then I turn my face away, unable to look any longer. I feel a deep silence grow inside me.

At first, when I look at Tris, her expression is like still water—like the images we just saw caused no ripples. But then her mouth quivers, and she presses her lips together to disguise it.

"Look at these weapons." Reggie brings up a photograph with a man in uniform holding a gun and points. "That kind of gun is incredibly old. The guns used in the Purity War were *much* more advanced. Even the Bureau would agree with that. It's gotta be from a really old conflict. Which must have been waged by genetically *pure* people, since genetic manipulation didn't exist back then."

"How do you hide a *war*?" I say.

"People are isolated, starving," Nita says quietly. "They know only what they're taught, they see only the information that's made available to them. And who controls all that? The government."

"Okay." Tris's head bobs, and she's talking too fast, nervous. "So they're lying about your—*our* history. That doesn't mean they're the enemy, it just means they're a group of grossly misinformed people trying to . . . better the world. In an ill-advised way."

Nita and Reggie glance at each other.

"That's the thing," Nita says. "They're hurting people."

She puts her hand on the counter and leans into it, leans toward us, and again I see the revolutionary building strength inside her, taking over the parts of her that are young woman and GD and laboratory worker.

"When the Abnegation wanted to reveal the great truth of their world sooner than they were supposed to," she says slowly, "and Jeanine wanted to stifle them . . . the Bureau was all too happy to provide her with an incredibly advanced simulation serum—the attack simulation that enslaved the minds of the Dauntless, that resulted in the destruction of Abnegation."

I take a moment to let that sink in.

"That can't be true," I say. "Jeanine told me that the highest proportion of Divergent—the genetically *pure*—in any faction was in Abnegation. You just said the Bureau values the genetically pure enough to send someone in to save them; why would they help Jeanine kill them?"

"Jeanine was wrong," Tris says distantly. "Evelyn said so. The highest proportion of Divergent was among the factionless, not Abnegation."

I turn to Nita.

"I still don't see why they would risk that many Divergent," I say. "I need evidence."

"Why do you think we came here?" Nita switches on

another set of lights that illuminate the drawers, and paces along the left wall. "It took me a long time to get clearance to go in here," she says. "Even longer to acquire the knowledge to understand what I saw. I had help from one of the GPs, actually. A sympathizer."

Her hand hovers over one of the low drawers. From it she takes a vial of orange liquid.

"Look familiar?" she asks me.

I try to remember the shot they gave me before the attack simulation began, right before the final round of Tris's initiation. Max did it, inserted the needle into the side of my neck as I had done myself dozens of times. Right before he did the glass vial caught the light, and it was orange, just like whatever Nita is holding.

"The colors match," I say. "So?"

Nita carries the vial to the microscope. Reggie takes a slide from a tray near the computer and, using a dropper, puts two drops of the orange liquid in its center, then seals the liquid in place with a second slide. As he places it on the microscope, his fingers are careful but certain; they are the movements of someone who has performed the same action hundreds of times.

Reggie taps the computer screen a few times, opening a program called "MicroScan."

"This information is free and available to anyone

who knows how to use this equipment and has the system password, which the GP sympathizer graciously gave me," Nita says. "So in other words, it's not all that hard to access, but no one would think to examine it very closely. And GDs don't have system passwords, so it's not like we would have known about it. This storage room is for obsolete experiments—failures, or outdated developments, or useless things."

She looks through the microscope, using a knob on the side to focus the lens.

"Go ahead," she says.

Reggie presses a button on the computer, and paragraphs of text appear under the "MicroScan" bar at the top of the screen. He points to a paragraph in the middle of the page, and I read it.

"'Simulation Serum v4.2. Coordinates a large number of targets. Transmits signals over long distances. Hallucinogen from original formula not included—simulated reality is predetermined by program master.'"

That's it.

That's the attack simulation serum.

"Now why would the Bureau have this unless they had developed it?" Nita says. "They were the ones who put the serums into the experiments, but they usually left the serums alone, let the city residents develop them further. If Jeanine was the one who developed it, they wouldn't have stolen it from her. If it's here, it's because *they* made it."

I stare at the illuminated slide in the microscope, at the orange droplet swimming in the eyepiece, and release a shaky breath.

Tris says, breathless, "Why?"

"Abnegation was about to reveal the truth to everyone inside the city. And you've seen what's happened now that the city knows the truth: Evelyn is effectively a dictator, the factionless are squashing the faction members, and I'm sure the factions will rise up against them sooner or later. Many people will die. Telling the truth risks the safety of the experiment, no question," Nita says. "So a few months ago, when the Abnegation were on the verge of causing that destruction and instability by revealing Edith Prior's video to your city, the Bureau probably thought, better that the Abnegation should suffer a great loss—even at the expense of several Divergent—than the whole city suffer a great loss. Better to end the lives of the Abnegation than to risk the experiment. So they reached out to someone who they knew would agree with them. Jeanine Matthews."

Her words surround me and bury themselves inside me.

I set my hands on the lab table, letting it cool my palms, and look at my distorted reflection in the brushed metal.

I may have hated my father for most of my life, but I never hated his faction. Abnegation's quiet, their community, their routine, always seemed good to me. And now most of those kind, giving people are dead. Murdered, at the hands of the Dauntless, at the urging of Jeanine, with the power of the Bureau to back her.

Tris's mother and father were among them.

Tris stands so still, her hands dangling limply, turning red with the flush of her blood.

"This is the problem with their blind commitment to these experiments," Nita says next to us, as if sliding the words into the empty spaces of our minds. "The Bureau values the experiments above GD lives. It's obvious. And now, things could get even worse."

"Worse?" I say. *"Worse* than killing most of the Abnegation? How?"

"The government has been threatening to shut down the experiments for almost a year now," Nita says. "The experiments keep falling apart because the communities can't live in peace, and David keeps finding ways to restore peace just in the nick of time. And if anything else goes wrong in Chicago, he can do it again. He can reset all the experiments at any time."

"*Reset* them," I say.

"With the Abnegation memory serum," Reggie says.

"Well, really, it's the Bureau's memory serum. Every man,

woman, and child will have to begin again."

Nita says tersely, "Their entire lives *erased*, against their will, for the sake of solving a genetic damage 'problem' that doesn't actually exist. These people have the power to do that. And no one should have that power."

I remember the thought I had, after Johanna told me about the Amity administering the memory serum to Dauntless patrols—that when you take a person's memories, you change who they are.

Suddenly I don't care what Nita's plan is, as long as it means striking the Bureau as hard as we can. What I have learned in the past few days has made me feel like there is nothing about this place worth salvaging.

"What's the plan?" says Tris, her voice flat, almost mechanical.

"I'll let my friends from the fringe in through the underground tunnel," Nita says. "Tobias, you will shut off the security system as I do, so that we aren't caught—it's nearly the same technology you worked with in the Dauntless control room; it should be easy for you. Then Rafi, Mary, and I will break into the Weapons Lab and steal the memory serum so the Bureau can't use it. Reggie's been helping behind the scenes, but he'll be opening the tunnel for us on the day of the attack."

"What will you do with a bunch of memory serum?" I say.

"Destroy it," Nita says, even-keeled.

I feel strange, empty like a deflated balloon. I don't know what I had in mind when Nita talked about her plan, but it wasn't this—this feels so small, so passive as an act of retaliation against the people responsible for the attack simulation, the people who told me that there was something wrong with me at my very core, in my genetic code.

"That's *all* you intend to do," Tris says, finally looking away from the microscope. She narrows her eyes at Nita. "You know that the Bureau is responsible for the murders of hundreds of people, and your plan is to . . . take away their memory serum?"

"I don't remember inviting your critique of my plan."

"I'm not critiquing your plan," Tris says. "I'm telling you I don't believe you. You hate these people. I can tell by the way you talk about them. Whatever you intend to do, I think it's far worse than stealing some serum."

"The memory serum is what they use to keep the experiments running. It's their greatest source of power over your city, and I want to take it away. I'd say that's a hard enough blow for now." Nita sounds gentle, like she's explaining something to a child. "I never said this was all I was ever going to do. It's not always wise to strike as hard as you can at the first opportunity. This is a long race, not a sprint."

Tris just shakes her head.

"Tobias, are you in?" Nita says.

I look from Tris, with her tense, stiff posture, to Nita, who is relaxed, ready. I don't see whatever Tris sees, or hear it. And when I think about saying no, I feel like my body will collapse in on itself. I have to do something. Even if it feels small, I have to do something, and I don't understand why Tris doesn't feel the same desperation inside her.

"Yes," I say. Tris turns to me, her eyes wide, incredulous. I ignore her. "I can disable the security system. I'll need some Amity peace serum, do you have access to that?"

"I do." Nita smiles a little. "I'll send you a message with the timing. Come on, Reggie. Let's leave these two to . . . talk."

Reggie nods to me, and then to Tris, and then he and Nita both leave the room, easing the door closed behind them so it doesn't make a sound.

Tris turns to me, her arms folded like two bars across her body, keeping me out.

"I can't believe you," she said. "She's *lying*. Why can't you see that?"

"Because it's not *there*," I say. "I can tell when someone's lying just as well as you can. And in this situation, I think your judgment might be clouded by something else. Something like jealousy."

"I am not *jealous!*" she says, scowling at me. "I am being smart. She has something bigger planned, and if I were you, I would run far away from anyone who lies to me about what they want me to participate in."

"Well, you're not me." I shake my head. "God, Tris. These people murdered your parents, and you're not going to do something about it?"

"I never said I wasn't going to do anything," she says tersely. "But I don't have to buy into the first plan I hear, either."

"You know, I brought you here because I wanted to be honest with you, not so that you could make snap judgments about people and tell me what to do!"

"Remember what happened last time you didn't trust my 'snap judgments'?" Tris says coldly. "You found out that I was right. I was right about Edith Prior's video changing everything, and I was right about Evelyn, and I'm right about this."

"Yeah. You're always right," I say. "Were you right about running into dangerous situations without weapons? Were you right about lying to me and going on a death march to Erudite headquarters in the middle of the night? Or about Peter, were you right about him?"

"Don't throw those things in my face." She points at

me, and I feel like I'm a child getting lectured by a parent. "I never said I was perfect, but you—you can't even see past your own desperation. You went along with Evelyn because you were desperate for a parent, and now you're going along with this because you're desperate not to be *damaged*—"

The word shivers through me.

"I am not damaged," I say quietly. "I can't believe you have so little faith in me that you would tell me not to trust myself." I shake my head. "And I don't need your *permission*."

I start toward the door, and as my hand closes around the handle, she says, "Just leaving so that you can have the last word, that's really mature!"

"So is being suspicious of someone's motives just because she's pretty," I say. "I guess we're even."

I leave the room.

I am not a desperate, unsteady child who throws his trust around. I am not damaged.

CHAPTER
TWENTY-SIX

TRIS

I TOUCH MY forehead to the eyepiece of the microscope. The serum swims before me, orange-brown.

I was so busy looking for Nita's lies that I barely registered the truth: In order to get their hands on this serum, the Bureau must have developed it, and somehow delivered it to Jeanine to use. I pull away. Why would Jeanine work with the Bureau when she so badly wanted to stay in the city, away from them?

But I guess the Bureau and Jeanine shared a common goal. Both wanted the experiment to continue. Both were terrified of what would happen if it didn't. Both were willing to sacrifice innocent lives to do it.

I thought this place could be home. But the Bureau is

full of killers. I rock back on my heels as if pushed back by some invisible force, then walk out of the room, my heart beating fast.

I ignore the few people dawdling in the corridor in front of me. I just push farther into the Bureau compound, farther and farther into the belly of the beast.

Maybe this place could be home, I hear myself saying to Christina.

These people murdered your parents, Tobias's words echo in my head.

I don't know where I'm going except that I need space, and air. I clutch my ID in my hand and half walk, half run past the security barrier to the sculpture. There is no light shining into the tank now, though the water still falls from it, one drop for every second that passes. I stand for a little while, watching it. And then, across the slab of stone, I see my brother.

"Are you all right?" he says tentatively.

I am not all right. I was beginning to feel that I had finally found a place to stay, a place that was not so unstable or corrupt or controlling that I could actually belong there. You would think that I would have learned by now—such a place does not exist.

"No," I say.

He starts to move around the stone block, toward me. "What is it?"

"What is it." I laugh. "Let me put it this way: I just found out you're not the worst person I know."

I drop into a crouch and push my fingers through my hair. I feel numb and terrified of my own numbness. The Bureau is responsible for my parents' deaths. Why do I have to keep repeating it to myself to believe it? What's wrong with me?

"Oh," he says. "I'm . . . sorry?"

All I can manage is a small grunt.

"You know what Mom told me once?" he says, and the way he says *Mom*, like he didn't *betray* her, sets my teeth on edge. "She said that everyone has some evil inside them, and the first step to loving anyone is to recognize the same evil in ourselves, so we're able to forgive them."

"Is that what you want me to do?" I say dully as I stand. "I may have done bad things, Caleb, but I would *never* deliver you to your own execution."

"You can't say that," he says, and it sounds like he's pleading with me, begging me to say that I am just like him, no better. "You didn't know how persuasive Jeanine was—"

Something inside me snaps like a brittle rubber band.

I punch him in the face.

All I can think about is how the Erudite stripped me of my watch and my shoes and led me to the bare table where they would take my life. A table that Caleb may as well have set up himself.

I thought I was beyond this kind of anger, but as he stumbles back with his hands on his face, I pursue him, grabbing the front of his shirt and slamming him against the stone sculpture and screaming that he is a coward and a traitor and that I will kill him, I will kill him.

One of the guards comes toward me, and all she has to do is put her hand on my arm and the spell is broken. I release Caleb's shirt. I shake out my stinging hand. I turn and walk away.

+ + +

There's a beige sweater draped over the empty chair in Matthew's lab, the sleeve brushing the floor. I've never met his supervisor. I'm beginning to suspect that Matthew does all the real work.

I sit on top of the sweater and examine my knuckles. A few of them are split from punching Caleb, and dotted with faint bruises. It seems fitting that the blow would leave a mark on both of us. That's how the world works.

Last night, when I went back to the dormitory, Tobias wasn't there, and I was too angry to sleep. In the hours that I lay awake, staring at the ceiling, I decided that while I wasn't going to participate in Nita's plan, I also wasn't going to stop it. The truth about the attack simulation brewed hate for the Bureau inside me, and I want to watch it break apart from within.

Matthew is talking science. I'm having trouble paying attention.

"—doing some genetic analysis, which is fine, but before, we were developing a way to make the memory compound behave as a virus," he says. "With the same rapid replication, the same ability to spread through the air. And then we developed a vaccination for it. Just a temporary one, only lasts for forty-eight hours, but still."

I nod. "So . . . you were making it so you could set up other city experiments more efficiently, right?" I say. "No need to inject everyone with the memory serum when you can just release it and let it spread."

"Exactly!" He seems excited that I'm actually interested in what he's saying. "And it's a better model for having the option to select particular members of a population to opt out—you inoculate them, the virus spreads within twenty-four hours, and it has no effect on them."

I nod again.

"You okay?" Matthew says, his coffee mug poised near his mouth. He puts it down. "I heard the security guards had to pull you off someone last night."

"It was my brother. Caleb."

"Ah." Matthew raises an eyebrow. "What did he do this time?"

"Nothing, really." I pinch the sweater sleeve between my fingers. Its edges are all fraying, wearing with time. "I was wired to explode anyway; he just got in the way."

I already know, by looking at him, the question he's asking, and I want to explain it all to him, everything that Nita showed me and told me. I wonder if I can trust him.

"I heard something yesterday," I say, testing the waters. "About the Bureau. About my city, and the simulations."

He straightens up and gives me a strange look.

"What?" I say.

"Did you hear that something from Nita?" he says.

"Yes. How did you know that?"

"I've helped her a couple times," he says. "I let her into that storage room. Did she tell you anything else?"

Matthew is Nita's informant? I stare at him. I never thought that Matthew, who went out of his way to show me the difference between my "pure" genes and Tobias's "damaged" genes, might be helping Nita.

"Something about a plan," I say slowly.

He gets up and walks toward me, oddly tense. I lean away from him by instinct.

"Is it happening?" he says. "Do you know when?"

"What's going on?" I say. "Why would you help Nita?"

"Because all this 'genetic damage' nonsense is ridiculous," he says. "It's very important that you answer my questions."

"It is happening. And I don't know when, but I think it will be soon."

"Shit." Matthew puts his hands on his face. "Nothing good can come of this."

"If you don't stop saying cryptic things, I'm going to slap you," I say, getting to my feet.

"I was helping Nita until she told me what she and those fringe people wanted to do," Matthew says. "They want to get to the Weapons Lab and—"

"—steal the memory serum, yeah, I heard."

"No." He shakes his head. "No, they don't want the memory serum, they want the death serum. Similar to the one the Erudite have—the one you were supposed to be injected with when you were almost executed. They're going to use it for assassinations, a lot of them. Set off an aerosol can and it's easy, see? Give it to the right people and you have an explosion of anarchy and violence, which is exactly what those fringe people want."

I do see. I see the tilt of a vial, the quick press of a button on an aerosol can. I see Abnegation bodies and Erudite bodies sprawled over streets and staircases. I see the little pieces of this world that we've managed to cling to bursting into flames.

"I thought I was helping her with something smarter," Matthew says. "If I had known I was helping her start another war, I wouldn't have done it. We have to do something about this."

"I told him," I say softly, but not to Matthew, to myself. "I told him she was lying."

"We may have a problem with the way we treat GDs in this country, but it's not going to be solved by killing a bunch of people," he says. "Now come on, we're going to David's office."

I don't know what's right or wrong. I don't know anything about this country or the way it works or what it needs to change. But I do know that a bunch of death serum in the hands of Nita and some people from the fringe is no better than a bunch of death serum in the Weapons Lab of the Bureau. So I chase Matthew down the hallway outside. We walk quickly in the direction of the front entrance, where I first entered this compound.

When we walk past the security checkpoint, I spot Uriah near the sculpture. He lifts a hand to wave to me, his mouth pressed into a line that could be a smile if he was trying harder. Above his head, light refracts through the water tank, the symbol of the compound's slow, pointless struggle.

I'm just passing the security checkpoint when I see the

wall next to Uriah explode.

It is like fire blossoming from a bud. Shards of glass and metal spray from the center of the bloom, and Uriah's body is among them, a limp projectile. A deep rumble moves through me like a shudder. My mouth is open; I am screaming his name, but I can't hear myself over the ringing in my ears.

Around me, everyone is crouched, their arms curled around their heads. But I am on my feet, watching the hole in the compound wall. No one comes through it.

Seconds later, everyone around me starts running away from the blast, and I hurl myself against them, shoulder first, toward Uriah. An elbow hits me in the side and I fall down, my face scraping something hard and metal—the side of a table. I struggle to my feet, wiping blood from my eyebrow with a sleeve. Fabric slides over my arms, and limbs, hair, and wide eyes are all I can see, except the sign over their heads that says COMPOUND EXIT.

"Signal the alarms!" one of the guards at the security checkpoint screams. I duck under an arm and trip to the side.

"I did!" another guard shouts. "They aren't working!"

Matthew grabs my shoulder and yells into my ear. "What are you doing? Don't go *toward*—"

I move faster, finding an empty channel where there

are no people to obstruct my path. Matthew runs after me.

"We shouldn't be going to the explosion site—whoever set it off is already in the building," he says. "Weapons Lab, now! Come on!"

The Weapons Lab. Holy words.

I think of Uriah lying on the tile surrounded by glass and metal. My body is straining toward him, every muscle, but I know there's nothing I can do for him right now. The more important thing for me to do is to use my knowledge of chaos, of attacks, to keep Nita and her friends from stealing the death serum.

Matthew was right. Nothing good can come of this.

Matthew takes the lead, plunging into the crowd like it is a pool of water. I try to look only at the back of his head, to keep track of him, but the oncoming faces distract me, the mouths and eyes rigid with terror. I lose him for a few seconds and then find him again, several yards ahead, turning right at the next hallway.

"Matthew!" I shout, and I push my way through another group of people. Finally I catch up, grabbing the back of his shirt. He turns and grabs my hand.

"Are you okay?" he says, staring just above my eyebrow. In the rush I almost forgot about my cut. I press my sleeve to it, and it comes away red, but I nod.

"I'm fine! Let's go!"

We sprint side by side down the hallway—this one is not as crowded as the others, but I can see that whoever infiltrated the building has been here already. There are guards lying on the floor, some alive and some not. I see a gun on the tile near a drinking fountain and lurch toward it, breaking my grip on Matthew's hand.

I grab the gun and offer it to Matthew. He shakes his head. "I've never fired one."

"Oh, for God's sake." My finger curls around the trigger. It's different from the guns we had in the city—it doesn't have a barrel that shifts to the side, or the same tension in the trigger, or even the same distribution of weight. It's easier to hold, as a result, because it doesn't spark the same memories.

Matthew is gasping for air. So am I, only I don't notice it the same way, because I've done this sprint through chaos so many times. The next hallway he guides us to is empty except for one fallen soldier. She's not moving.

"It's not far," he says, and I touch my finger to my lips to tell him to be quiet.

We slow to a walk, and I squeeze the gun, my sweat making it slip. I don't know how many bullets are in it, or how to check. When we pass the soldier, I pause to search her for a weapon. I find a gun tucked under her hip, where she fell on her own wrist. Matthew stares at her, unblinking, as I take her weapon.

"Hey," I say quietly. "Just keep moving. Move now, process later."

I elbow him and lead the way down the hallway. Here the hallways are dim, the ceilings crossed with bars and pipes. I can hear people ahead and don't need Matthew's whispered directions to find them.

When we reach the place where we're supposed to turn, I press against the wall and look around the corner, careful to keep myself as hidden as possible.

There's a set of double-walled glass doors that look as heavy as metal doors would be, but they're open. Beyond them is a cramped hallway, empty except for three people in black. They wear heavy clothing and carry guns so big I'm not sure I would be able to lift one. Their faces are covered with dark fabric, disguising all but their eyes.

On his knees before the double doors is David, a gun barrel pressed to his temple, blood trailing down his chin. And standing among the invaders, wearing the same mask as the others, is a girl with a dark ponytail.

Nita.

CHAPTER
TWENTY-SEVEN

TRIS

"GET US IN, David," Nita says, her voice garbled by the mask.

David's eyes slide lazily to the side, to the man pointing the gun at him.

"I don't believe you'll shoot me," he says. "Because I'm the only one in this building who knows this information, and you want that serum."

"Won't shoot you in the head, maybe," the man says, "but there are other places."

The man and Nita exchange a look. Then the man shifts the gun down, to David's feet, and fires. I squeeze my eyes shut as David's screams fill the hallway. He might be one of the people who offered Jeanine Matthews the attack simulation, but I still don't relish his screams of pain.

I stare at the guns I carry, one in each hand, my fingers pale against the black triggers. I imagine myself trimming back all the stray branches of my thoughts, focusing on just this place, just this time.

I put my mouth right next to Matthew's ear and mutter, "Go for help. Now."

Matthew nods and starts down the hallway. To his credit, he moves quietly, his footsteps silent on the tile. At the end of the hallway he looks back at me, and then disappears around the bend.

"I'm sick of this shit," the red-haired woman says. "Just blow up the doors."

"An explosion would activate one of the backup security measures," says Nita. "We need the pass code."

I look around the corner again, and this time, David's eyes shift to mine. His face is pale and shiny with sweat, and there is a wide pool of blood around his ankles. The others are looking at Nita, who takes a black box from her pocket and opens it to reveal a syringe and needle.

"Thought you said that stuff doesn't work on him," the man with the gun says.

"I said he could *resist* it, not that it didn't work at all," she says. "David, this is a very potent blend of truth serum and fear serum. I'm going to stick you with it if you don't tell us the pass code."

"I know this is just the fault of your genes, Nita," David

says weakly. "If you stop now, I can help you, I can—"

Nita smiles a twisted smile. With relish, she sticks the needle in his neck and presses the plunger. David slumps over, and then his body shudders, and shudders again.

He opens his eyes wide and screams, staring at the empty air, and I know what he's seeing, because I've seen it myself, in Erudite headquarters, under the influence of the terror serum. I watched my worst fears come to life.

Nita kneels in front of him and grabs his face.

"David!" she says urgently. "I can make it stop if you tell us how to get into this room. Hear me?"

He pants, and his eyes aren't focused on her, but rather on something over her shoulder. "Don't do it!" he shouts, and he lunges forward, toward whatever phantom the serum is showing him. Nita puts an arm across his chest to keep him steady, and he screams, "Don't—!"

Nita shakes him. "I'll stop them from doing it if you tell me how to get in!"

"Her!" David says, and tears gleam in his eyes. "The—the name—"

"Whose name?"

"We're running out of time!" the man with the gun trained on David says. "Either we get the serum or we kill him—"

"*Her,*" David says, pointing at the space in front of him. Pointing at me.

I stretch my arms around the corner of the wall and fire twice. The first bullet hits the wall. The second hits the man in the arm, so the huge weapon topples to the floor. The red-haired woman points her weapon at me—or the part of me that she can see, half hidden by the wall—and Nita screams, "Hold your fire!"

"Tris," Nita says, "you don't know what you're doing—"

"You're probably right," I say, and I fire again. This time my hand is steadier, my aim is better; I hit Nita's side, right above her hip. She screams into her mask and clutches the hole in her skin, sinking to her knees, her hands covered in blood.

David surges toward me with a grimace of pain as he puts weight on his injured leg. I wrap my arm around his waist and swing his body around so he's between me and the remaining soldiers. Then I press one of my guns to the back of his head.

They all freeze. I can feel my heartbeat in my throat, in my hands, behind my eyes.

"Fire, and I'll shoot him in the head," I say.

"You wouldn't kill your own leader," the red-haired woman says.

"He's not my leader. I don't care if he lives or dies," I say. "But if you think I'm going to let you gain control of that death serum, you're insane."

I start to shuffle backward, with David whimpering in

front of me, still under the influence of the serum cocktail. I duck my head and turn my body sideways so it's safely behind his. I keep one of the guns against his head.

We reach the end of the hallway, and the woman calls my bluff. She fires, and hits David just above the knee, in his other leg. He collapses with a scream, and I am exposed. I dive to the ground, slamming my elbows into the floor, as a bullet goes past me, the sound vibrating inside my head.

Then I feel something hot spreading through my left arm, and I see blood and my feet scramble on the floor, searching for traction. I find it and fire blindly down the hallway. I grab David by the collar and drag him around the corner, pain searing through my left arm.

I hear running footsteps and groan. But they aren't coming from behind me; they're coming from in front. People surround me, Matthew among them, and some of them pick David up and run with him down the hallway. Matthew offers me his hand.

My ears are ringing. I can't believe I did it.

CHAPTER TWENTY-EIGHT

TRIS

THE HOSPITAL IS packed with people, all of them yelling or racing back and forth or yanking curtains shut. Before I sat down I checked all the beds for Tobias. He wasn't in any of them. I am still shaking with relief.

Uriah is not here either. He is in one of the other rooms, and the door is closed—not a good sign.

The nurse who dabs my arm with antiseptic is breathless and looks around at all the activity instead of at my wound. I'm told it's a minor graze, nothing to worry about.

"I can wait, if you need to do something else," I say. "I have to find someone anyway."

She purses her lips, then says, "You need stitches."

"It's just a graze!"

"Not your arm, your head," she says, pointing to a spot above my eye. I had almost forgotten about the cut in all the chaos, but it still hasn't stopped bleeding.

"Fine."

"I'm going to have to give you a shot of this numbing agent," she says, holding up a syringe.

I am so used to needles that I don't even react. She dabs my forehead with antiseptic—they are so careful about germs here—and I feel the sting and prickle of the needle, diminishing by the second as the numbing agent does its work.

I watch the people rush past as she stitches my skin—a doctor pulls off a pair of bloodstained rubber gloves; a nurse carries a tray of gauze, his shoes nearly slipping on the tile; a family member of someone injured wrings her hands. The air smells like chemicals and old paper and warm bodies.

"Any updates on David?" I say.

"He'll live, but it will take him a long time to walk again," she says. Her lips stop puckering, just for a few seconds. "Could have been a lot worse, if you hadn't been there. You're all set."

I nod. I wish I could tell her that I'm not a hero, that I was using him as a shield, like a wall of meat. I wish I could confess to being a person full of hate for the Bureau and for David, a person who would let someone else get riddled with bullets to save herself. My parents would be ashamed.

She places a bandage over the stitches to protect the wound, and gathers all the wrappers and soaked cotton balls into her fists to throw them away.

Before I can thank her, she is gone, off to the next bed, the next patient, the next injury.

Injured people line the hallway outside the emergency ward. I have gathered from the evidence that there was another explosion set off at the same time as the one near the entrance. Both were diversions. Our attackers got in through the underground tunnel, as Nita said they would. She never mentioned blowing holes in walls.

The doors at the end of the hallway open, and a few people rush in, carrying a young woman—Nita—between them. They put her on a cot near one of the walls. She groans, clutching at a roll of gauze that is pressed to the wound in her side. I feel strangely separate from her pain. I shot her. I had to. That's the end of it.

As I walk down the aisle between the wounded, I notice the uniforms. Everyone sitting here wears green. With few exceptions, they are all support staff. They are clutching bleeding arms or legs or heads, their injuries no better than my own, some much worse.

I catch my reflection in the windows just beyond the main corridor—my hair is stringy and limp, and the bandage dominates my forehead. David's blood and my blood smear my clothes in places. I need to shower and change, but first I have to find Tobias and Christina. I haven't seen either of them since before the invasion.

It doesn't take me long to find Christina—she is sitting in the waiting room when I walk out of the emergency ward, her knee jiggling so much that the person next to her is giving her dirty looks. She lifts a hand to greet me, but her eyes shift away from mine and toward the doors right afterward.

"You all right?" she asks me.

"Yeah," I say. "There's still no update on Uriah. I couldn't get into the room."

"These people make me crazy, you know that?" she says. "They won't tell anyone anything. They won't let us see him. It's like they think they own him and everything that happens to him!"

"They work differently here. I'm sure they'll tell you when they know something concrete."

"Well, they would tell *you*," she says, scowling. "But I'm not convinced they would give *me* a second look."

A few days ago I might have disagreed with her, unsure how influential their belief in genetic damage was on their behavior. I'm not sure what to do—not sure how to talk to her now that I have these advantages and she does not and there's nothing either of us can do about it. All I can think to do is be near her.

"I have to find Tobias, but I'll come back after I do and sit with you, okay?"

She finally looks at me, and her knee goes still. "They didn't tell you?"

My stomach clenches with fear. "Tell me what."

"Tobias was arrested," she says quietly. "I saw him sitting with the invaders right before I came in here. Some people saw him at the control room before the attack—they say he was disabling the alarm system."

There is a sad look in her eyes, like she pities me. But I already knew what Tobias did.

"Where are they?" I say.

I need to talk to him. And I know what I need to say.

CHAPTER
TWENTY-NINE

TOBIAS

MY WRISTS STING from the plastic tie the guard squeezed around them. I probe my jaw with just my fingertips, testing the skin for blood.

"All right?" Reggie says.

I nod. I have dealt with worse injuries than this—I have been hit harder than I was by the soldier who slammed the butt of his gun into my jaw while he was arresting me. His eyes were wild with anger when he did it.

Mary and Rafi sit a few feet away, Rafi clutching a handful of gauze to his bleeding arm. A guard stands between us and them, keeping us separate. As I look at them, Rafi meets my eyes and nods. As if to say, *Well done.*

If I did well, why do I feel sick to my stomach?

"Listen," Reggie says, shifting so he's closer to me. "Nita and the fringe people are taking the fall. It'll be all right."

I nod again, without conviction. We had a backup plan for our probable arrest, and I'm not worried about its success. What I am worried about is how long it's taking them to deal with us, and how casual it has been—we have been sitting against a wall in an empty corridor since they caught the invaders more than an hour ago, and no one has come to tell us what will happen to us, or to ask us any questions. I haven't even seen Nita yet.

It puts a sour taste in my mouth. Whatever we did, it seems to have shaken them up, and I know of nothing that shakes people up as much as lost lives.

How many of those am I responsible for, because I participated in this?

"Nita told me they were going to steal memory serum," I say to Reggie, and I'm afraid to look at him. "Was that true?"

Reggie eyes the guard who stands a few feet away. We have already been yelled at once for talking.

But I know the answer.

"It wasn't, was it," I say. Tris was right. Nita was lying.

"Hey!" The guard marches toward us and sticks the barrel of her gun between us. "Move aside. No conversation allowed."

Reggie shifts to the right, and I make eye contact with the guard.

"What's going on?" I say. "What happened?"

"Oh, like you don't know," she answers. "Now keep your mouth shut."

I watch her walk away, and then I see a small blond girl appear at the end of the hallway. Tris. A bandage stretches across her forehead, and blood smears her clothes in the shape of fingers. She clutches a piece of paper in her fist.

"Hey!" the guard says. "What are you doing here?"

"Shelly," the other guard says, jogging over. "Calm down. That's the girl who saved David."

The girl who saved David—from what, exactly?

"Oh." Shelly puts her gun down. "Well, it's still a valid question."

"They asked me to bring you guys an update," Tris says, and she offers Shelly the piece of paper. "David is in recovery. He'll live, but they're not sure when he'll walk again. Most of the other injured have been cared for."

The sour taste in my mouth grows stronger. David can't walk. And what they've been doing all this time is caring for the injured. All this destruction, and for what? I don't even know. I don't know the truth.

What did I do?

"Do they have a casualty count?" Shelly asks.

"Not yet," Tris replies.

"Thanks for letting us know."

"Listen." She shifts her weight to one foot. "I need to talk to him."

She jerks her head toward me.

"We can't really—" Shelly starts.

"Just for a second, I promise," Tris says. "Please."

"Let her," the other guard says. "What could it hurt?"

"Fine," Shelly says. "I'll give you two minutes."

She nods to me, and I use the wall to push myself to my feet, my hands still bound in front of me. Tris comes closer, but not that close—the space, and her folded arms, form a barrier between us that may as well be a wall. She looks somewhere south of my eyes.

"Tris, I—"

"Want to know what your friends did?" she says. Her voice shakes, and I do not make the mistake of thinking it's from tears. It's from anger. "They weren't after the memory serum. They were after poison—death serum. So that they could kill a bunch of important government people and start a war."

I look down, at my hands, at the tile, at the toes of her shoes. A war. "I didn't know—"

"I was right. I was right, and you didn't listen. Again," she says, quiet. Her eyes lock on mine, and I find that I do not want the eye contact I craved, because it takes me apart, piece by piece. "Uriah was standing right in front of one of the explosives they set off as diversions. He's unconscious and they're not sure he'll wake up."

It's strange how a word, a phrase, a sentence, can feel like a blow to the head.

"What?"

All I can see is Uriah's face when he hit the net after the Choosing Ceremony, the giddy smile he wore as Zeke and I pulled him onto the platform next to the net. Or him sitting in the tattoo parlor, his ear taped forward so it wouldn't get in Tori's way as she drew a snake on his skin. Uriah might not wake up? Uriah, gone forever?

And I promised. I promised Zeke I would look after him, I *promised* . . .

"He's one of the last friends I have," she says, her voice breaking. "I don't know if I'll ever be able to look at you the same way again."

She walks away. I hear Shelly's muffled voice telling me to sit down, and I sink to my knees, letting my wrists rest on my legs. I struggle to find a way to escape this, the horror of what I've done, but there is no sophisticated logic that can liberate me; there is no way out.

I put my face in my hands and try not to think, try not to imagine anything at all.

+ + +

The overhead light in the interrogation room reflects a muddled circle in the center of the table. That is where I keep my eyes as I recite the story Nita gave me, the one that is so close to true I have no trouble telling it. When I'm finished, the man recording it taps out my last sentences on his screen, the glass lighting up with letters where his fingers touch it. Then the woman acting as David's proxy—Angela—says, "So you didn't know the reason Juanita asked you to disable the security system?"

"No," I say, which is true. I didn't know the real reason; I only knew a lie.

They put all the others under truth serum, but not me. The genetic anomaly that makes me aware during simulations also suggests I could be resistant to serums, so my truth serum testimony might not be reliable. As long as my story fits with the others, they will assume it's true. They don't know that, a few hours ago, all of us were inoculated against truth serum. Nita's informant among the GPs provided her with the inoculation serum months ago.

"How, then, did she compel you to do it?"

"We're friends," I say. "She is—was—one of the only friends I had here. She asked me to trust her, told me it was for a good reason, so I did it."

"And what do you think about the situation now?"

I finally look at her. "I've never regretted something so much in my life."

Angela's hard, bright eyes soften a little. She nods. "Well, your story fits with what the others told us. Given your newness to this community, your ignorance of the master plan, and your genetic deficiency, we are inclined to be lenient. Your sentence is parole—you must work for the good of this community, and stay on your best behavior, for one year. You will not be allowed to enter any private laboratories or rooms. You will not leave the confines of this compound without permission. You will check in every month with a parole officer who will be assigned to you at the conclusion of our proceedings. Do you understand these terms?"

With the words "genetic deficiency" lingering in my mind, I nod and say, "I do."

"Then we're finished here. You're free to go." She stands, pushing her chair back. The recorder also stands, and slips his screen into his bag. Angela touches the table so that I look up at her again.

"Don't be so hard on yourself," she says. "You're very young, you know."

I don't think my youth excuses it, but I accept her attempt at kindness without objection.

"Can I ask what's going to happen to Nita?" I say.

Angela presses her lips together. "Once she recovers from her substantial injuries, she will be transferred to our prison and will spend the duration of her life there," she says.

"She won't be executed?"

"No, we don't believe in capital punishment for the genetically damaged." Angela moves toward the door. "We can't have the same behavioral expectations for those with damaged genes as we do for those with pure genes, after all."

With a sad smile, she leaves the room, and doesn't close the door behind her. I stay in my seat for a few seconds, absorbing the sting of her words. I wanted to believe they were all wrong about me, that I was not limited by my genes, that I was no more damaged than any other person. But how can that be true, when my actions landed Uriah in the hospital, when Tris can't even look me in the eye, when so many people died?

I cover my face and grit my teeth as the tears fall, bearing the wave of despair like it is a fist, striking me. By the time I get up to leave, the cuffs of my sleeves, used to wipe my cheeks, are damp, and my jaw aches.

CHAPTER
THIRTY

TRIS

"HAVE YOU BEEN in yet?"

Cara stands beside me, her arms folded. Yesterday Uriah was transferred from his secure room to a room with a viewing window, I suspect to keep us from asking to see him all the time. Christina sits by his bed now, grasping his limp hand.

I thought he would have come apart like a rag doll with a pulled thread, but he doesn't look that different, except for some bandages and scrapes. I feel like he could wake up at any moment, smiling and wondering why we're all staring at him.

"I was in there last night," I say. "It just didn't seem right to leave him alone."

"There is some evidence to suggest that, depending on the extent of his brain damage, he can on some level hear and feel us," says Cara. "Though I was told his prognosis is not good."

Sometimes I still want to smack her. As if I need to be reminded that Uriah is unlikely to recover. "Yeah."

After I left Uriah's side last night, I wandered the compound without any sense of direction. I should have been thinking of my friend, teetering between this world and whatever comes next, but instead I thought of what I said to Tobias. And how I felt when I looked at him, like something was breaking.

I didn't tell him it was the end of our relationship. I meant to, but when I was looking at him, the words were impossible to say. I feel tears welling up again, as they have every hour or so since yesterday, and I push them away, swallow them down.

"So you saved the Bureau," Cara says, turning to me. "You seem to get involved in a lot of conflict. I suppose we should all be grateful that you are steady in a crisis."

"I didn't save the Bureau. I have no interest in saving the Bureau," I retort. "I kept a weapon out of some dangerous hands, that's all." I wait a beat. "Did you just compliment me?"

"I am capable of recognizing another person's

strengths," Cara replies, and she smiles. "Additionally, I think *our* issues are now resolved, both on a logical and an emotional level." She clears her throat a little, and I wonder if it's finally acknowledging that she has emotions that makes her uncomfortable, or something else. "It sounds like you know something about the Bureau that has made you angry. I wonder if you could tell me what it is."

Christina rests her head on the edge of Uriah's mattress, her slender body collapsing sideways. I say wryly, "I wonder. We may never know."

"Hmm." The crease between Cara's eyebrows appears when she frowns, making her look so much like Will that I have to look away. "Maybe I should say please."

"Fine. You know Jeanine's simulation serum? Well, it wasn't hers." I sigh. "Come on. I'll show you. It'll be easier that way."

It would be just as easy to tell her what I saw in that old storage room, nestled deep in the Bureau laboratories. But the truth is, I just want to keep myself busy, so I don't think about Uriah. Or Tobias.

"It seems like we'll never reach the end of all these deceptions," Cara says as we walk toward the storage room. "The factions, the video Edith Prior left us . . . all lies, designed to make us behave a particular way."

"Is that what you really think about the factions?" I say. "I thought you loved being an Erudite."

"I did." She scratches the back of her neck, leaving little red lines on her skin from her fingernails. "But the Bureau made me feel like a fool for fighting for any of it, and for what the Allegiant stood for. And I don't like to feel foolish."

"So you don't think any of it was worthwhile," I say. "Any of the Allegiant stuff."

"You do?"

"It got us out," I say, "and it got us to the truth, and it was better than the factionless commune Evelyn had in mind, where no one gets to choose anything at all."

"I suppose," she says. "I just pride myself on being someone who can see through things, the faction system included."

"You know what the Abnegation used to say about pride?"

"Something unfavorable, I assume."

I laugh. "Obviously. They said it blinds people to the truth of what they are."

We reach the door to the labs, and I knock a few times so Matthew will hear me and let us in. As I wait for him to open the door, Cara gives me a strange look.

"The old Erudite writings said the same thing, more or less," she says.

I never thought the Erudite would say anything about pride—that they would even concern themselves with morality. It sounds like I was wrong. I want to ask her more, but then the door opens, and Matthew stands in the hallway, chewing on an apple core.

"Can you let me into the storage room?" I say. "I need to show Cara something."

He bites off the end of the apple core and nods. "Of course."

I cringe, imagining the bitter taste of apple seeds, and follow him.

CHAPTER
THIRTY-ONE

TOBIAS

I CAN'T GO back to the staring eyes and unspoken questions of the dormitory. I know I shouldn't return to the scene of my great crime, even though it's not one of the secure areas I'm barred from entering, but I feel like I need to see what's happening inside the city. Like I need to remember that there is a world outside this one, where I am not hated.

I walk to the control room and sit in one of the chairs. Each screen in the grid above me shows a different part of the city: the Merciless Mart, the lobby of Erudite headquarters, Millennium Park, the pavilion outside the Hancock building.

For a long time I watch the people milling around inside

Erudite headquarters, their arms covered in factionless armbands, weapons at their hips, exchanging quick conversation or handing off cans of food for dinner, an old factionless habit.

Then I hear someone at the control room desks say, "There he is," to one of her coworkers, and I scan the screens to see what she's talking about. Then I see him, standing in front of the Hancock building: Marcus, near the front doors, checking his watch.

I get up and tap the screen with my index finger to turn on the sound. For a moment only the rush of air comes through the speakers just below the screen, but then, footsteps. Johanna Reyes approaches my father. He stretches his hand out for her to shake, but she doesn't, and my father is left with his hand dangling in the air, a piece of bait she did not take.

"I *knew* you stayed in the city," she says. "They're looking all over for you."

A few of the people milling around the control room gather behind me to watch. I hardly notice them. I am watching my father's arm return to his side in a fist.

"Have I done something to offend you?" Marcus says. "I contacted you because I thought you were a friend."

"I thought you contacted me because you know I'm still the leader of the Allegiant, and you want an ally," Johanna says, bending her neck so a lock of hair falls over her scarred eye. "And depending on what your aim is, I am still that, Marcus, but I think our friendship is over."

Marcus's eyebrows pinch together. My father has the look of a man who used to be handsome, but as he has aged, his cheeks have become hollow, his features harsh and strict. His hair, cropped close to his skull in the Abnegation style, does not help this impression.

"I don't understand," Marcus says.

"I spoke to some of my Candor friends," Johanna says. "They told me what your boy said when he was under truth serum. That nasty rumor Jeanine Matthews spread about you and your son . . . it was true, wasn't it?"

My face feels hot, and I shrink into myself, my shoulders curving in.

Marcus is shaking his head. "No, Tobias is—"

Johanna holds up a hand. She speaks with her eyes closed, like she can't stand to look at him. "Please. I have watched how your son behaves, how your wife behaves. I know what people who are stained with violence look like." She pushes her hair behind her ear. "We recognize our own."

"You can't possibly believe—" Marcus starts. He shakes his head. "I'm a disciplinarian, yes, but I only wanted what was best—"

"A husband should not *discipline* his wife," Johanna says. "Not even in Abnegation. And as for your son . . . well, let us say that I *do* believe it of you."

Johanna's fingers skip over the scar on her cheek. My heart overwhelms me with its rhythm. She knows. She knows, not because she heard me confess to my shame in the Candor interrogation room, but because she *knows*, she has experienced it herself, I'm sure of it. I wonder who it was for her—mother? Father? Someone else?

Part of me always wondered what my father would do if directly confronted with the truth. I thought he might shift from the self-effacing Abnegation leader to the nightmare I knew at home, that he might lash out and reveal himself for who he is. It would be a satisfying reaction for me to see, but it is not his real reaction.

He just stands there looking confused, and for a moment I wonder if he *is* confused, if in his sick heart he believes his own lies about disciplining me. The thought creates a storm inside me, a rumbling of thunder and a rush of wind.

"Now that I've been honest," Johanna says, a little more calm now, "you can tell me why you asked me to come here."

Marcus shifts to a new subject like the old one was never discussed. I see in him a man who divides himself into compartments and can switch between them on command. One of those compartments was reserved only for my mother and me.

The Bureau employees move the camera in closer, so that the Hancock building is just a black backdrop behind Marcus's and Johanna's torsos. I follow a girder diagonally across the screen so I don't have to look at him.

"Evelyn and the factionless are tyrants," Marcus says. "The peace we experienced among the factions, before Jeanine's first attack, *can* be restored, I'm sure of it. And I want to try to restore it. I think this is something you want too."

"It is," Johanna says. "How do you think we should go about it?"

"This is the part you might not like, but I hope you will keep an open mind," Marcus says. "Evelyn controls the city because she controls the weapons. If we take those weapons away, she won't have nearly as much power, and she can be challenged."

Johanna nods, and scrapes her shoe against the pavement. I can only see the smooth side of her face from this angle, the limp but curled hair, the full mouth.

"What would you like me to do?" she says.

"Let me join you in leading the Allegiant," he says. "I was an Abnegation leader. I was practically the leader of this entire city. People will rally behind me."

"People have rallied already," Johanna points out. "And not behind a person, but behind the desire to reinstate the factions. Who says I need you?"

"Not to diminish your accomplishments, but the Allegiant are still too insignificant to be any more than a small uprising," Marcus says. "There are more faction-less than any of us knew. You do need me. You know it."

My father has a way of persuading people with-out charm that has always confused me. He states his opinions as if they're facts, and somehow his complete lack of doubt makes you believe him. That quality fright-ens me now, because I know what he told me: that I was broken, that I was worthless, that I was nothing. How many of those things did he make me believe?

I can see Johanna beginning to believe him, think-ing of the small cluster of people she has gathered to the Allegiant cause. Thinking of the group she sent out-side the fence, with Cara, and never heard from again. Thinking of how alone she is, and how rich his history of leadership is. I want to scream at her through the screens not to trust him, to tell her that he only wants the factions back because he knows he can then take up his place as their leader again. But my voice can't reach her, wouldn't be able to even if I was standing right next to her.

Carefully, Johanna says to him, "Can you promise me that you will, wherever possible, try to limit the destruction we will cause?"

Marcus says, "Of course."

She nods again, but this time it looks like she's nodding to herself.

"Sometimes we need to fight for peace," she says, more to the pavement than to Marcus. "I think this is one of those times. And I do think you would be useful for people to rally behind."

It's the beginning of the Allegiant rebellion I've been expecting since I first heard the group had formed. Even though it has seemed inevitable to me since I saw how Evelyn chose to rule, I feel sick. It seems like the rebellions never stop, in the city, in the compound, anywhere. There are just breaths between them, and foolishly, we call those breaths "peace."

I move away from the screen, intending to leave the control room behind me, to get some fresh air wherever I can.

But as I walk away, I catch sight of another screen, showing a dark-haired woman pacing back and forth in an office in Erudite headquarters. Evelyn—of course they keep footage of Evelyn on the most prominent screens in the control room, it only makes sense.

Evelyn pushes her hands into her hair, clenching her fingers around the thick locks. She drops to a crouch, papers littering the floor all around her, and I think, *She's crying*, but I'm not sure why, since I don't see her shoulders shake.

I hear, through the screen speakers, a knock on the office door. Evelyn straightens, pats her hair, wipes her face, and says, "Come in!"

Therese comes in, her factionless armband askew. "Just got an update from the patrols. They say they haven't seen any sign of him."

"Great." Evelyn shakes her head. "I exile him, and he stays inside the city. He must be doing this just to spite me."

"Or he's joined the Allegiant, and they're harboring him," Therese says, slinging her body across one of the office chairs. She twists paper into the floor with her boot soles.

"Well, obviously." Evelyn puts her arm against the window and leans into it, looking out over the city and beyond it, the marsh. "Thank you for the update."

"We'll find him," Therese says. "He can't have gone far. I swear we'll find him."

"I just want him to be gone," Evelyn says, her voice tight and small, like a child's. I wonder if she's still afraid of him, in the way that I'm still afraid of him, like a

nightmare that keeps resurfacing during the day. I wonder how similar my mother and I are, deep down where it
counts.

"I know," Therese says, and she leaves.

I stand for a long time, watching Evelyn stare out the
window, her fingers twitching at her side.

I feel like what I have become is halfway between my
mother and my father, violent and impulsive and desperate and afraid. I feel like I have lost control of what I have
become.

CHAPTER
THIRTY-TWO

TRIS

DAVID SUMMONS ME to his office the next day, and I am afraid that he remembers how I used him as a shield when I was backing away from the Weapons Lab, how I pointed a gun at his head and said I didn't care if he lived or died.

Zoe meets me in the hotel lobby and leads me through the main hallway and down another one, long and narrow, with windows on my right that show the small fleet of airplanes perched in rows on the concrete. Light snow touches the glass, an early taste of winter, and melts within seconds.

I sneak looks at her as we walk, hoping to see what she is like when she doesn't think anyone is watching, but she seems just the same as always—chipper, but businesslike. Like the attack never happened.

"He'll be in a wheelchair," she says when we reach the end of the narrow hallway. "It's best not to make a big deal of it. He doesn't like to be pitied."

"I don't pity him." I struggle to keep the anger out of my voice. It would make her suspicious. "He's not the first person to ever be hit with a bullet."

"I always forget that you have seen far more violence than we have," Zoe says, and she scans her card at the next security barrier we reach. I stare through the glass at the guards on the other side—they stand erect, their guns at their shoulders, facing forward. I get the sense they have to stand that way all day.

I feel heavy and achy, like my muscles are communicating a deeper, emotional pain. Uriah is still in a coma. I still can't look at Tobias when I see him in the dormitory, in the cafeteria, in the hallway, without seeing the exploded wall next to Uriah's head. I'm not sure when, or if, anything will ever get better, not sure if these wounds are the kind that can heal.

We walk past the guards, and the tile turns to wood beneath my feet. Small paintings with gilded frames line the walls, and just outside David's office is a pedestal with a bouquet of flowers on it. They are small touches, but the effect is that I feel like my clothes are smudged with dirt.

Zoe knocks, and a voice within calls out, "Come in!"

She opens the door for me but doesn't follow me in. David's office is spacious and warm, the walls lined with books where they are not lined with windows. On the left side is a desk with glass screens suspended above it, and on the right side is a small laboratory with wood furnishings instead of metal ones.

David sits in a wheelchair, his legs covered in a stiff material—to keep the bones in place so they can heal, I assume. He looks pale and wan, but healthy enough. Though I know that he had something to do with the attack simulation, and with all those deaths, I find it difficult to pair those actions with the man I see in front of me. I wonder if this is how it is with all evil men, that to someone, they look just like good men, talk like good men, are just as likable as good men.

"Tris." He pushes himself toward me and presses one of my hands between his. I keep my hand firmly in his, though his skin feels dry as paper and I am repulsed by him.

"You are so very brave," he says, and then he releases my hand. "How are your injuries?"

I shrug. "I've had worse. How are yours?"

"It will take me some time to walk again, but they're confident that I will. Some of our people are developing sophisticated leg braces anyway, so I can be their first test case if I have to," he says, the corners of his eyes crinkling. "Could you push me behind the desk again? I am still having trouble steering."

I do, guiding his stiff legs under the tabletop and letting the rest of him follow. When I'm sure he's positioned correctly, I sit in the chair across from him and try to smile. In order to find some way to avenge my parents, I need to keep his trust and his fondness for me intact. And I won't do that with a scowl.

"I asked you to come here mostly so that I could thank you," he says. "I can't think of many young people who would have come after me instead of running for cover, or who would have been able to save this compound the way you did."

I think of pressing a gun to his head and threatening his life, and swallow hard.

"You and the people you came with have been in a regrettable state of flux since your arrival," he says. "We aren't quite sure what to do with all of you, to be honest, and I'm sure you don't know what to do with yourselves, but I have thought of something I would like *you* to do. I am the official leader of this compound, but apart from that, we have a similar system of governance to the Abnegation, so I am advised by a small group of councilors. I would like you to begin training for that position."

My hands tighten around the armrests.

"You see, we are going to need to make some changes around here now that we have been attacked," he says. "We are going to have to take a stronger stand for our cause. And I think you know how to do that."

I can't argue with that.

"What . . ." I clear my throat. "What would training for that entail?"

"Attending our meetings, for one thing," he says, "and learning the ins and outs of our compound—how we function, from top to bottom, our history, our values, and so on. I can't allow you to be a part of the council in any official capacity at such a young age, and there is a track you must follow—assisting one of the current council members—but I am inviting you to travel down the road, if you would like to."

His eyes, not his voice, ask me the question.

The councilors are probably the same people who authorized the attack simulation and ensured that it was passed on to Jeanine at the right time. And he wants me to sit among them, learn to become them. Even though I can taste bile in the back of my mouth, I have no trouble answering.

"Of course," I say, and smile. "I would be honored."

If someone offers you an opportunity to get closer to your enemy, you always take it. I know that without having learned it from anyone.

He must believe my smile, because he grins.

"I thought you would say yes," he says. "It's something I wanted your mother to do with me, before she volunteered to enter the city. But I think she had fallen in love with the place from afar and couldn't resist it."

"Fallen in love . . . with the city?" I say. "No accounting for taste, I suppose."

It's just a joke, but my heart isn't in it. Still, David laughs, and I know I've said the right thing.

"You were . . . close with my mother, while she was here?" I say. "I've been reading her journal, but she's not very wordy."

"No, she wouldn't be, would she? Natalie was always very straightforward. Yes, we were close, your mother and I." His voice softens when he talks about her—he is no longer the toughened leader of this compound, but an old man, reflecting on some fonder past.

The past that happened before he got her killed.

"We had a similar history. I was also plucked right out of the damaged world as a child . . . my parents were severely dysfunctional people who were both taken to prison when I was young. Rather than succumbing to an adoption system overburdened with orphans, my siblings and I ran to the fringe—the same place where your mother also took refuge, years later—and only I came out of there alive."

I don't know what to say to that—I don't know what to do with the sympathy growing within me, for a man I know has done terrible things. I just stare at my hands, and I imagine that my insides are liquid metal hardening in the air, taking a shape they will never leave again.

"You'll have to go out there with our patrols tomorrow. You can see the fringe for yourself," he says. "It's something that's important for a future council member to see."

"I'd be very interested," I say.

"Lovely. Well, I hate to end our time together, but I have quite a bit of work to catch up on," he says. "I'll have someone notify you about the patrols, and our first council meeting is on Friday at ten in the morning, so I'll be seeing you soon."

I feel frantic—I didn't ask him what I wanted to ask him. I don't think there was ever an opportunity. It's too late now, anyway. I get up and move toward the doorway, but then he speaks again.

"Tris, I feel like I should be open with you, if we are to trust each other," he says.

For the first time since I've met him, David looks almost . . . afraid. His eyes are wide open, like a child's. But a moment later, the expression is gone.

"I may have been under the influence of a serum cocktail at the time," he says, "but I know what you said to them to keep them from shooting at us. I know you told them you would kill me to protect what was in the Weapons Lab."

My throat feels so tight I can hardly breathe.

"Don't be alarmed," he says. "It's one of the reasons why I offered you this opportunity."

"W-why?"

"You demonstrated the quality I most need in my advisers," he says. "Which is the ability to make sacrifices for the greater good. If we are going to win this fight against genetic damage, if we are going to save the experiments from being shut down, we will need to make sacrifices. You understand that, don't you?"

I feel a flash of anger and force myself to nod. Nita already told us that the experiments were in danger of being disbanded, so I am not surprised to hear it's true. But David's desperation to save his life's work doesn't excuse killing off a faction, *my* faction.

For a moment I stand with my hand on the doorknob, trying to gather myself together, and then I decide to take a risk.

"What would have happened, if they had set off another explosion to get into the Weapons Lab?" I say. "Nita said it would trigger a backup security measure if they did, but it seemed like the most obvious solution to their problem, to me."

"A serum would have been released into the air . . . one that masks could not have protected against, because it is absorbed into the skin," says David. "One that even the genetically pure cannot fight off. I don't know how Nita knows about it, since it's not supposed to be public knowledge, but I suppose we'll find out some other time."

"What does the serum do?"

His smile turns into a grimace. "Let's just say it's bad enough that Nita would rather be in prison for the rest of her life than come into contact with it."

He's right. He doesn't have to say anything more.

CHAPTER
THIRTY-THREE

TOBIAS

"Look who it is," Peter says as I walk into the dormitory.
"The traitor."

There are maps spread across his cot and the one next
to his. They are white and pale blue and dull green, and
they draw me to them by some strange magnetism. On
each one Peter has drawn a wobbly circle—around our
city, around Chicago. He's marking the limits of where
he's been.

I watch that circle shrink into each map, until it's just a
bright red dot, like a drop of blood.

And then I back away, afraid of what it means that I am
so small.

"If you think you're standing on some kind of moral

high ground, you're wrong," I say to Peter. "Why all the maps?"

"I'm having trouble wrapping my head around it, the size of the world," he says. "Some of the Bureau people have been helping me learn more about it. Planets and stars and bodies of water, things like that."

He says it casually, but I know from the frantic scribbling on maps that his interest isn't casual—it's obsessive. I was obsessive about my fears, once, in the same way, always trying to make sense of them, over and over again.

"Is it helping?" I say. I realize that I've never had a conversation with Peter that didn't involve yelling at him. Not that he didn't deserve it, but I don't know anything about him. I barely remember his last name from the initiate roster. Hayes. Peter Hayes.

"Sort of." He picks up one of the bigger maps. It shows the entire globe, pressed flat like kneaded dough. I stare at it long enough to make sense of the shapes on it, the blue stretches of water and the multicolored pieces of land. On one of the pieces is a red dot. He points at it. "That dot covers all the places we've ever been. You could cut that piece of land out of the ground and sink it into this ocean and no one would even notice."

I feel that fear again, the fear of my own size. "Right. So?"

"So? So everything I've ever worried about or said or

done, how can it possibly matter?" He shakes his head. "It doesn't."

"Of course it does," I say. "All that land is filled with people, every one of them different, and the things they do to each other matter."

He shakes his head again, and I wonder, suddenly, if this is how he comforts himself: by convincing himself that the bad things he's done don't matter. I see how the mammoth planet that terrifies me seems like a haven to him, a place where he can disappear into its great space, never distinguishing himself, and never being held responsible for his actions.

He bends over to untie his shoes. "So, have you been ostracized from your little crowd of devotees?"

"No," I say automatically. Then I add, "Maybe. But they aren't my devotees."

"Please. They're like the Cult of Four."

I can't help but laugh. "Jealous? Wish you had a Cult of Psychopaths to call your very own?"

One of his eyebrows twitches up. "If I was a psychopath, I would have killed you in your sleep by now."

"And added my eyeballs to your eyeball collection, no doubt."

Peter laughs too, and I realize that I am exchanging jokes and conversation with the initiate who stabbed

Edward in the eye and tried to kill my girlfriend—if she's still that. But then, he's also the Dauntless who helped us end the attack simulation and saved Tris from a horrible death. I am not sure which actions should weigh more heavily on my mind. Maybe I should forget them all, let him begin again.

"Maybe you should join my little group of hated people," says Peter. "So far Caleb and I are the only members, but given how easy it is to get on that girl's bad side, I'm sure our numbers will grow."

I stiffen. "You're right, it is easy to get on her bad side. All you have to do is try to get her killed."

My stomach clenches. *I* almost got her killed. If she had been standing closer to the explosion, she might be like Uriah, hooked up to tubes in the hospital, her mind quiet.

No wonder she doesn't know if she wants to stay with me or not.

The ease of a moment ago is gone. I cannot forget what Peter did, because he has not changed. He is still the same person who was willing to kill and maim and destroy to climb to the top of his initiate class. And I can't forget what I did either. I stand.

Peter leans against the wall and laces his fingers over his stomach. "I'm just saying, if she decides someone is worthless, everyone follows suit. That's a strange talent, for someone who used to be just another boring Stiff, isn't it? And maybe too much power for one person to have, right?"

"Her talent isn't for controlling other people's opinions," I say, "it's for usually being right about people."

He closes his eyes. "Whatever you say, Four."

All my limbs feel brittle with tension. I leave the dormitory and the maps with their red circles, though I'm not sure where else to go.

To me, Tris has always seemed magnetic in a way I could not describe, and that she was not aware of. I have never feared or hated her for it, the way Peter does, but then, I have always been in a position of strength myself, not threatened by her. Now that I have lost that position, I can feel the tug toward resentment, as strong and sure as a hand around my arm.

I find myself in the atrium garden again, and this time, light glows behind the windows. The flowers look beautiful and savage in the daylight, like vicious creatures suspended in time, motionless.

Cara jogs into the atrium, her hair askew and floating over her forehead. "There you are. It is frighteningly easy to lose people in this place."

"What is it?"

"Well—are you all right, Four?"

I bite down on my lip so hard I feel a pinch. "I'm fine. What is it?"

"We're having a meeting, and your presence is required."

"Who is 'we,' exactly?"

"GDs and GD sympathizers who don't want to let the Bureau get away with certain things," she says, and then she cocks her head to the side. "But better planners than the last ones you fell in with."

I wonder who told her. "You know about the attack simulation?"

"Better still, I recognized the simulation serum in the microscope when Tris showed it to me," Cara says. "Yes, I know."

I shake my head. "Well, I'm not getting involved in this again."

"Don't be a fool," she says. "The truth you heard is still true. These people are still responsible for the deaths of most of the Abnegation and the mental enslavement of the Dauntless and the utter destruction of our way of life, and something has to be done about them."

I'm not sure I want to be in the same room with Tris, knowing that we might be on the verge of ending, like standing on the edge of a cliff. It's easier to pretend it's not happening when I'm not around her. But Cara says it so simply I have to agree with her: yes, something has to be done.

She takes my hand and leads me down the hotel hallway. I know she's right, but I'm uncertain, uneasy about participating in another attempt at resistance. Still, I am already moving toward it, part of me eager for a chance to move again, instead of standing frozen before the surveillance footage of our city, as I have been.

When she's sure I'm following her, she releases my hand and tucks her stray hair behind her ears.

"It's still strange not to see you in blue," I say.

"It's time to let all that go, I think," she answers. "Even if I could go back, I wouldn't want to, at this point."

"You don't miss the factions?"

"I do, actually." She glances at me. Enough time has passed between Will's death and now that I no longer see him when I look at her, I just see Cara. I have known her far longer than I knew him. She has just a touch of his good-naturedness, enough to make me feel like I can tease her without offending her. "I thrived in Erudite. So many people devoted to discovery and innovation—it was lovely. But now that I know how large the world is . . . well. I suppose I have grown too large for my faction, as a consequence." She frowns. "I'm sorry, was that arrogant?"

"Who cares?"

"Some people do. It's nice to know you aren't one of them."

I notice, because I can't help it, that some of the people we pass on the way to the meeting give me nasty looks, or a wide berth. I have been hated and avoided before, as the son of Evelyn Johnson, factionless tyrant, but it bothers me more now. Now I know that I have done something to make myself worthy of that hatred; I have betrayed them all.

Cara says, "Ignore them. They don't know what it is to make a difficult decision."

"You wouldn't have done it, I bet."

"That is only because I have been taught to be cautious when I don't know all the information, and you have been taught that risks can produce great rewards." She looks at me sideways. "Or, in this case, no rewards."

She pauses at the door to the labs Matthew and his supervisor use, and knocks. Matthew tugs it open and takes a bite out of the apple he's holding. We follow him into the room where I found out I was not Divergent.

Tris is there, standing beside Christina, who looks at me like I am something rotten that needs to be discarded. And in the corner by the door is Caleb, his face stained with bruises. I am about to ask what happened to him when I realize that Tris's knuckles are also discolored, and that she very intentionally isn't looking at him.

Or at me.

"I think that's everyone," Matthew says. "Okay . . . so . . . um. Tris, I suck at this."

"You do, actually," she says with a grin. I feel a flare of jealousy. She clears her throat. "So, we know that these people are responsible for the attack on Abnegation, and that they can't be trusted to safeguard our city any longer. We know that we want to do something about it, and that the previous attempt to do something was . . ." Her eyes drift to mine, and her stare carves me into a smaller man. "Ill-advised," she finishes. "We can do better."

"What do you propose?" Cara says.

"All I know right now is that I want to expose them for what they are," Tris says. "The entire compound can't possibly know what their leaders have done, and I think we should show them. Maybe then they'll elect new leaders, ones who won't treat the people inside the experiments as expendable. I thought, maybe a widespread truth serum 'infection,' so to speak—"

I remember the weight of the truth serum, filling me in all my empty places, lungs and belly and face. I remember how impossible it seemed to me that Tris had lifted that weight enough to lie.

"Won't work," I say. "They're GPs, remember? GPs can resist truth serum."

"That's not necessarily true," Matthew says, pinching the string around his neck and then twisting it. "We don't see that many Divergent resisting truth serum. Just Tris, in recent memory. The capacity for serum resistance seems to be higher in some people than others—take yourself, for example, Tobias." Matthew shrugs. "Still, this is why I invited *you*, Caleb. You've worked on the serums before. You might know them as well as I do. Maybe we can develop a truth serum that is more difficult to resist."

"I don't want to do that kind of work anymore," Caleb says.

"Oh, shut—" starts Tris, but Matthew interrupts her.

"Please, Caleb," he says.

Caleb and Tris exchange a look. The skin on his face and on her knuckles is nearly the same color, purple-blue-green, as if drawn with ink. This is what happens when siblings collide—they injure each other the same way. Caleb sinks back against the countertop edge, touching the back of his head to the metal cabinets.

"Fine," Caleb says. "As long as you promise not to use this against me, Beatrice."

"Why would I?" Tris says.

"I can help," Cara says, lifting a hand. "I've worked on serums too, as an Erudite."

"Great." Matthew claps his hands together. "Meanwhile, Tris will be playing the spy."

"What about me?" Christina says.

"I was hoping you and Tobias could get in with Reggie," Tris says. "David wouldn't tell me about the backup security measures in the Weapons Lab, but Nita can't have been the only one who knew about them."

"You want me to get *in* with the guy who set off the explosives that put Uriah in a coma?" Christina says.

"You don't have to be friends," Tris says, "you just need to talk to him about what he knows. Tobias can help you."

"I don't need Four; I can do it myself," Christina says.

She shifts on the exam table, tearing the paper beneath her with her thigh, and gives me another sour look. I know it must be Uriah's blank face she sees when she looks at me. I feel like there is something stuck in my throat.

"You do need me, actually, because he already trusts me," I say. "And those people are very secretive, which means this will require subtlety."

"I can be subtle," Christina says.

"No, you can't."

"He's got a *point* . . ." Tris sings with a smile.

Christina smacks her arm, and Tris smacks her back.

"It's all settled, then," Matthew says. "I think we should meet again after Tris has been to the council meeting, which is on Friday. Come here at five."

He approaches Cara and Caleb and says something

about chemical compounds I don't quite understand. Christina walks out, bumping me with her shoulder as she leaves. Tris lifts her eyes to mine.

"We should talk," I say.

"Fine," she says, and I follow her into the hallway.

We stand next to the door until everyone else leaves. Her shoulders are drawn in like she's trying to make herself even smaller, trying to evaporate on the spot, and we stand too far apart, the entire width of the hallway between us. I try to remember the last time I kissed her and I can't.

Finally we're alone, and the hallway is quiet. My hands start to tingle and go numb, the way they always do when I panic.

"Do you think you'll ever forgive me?" I say.

She shakes her head, but says, "I don't know. I think that's what I need to figure out."

"You know . . . you *know* I never wanted Uriah to get hurt, right?" I look at the stitches crossing her forehead and I add, "Or you. I never wanted you to get hurt either."

She's tapping her foot, her body shifting with the movement. She nods. "I know that."

"I had to do something," I say. "I *had* to."

"A lot of people got hurt," she says. "All because you dismissed what I said, because—and this is the worst part, Tobias—because you thought I was being petty and *jealous*. Just some silly sixteen-year-old girl, right?" She shakes her head.

"I would never call you silly or petty," I say sternly. "I thought your judgment was clouded, yes. But that's all."

"That's enough." Her fingers slide through her hair and wrap around it. "It's just the same thing all over again, isn't it? You don't respect me as much as you say you do. When it comes down to it, you still believe I can't think rationally—"

"That is *not* what's happening!" I say hotly. "I respect you more than anyone. But right now I'm wondering what bothers you more, that I made a stupid decision or that I didn't make *your* decision."

"What's that supposed to mean?"

"It means," I say, "that you may have said you just wanted us to be honest with each other, but I think you really wanted me to always agree with you."

"I can't believe you would say that! You were *wrong*—"

"Yeah, I was wrong!" I'm shouting now, and I don't know where the anger came from, except that I can feel it swirling around inside me, violent and vicious and the strongest I have felt in days. "I was wrong, I made a huge mistake! My best friend's brother is as good as dead! And now you're acting like a parent, punishing me for it because I didn't do as I was told. Well, you are not my parent, Tris, and you don't get to tell me what to do, what to choose—!"

"Stop yelling at me," she says quietly, and she finally looks at me. I used to see all kinds of things in her eyes, love and longing and curiosity, but now all I see is anger. "Just stop."

Her quiet voice stalls the anger inside me, and I relax into the wall behind me, shoving my hands into my pockets. I didn't mean to yell at her. I didn't mean to get angry at all.

I stare, shocked, as tears touch her cheeks. I haven't seen her cry in a long time. She sniffs, and gulps, and tries to sound normal, but she doesn't.

"I just need some time," she says, choking on each word. "Okay?"

"Okay," I say.

She wipes her cheeks with her palms and walks down the hallway. I watch her blond head until it disappears around the bend, and I feel bare, like there's nothing left to protect me against pain. Her absence stings worst of all.

CHAPTER THIRTY-FOUR

TRIS

"THERE SHE IS," Amar says as I approach the group. "Here, I'll get you your vest, Tris."

"My . . . vest?" As promised by David yesterday, I'm going to the fringe this afternoon. I don't know what to expect, which usually makes me nervous, but I'm too worn-out from the past few days to feel much of anything.

"Bulletproof vest. The fringe is not all that safe," he says, and he reaches into a crate near the doors, sorting through a stack of thick black vests to find the right size. He emerges with one that still looks far too big for me. "Sorry, not much variety here. This will work just fine. Arms up."

He guides me into the vest and tightens the straps at my sides.

"I didn't know you would be here," I say.

"Well, what did you think I did at the Bureau? Just wandered around cracking jokes?" He smiles. "They found a good use for my Dauntless expertise. I'm part of the security team. So is George. We usually just handle compound security, but any time anyone wants to go to the fringe, I volunteer."

"Talking about me?" George, who was standing in the group by the doors. "Hi, Tris. I hope he's not saying anything bad."

George puts his arm across Amar's shoulders, and they grin at each other. George looks better than the last time I saw him, but grief leaves its mark on his expression, taking the crinkles out of the corners of his eyes when he smiles, taking the dimple from his cheek.

"I was thinking we should give her a gun," Amar says. He glances at me. "We don't normally give potential future council members weapons, because they have no clue how to use them, but it's pretty clear that you do."

"It's really all right," I say. "I don't need—"

"No, you're probably a better shot than most of them," George says. "We could use another Dauntless on board with us. Let me go get one."

A few minutes later I am armed and walking with Amar to the truck. He and I get in the far back, George and a woman named Ann get in the middle, and two older security officers named Jack and Violet get in the front. The back of the truck is covered with a hard black material. The back doors look opaque and black from the outside, but from the inside they're transparent, so we can see where we're going. I am nestled between Amar and stacks of equipment that block our view of the front of the truck. George peers over the equipment and grins when the truck starts, but other than that, it's just Amar and me.

I watch the compound disappear behind us. We drive through the gardens and outbuildings that surround it, and peeking out from behind the edge of the compound are the airplanes, white and stationary. We reach the fence, and the gates open for us. I hear Jack speaking to the soldier at the outer fence, telling him our plans and the contents of the vehicle—a series of words I don't understand—before we can be released into the wild.

I ask, "What's the purpose of this patrol? Beyond showing me how things work, I mean."

"We've always kept an eye on the fringe, which is the nearest genetically damaged area outside the compound. Mostly just research, studying how the genetically damaged behave," Amar says. "But after the attack, David and the council decided we needed more extensive surveillance set up there so we can prevent an attack from happening again."

344

We drive past the same kind of ruins I saw when we left the city—the buildings collapsing under their own weight, and the plants roaming wild over the land, breaking through concrete.

I don't know Amar, and I don't exactly trust him, but I have to ask:

"So you believe it all? All the stuff about genetic damage being the cause of . . . *this*?"

All his old friends in the experiment were GDs. Can he possibly believe that they're damaged, that there's something wrong with them?

"You don't?" Amar says. "The way I see it, the earth has been around for a long, long time. Longer than we can imagine. And before the Purity War, no one had ever done *this*, right?" He waves his hand to indicate the world outside.

"I don't know," I say. "I find it hard to believe that they didn't."

"Such a grim view of human nature you have," he says.

I don't respond.

He continues, "Anyway, if something like that had happened in our history, the Bureau would know about it."

That strikes me as naive, for someone who once lived in my city and saw, at least on the screens, how many secrets we kept from one another. Evelyn tried to control people by controlling weapons, but Jeanine was more ambitious—she knew that when you control information, or manipulate it, you don't need force to keep people under your thumb. They stay there willingly.

That is what the Bureau—and the entire government, probably—is doing: conditioning people to be happy under its thumb.

We ride in silence for a while, with just the sound of jiggling equipment and the engine to accompany us. At first I look at every building we pass, wondering what it once housed, and then they start to blend together for me. How many different kinds of ruin do you have to see before you resign yourself to calling it all "ruin"?

"We're almost at the fringe," George calls from the middle of the truck. "We're going to stop here and advance on foot. Everyone take some equipment and set it up—except Amar, who should just look after Tris. Tris, you're welcome to get out and have a look, but stay with Amar."

I feel like all my nerves are too close to the surface, and the slightest touch will make them fire. The fringe is where my mother retreated after witnessing a murder—it is where the Bureau found her and rescued her because they suspected her genetic code was sound. Now I will walk there, to the place where, in some ways, it all began.

The truck stops, and Amar shoves the doors open. He

holds his gun in one hand and beckons to me with the other. I jump out behind him.

There are buildings here, but they are not nearly as prominent as the makeshift homes, made of scrap metal and plastic tarps, piled up right next to one another like they are holding one another upright. In the narrow aisles between them are people, mostly children, selling things from trays, or carrying buckets of water, or cooking over open fires.

When the ones nearest to us see us, a young boy takes off running and screams, "Raid! Raid!"

"Don't worry about that," Amar says to me. "They think we're soldiers. Sometimes they raid to transport the kids to orphanages."

I barely acknowledge the comment. Instead I start walking down one of the aisles, as most people take off or shut themselves inside their lean-tos with cardboard or more tarp. I see them through the cracks between the walls, their houses not much more than a pile of food and supplies on one side and sleeping mats on the other. I wonder what they do in the winter. Or what they do for a toilet.

I think of the flowers inside the compound, and the wood floors, and all the beds in the hotel that are unoccupied, and say, "Do you ever help them?"

"We believe that the best way to help our world is to fix its genetic deficiencies," Amar says, like he's reciting it from memory. "Feeding people is just putting a tiny bandage on a gaping wound. It might stop the bleeding for a while, but ultimately the wound will still be there."

I can't respond. All I do is shake my head a little and keep walking. I am beginning to understand why my mother joined Abnegation when she was supposed to join Erudite. If she had really craved safety from Erudite's growing corruption, she could have gone to Amity or Candor. But she chose the faction where she could help the helpless, and dedicated most of her life to making sure the factionless were provided for.

They must have reminded her of this place, of the fringe.

I turn my head away from Amar so he won't see the tears in my eyes. "Let's go back to the truck."

"You all right?"

"Yeah."

We both turn around to head back to the truck, but then we hear gunshots.

And right after them, a shout. "Help!"

Everyone around us scatters.

"That's George," Amar says, and he takes off running down one of the aisles on our right. I chase him into the scrap-metal structures, but he's too quick for me, and this place is a maze—I lose him in seconds, and then I am alone.

As much automatic, Abnegation-bred sympathy as I have for the people living in this place, I am also afraid of them. If they are like the factionless, then they are surely desperate like the factionless, and I am wary of desperate people.

A hand closes around my arm and drags me backward, into one of the aluminum lean-tos. Inside everything is tinted blue from the tarp that covers the walls, insulating the structure against the cold. The floor is covered with plywood, and standing in front of me is a small, thin woman with a grubby face.

"You don't want to be out there," she says. "They'll lash out at anyone, no matter how young she is."

"They?" I say.

"Lots of angry people here in the fringe," the woman says. "Some people's anger makes them want to kill everyone they perceive as an enemy. Some people's makes them more constructive."

"Well, thank you for the help," I say. "My name is Tris."

"Amy. Sit."

"I can't," I say. "My friends are out there."

"Then you should wait until the hordes of people run

to wherever your friends are, and then sneak up on them from behind."

That sounds smart.

I sink to the floor, my gun digging into my leg. The bulletproof vest is so stiff it's hard to get comfortable, but I do the best I can to seem relaxed. I hear people running outside and shouting. Amy flicks the corner of the tarp back to see outside.

"So you and your friends aren't soldiers," Amy says, still looking outside. "Which means you must be Genetic Welfare types, right?"

"No," I say. "I mean, they are, but I'm from the city. I mean, Chicago."

Amy's eyebrows pop up high. "Damn. Has it been disbanded?"

"Not yet."

"That's unfortunate."

"Unfortunate?" I frown at her. "That's my home you're talking about, you know."

"Well your home is perpetuating the belief that genetically damaged people need to be fixed—that they're *damaged*, period, which they—we—are not. So yes, it's unfortunate that the experiments still exist. I won't apologize for saying so."

I hadn't thought about it that way. To me Chicago has

to keep existing because the people I have lost lived there, because the way of life I once loved continues there, though in a broken form. But I didn't realize that Chicago's very existence could be harmful to people outside who just want to be thought of as whole.

"It's time for you to go," Amy says, dropping the corner of the tarp. "They're probably in one of the meeting areas, northwest of here."

"Thank you again," I say.

She nods to me, and I duck out of her makeshift home, the boards creaking beneath my feet.

I move through the aisles, fast, glad that all the people scattered when we arrived so there is no one to block my way. I jump over a puddle of—well, I don't want to know what it is—and emerge into a kind of courtyard, where a tall, gangly boy has a gun pointed at George.

A small crowd of people surrounds the boy with the gun. They have distributed among them the surveillance equipment George was carrying, and they're destroying it, hitting it with shoes or rocks or hammers.

George's eyes shift to me, but I touch a finger to my lips, hastily. I am behind the crowd now; the one with the gun doesn't know I'm there.

"Put the gun down," George says.

"No!" the boy answers. His pale eyes keep shifting

from George to the people around him and back. "Went to a lot of trouble to get this, not gonna give it to you now."

"Then just . . . let me go. You can keep it."

"Not until you tell us where you've been taking our people!" the boy says.

"We haven't taken any of your people," George says. "We're not soldiers. We're just scientists."

"Yeah, right," the boy says. "A bulletproof vest? If that's not soldier shit, then I'm the richest kid in the States. Now tell me what I need to know!"

I move back so I'm standing behind one of the lean-tos, then put my gun around the edge of the structure and say, "Hey!"

Everyone in the crowd turns at once, but the boy with the gun doesn't stop aiming at George, like I'd hoped.

"I've got you in my sights," I say. "Leave now and I'll let you go."

"I'll shoot him!" the boy says.

"I'll shoot *you*," I say. "We're with the government, but we aren't soldiers. We don't know where your people are. If you let him go, we'll all leave quietly. If you kill him, I guarantee there *will* be soldiers here soon to arrest you, and they won't be as forgiving as we are."

At that moment Amar emerges into the courtyard behind George, and someone in the crowd screeches,

"There are more of them!" And everyone scatters. The boy with the gun dives into the nearest aisle, leaving George, Amar, and me alone. Still, I keep my gun up by my face, in case they decide to come back.

Amar wraps his arms around George, and George thumps his back with a fist. Amar looks at me, his face over George's shoulder. "Still don't think genetic damage is to blame for any of these troubles?"

I walk past one of the lean-tos and see a little girl crouching just inside the door, her arms wrapped around her knees. She sees me through the crack in the layered tarps and whimpers a little. I wonder who taught these people to be so terrified of soldiers. I wonder what made a young boy desperate enough to aim a gun at one of them.

"No," I say. "I don't."

I have better people to blame.

+ + +

By the time we get back to the truck, Jack and Violet are setting up a surveillance camera that wasn't stolen by people in the fringe. Violet has a screen in her hands with a long list of numbers on it, and she reads them to Jack, who programs them into his screen.

"Where have you guys been?" he says.

"We were attacked," George says. "We have to leave, now."

"Luckily, that's the last set of coordinates," Violet says. "Let's get going."

We pile into the truck again. Amar draws the doors shut behind us, and I set my gun on the floor with the safety on, glad to be rid of it. I didn't think I would be aiming a dangerous weapon at someone today when I woke up. I didn't think I would witness those kinds of living conditions, either.

"It's the Abnegation in you," Amar says. "That makes you hate that place. I can tell."

"It's a lot of things in me."

"It's just something I noticed in Four, too. Abnegation produces deeply serious people. People who automatically see things like need," he says. "I've noticed that when people switch to Dauntless, it creates some of the same types. Erudite who switch to Dauntless tend to turn cruel and brutal. Candor who switch to Dauntless tend to become boisterous, fight-picking adrenaline junkies. And Abnegation who switch to Dauntless become . . . I don't know, soldiers, I guess. Revolutionaries.

"That's what he could be, if he trusted himself more," he adds. "If Four wasn't so plagued with self-doubt, he would be one hell of a leader, I think. I've always thought that."

"I think you're right," I say. "It's when he's a follower

that he gets himself into trouble. Like with Nita. Or Evelyn."

What about you? I ask myself. *You wanted to make him a follower too.*

No, I didn't, I tell myself, but I'm not sure if I believe it.

Amar nods.

Images from the fringe keep rising up inside me like hiccups. I imagine the child my mother was, crouched in one of those lean-tos, scrambling for weapons because they meant an ounce of safety, choking on smoke to keep warm in the winter. I don't know why she was so willing to abandon that place after she was rescued. She became absorbed into the compound, and then worked on its behalf for the rest of her life. Did she forget about where she came from?

She couldn't have. She spent her entire life trying to help the factionless. Maybe it wasn't a fulfillment of her duty as an Abnegation—maybe it came from a desire to help people like the ones she had left.

Suddenly I can't stand to think of her, or that place, or the things I saw there. I grab on to the first thought that comes to my mind, to distract myself.

"So you and Tobias were good friends?"

"Is anyone good friends with him?" Amar shakes his head. "I gave him his nickname, though. I watched him face his fears and I saw how troubled he was, and I figured he could use a new life, so I started calling him 'Four.' But no, I wouldn't say we were good friends. Not as good as I wanted to be."

Amar leans his head back against the wall and closes his eyes. A small smile curls his lips.

"Oh," I say. "Did you . . . *like* him?"

"Now why would you ask that?"

I shrug. "Just the way you talk about him."

"I don't *like* him anymore, if that's what you're really asking. But yes, at one time I did, and it was clear that he did not return that particular sentiment, so I backed off," Amar says. "I'd prefer it if you didn't say anything."

"To Tobias? Of course I won't."

"No, I mean, don't say anything to anyone. And I'm not talking about just the thing with Tobias."

He looks at the back of George's head, now visible above the considerably diminished pile of equipment.

I raise an eyebrow at him. I'm not surprised he and George were drawn to each other. They're both Divergent who had to fake their own deaths to survive. Both outsiders in an unfamiliar world.

"You have to understand," Amar says. "The Bureau is obsessed with procreation—with passing on genes. And George and I are both GPs, so any entanglement that can't produce a stronger genetic code . . . It's not encouraged, that's all."

"Ah." I nod. "You don't have to worry about me. I'm not obsessed with producing strong genes." I smile wryly.

"Thank you," he says.

For a few seconds we sit quietly, watching the ruins turn to a blur as the truck picks up speed.

"I think you're good for Four, you know," he says.

I stare at my hands, curled in my lap. I don't feel like explaining to him that we're on the verge of breaking up—I don't know him, and even if I did, I wouldn't want to talk about it. All I can manage to say is, "Oh?"

"Yeah. I can see what you bring out in him. You don't know this because you've never experienced it, but Four without you is a much different person. He's . . . obsessive, explosive, insecure . . ."

"Obsessive?"

"What else do you call someone who repeatedly goes through his own fear landscape?"

"I don't know . . . determined." I pause. "Brave."

"Yeah, sure. But also a little bit crazy, right? I mean, most Dauntless would rather leap into the chasm than keep going through their fear landscapes. There's bravery and then there's masochism, and the line got a little hazy with him."

"I'm familiar with the line," I say.

"I know." Amar grins. "Anyway, all I'm saying is, any time you mash two different people against each other, you'll get problems, but I can see that what you guys have is worthwhile, that's all."

I wrinkle my nose. "*Mash* people against each other, really?"

Amar presses his palms together and twists them back and forth, to illustrate. I laugh, but I can't ignore the achy feeling in my chest.

CHAPTER
THIRTY-FIVE

TOBIAS

I WALK TO the cluster of chairs closest to the windows in the control room and bring up the footage from different cameras throughout the city, one by one, searching for my parents. I find Evelyn first—she is in the lobby of Erudite headquarters, talking in a close huddle with Therese and a factionless man, her second and third in command now that I am gone. I turn up the volume on the microphone, but I still can't hear anything but muttering.

Through the windows along the back of the control room, I see the same empty night sky as the one above the city, interrupted only by small blue and red lights marking the runways for airplanes. It's strange to think we have that in common when everything else is so different here.

By now the people in the control room know that I was the one who disabled the security system the night before the attack, though I wasn't the one who slipped one of their night shift workers peace serum so that I could do it—that was Nita. But for the most part, they ignore me, as long as I stay away from their desks.

On another screen, I scroll through the footage again, looking for Marcus or Johanna, anything that can show me what's happening with the Allegiant. Every part of the city shows up on the screen, the bridge near the Merciless Mart and the Pire and the main thoroughfare of the Abnegation sector, the Hub and the Ferris wheel and the Amity fields, now worked by all the factions. But none of the cameras shows me anything.

"You've been coming here a lot," Cara says as she approaches. "Are you afraid of the rest of the compound? Or of something else?"

She's right, I have been coming to the control room a lot. It's just something to pass the time as I wait for my sentence from Tris, as I wait for our plan to strike the Bureau to come together, as I wait for something, *anything*.

"No," I say. "I'm just keeping an eye on my parents."

"The parents you hate?" She stands next to me, her arms folded. "Yes, I can see why you would want to spend every waking hour staring at people you want nothing to do with. It makes perfect sense."

"They're dangerous," I say. "More dangerous because no one else knows how dangerous they are but me."

"And what are you going to do from here, if they do something terrible? Send a smoke signal?"

I glare at her.

"Fine, fine." She puts up her hands in surrender. "I'm just trying to remind you that you aren't in their world anymore, you're in this one. That's all."

"Point taken."

I never thought of the Erudite as being particularly perceptive about relationships, or emotions, but Cara's discerning eyes see all kinds of things. My fear. My search for a distraction in my past. It's almost alarming.

I scroll past one of the camera angles and then pause, and scroll back. The scene is dark, because of the hour, but I see people alighting like a flock of birds around a building I don't recognize, their movements synchronized.

"They're doing it," Cara says, excited. "The Allegiant are actually attacking."

"Hey!" I shout to one of the women at the control room desks. The older one, who always gives me a nasty look when I show up, lifts her head. "Camera twenty-four! Hurry!"

She taps her screen, and everyone milling around the

surveillance area gathers around her. People passing by in the hallway stop to see what's happening, and I turn to Cara.

"Can you go get the others?" I say. "I think they should see this."

She nods, her eyes wild, and rushes away from the control room.

The people around the unfamiliar building wear no uniform to distinguish them, but they don't wear factionless armbands either, and they carry guns. I try to pick out a face, anything I recognize, but the footage is too blurry. I watch them arrange themselves, motioning to one another to communicate, dark arms waving in the darker night.

I wedge my thumbnail between my teeth, impatient for something, anything to happen. A few minutes later Cara arrives with the others at her back. When they reach the crowd of people around the primary screens, Peter says, "Excuse me!" loud enough to make people turn around. When they see who he is, they part for him.

"What's up?" Peter says to me when he's closer. "What's going on?"

"The Allegiant have formed an army," I say, pointing at the screen on the left. "There are people from every faction in it, even Amity and Erudite. I've been watching a lot lately."

"Erudite?" Caleb says.

"The Allegiant are the enemies of the new enemies, the factionless," Cara replies. "Which gives the Erudite and the Allegiant a common goal: to usurp Evelyn."

"Did you say there were Amity in an *army*?" Christina asks me.

"They're not really participating in the violence," I say. "But they are participating in the effort."

"The Allegiant raided their first weapons storehouse a few days ago," the young woman sitting at the control room desk nearest to us says over her shoulder. "This is their second. That's where they got those weapons. After the first raid, Evelyn had most of the weapons relocated, but this storehouse didn't make it in time."

My father knows what Evelyn knew: that the power to make people fear you is the only power you need. Weapons will do that for him.

"What's their goal?" Caleb says.

"The Allegiant are motivated by the desire to return to our original purpose in the city," Cara says. "Whether that means sending a group of people outside of it, as instructed by Edith Prior—which we thought was important at the time, though I've since learned that her instructions didn't really matter—or reinstating the factions by force. They're building up to an attack on the factionless stronghold. That's what Johanna and I discussed before I left. We did *not* discuss allying with your father, Tobias, but I suppose she's capable of making her own decisions."

I almost forgot that Cara was the leader of the Allegiant, before we left. Now I'm not sure she cares whether the factions survive or not, but she still cares about the people. I can tell by the way she watches the screens, eager but afraid.

Even over the chatter of the people around us, I hear the gunfire when it starts, just snaps and claps in the microphones. I tap the glass in front of me a few times, and the camera angle switches to one inside the building the invaders have just forced their way into. On a table within is a pile of small boxes—ammunition—and a few pistols. It's nothing compared to the guns the people here have, in all their abundance, but in the city, I know it's valuable.

Several men and women with factionless armbands guard the table, but they are falling fast, outnumbered by the Allegiant. I recognize a familiar face among them— Zeke, slamming the butt of his gun into a factionless man's jaw. The factionless are overcome within two minutes, falling to bullets I see only when they're already buried in flesh. The Allegiant spread through the room, stepping over bodies like they are just more debris, and gather everything they can. Zeke piles stray guns on the table, a hard look on his face that I've only seen a few times.

He doesn't even know what happened to Uriah.

The woman at the desk taps the screen in a few places. On one of the smaller screens above her is an image—a piece of the surveillance footage we just watched, frozen at a particular moment in time. She taps again, and the image moves closer to its targets, a man with close-cropped hair and a woman with long, dark hair covering one side of her face.

Marcus, of course. And Johanna—carrying a gun.

"Between them, they have managed to rally most of the loyal faction members to their cause. Surprisingly, though, the Allegiant still don't outnumber the faction-less." The woman leans back in her chair and shakes her head. "There were far more factionless than we ever anticipated. It's difficult to get an accurate population count on a scattered population, after all."

"Johanna? Leading a rebellion? With a weapon? That makes no sense," Caleb says.

Johanna told me once that if the decisions had been up to her, she would have supported action against Erudite instead of the passivity the rest of her faction advocated. But she was at the mercy of her faction and their fear. Now, with the factions disbanded, it seems she has become something other than the mouthpiece of Amity or even the leader of the Allegiant. She has become a soldier.

"Makes more sense than you'd think," I say, and Cara nods along with my words.

I watch them empty the room of weapons and ammunition and move on, fast, scattering like seeds on the wind. I feel heavier, like I am bearing a new burden. I wonder if the people around me—Cara, Christina, Peter, even Caleb—feel the same way. The city, our city, is even closer to total destruction than it was before.

We can pretend that we don't belong there anymore, while we're living in relative safety in this place, but we do. We always will.

CHAPTER
THIRTY-SIX

TRIS

IT'S DARK AND snowing when we drive up to the entrance of
the compound. The flakes blow across the road, as light
as powdered sugar. It's just an early autumn snow; it will
be gone in the morning. I take off my bulletproof vest as
soon as I get out, and offer it to Amar along with my gun.
I'm uncomfortable holding it now, and I used to think that
my discomfort would go away with time, but now I'm not
so sure. Maybe it never will, and maybe that's all right.

Warm air surrounds me as I pass through the doors.
The compound looks cleaner than ever before, now that
I've seen the fringe. The comparison is unsettling. How
can I walk these squeaky floors and wear these starchy
clothes when I know that those people are out there,

wrapping their houses in tarp to stay warm?

But by the time I reach the hotel dormitory, the unsettled feeling is gone.

I scan the room for Christina, or for Tobias, but neither of them is there. Only Peter and Caleb are, Peter with a large book on his lap, scribbling notes on a nearby notepad, and Caleb reading our mother's journal on the screen, his eyes glassy. I try to ignore that.

"Have either of you seen . . ." But who do I want to talk to, Christina or Tobias?

"Four?" Caleb says, deciding for me. "I saw him in the genealogy room earlier."

"The . . . what room?"

"They have our ancestors' names on display in a room. Can I get a piece of paper?" he asks Peter.

Peter tears a sheet from the back of his notepad and hands it to Caleb, who scribbles something on it—directions. Caleb says, "I found our parents' names there earlier. On the right side of the room, second panel from the door."

He hands me the directions without looking at me. I look at his neat, even letters. Before I punched him, Caleb would have insisted on walking me himself, desperate for time to explain himself to me. But recently he has kept his distance, either because he's afraid of me or because he has finally given up.

Neither option makes me feel good.

"Thank you," I say. "Um . . . how's your nose?"

"It's fine," he says. "I think the bruise really brings out my eyes, don't you?"

He smiles a little, and so do I. But it's clear that neither of us knows what to do from here, because we've both run out of words.

"Wait, you were gone today, right?" he says after a second. "Something's happening in the city. The Allegiant rose up against Evelyn, attacked one of her weapons storehouses."

I stare at him. I haven't wondered about what was happening in the city for a few days now; I've been too wrapped up in what's happening here.

"The Allegiant?" I say. "The people currently led by *Johanna Reyes* . . . attacked a storehouse?"

Before we left, I was sure the city was about to explode into another conflict. I guess now it has. But I feel detached from it—almost everyone I care about is here.

"Led by Johanna Reyes and Marcus Eaton," Caleb says. "But Johanna was there, holding a gun. It was ludicrous. The Bureau people seemed really disturbed by it."

"Wow." I shake my head. "I guess it was just a matter of time."

We lapse into silence again, then walk away from each other at the same time, Caleb returning to his cot and me walking down the hallway, following Caleb's directions.

I see the genealogy room from a distance. The bronze walls seem to glow with warm light. Standing in the doorway, I feel like I am inside a sunset, the radiance surrounding me. Tobias's finger runs along the lines of his family tree—I assume—but idly, like he's not really paying attention to it.

I feel like I can see that obsessive streak Amar was referring to. I know that Tobias has been watching his parents on the screens, and now he is staring at their names, though there's nothing in this room he didn't already know. I was right to say that he was desperate, desperate for a connection to Evelyn, desperate not to be damaged, but I never thought about how those things were connected. I don't know how it would feel, to hate your own history and to crave love from the people who gave that history to you at the same time. How have I never seen the schism inside his heart? How have I never realized before that for all the strong, kind parts of him, there are also hurting, broken parts?

Caleb told me that our mother said there was evil in everyone, and the first step to loving someone else is to recognize that evil in ourselves, so we can forgive them.

So how can I hold Tobias's desperation against him, like I'm better than him, like I've never let my own broken-ness blind me?

"Hey," I say, crushing Caleb's directions into my back pocket.

He turns, and his expression is stern, familiar. It looks the way it did the first few weeks I knew him, like a sentry guarding his innermost thoughts.

"Listen," I say. "I thought I was supposed to figure out if I could forgive you or not, but now I'm thinking you didn't do anything to me that I need to forgive, except maybe accusing me of being jealous of Nita. . . ."

He opens his mouth to interject, but I hold up a hand to stop him.

"If we stay together, I'll have to forgive you over and over again, and if you're still in this, you'll have to forgive me over and over again too," I say. "So forgiveness isn't the point. What I really should have been trying to figure out is whether we were still good for each other or not."

All the way home I thought about what Amar said, about every relationship having its problems. I thought about my parents, who argued more often than any other Abnegation parents I knew, who nonetheless went through each day together until they died.

Then I thought of how strong I have become, how

secure I feel with the person I now am, and how all along the way he has told me that I am brave, I am respected, I am loved and worth loving.

"And?" he says, his voice and his eyes and his hands a little unsteady.

"And," I say, "I think you're still the only person sharp enough to sharpen someone like me."

"I am," he says roughly.

And I kiss him.

His arms slip around me and hold me tight, lifting me onto the tips of my toes. I bury my face in his shoulder and close my eyes, just breathing in the clean smell of him, the smell of wind.

I used to think that when people fell in love, they just landed where they landed, and they had no choice in the matter afterward. And maybe that's true of beginnings, but it's not true of this, now.

I fell in love with him. But I don't just stay with him by default as if there's no one else available to me. I stay with him because I choose to, every day that I wake up, every day that we fight or lie to each other or disappoint each other. I choose him over and over again, and he chooses me.

CHAPTER
THIRTY-SEVEN

I ARRIVE AT David's office for my first council meeting just as my watch shifts to ten, and he pushes himself into the hallway soon afterward. He looks even paler than he did the last time I saw him, and the dark circles under his eyes are pronounced, like bruises.

"Hello, Tris," he says. "Eager, are you? You're right on time."

I still feel a little weight in my limbs from the truth serum Cara, Caleb, and Matthew tested on me earlier, as part of our plan. They're trying to develop a powerful truth serum, one that even GPs as serum-resistant as I am are not immune to. I ignore the heavy feeling and say, "Of course I'm eager. It's my first meeting. Want help? You look tired."

"Fine, fine."

I move behind him and press into the handles of the wheelchair to get it moving.

He sighs. "I suppose I am tired. I was up all night dealing with our most recent crisis. Take a left here."

"What crisis is that?"

"Oh, you'll find out soon enough, let's not rush it."

We maneuver through the dim hallways of Terminal 5, as it is labeled—"an old name," David says—which have no windows, no hint of the world outside. I can almost feel the paranoia emanating from the walls, like the terminal itself is terrified of unfamiliar eyes. If only they knew what *my* eyes were searching for.

As I walk, I get a glimpse of David's hands, pressed to the armrests. The skin around his fingernails is raw and red, like he chewed it away overnight. The fingernails themselves are jagged. I remember when my own hands looked that way, when the memories of fear simulations crept into every dream and every idle thought. Maybe it's David's memories of the attack that are doing this to him.

I don't care, I think. *Remember what he did. What he would do again.*

"Here we are," David says. I push him through a set of double doors, propped open with doorstops. Most of the council members seem to be there, stirring tiny sticks in tiny cups of coffee, the majority of them men and women David's age. There are some younger members—Zoe is there, and she gives me a strained, but polite, smile when I walk in.

"Let's come to order!" David says as he wheels himself to the head of the conference table. I sit in one of the chairs along the edge of the room, next to Zoe. It's clear we're not supposed to be at the table with all the important people, and I'm okay with that—it'll be easier to doze off if things get boring, though if this new crisis is serious enough to keep David awake at night, I doubt it will.

"Last night I received a frantic call from the people in our control room," David says. "Evidently Chicago is about to erupt into violence again. Faction loyalists calling themselves the Allegiant have rebelled against faction-less control, attacking weapons safe houses. What they don't know is that Evelyn Johnson has discovered a new weapon—stores of death serum kept hidden in Erudite headquarters. As we know, no one is capable of resisting death serum, not even the Divergent. If the Allegiant attack the factionless government, and Evelyn Johnson retaliates, the casualties will obviously be catastrophic."

I stare at the floor in front of my feet as the room bursts into conversation.

"Quiet," says David. "The experiments are already in

danger of being shut down if we cannot prove to our superiors that we are capable of controlling them. Another revolution in Chicago would only cement their belief that this endeavor has outlived its usefulness—something we cannot allow to happen if we want to continue to fight genetic damage."

Somewhere behind David's exhausted, haggard expression is something harder, stronger. I believe him. I believe that he will not allow it to happen.

"It's time to use the memory serum virus for a mass reset," he says. "And I think we should use it against all four experiments."

"*Reset* them?" I say, because I can't help myself. Everyone in the room looks at me at once. They seem to have forgotten that I, a former member of the experiments they're referring to, am in the room.

"'Resetting' is our word for widespread memory erasure," David says. "It is what we do when the experiments that incorporate behavioral modification are in danger of falling apart. We did it when we first created each experiment that had a behavioral modification component, and the last one in Chicago was done a few generations before yours." He gives me an odd smile. "Why did you think there was so much physical devastation in the factionless sector? There was an uprising, and we had to quell it as cleanly as possible."

I sit stunned in my chair, picturing the broken roads and shattered windows and toppled streetlights in the factionless sector of the city, the destruction that is evident nowhere else—not even north of the bridge, where the buildings are empty but seem to have been vacated peacefully. I always just took the broken-down sectors of Chicago in stride, as evidence of what happens when people are without community. I never dreamed that they were the result of an uprising—and a subsequent *resetting*.

I feel sick with anger. That they want to stop a revolution, not to save lives, but to save their precious experiment, would be enough. But why do they believe they have the right to rip people's memories, their identities, out of their heads, just because it's convenient for them?

But of course, I know the answer to that question. To them, the people in our city are just containers of genetic material—just GDs, valuable for the corrected genes they pass on, and not for the brains in their heads or the hearts in their chests.

"When?" one of the council members says.

"Within the next forty-eight hours," David says.

Everyone nods as if this is sensible.

I remember what he said to me in his office. *If we are*

going to win this fight against genetic damage, we will need to make sacrifices. You understand that, don't you? I should have known, then, that he would gladly trade thousands of GD memories—lives—for control of the experiments. That he would trade them without even thinking of alternatives— without feeling like he needed to bother to save them.

They're *damaged*, after all.

CHAPTER
THIRTY-EIGHT

TOBIAS

I PROP UP my shoe on the edge of Tris's bed and tighten the laces. Through the large windows I see afternoon light winking in the side panels of the parked airplanes on the landing strip. GDs in green suits walk across the wings and crawl under the noses, checking the planes before takeoff.

"How's your project with Matthew going?" I say to Cara, who is two beds away. Tris let Cara, Caleb, and Matthew test their new truth serum on her this morning, but I haven't seen her since then.

Cara is pushing a brush through her hair. She glances around the room to make sure it's empty before she answers. "Not well. So far Tris was immune to the new version of the serum we created—it had no effect whatsoever. It's very strange that a person's genes would make them so resistant to mind manipulation of any kind."

"Maybe it's not her genes," I say, shrugging. I switch feet. "Maybe it's some kind of superhuman stubbornness."

"Oh, are we at the insult part of the breakup?" she says. "Because I got in a lot of practice after what happened with Will. I have several choice things to say about her nose."

"We didn't break up." I grin. "But it's nice to know you have such warm feelings for my girlfriend."

"I apologize, I don't know why I jumped to that conclusion." Cara's cheeks flush. "My feelings toward your girlfriend are mixed, yes, but for the most part I have a lot of respect for her."

"I know. I was just kidding. It's nice to see you get flustered every once in a while."

Cara glares at me.

"Besides," I say, "what's wrong with her nose?"

The door to the dormitory opens, and Tris walks in, hair unkempt and eyes wild. It unsettles me to see her so agitated, like the ground I'm standing on is no longer solid. I get up and smooth my hand over her hair to put it back into place. "What happened?" I say, my hand coming to rest on her shoulder.

"Council meeting," Tris says. She covers my hand with hers, briefly, then sits on one of the beds, her hands dangling between her knees.

"I hate to be repetitive," Cara says, "but . . . what happened?"

Tris shakes her head like she's trying to shake the dust out of it. "The council has made plans. Big ones."

She tells us, in fits and starts, about the council's plan to reset the experiments. As she speaks she wedges her hands under her legs and presses forward into them until her wrists turn red.

When she finishes I move to sit beside her, putting my arm across her shoulders. I look out the window, at the planes perched on the runway, gleaming and poised for flight. In less than two days those planes will probably drop the memory serum virus over the experiments.

Cara says to Tris, "What do you intend to do about it?"

"I don't know," Tris says. "I feel like I don't know what's right anymore."

They're similar, Cara and Tris, two women sharpened by loss. The difference is that Cara's pain has made her certain of everything, and Tris has guarded her uncertainty, protected it, despite all she's been through. She still approaches everything with a question instead of an answer. It is something I admire about her—something I should probably admire more.

For a few seconds we stew in silence, and I follow the path of my thoughts as they turn over and over one another.

"They can't do this," I say. "They can't erase everyone. They shouldn't have the power to do that." I pause. "All I can think is that this would be so much easier if we were dealing with a completely different set of people who could actually see *reason*. Then we might be able to find a balance between protecting the experiments and opening themselves up to other possibilities."

"Maybe we should import a new group of scientists," Cara says, sighing. "And discard the old ones."

Tris's face twists, and she touches a hand to her forehead, as if rubbing out some brief and inconvenient pain. "No," she says. "We don't even need to do that."

She looks up at me, her bright eyes holding me still.

"Memory serum," she says. "Alan and Matthew came up with a way to make the serums behave like viruses, so they could spread through an entire population without injecting everyone. That's how they're planning to reset the experiments. But we could reset *them*." She speaks faster as the idea takes shape in her mind, and her excitement is contagious; it bubbles inside me like the idea is mine and not hers. But to me it doesn't feel like she's suggesting a solution to our problem. It feels like she's suggesting that we cause yet another problem. "Reset the Bureau, and reprogram them without the propaganda, without the disdain for GDs. Then they'll never risk the memories of the people in the experiments again. The danger will be gone forever."

Cara raises her eyebrows. "Wouldn't erasing their memories also erase all of their knowledge? Thus rendering them useless?"

"I don't know. I think there's a way to target memories, depending on where the knowledge is stored in the brain, otherwise the first faction members wouldn't have known how to speak or tie their shoes or anything." Tris comes to her feet. "We should ask Matthew. He knows how it works better than I do."

I get up too, putting myself in her path. The streaks of sun caught on the airplane wings blind me so I can't see her face.

"Tris," I say. "Wait. You really want to erase the memories of a whole population against their will? That's the same thing *they're* planning to do to our friends and family."

I shield my eyes from the sun to see her cold look—the expression I saw in my mind even before I looked at her. She looks older to me than she ever has, stern and tough and worn by time. I feel that way, too.

"These people have no regard for human life," she says. "They're about to wipe the memories of all our friends and neighbors. They're responsible for the deaths of a large majority of our old faction." She sidesteps me and marches toward the door. "I think they're lucky I'm not going to kill them."

CHAPTER
THIRTY-NINE

TRIS

Matthew clasps his hands behind his back.

"No, no, the serum doesn't erase all of a person's knowledge," he says. "Do you think we would design a serum that makes people forget how to speak or walk?" He shakes his head. "It targets explicit memories, like your name, where you grew up, your first teacher's name, and leaves implicit memories—like how to speak or tie your shoes or ride a bicycle—untouched."

"Interesting," Cara says. "That actually works?"

Tobias and I exchange a look. There's nothing like a conversation between an Erudite and someone who may as well be an Erudite. Cara and Matthew are standing too close together, and the longer they talk, the more hand gestures they make.

"Inevitably, some important memories will be lost," Matthew says. "But if we have a record of people's scientific discoveries or histories, they can relearn them in the hazy period after their memories are erased. People are very pliable then."

I lean against the wall.

"Wait," I say. "If the Bureau is going to load all of those planes with the memory serum virus to reset the experiments, will there be any serum left to use against the compound?"

"We'll have to get it first," Matthew says. "In less than forty-eight hours."

Cara doesn't appear to hear what I said. "After you erase their memories, won't you have to program them with new memories? How does that work?"

"We just have to reteach them. As I said, people tend to be disoriented for a few days after being reset, which means they'll be easier to control." Matthew sits, and spins in his chair once. "We can just give them a new history class. One that teaches facts rather than propaganda."

"We could use the fringe's slide show to supplement a basic history lesson," I say. "They have photographs of a war caused by GPs."

"Great." Matthew nods. "Big problem, though. The memory serum virus is in the Weapons Lab. The one Nita just tried—and *failed*—to break into."

"Christina and I were supposed to talk to Reggie," Tobias says, "but I think, given this new plan, we should talk to Nita instead."

"I think you're right," I say. "Let's go find out where she went wrong."

+ + +

When I first arrived here, I felt like the compound was huge and unknowable. Now I don't even have to consult the signs to remember how to get to the hospital, and neither does Tobias, who keeps stride with me on the way. It's strange how time can make a place shrink, make its strangeness ordinary.

We don't say anything to each other, though I can feel a conversation brewing between us. Finally I decide to ask.

"What's wrong?" I say. "You hardly said anything during the meeting."

"I just . . ." He shakes his head. "I'm not sure this is the right thing to do. They want to erase our friends' memories, so we decide to erase theirs?"

I turn to him and touch his shoulders lightly. "Tobias, we have forty-eight hours to stop them. If you can think of any other idea, anything else that could save our city, I'm open to it."

"I can't." His dark blue eyes look defeated, sad. "But we're acting out of desperation to save something that's important to us—just like the Bureau is. What's the difference?"

"The difference is what's right," I say firmly. "The people in the city, as a whole, are innocent. The people in the Bureau, who supplied Jeanine with the attack simulation, are not innocent."

His mouth puckers, and I can tell he doesn't completely buy it.

I sigh. "It's not a perfect situation. But when you have to choose between two bad options, you pick the one that saves the people you love and believe in most. You just do. Okay?"

He reaches for my hand, his hand warm and strong. "Okay."

"Tris!" Christina pushes through the swinging doors to the hospital and jogs toward us. Peter is on her heels, his dark hair combed smoothly to the side.

At first I think she's excited, and I feel a swell of hope—what if Uriah is awake?

But the closer she gets, the more obvious it is that she isn't excited. She's frantic. Peter lingers behind her, his arms crossed.

"I just spoke to one of the doctors," she says, breathless. "The doctor says Uriah's not going to wake up.

Something about . . . no brain waves."

A weight settles on my shoulders. I knew, of course, that Uriah might never wake up. But the hope that kept the grief at bay is dwindling, slipping away with each word she speaks.

"They were going to take him off life support right away, but I pleaded with them." She wipes one of her eyes fiercely with the heel of her hand, catching a tear before it falls. "Finally the doctor said he would give me four days. So I can tell his family."

His family. Zeke is still in the city, and so is their Dauntless mother. It never occurred to me before that they don't know what happened to him, and we never bothered to tell them, because we were all so focused on—

"They're going to reset the city in forty-eight hours," I say suddenly, and I grab Tobias's arm. He looks stunned. "If we can't stop them, that means Zeke and his mother will *forget him*."

They'll forget him before they have a chance to say good-bye to him. It will be like he never existed.

"What?" Christina demands, her eyes wide. "My *family* is in there. They can't reset everyone! How could they do that?"

"Pretty easily, actually," Peter says. I had forgotten that he was there.

"What are you even doing here?" I demand.

"I went to see Uriah," he says. "Is there a law against it?"

"You didn't even care about him," I spit. "What right do you have—"

"Tris." Christina shakes her head. "Not now, okay?"

Tobias hesitates, his mouth open like there are words waiting on his tongue.

"We have to go in," he says. "Matthew said we could inoculate people against the memory serum, right? So we'll go in, inoculate Uriah's family just in case, and take them back to the compound to say good-bye to him. We have to do it tomorrow, though, or we'll be too late." He pauses. "And you can inoculate your family too, Christina. I should be the one who tells Zeke and Hana, anyway."

Christina nods. I squeeze her arm, in an attempt at reassurance.

"I'm going too," Peter says. "Unless you want me to tell David what you're planning."

We all pause to look at him. I don't know what Peter wants with a journey into the city, but it can't be good. At the same time, we can't afford for David to find out what we're doing, not now, when there's no time.

"Fine," Tobias says. "But if you cause any trouble, I reserve the right to knock you unconscious and lock you in an abandoned building somewhere."

Peter rolls his eyes.

"How do we get there?" Christina says. "It's not like they just let people borrow cars."

"I bet we could get Amar to take you," I say. "He told me today that he always volunteers for patrols. So he knows all the right people. And I'm sure he would agree to help Uriah and his family."

"I should go ask him now. And someone should probably sit with Uriah . . . make sure that doctor doesn't go back on his word. Christina, not Peter." Tobias rubs the back of his neck, pawing at the Dauntless tattoo like he wants to tear it from his body. "And then I should figure out how to tell Uriah's family that he got killed when I was supposed to be looking out for him."

"Tobias—" I say, but he holds up a hand to stop me.

He starts to move away. "They probably won't let me visit Nita anyway."

Sometimes it's hard to know how to take care of people. As I watch Peter and Tobias walk away—keeping their distance from each other—I think it's possible that Tobias needs someone to run after him, because people have been letting him walk away, letting him withdraw, his entire life. But he's right: He needs to do this for Zeke, and I need to talk to Nita.

"Come on," Christina says. "Visiting hours are almost over. I'm going back to sit with Uriah."

+ + +

Before I go to Nita's room—identifiable by the security guard sitting by the door—I stop by Uriah's room with Christina. She sits in the chair next to him, which is creased with the contours of her legs.

It's been a long time since I've spoken to her like a friend, a long time since we laughed together. I was lost in the fog of the Bureau, in the promise of belonging.

I stand next to her and look at him. He doesn't really look injured anymore—there are some bruises, some cuts, but nothing serious enough to kill him. I tilt my head to see the snake tattoo wrapped around his ear. I know it's him, but he doesn't look much like Uriah without a wide smile on his face and his dark eyes bright, alert.

"He and I weren't really even that close," she says. "Just at the . . . the very end. Because he had lost someone who died, and so had I . . ."

"I know," I say. "You really helped him."

I drag a chair over to sit next to her. She clutches Uriah's hand, which stays limp on the sheets.

"Sometimes I just feel like I've lost all my friends," she says.

"You haven't lost Cara," I say. "Or Tobias. And Christina, you haven't lost me. You'll never lose me."

She turns to me, and somewhere in the haze of grief

we wrap our arms around each other, in the same desperate way we did when she told me she had forgiven me for killing Will. Our friendship has held up under an incredible weight, the weight of me shooting someone she loved, the weight of so many losses. Other bonds would have broken. For some reason, this one hasn't.

We stay clutched together for a long time, until the desperation fades.

"Thanks," she says. "You won't lose me, either."

"I'm pretty sure if I was going to, I would have already." I smile. "Listen, I have some things to catch you up on."

I tell her about our plan to stop the Bureau from resetting the experiments. As I speak, I think of the people she stands to lose—her father and mother, her sister—all those connections, forever altered or discarded, in the name of genetic purity.

"I'm sorry," I say when I finish. "I know you probably want to help us, but . . ."

"Don't be sorry." She stares at Uriah. "I'm still glad I'm going into the city." She nods a few times. "You'll stop them from resetting the experiment. I know you will."

I hope she's right.

+ + +

I only have ten minutes until visiting hours are over when I arrive at Nita's room. The guard looks up from his book and raises his eyebrow at me.

"Can I go in?" I say.

"Not really supposed to let people in there," he says.

"I'm the one who shot her," I say. "Does that count for anything?"

"Well." He shrugs. "As long as you promise not to shoot her again. And get out within ten minutes."

"It's a deal."

He has me take off my jacket to show that I'm not carrying any weapons, and then he lets me into the room. Nita jerks to attention—as much as she can, anyway. Half her body is encased in plaster, and one of her hands is cuffed to the bed, as if she could escape even if she wanted to. Her hair is messy, knotted, but of course, she's still pretty.

"What are you doing here?" she says.

I don't answer—I check the corners of the room for cameras, and there's one across from me, pointed at Nita's hospital bed.

"There aren't microphones," she says. "They don't really do that here."

"Good." I pull up a chair and sit beside her. "I'm here because I need important information from you."

"I already told them everything I felt like telling them." She glares at me. "I've got nothing more to say. Especially not to the person who shot me."

"If I hadn't shot you, I wouldn't be David's favorite person, and I wouldn't know all the things I know." I glance at the door, more from paranoia than an actual concern that someone is listening in. "We've got a new plan. Matthew and I. And Tobias. And it will require getting into the Weapons Lab."

"And you thought I could help you with that?" She shakes her head. "I couldn't get in the first time, remember?"

"I need to know what the security is like. Is David the only person who knows the pass code?"

"Not like . . . the only person ever," she says. "That would be stupid. His superiors know it, but he's the only person in the compound, yes."

"Okay, then what's the backup security measure? The one that is activated if you explode the doors?"

She presses her lips together so they almost disappear, and stares at the half-body cast covering her. "It's the death serum," she says. "In aerosol form, it's practically unstoppable. Even if you wear a clean suit or something, it works its way in eventually. It just takes a little more time that way. That's what the lab reports said."

"So they just automatically *kill* anyone who makes their way into that room without the pass code?" I say.

"It surprises you?"

"I guess not." I balance my elbows on my knees. "And there's no other way in except with David's code."

"Which, as you found out, he is completely unwilling to share," she says.

"There's no chance a GP could resist the death serum?" I say.

"No. Definitely not."

"Most GPs can't resist the truth serum, either," I say. "But I can."

"If you want to go flirt with death, be my guest." She leans back into the pillows. "I'm done with that now."

"One more question," I say. "Say I do want to flirt with death. Where do I get explosives to break through the doors?"

"Like I'm going to tell you that."

"I don't think you get it," I say. "If this plan succeeds, you won't be imprisoned for life anymore. You'll recover and you'll go free. So it's in your best interest to help me."

She stares at me like she is weighing and measuring me. Her wrist tugs against the handcuff, just enough that the metal carves a line into her skin.

"Reggie has the explosives," she says. "He can teach you how to use them, but he's no good in action, so for God's sake, don't bring him along unless you feel like babysitting."

"Noted," I say.

"Tell him it will require twice as much firepower to get through those doors than any others. They're extremely sturdy."

I nod. My watch beeps on the hour, signaling that my time is up. I stand and push my chair back to the corner where I found it.

"Thank you for the help," I say.

"What is the plan?" she says. "If you don't mind telling me."

I pause, hesitating over the words.

"Well," I say eventually. "Let's just say it will erase the phrase 'genetically damaged' from everyone's vocabulary."

The guard opens the door, probably to yell at me for overstaying my welcome, but I'm already making my way out. I look over my shoulder just once before going, and I see that Nita is wearing a small smile.

CHAPTER
FORTY

TOBIAS

AMAR AGREES TO help us get into the city without requiring much persuasion, eager for an adventure, as I knew he would be. We agree to meet that evening for dinner to talk through the plan with Christina, Peter, and George, who will help us get a vehicle.

After I talk to Amar, I walk to the dormitory and lay with a pillow over my head for a long time, cycling through a script of what I will say to Zeke when I see him. *I'm sorry, I was doing what I thought I had to do, and everyone else was looking after Uriah, and I didn't think . . .*

People come into the room and leave it, the heat switches on and pushes through the vents and then turns off again, and all the while I am thinking through that script, concocting excuses and then discarding them, choosing the right tone, the right gestures. Finally I grow frustrated and take the pillow from my face and fling it against the opposite wall. Cara, who is just smoothing a clean shirt down over her hips, jumps back.

"I thought you were asleep," she says.

"Sorry."

She touches her hair, ensuring that each strand is secure. She is so careful in her movements, so precise—it reminds me of the Amity musicians plucking at banjo strings.

"I have a question." I sit up. "It's kind of personal."

"Okay." She sits across from me, on Tris's bed. "Ask it."

"How were you able to forgive Tris, after what she did to your brother?" I say. "Assuming you have, that is."

"Hmm." Cara hugs her arms close to her body. "Sometimes I think I have forgiven her. Sometimes I'm not certain I have. I don't know how—that's like asking how you continue on with your life after someone dies. You just do it, and the next day you do it again."

"Is there . . . any way she could have made it easier for you? Or any way she did?"

"Why are you asking this?" She sets her hand on my knee. "Is it because of Uriah?"

"Yes," I say firmly, and I shift my leg a little so her hand falls away. I don't need to be patted or consoled, like a child. I don't need her raised eyebrows, her soft voice, to coax an emotion from me that I would prefer to contain.

"Okay." She straightens, and when she speaks again, she sounds casual, the way she usually does. "I think the most crucial thing she did—admittedly without meaning to—was confess. There is a difference between admitting and confessing. Admitting involves softening, making excuses for things that cannot be excused; confessing just names the crime at its full severity. That was something I needed."

I nod.

"And after you've confessed to Zeke," she says, "I think it would help if you leave him alone for as long as he wants to be left alone. That's all you can do."

I nod again.

"But, Four," she adds, "you didn't kill Uriah. You didn't set off the bomb that injured him. You didn't make the plan that led to that explosion."

"But I did participate in the plan."

"Oh, shut up, would you?" She says it gently, smiling at me. "It happened. It was awful. You aren't perfect. That's all there is. Don't confuse your grief with guilt."

We stay in the silence and the loneliness of the otherwise empty dormitory for a few more minutes, and I try to let her words work themselves into me.

I eat dinner with Amar, George, Christina, and Peter in the cafeteria, between the beverage counter and a row of trash cans. The bowl of soup before me went cold before I could eat all of it, and there are still crackers swimming in the broth.

Amar tells us where and when to meet, then we go to the hallway near the kitchens so we won't be seen, and he takes out a small black box with syringes inside it. He gives one to Christina, Peter, and me, along with an individually packaged antibacterial wipe, something I suspect only Amar will bother with.

"What's this?" Christina says. "I'm not going to inject it into my body unless I know what it is."

"Fine." Amar folds his hands. "There's a chance that we will still be in the city when a memory serum virus is deployed. You'll need to inoculate yourself against it unless you want to forget everything you now remember. It's the same thing you'll be injecting into your family's arms, so don't worry about it."

Christina turns her arm over and slaps the inside of her elbow until a vein stands at attention. Out of habit, I stick the needle into the side of my neck, the same way I did every time I went through my fear landscape—which was several times a week, at one point. Amar does the same thing.

I notice, however, that Peter only pretends to inject himself—when he presses the plunger down, the fluid runs down his throat, and he wipes it casually with a sleeve.

I wonder what it feels like to volunteer to forget everything.

+ + +

After dinner Christina walks up to me and says, "We need to talk."

We walk down the long flight of stairs that leads to the underground GD space, our knees bouncing in unison with each step, and down the multicolored hallway. At the end, Christina crosses her arms, purple light playing over her nose and mouth.

"Amar doesn't know we're going to try to stop the reset?" she says.

"No," I say. "He's loyal to the Bureau. I don't want to involve him."

"You know, the city is still on the verge of revolution," she says, and the light turns blue. "The Bureau's whole reason for resetting our friends and families is to stop them from killing each other. If we stop the reset, the Allegiant will attack Evelyn, Evelyn will turn the death serum loose, and a lot of people will die. I may still be mad at you, but I don't think you want that many people in the city to die. Your parents in particular."

I sigh. "Honestly? I don't really care about them."

"You can't be serious," she says, scowling. "They're your *parents*."

"I can be, actually," I say. "I want to tell Zeke and his mother what I did to Uriah. Apart from that, I really don't care what happens to Evelyn and Marcus."

"You may not care about your permanently messed-up family, but you should care about everyone else!" she says. She takes my arm in one strong hand and jerks me so that I look at her. "Four, my little sister is in there. If Evelyn and the Allegiant smack into each other, she could get hurt, and I won't be there to protect her."

I saw Christina with her family on Visiting Day, when she was still just a loudmouthed Candor transfer to me. I watched her mother fix the collar of Christina's shirt with a proud smile. If the memory serum virus is deployed, that memory will be erased from her mother's mind. If it's not, her family will be caught in the middle of another citywide battle for control.

I say, "So what are you suggesting we do?"

She releases me. "There has to be a way to prevent a huge blowup that doesn't involve forcibly erasing everyone's memories."

"Maybe," I concede. I hadn't thought about it because it didn't seem necessary. But it is necessary, of course it's necessary. "Did you have an idea for how to stop it?"

"It's basically one of your parents against the other one," Christina says. "Isn't there something you can say to them that will stop them from trying to kill each other?"

"Something I can *say* to them?" I say. "Are you kidding? They don't listen to anyone. They don't do anything that doesn't directly benefit them."

"So there's nothing you can do. You're just going to let the city rip itself to shreds."

I stare at my shoes, bathed in green light, mulling it over. If I had different parents—if I had reasonable parents, less driven by pain and anger and the desire for revenge—it might work. They might be compelled to listen to their son. Unfortunately, I do not have different parents.

But I could. I could if I wanted them. Just a slip of the memory serum in their morning coffee or their evening water, and they would be new people, clean slates, unblemished by history. They would have to be taught that they even had a son to begin with; they would need to learn my name again.

It's the same technique we're using to heal the compound. I could use it to heal them.

I look up at Christina.

"Get me some memory serum," I say. "While you, Amar, and Peter are looking for your family and Uriah's family, I'll take care of it. I probably won't have enough time to get to both of my parents, but one of them will do."

"How will you get away from the rest of us?"

"I need . . . I don't know, we need to add a complication. Something that requires one of us leaving the pack."

"What about flat tires?" Christina says. "We're going at night, right? So I can tell Amar to stop so I can go to the bathroom or something, slash the tires, and then we'll have to split up, so you can find another truck."

I consider this for a moment. I could tell Amar what's really going on, but that would require undoing the dense knot of propaganda and lies the Bureau has tied in his mind. Assuming I could even do it, we don't have time for that.

But we do have time for a well-told lie. Amar knows that my father taught me how to start a car with just the wires when I was younger. He wouldn't question me volunteering to find us another vehicle.

"That will work," I say.

"Good." She tilts her head. "So you're really going to erase one of your parents' memories?"

"What do you do when your parents are evil?" I say.

"Get a new parent. If one of them doesn't have all the baggage they currently have, maybe the two of them can negotiate a peace agreement or something."

She frowns at me for a few seconds like she wants to say something, but eventually, she just nods.

CHAPTER
FORTY-ONE

TRIS

THE SMELL OF bleach tingles in my nose. I stand next to a mop in a storage room in the basement; I stand in the wake of what I just told everyone, which is that whoever breaks into the Weapons Lab will be going on a suicide mission. The death serum is unstoppable.

"The question is," Matthew says, "is this something we're willing to sacrifice a life for."

This is the room where Matthew, Caleb, and Cara were developing the new serum, before the plan changed. Vials and beakers and scribbled-on notebooks are scattered across the lab table in front of Matthew. The string he wears tied around his neck is in his mouth now, and he chews it absentmindedly.

Tobias leans against the door, his arms crossed. I

remember him standing that way during initiation, as he watched us fight each other, so tall and so strong I never dreamed he would give me more than a cursory glance.

"It's not just about revenge," I say. "It's not about what they did to the Abnegation. It's about stopping them before they do something equally bad to the people in all the experiments—about taking away their power to control thousands of lives."

"It is worth it," Cara says. "One death, to save thousands of people from a terrible fate? And cut the compound's power off at the knees, so to speak? Is it even a question?"

I know what she is doing—weighing a single life against so many lifetimes and memories, drawing an obvious conclusion from the scales. That is the way an Erudite mind works, and the way an Abnegation mind works, but I am not sure if they are the minds we need right now. One life against thousands of memories, of course the answer is easy, but does it have to be one of our lives? Do we have to be the ones who act?

But because I know what my answer will be to that question, my thoughts turn to another question. If it has to be one of us, who should it be?

My eyes shift from Matthew and Cara, standing behind the table, to Tobias, to Christina, her arm slung over a broom handle, and land on Caleb.

Him.

A second later I feel sick with myself.

"Oh, just come out with it," Caleb says, lifting his eyes to mine. "You want me to do it. You all do."

"No one said that," Matthew says, spitting out the string necklace.

"Everyone's staring at me," Caleb says. "Don't think I don't know it. I'm the one who chose the wrong side, who worked with Jeanine Matthews; I'm the one none of you care about, so I should be the one to die."

"Why do you think Tobias offered to get you out of the city before they executed you?" My voice comes out cold, quiet. The odor of bleach plays over my nose. "Because I don't care whether you live or die? Because I don't care about you at all?"

He should be the one to die, part of me thinks.

I don't want to lose him, another part argues.

I don't know which part to trust, which part to believe.

"You think I don't know hatred when I see it?" Caleb shakes his head. "I see it every time you look at me. On the rare occasions when you do look at me."

His eyes are glossy with tears. It's the first time since my near execution that I've seen him remorseful instead of defensive or full of excuses. It might also be the first time since then that I've seen him as my brother instead of the coward who sold me out to Jeanine Matthews. Suddenly I have trouble swallowing.

"If I do this . . ." he says.

I shake my head no, but he holds up a hand.

"Stop," he says. "Beatrice, if I do this . . . will you be able to forgive me?"

To me, when someone wrongs you, you both share the burden of that wrongdoing—the pain of it weighs on both of you. Forgiveness, then, means choosing to bear the full weight all by yourself. Caleb's betrayal is something we both carry, and since he did it, all I've wanted is for him to take its weight away from me. I am not sure that I'm capable of shouldering it all myself—not sure that I am strong enough, or good enough.

But I see him steeling himself against this fate, and I know that I *have* to be strong enough, and good enough, if he is going to sacrifice himself for us all.

I nod. "Yes," I choke out. "But that's not a good reason to do this."

"I have plenty of reasons," Caleb says. "I'll do it. Of course I will."

+ + +

I am not sure what just happened.

Matthew and Caleb stay behind to fit Caleb for the clean suit—the suit that will keep him alive in the Weapons Lab long enough to set off the memory serum virus. I wait

410

until the others leave before leaving myself. I want to walk back to the dormitory with only my thoughts as company.

A few weeks ago, I would have volunteered to go on the suicide mission myself—and I did. I volunteered to go to Erudite headquarters, knowing that death waited for me there. But it wasn't because I was selfless, or because I was brave. It was because I was guilty and a part of me wanted to lose everything; a grieving, ailing part of me wanted to die. Is that what's motivating Caleb now? Should I really allow him to die so that he feels like his debt to me is repaid?

I walk the hallway with its rainbow of lights and go up the stairs. I can't even think of an alternative—would I be any more willing to lose Christina, or Cara, or Matthew? No. The truth is that I would be less willing to lose them, because they have been good friends to me and Caleb has not, not for a long time. Even before he betrayed me, he left me for the Erudite and didn't look back. I was the one who went to visit *him* during my initiation, and he spent the whole time wondering why I was there.

And I don't want to die anymore. I am up to the challenge of bearing the guilt and the grief, up to facing the difficulties that life has put in my path. Some days are harder than others, but I am ready to live each one of them. I can't sacrifice myself, this time.

In the most honest parts of me, I am able to admit that it was a relief to hear Caleb volunteer.

Suddenly I can't think about it anymore. I reach the hotel entrance and walk to the dormitory, hoping that I can just collapse into my bed and sleep, but Tobias is waiting in the hallway for me.

"You okay?" he says.

"Yes," I say. "But I shouldn't be." I touch a hand, briefly, to my forehead. "I feel like I've already been mourning him. Like he died the second I saw him in Erudite headquarters while I was there. You know?"

I confessed to Tobias, soon after that, that I had lost my entire family. And he assured me that he was my family now.

That is how it feels. Like everything between us is twisted together, friendship and love and family, so I can't tell the difference between any of them.

"The Abnegation have teachings about this, you know," he says. "About when to let others sacrifice themselves for you, even if it's selfish. They say that if the sacrifice is the ultimate way for that person to show you that they love you, you should let them do it." He leans one shoulder into the wall. "That, in that situation, it's the greatest gift you can give them. Just as it was when both of your parents died for you."

"I'm not sure it's love that's motivating him, though." I close my eyes. "It seems more like guilt."

"Maybe," Tobias admits. "But why would he feel guilty for betraying you if he didn't love you?"

I nod. I know that Caleb loves me, and always has, even when he was hurting me. I know that I love him, too. But this feels wrong anyway.

Still, I am able to be momentarily placated, knowing that this is something my parents might have understood, if they were here right now.

"This may be a bad time," he says, "but there's something I want to say to you."

I tense immediately, afraid that he's going to name some crime of mine that went unacknowledged, or a confession that's eating away at him, or something equally difficult. His expression is unreadable.

"I just want to thank you," he says, his voice low. "A group of scientists told you that my genes were damaged, that there was something wrong with me—they showed you test results that proved it. And even I started to believe it."

He touches my face, his thumb skimming my cheekbone, and his eyes are on mine, intense and insistent.

"You never believed it," he says. "Not for a second. You always insisted that I was . . . I don't know, whole."

I cover his hand with my own. "Well, you are."

"No one has ever told me that before," he says softly.

"It's what you deserve to hear," I say firmly, my eyes going cloudy with tears. "That you're whole, that you're worth loving, that you're the best person I've ever known."

Just as the last word leaves my mouth, he kisses me.

I kiss him back so hard it hurts, and twist my fingers into his shirt. I push him down the hallway and through one of the doors to a sparsely furnished room near the dormitory. I kick the door shut with my heel.

Just as I have insisted on his worth, he has always insisted on my strength, insisted that my capacity is greater than I believe. And I know, without being told, that's what love does, when it's right—it makes you more than you were, more than you thought you could be.

This is right.

His fingers slide over my hair and curl into it. My hands shake, but I don't care if he notices, I don't care if he knows that I'm afraid of how intense this feels. I draw his shirt into my fists, tugging him closer, and sigh his name against his mouth.

I forget that he is another person; instead it feels like he is another part of me, just as essential as a heart or an eye or an arm. I pull his shirt up and over his head. I run my hands over the skin I expose like it is my own.

414

His hands clutch at my shirt and I am removing it and then I remember, I remember that I am small and flat-chested and sickly pale, and I pull back.

He looks at me, not like he's waiting for an explanation, but like I am the only thing in the room worth looking at.

I look at him, too, but everything I see makes me feel worse—he is so handsome, and even the black ink curling over his skin makes him into a piece of art. A moment ago I was convinced that we were perfectly matched, and maybe we still are—but only with our clothes on.

But he is still looking at me that way.

He smiles, a small, shy smile. Then he puts his hands on my waist and draws me toward him. He bends down and kisses between his fingers and whispers "beautiful" against my stomach.

And I believe him.

He stands and presses his lips to mine, his mouth open, his hands on my bare hips, his thumbs slipping under the top of my jeans. I touch his chest, lean into him, feel his sigh singing in my bones.

"I love you, you know," I say.

"I know," he replies.

With a quirk of his eyebrows, he bends and wraps an arm around my legs, throwing me over his shoulder. A laugh bursts from my mouth, half joy and half nerves, and

he carries me across the room, dropping me unceremoni-
ously on the couch.

He lies down next to me, and I run my fingers over the
flames wrapping around his rib cage. He is strong, and
lithe, and certain.

And he is mine.

I fit my mouth to his.

+ + +

I was so afraid that we would just keep colliding over and
over again if we stayed together, and that eventually the
impact would break me. But now I know I am like the
blade and he is like the whetstone—

I am too strong to break so easily, and I become better,
sharper, every time I touch him.

CHAPTER
FORTY-TWO

TOBIAS

THE FIRST THING I see when I wake, still on the couch in the hotel room, are the birds flying over her collarbone. Her shirt, retrieved from the floor in the middle of the night because of the cold, is pulled down on one side from where she's lying on it.

We have slept close to each other before, but this time feels different. Every other time we were there to comfort each other or to protect each other; this time we're here just because we want to be—and because we fell asleep before we could go back to the dormitory.

I stretch out my hand and touch my fingertips to her tattoos, and she opens her eyes.

She wraps an arm around me and pulls herself across

the cushions so she's right up against me, warm and soft and pliable.

"Morning," I say.

"Shh," she says. "If you don't acknowledge it, maybe it will go away."

I draw her toward me, my hand on her hip. Her eyes are wide, alert, despite just having opened. I kiss her cheek, then her jaw, then her throat, lingering there for a few seconds. Her hands tighten around my waist, and she sighs into my ear.

My self-control is about to disappear in five, four, three . . .

"Tobias," she whispers, "I hate to say this, but . . . I think we have just a *few* things to do today."

"They can wait," I say against her shoulder, and I kiss the first tattoo, slowly.

"No, they can't!" she says.

I flop back onto the cushions, and I feel cold without her body parallel to mine. "Yeah. About that—I was thinking your brother could use some target practice. Just in case."

"That might be a good idea," she says quietly. "He's only fired a gun . . . what, once? Twice?"

"I can teach him," I say. "If there's one thing I'm good at, it's aiming. And it might make him feel better to do something."

"Thank you," she says. She sits up and puts her fingers through her hair to comb it. In the morning light its color looks brighter, like it's threaded with gold. "I know you don't like him, but . . ."

"But if you're going to let what he did go," I say, taking her hand, "then I'm going to try to do the same."

She smiles, and kisses my cheek.

+ + +

I skim the lingering shower water from the back of my neck with my palm. Tris, Caleb, Christina, and I are in the training room in the GD area underground—it's cold and dim and full of equipment, training weapons and mats and helmets and targets, everything we could ever need. I select the right practice gun, the one about the size of a pistol, but bulkier, and offer it to Caleb.

Tris's fingers slide between mine. Everything comes easily this morning, every smile and every laugh, every word and every motion.

If we succeed in what we attempt tonight, tomorrow Chicago will be safe, the Bureau will be forever changed, and Tris and I will be able to build a new life for ourselves somewhere. Maybe it will even be a place where I trade my guns and knives for more productive tools, screwdrivers and nails and shovels. This morning I feel like I could be so fortunate. I could.

"It doesn't shoot real bullets," I say, "but it seems like they designed it so it would be as close as possible to one of the guns you'll be using. It feels real, anyway."

Caleb holds the gun with just his fingertips, like he's afraid it will shatter in his hands.

I laugh. "First lesson: Don't be afraid of it. Grab it. You've held one before, remember? You got us out of the Amity compound with that shot."

"That was just lucky," Caleb says, turning the gun over and over to see it from every angle. His tongue pushes into his cheek like he's solving a problem. "Not the result of skill."

"Lucky is better than unlucky," I say. "We can work on skill now."

I glance at Tris. She grins at me, then leans in to whisper something to Christina.

"Are you here to help or what, Stiff?" I say. I hear myself speaking in the voice I cultivated as an initiation instructor, but this time I use it in jest. "You could use some practice with that right arm, if I recall correctly. You too, Christina."

Tris makes a face at me, then she and Christina cross the room to get their own weapons.

"Okay, now face the target and turn the safety off," I say. There is a target across the room, more sophisticated than the wooden-board target in the Dauntless training rooms. It has three rings in three different colors, green, yellow, and red, so it's easier to tell where the bullets hit. "Let me see how you would naturally shoot."

He lifts up the gun with one hand, squares off his feet and shoulders to the target like he's about to lift something heavy, and fires. The gun jerks back and up, firing the bullet near the ceiling. I cover my mouth with my hand to disguise my smile.

"There's no need to *giggle*," Caleb says irritably.

"Book learning doesn't teach you everything, does it?" Christina says. "You have to hold it with *both* hands. It doesn't look as cool, but neither does attacking the ceiling."

"I wasn't trying to look cool!"

Christina stands, her legs slightly uneven, and lifts both arms. She stares at the target for a moment, then fires. The training bullet hits the outer circle of the target and bounces off, rolling on the floor. It leaves a circle of light on the target, marking the impact site. I wish I'd had this technology during initiation training.

"Oh, good," I say. "You hit the air around your target's body. How useful."

"I'm a little rusty," Christina admits, grinning.

"I think the easiest way for you to learn would be to

mimic me," I say to Caleb. I stand the way I always stand, easy, natural, and lift both my arms, squeezing the gun with one hand and steadying it with the other.

Caleb tries to match me, beginning with his feet and moving up with the rest of him. As eager as Christina was to tease him, it's his ability to analyze that makes him successful—I can see him changing angles and distances and tension and release as he looks me over, trying to get everything right.

"Good," I say when he's finished. "Now focus on what you're trying to hit, and nothing else."

I stare at the center of the target and try to let it swallow me. The distance doesn't trouble me—the bullet will travel straight, just like it would if I was closer. I inhale and brace myself, exhale and fire, and the bullet goes right where I meant to put it: in the red circle, in the center of the target.

I step back to watch Caleb try it. He has the right way of standing, the right way of holding the gun, but he is rigid there, a statue with a gun in hand. He sucks in a breath and holds it as he fires. This time the kickback doesn't startle him as much, and the bullet nicks the top of the target.

"Good," I say again. "I think what you mostly need is to get comfortable with it. You're very tense."

"Can you blame me?" he says. His voice trembles, but just at the end of each word. He has the look of someone who is trapping terror inside. I watched two classes of initiates with that expression, but none of them was ever facing what Caleb is facing now.

I shake my head and say quietly, "Of course not. But you have to realize that if you can't let that tension go tonight, you might not make it to the Weapons Lab, and what good would that do anyone?"

He sighs.

"The physical technique is important," I say. "But it's mostly a mental game, which is lucky for you, because you know how to play those. You don't just practice the shooting, you also practice the focus. And then, when you're in a situation where you're fighting for your life, the focus will be so ingrained that it will happen naturally."

"I didn't know the Dauntless were so interested in training the brain," Caleb says. "Can I see you try it, Tris? I don't think I've ever really seen you shoot something without a bullet wound in your shoulder."

Tris smiles a little and faces the target. When I first saw her shoot during Dauntless training, she looked awkward, birdlike. But her thin, fragile form has become slim but muscular, and when she holds the gun, it looks easy. She squints one eye a little, shifts her weight, and fires. Her bullet strays from the target's center, but only by inches. Obviously impressed, Caleb raises his eyebrows.

"Don't look so surprised!" Tris says.

"Sorry," he says. "I just . . . you used to be so clumsy, remember? I don't know how I missed that you weren't like that anymore."

Tris shrugs, but when she looks away, her cheeks are flushed and she looks pleased. Christina shoots again, and this time hits the target closer to the middle.

I step back to let Caleb practice, and watch Tris fire again, watch the straight lines of her body as she lifts the gun, and how steady she is when it goes off. I touch her shoulder and lean in close to her ear. "Remember during training, how the gun almost hit you in the face?"

She nods, smirking.

"Remember during training, when I did *this*?" I say, and I reach around her to press my hand to her stomach. She sucks in a breath.

"I'm not likely to forget that anytime soon," she mutters.

She twists around and draws my face toward hers, her fingertips on my chin. We kiss, and I hear Christina say something about it, but for the first time, I don't care at all.

+++

There isn't much to do after target practice but wait. Tris and Christina get the explosives from Reggie and teach Caleb how to use them. Then Matthew and Cara pore over a map, examining different routes to get through the compound to the Weapons Lab. Christina and I meet with Amar, George, and Peter to go over the route we're going to take through the city that evening. Tris is called to a last-minute council meeting. Matthew inoculates people against the memory serum all throughout the day, Cara and Caleb and Tris and Nita and Reggie and himself.

There isn't enough time to think about the significance of what we're going to try to do: stop a revolution, save the experiments, change the Bureau forever.

While Tris is gone, I go to the hospital to see Uriah one last time before I bring his family back to him.

When I get there, I can't go in. From here, through the glass, I can pretend that he is just asleep, and that if I touched him, he would wake up and smile and make a joke. In there, I would be able to see how lifeless he is now, how the shock to his brain took the last parts of him that were Uriah.

I squeeze my hands into fists to disguise their shaking.

Matthew approaches from the end of the hallway, his hands in the pockets of his dark blue uniform. His gait is relaxed, his footsteps heavy. "Hey."

"Hi," I say.

"I was just inoculating Nita," he says. "She's in better spirits today."

"Good."

Matthew taps the glass with his knuckles. "So . . . you're going to go get his family later? That's what Tris told me."

I nod. "His brother and his mom."

I've met Zeke and Uriah's mother before. She is a small woman with power in her bearing, and one of the rare Dauntless who goes about things quietly and without ceremony. I liked her and I was afraid of her at the same time.

"No dad?" Matthew says.

"Died when they were young. Not surprising, among the Dauntless."

"Right."

We stand in silence for a little while, and I'm grateful for his presence, which keeps me from being overwhelmed by grief. I know that Cara was right yesterday to tell me that I didn't kill Uriah, not really, but it still *feels* like I did, and maybe it always will.

"I've been meaning to ask you," I say after a while. "Why are you helping us with this? It seems like a big risk for someone who isn't personally invested in the outcome."

"I am, though," Matthew says. "It's sort of a long story."

He crosses his arms, then tugs at the string around

his throat with his thumb.

"There was this girl," he says. "She was genetically damaged, and that meant I wasn't supposed to go out with her, right? We're supposed to make sure that we match ourselves with 'optimal' partners, so we produce genetically superior offspring, or something. Well I was feeling rebellious, and there was something appealing about how forbidden it was, so she and I started dating. I never meant for it to become anything serious, but . . ."

"But it did," I supply.

He nods. "It did. She, more than anything else, convinced me that the compound's position on genetic damage was twisted. She was a better person than I was, than I'll ever be. And then she got attacked. A bunch of GPs beat her up. She had kind of a smart mouth, she was never content to just stay where she was—I think that had something to do with it, or maybe nothing did, maybe people just do things like that out of nowhere, and trying to find a reason just frustrates the mind."

I look closely at the string he's toying with. I always thought it was black, but when I look closely, I see that it's actually green—the color of the support staff uniforms.

"Anyway, she was injured pretty badly, but one of the GPs was a council member's kid. He claimed the attack was provoked, and that was the excuse they used when they let him and the other GPs off with some community service, but I knew better." He starts nodding along with his own words. "I knew that they let them off because they thought of her as something less than them. Like if the GPs had beat up an animal."

A shiver starts at the top of my spine and travels down my back. "What . . ."

"What happened to her?" Matthew glances at me. "She died a year later during a surgical procedure to fix some of the damage. It was a fluke—an infection." He drops his hands. "The day she died was the day I started helping Nita. I didn't think her recent plan was a good one, though, which is why I didn't help out with it. But then, I also didn't try that hard to stop her."

I cycle through the things you're supposed to say at times like these, the apologies and the sympathy, and I don't find a single phrase that feels right to me. Instead I just let the silence stretch out between us. It's the only adequate response to what he just told me, the only thing that does the tragedy justice instead of patching it up hastily and moving on.

"I know it doesn't seem like it," Matthew says, "but I hate them."

The muscles in his jaw stand at attention. He has never struck me as a warm person, but he's never been cold, either. That is what he's like now, a man encased in ice, his eyes hard and his voice like a frosty exhale.

"And I would have volunteered to die instead of Caleb . . . if not for the fact that I really want to see them suffer the repercussions. I want to watch them fumble around under the memory serum, not knowing who they are anymore, because that's what happened to me when she died."

"That sounds like an adequate punishment," I say.

"More adequate than killing them would be," Matthew says. "And besides, I'm not a murderer."

I feel uneasy. It's not often you encounter the real person behind a good-natured mask, the darkest parts of someone. It's not comfortable when you do.

"I'm sorry for what happened to Uriah," Matthew says. "I'll leave you with him."

He puts his hands back in his pockets and continues down the hallway, his lips puckered in a whistle.

CHAPTER
FORTY-THREE

TRIS

THE EMERGENCY COUNCIL meeting is more of the same: confirmation that the viruses will be dropped over the cities this evening, discussions about what planes will be used and at what times. David and I exchange friendly words when the meeting is over, and then I slip out while the others are still sipping coffee and walk back to the hotel.

Tobias takes me to the atrium near the hotel dormitory, and we spend some time there, talking and kissing and pointing out the strangest plants. It feels like something that normal people do—go on dates, talk about small things, laugh. We have had so few of those moments. Most of our time together has been spent running from one threat or another, or running toward one threat or

430

another. But I can see a time on the horizon when that won't need to happen anymore. We will reset the people in the compound, and work to rebuild this place together. Maybe then we can find out if we do as well with the quiet moments as we have with the loud ones.

I am looking forward to it.

Finally the time comes for Tobias to leave. I stand on the higher step in the atrium and he stands on the lower one, so we're on the same plane.

"I don't like that I can't be with you tonight," he says. "It doesn't feel right to leave you alone with something this huge."

"What, you don't think I can handle it?" I say, a little defensive.

"Obviously that is not what I think." He touches his hands to my face and leans his forehead against mine. "I just don't want you to have to bear it alone."

"I don't want you to have to bear Uriah's family alone," I say softly. "But I think these are things we have to do separately. I'm glad I'll get to be with Caleb before . . . you know. It'll be nice not having to worry about you at the same time."

"Yeah." He closes his eyes. "I can't wait until tomorrow, when I'm back and you've done what you set out to do and we can decide what comes next."

"I can tell you it will involve a lot of this," I say, and I press my lips to his.

His hands shift from my cheeks to my shoulders and then slide painstakingly down my back. His fingers find the hem of my shirt, then slip under it, warm and insistent.

I feel aware of everything at once, of the pressure of his mouth and the taste of our kiss and the texture of his skin and the orange light glowing against my closed eyelids and the smell of green things, growing things, in the air. When I pull away, and he opens his eyes, I see everything about them, the dart of light blue in his left eye, the dark blue that makes me feel like I am safe inside it, like I am dreaming.

"I love you," I say.

"I love you, too," he says. "I'll see you soon."

He kisses me again, softly, and then leaves the atrium. I stand in that shaft of sunlight until the sun disappears.

It's time to be with my brother now.

CHAPTER
FORTY-FOUR

TOBIAS

I CHECK THE screens before I go to meet Amar and George. Evelyn is holed up in Erudite headquarters with her factionless supporters, leaning over a map of the city. Marcus and Johanna are in a building on Michigan Avenue, north of the Hancock building, conducting a meeting.

I hope that's where they both are in a few hours when I decide which of my parents to reset. Amar gave us a little over an hour to find and inoculate Uriah's family and get back to the compound unnoticed, so I only have time for one of them.

+ + +

Snow swirls over the pavement outside, floating on the wind. George offers me a gun.

"It's dangerous in there right now," he says. "With all that Allegiant stuff going on."

I take the gun without even looking at it.

"You are all familiar with the plan?" George says. "I'm going to be monitoring you from here, from the small control room. We'll see how useful I am tonight, though, with all this snow obscuring the cameras."

"And where will the other security people be?"

"Drinking?" George shrugs. "I told them to take the night off. No one will notice the truck is gone. It'll be fine, I promise."

Amar grins. "All right, let's pile in."

George squeezes Amar's arm and waves at the rest of us. As the others follow Amar to the parked truck outside, I grab George and hold him back. He gives me a strange look.

"Don't ask me any questions about this, because I won't answer them," I say. "But inoculate yourself against the memory serum, okay? As soon as possible. Matthew can help you."

He frowns at me.

"Just do it," I say, and I go out to the truck.

Snowflakes cling to my hair, and vapor curls around my mouth with each breath. Christina bumps into me on our way to the truck and slips something into my pocket. A vial.

I see Peter's eyes on us as I get in the passenger's seat. I'm still not sure why he was so eager to come with us, but I know I need to be wary of him.

The inside of the truck is warm, and soon we are all covered with beads of water instead of snow.

"Lucky you," Amar says. He hands me a glass screen with bright lines tangled across it like veins. I look closer and see that they are streets, and the brightest line traces our path through them. "You get to man the map."

"You need a map?" I raise my eyebrows. "Has it not occurred to you to just . . . aim for the giant buildings?"

Amar makes a face at me. "We aren't just driving straight into the city, we're taking a stealth route. Now shut up and man the map."

I find a blue dot on the map that marks our position. Amar urges the truck into the snow, which falls so fast I can only see a few feet in front of us.

The buildings we drive past look like dark figures peeking through a white shroud. Amar drives fast, trusting the weight of the truck to keep us steady. Between snowflakes, I see the city lights up ahead. I had forgotten how close we were to it, because everything is so different just outside its limits.

"I can't believe we're going back," Peter says quietly, like he doesn't expect a response.

"Me either," I say, because it's true.

The distance the Bureau has kept from the rest of the world is an evil separate from the war they intend to wage against our memories—more subtle, but, in its way, just as sinister. They had the capacity to help us, languishing in our factions, but instead they let us fall apart. Let us die. Let us kill one another. Only now that we are about to destroy more than an acceptable level of genetic material are they deciding to intervene.

We bounce back and forth in the truck as Amar drives over the railroad tracks, staying close to the high cement wall on our right.

I look at Christina in the rearview mirror. Her right knee bounces fast.

+ + +

I still don't know whose memory I'm going to take: Marcus's, or Evelyn's?

Usually I would try to decide what the most selfless choice would be, but in this case either choice feels selfish. Resetting Marcus would mean erasing the man I hate and fear from the world. It would mean my freedom from his influence.

Resetting Evelyn would mean making her into a new mother—one who wouldn't abandon me, or make decisions out of a desire for revenge, or control everyone in an effort not to have to trust them.

Either way, with either parent gone, I am better off. But what would help the city most?

I no longer know.

+ + +

I hold my hands over the air vents to warm them as Amar continues to drive, over the railroad tracks and past the abandoned train car we saw on our way in, reflecting the headlights in its silver panels. We reach the place where the outside world ends and the experiment begins, as abrupt a shift as if someone had drawn a line in the ground.

Amar drives over that line like it isn't there. For him, I suppose, it has faded with time, as he grows more and more used to his new world. For me, it feels like driving from truth into a lie, from adulthood into childhood. I watch the land of pavement and glass and metal turn into an empty field. The snow is falling softly now, and I can faintly see the city's skyline up ahead, the buildings just a shade darker than the clouds.

"Where should we go to find Zeke?" Amar says.

"Zeke and his mother joined up with the revolt," I say. "So wherever most of them are is my best bet."

"Control room people said most of them have taken up

residence north of the river, near the Hancock building," Amar says. "Feel like going zip lining?"

"Absolutely not," I say.

Amar laughs.

It takes us another hour to get close. Only when I see the Hancock building in the distance do I start to feel nervous.

"Um . . . Amar?" Christina says from the back. "I hate to say this, but I really need to stop. And . . . you know. Pee."

"Right now?" Amar says.

"Yeah. It came on all of a sudden."

He sighs, but pulls the truck over to the side of the road.

"You guys stay here, and don't look!" Christina says as she gets out.

I watch her silhouette move to the back of the truck, and wait. All I feel when she slashes the tires is a slight bounce in the truck, so small I'm sure I only felt it because I was waiting for it. When Christina gets back in, brushing snowflakes from her jacket, she wears a small smile.

Sometimes, all it takes to save people from a terrible fate is one person willing to do something about it. Even if that "something" is a fake bathroom break.

Amar drives for a few more minutes before anything happens. Then the truck shudders and starts to bounce like we're going over bumps.

"Shit," Amar says, scowling at the speedometer. "I can't believe this."

"Flat?" I say.

"Yeah." He sighs, and eases on the brakes so the car slips to a stop by the side of the road.

"I'll check it," I say. I jump down from the passenger's seat and walk to the back of the truck. The back tires are completely flat, flayed by the knife Christina brought with her. I peer through the back windows to make sure there's only one spare tire, then return to my open door to give the news.

"Both back tires are flat and we only have one spare," I say. "We're going to have to abandon the truck and get a new one."

"Shit!" Amar smacks the steering wheel. "We don't have time for this. We have to make sure Zeke and his mother and Christina's family are all inoculated before the memory serum is released, or they'll be useless."

"Calm down," I say. "I know where we can find another vehicle. Why don't you guys keep going on foot and I'll go find something to drive?"

Amar's expression brightens. "Good idea."

Before moving away from the truck I make sure that there are bullets in my gun, even though I'm not sure if I'll need them. Everyone piles out of the truck, Amar shivering in the cold and bouncing on his toes.

I check my watch. "So you need to inoculate them by what time?"

"George's schedule says we've got an hour before we reset the city," Amar says, checking his watch too, to make sure. "If you want us to spare Zeke and his mother the grief and let them get reset, I wouldn't blame you. I'll do it if you need me to."

I shake my head. "Couldn't do that. They wouldn't be in pain, but it wouldn't be real."

"As I've always said," Amar says, smiling, "once a Stiff, always a Stiff."

"Can you . . . not tell them what happened? Just until I get there," I say. "Just inoculate them? I want to be the one who tells them."

Amar's smile shrinks a little. "Sure. Of course."

My shoes are already soaked through from checking the tires, and my feet ache when they touch the cold ground again. I'm about to walk away from the truck when Peter speaks up.

"I'm coming with you," he says.

"What? Why?" I glare at him.

"You might need help finding a truck," he says. "It's a big city."

I look at Amar, who shrugs. "Man's got a point."

Peter leans in closer and speaks quietly, so only I can

hear. "And if you don't want me to tell him you're planning something, you won't object."

His eyes drift to my jacket pocket, where the memory serum is.

I sigh. "Fine. But you do what I say."

I watch Amar and Christina walk away without us, heading toward the Hancock building. Once they're too far away to see us, I take a few steps back, slipping my hand into my pocket to protect the vial.

"I'm not going to look for a truck," I say. "You might as well know that now. Are you going to help me with what I'm doing, or do I have to shoot you?"

"Depends what you're doing."

It's hard to come up with an answer when I'm not even sure. I stand facing the Hancock building. To my right are the factionless, Evelyn, and her collection of death serum. To my left are the Allegiant, Marcus, and the insurrection plan.

Where do I have the greatest influence? Where can I make the biggest difference? Those are the questions I should be asking myself. Instead I am asking myself whose destruction I am more desperate for.

"I'm going to stop a revolution," I say.

I turn right, and Peter follows me.

CHAPTER
FORTY-FIVE

MY BROTHER STANDS behind the microscope, his eye pressed to the eyepiece. The light in the microscope platform casts strange shadows on his face, making him look years older.

"This is definitely it," he says. "The attack simulation serum, I mean. No question."

"It's always good to have another person verify," Matthew says.

I am standing with my brother in the hours before he dies. And he is analyzing serums. It's so stupid.

I know why Caleb wanted to come here: to make sure that he was giving his life for a good reason. I don't blame him. There are no second chances after you've died for something, at least as far as I know.

"Tell me the activation code again," Matthew says. The activation code will enable the memory serum weapon, and another button will deploy it instantly. Matthew has made Caleb repeat them both every few minutes since we got here.

"I have no trouble memorizing sequences of numbers!" Caleb says.

"I don't doubt that. But we don't know what state of mind you'll be in when the death serum begins to take its course, and these codes need to be deeply ingrained."

Caleb flinches at the words "death serum." I stare at my shoes.

"080712," Caleb says. "And then I press the green button."

Right now Cara is spending some time with the people in the control room so she can spike their beverages with peace serum and shut off the lights in the compound while they're too drunk to notice, just like Nita and Tobias did a few weeks ago. When she does that, we'll run for the Weapons Lab, unseen by the cameras in the dark.

Sitting across from me on the lab table are the explosives Reggie gave us. They look so ordinary—inside a black box with metal claws on the edges and a remote detonator. The claws will attach the box to the second set of laboratory doors. The first set still hasn't been repaired since the attack.

"I think that's it," Matthew says. "Now all we have to do is wait for a little while."

"Matthew," I say. "Do you think you could leave us alone for a bit?"

"Of course." Matthew smiles. "I'll come back when it's time."

He closes the door behind him. Caleb runs his hands over the clean suit, the explosives, the backpack they go in. He puts them all in a straight line, fixing this corner and that one.

"I keep thinking about when we were young and we played 'Candor,'" he says. "How I used to sit you down in a chair in the living room and ask you questions? Remember?"

"Yes," I say. I lean my hips into the lab table. "You used to find the pulse in my wrist and tell me that if I lied, you would be able to tell, because the Candor can always tell when other people are lying. It wasn't very nice."

Caleb laughs. "That one time, you confessed to stealing a book from the school library just as Mom came home—"

"And I had to go to the librarian and apologize!" I laugh too. "That librarian was awful. She always called everyone 'young lady' or 'young man.'"

"Oh, she loved me, though. Did you know that when I was a library volunteer and was supposed to be shelving books during my lunch hour, I was really just standing in the aisles and reading? She caught me a few times and never said anything about it."

"Really?" I feel a twinge in my chest. "I didn't know that."

"There was a lot we didn't know about each other, I guess." He taps his fingers on the table. "I wish we had been able to be more honest with each other."

"Me too."

"And it's too late now, isn't it." He looks up.

"Not for everything." I pull out a chair from the lab table and sit in it. "Let's play Candor. I'll answer a question and then you have to answer a question. Honestly, obviously."

He looks a little exasperated, but he plays along. "Okay. What did you really do to break those glasses in the kitchen when you claimed that you were taking them out to clean water spots off them?"

I roll my eyes. "That's the one question you want an honest answer to? Come on, Caleb."

"Okay, fine." He clears his throat, and his green eyes fix on mine, serious. "Have you really forgiven me, or are you just saying that you have because I'm about to die?"

I stare at my hands, which rest in my lap. I have been able to be kind and pleasant to him because every time I think of what happened in Erudite headquarters, I immediately push the thought aside. But that can't be forgiveness—if I had forgiven him, I would be able to think of what happened without that hatred I can feel in my gut, right?

Or maybe forgiveness is just the continual pushing aside of bitter memories, until time dulls the hurt and the anger, and the wrong is forgotten.

For Caleb's sake, I choose to believe the latter.

"Yes, I have," I say. I pause. "Or at least, I desperately want to, and I think that might be the same thing."

He looks relieved. I step aside so he can take my place in the chair. I know what I want to ask him, and have since he volunteered to make this sacrifice.

"What is the biggest reason that you're doing this?" I say. "The most important one?"

"Don't ask me that, Beatrice."

"It's not a trap," I say. "It won't make me un-forgive you. I just need to know."

Between us are the clean suit, the explosives, and the backpack, arranged in a line on the brushed steel. They are the instruments of his going and not coming back.

"I guess I feel like it's the only way I can escape the guilt

446

for all the things I've done," he says. "I've never wanted anything more than I want to be rid of it."

His words ache inside me. I was afraid he would say that. I knew he would say that all along. I wish he hadn't said it.

A voice speaks through the intercom in the corner. "Attention all compound residents. Commence emergency lockdown procedure, effective until five o'clock a.m. I repeat, commence emergency lockdown procedure, effective until five o'clock a.m."

Caleb and I exchange an alarmed look. Matthew shoves the door open.

"Shit," he says. And then, louder: "Shit!"

"Emergency lockdown?" I say. "Is that the same as an attack drill?"

"Basically. It means we have to go *now*, while there's still chaos in the hallways and before they increase security," Matthew says.

"Why would they do this?" Caleb says.

"Could be they just want to increase security before releasing the viruses," Matthew says. "Or it could be that they figured out we're going to try something—only, if they knew that, they probably would have come to arrest us."

I look at Caleb. The minutes I had left with him fall away like dead leaves pulled from branches.

I cross the room and retrieve our guns from the counter, but itching at the back of my mind is what Tobias said yesterday—that the Abnegation say you should only let someone sacrifice himself for you if it's the ultimate way for them to show they love you.

And for Caleb, that's not what this is.

CHAPTER FORTY-SIX

TOBIAS

MY FEET SLIP on the snowy pavement.

"You didn't inoculate yourself yesterday," I say to Peter.

"No, I didn't," Peter says.

"Why not?"

"Why should I tell you?"

I run my thumb over the vial and say, "You came with me because you know I have the memory serum, right? If you want me to give it to you, it couldn't hurt to give me a reason."

He looks at my pocket again, like he did earlier. He must have seen Christina give it to me. He says, "I'd rather just *take* it from you."

"Please." I lift my eyes up, to watch the snow spilling over the edges of the buildings. It's dark, but the moon provides just enough light to see by. "You might think you're pretty good at fighting, but you aren't good enough to beat me, I promise you."

Without warning he shoves me, hard, and I slip on the snowy ground and fall. My gun clatters to the ground, half buried in the snow. *That'll teach me to get cocky,* I think, and I scramble to my feet. He grabs my collar and yanks me forward so I slide again, only this time I keep my balance and elbow him in the stomach. He kicks me hard in the leg, making it go numb, and grabs the front of my jacket to pull me toward him.

His hand fumbles for my pocket, where the serum is. I try to push him away, but his footing is too sure and my leg is still too numb. With a groan of frustration, I bring my free arm back by my face and slam my elbow into his mouth. Pain spreads through my arm—it hurts to hit someone in the teeth—but it was worth it. He yells, sliding back onto the street, his face clutched in both hands.

"You know why you won fights as an initiate?" I say as I get to my feet. "Because you're cruel. Because you like to hurt people. And you think you're special, you think everyone around you is a bunch of sissies who can't make the tough choices like you can."

He starts to get up, and I kick him in the side so he goes sprawling again. Then I press my foot to his chest, right under his throat, and our eyes meet, his wide and innocent and nothing like what's inside him.

"You are not special," I say. "I like to hurt people too. I can make the cruelest choice. The difference is, sometimes I don't, and you always do, and that makes you evil."

I step over him and start down Michigan Avenue again. But before I take more than a few steps, I hear his voice.

"That's why I want it," he says, his voice shaking.

I stop. I don't turn around. I don't want to see his face right now.

"I want the serum because I'm sick of being this way," he says. "I'm sick of doing bad things and liking it and then wondering what's wrong with me. I want it to be over. I want to start again."

"And you don't think that's the coward's way out?" I say over my shoulder.

"I think I don't care if it is or not," Peter says.

I feel the anger that was swelling within me deflate as I turn the vial over in my fingers, inside my pocket. I hear him get to his feet and brush the snow from his clothes.

"Don't try to mess with me again," I say, "and I promise I'll let you reset yourself, when all this is said and done. I have no reason not to."

He nods, and we continue through the unmarked snow to the building where I last saw my mother.

CHAPTER FORTY-SEVEN

TRIS

THERE IS A nervous kind of quiet in the hallway, though there are people everywhere. One woman bumps me with her shoulder and then mutters an apology, and I move closer to Caleb so I don't lose sight of him. Sometimes all I want is to be a few inches taller so the world does not look like a dense collection of torsos.

We move quickly, but not too quickly. The more security guards I see, the more pressure I feel building inside me. Caleb's backpack, with the clean suit and explosives inside it, bounces against his lower back as we walk. People are moving in all different directions, but soon, we will reach a hallway that no one has any reason to walk down.

"I think something must have happened to Cara," Matthew says. "The lights were supposed to be off by now."

I nod. I feel the gun digging into my back, disguised by my baggy shirt. I had hoped that I wouldn't have to use it, but it seems that I will, and even then it might not be enough to get us to the Weapons Lab.

I touch Caleb's arm, and Matthew's, stopping all three of us in the middle of the hallway.

"I have an idea," I say. "We split up. Caleb and I will run to the lab, and Matthew, cause some kind of diversion."

"A diversion?"

"You have a gun, don't you?" I say. "Fire into the air."

He hesitates.

"Do it," I say through gritted teeth.

Matthew takes his gun out. I grab Caleb's elbow and steer him down the hallway. Over my shoulder I watch Matthew lift the gun over his head and fire straight up, at one of the glass panels above him. At the sharp bang, I burst into a run, dragging Caleb with me. Screams and shattering glass fill the air, and security guards run past us without noticing that we are running away from the dormitories, running toward a place we should not be.

It's a strange thing to feel my instincts and Dauntless training kick in. My breathing becomes deeper, more even, as we follow the route we determined this morning.

My mind feels sharper, clearer. I look at Caleb, expecting to see the same thing happening to him, but all the blood seems to have drained from his face, and he is gasping. I keep my hand firm on his elbow to steady him.

We round a corner, shoes squeaking on the tile, and an empty hallway with a mirrored ceiling stretches out in front of us. I feel a surge of triumph. I know this place. We aren't far now. We're going to make it.

"Stop!" a voice shouts from behind me.

The security guards. They found us.

"Stop or we'll shoot!"

Caleb shudders and lifts his hands. I lift mine, too, and look at him.

I feel everything slowing down inside me, my racing thoughts and the pounding of my heart.

When I look at him, I don't see the cowardly young man who sold me out to Jeanine Matthews, and I don't hear the excuses he gave afterward.

When I look at him, I see the boy who held my hand in the hospital when our mother broke her wrist and told me it would be all right. I see the brother who told me to make my own choices, the night before the Choosing Ceremony. I think of all the remarkable things he is—smart and enthusiastic and observant, quiet and earnest and kind.

He is a part of me, always will be, and I am a part of him, too. I don't belong to Abnegation, or Dauntless, or even the Divergent. I don't belong to the Bureau or the experiment or the fringe. I belong to the people I love, and they belong to me—they, and the love and loyalty I give them, form my identity far more than any word or group ever could.

I love my brother. I love him, and he is quaking with terror at the thought of death. I love him and all I can think, all I can hear in my mind, are the words I said to him a few days ago: *I would never deliver you to your own execution.*

"Caleb," I say. "Give me the backpack."

"What?" he says.

I slip my hand under the back of my shirt and grab my gun. I point it at him. "Give me the backpack."

"Tris, no." He shakes his head. "No, I won't let you do that."

"Put down your weapon!" the guard screams at the end of the hallway. "Put down your weapon or we will fire!"

"I might survive the death serum," I say. "I'm good at fighting off serums. There's a chance I'll survive. There's no chance you would survive. Give me the backpack or I'll shoot you in the leg and take it from you."

Then I raise my voice so the guards can hear me. "He's my hostage! Come any closer and I'll kill him!"

In that moment he reminds me of our father. His eyes are tired and sad. There's a shadow of a beard on his chin. His hands shake as he pulls the backpack to the front of his body and offers it to me.

I take it and swing it over my shoulder. I keep my gun pointed at him and shift so he's blocking my view of the soldiers at the end of the hallway.

"Caleb," I say, "I love you."

His eyes gleam with tears as he says, "I love you, too, Beatrice."

"Get down on the floor!" I yell, for the benefit of the guards.

Caleb sinks to his knees.

"If I don't survive," I say, "tell Tobias I didn't want to leave him."

I back up, aiming over Caleb's shoulder at one of the security guards. I inhale and steady my hand. I exhale and fire. I hear a pained yell, and sprint in the other direction with the sound of gunfire in my ears. I run a crooked path so it's harder to hit me, and then dive around the corner. A bullet hits the wall right behind me, putting a hole in it.

As I run, I swing the backpack around my body and open the zipper. I take out the explosives and the detonator. There are shouts and running footsteps behind me. I don't have any time. I don't have any time.

I run harder, faster than I thought I could. The impact of each footstep shudders through me and I turn the next corner, where there are two guards standing by the doors Nita and the invaders broke. Clutching the explosives and detonator to my chest with my free hand, I shoot one guard in the leg and the other in the chest.

The one I shot in the leg reaches for his gun, and I fire again, closing my eyes after I aim. He doesn't move again.

I run past the broken doors and into the hallway between them. I slam the explosives against the metal bar where the two doors join, and clamp down the claws around the edge of the bar so it will stay. Then I run back to the end of the hallway and around the corner and crouch, my back to the doors, as I press the detonation button and shield my ears with my palms.

The noise vibrates in my bones as the small bomb detonates, and the force of the blast throws me sideways, my gun sliding across the floor. Pieces of glass and metal spray through the air, falling to the floor where I lie, stunned. Even though I sealed off my ears with my hands, I still hear ringing when I take them away, and I feel unsteady on my feet.

At the end of the hallway, the guards have caught up with me. They fire, and a bullet hits me in the fleshy part of my arm. I scream, clapping my hand over the wound, and my vision goes spotty at the edges as I throw myself around the corner again, half walking and half stumbling to the blasted-open doors.

Beyond them is a small vestibule with a set of sealed, lockless doors at the other end. Through the windows in those doors I see the Weapons Lab, the even rows of machinery and dark devices and serum vials, lit from beneath like they're on display. I hear a spraying sound and know that the death serum is floating through the air, but the guards are behind me, and I don't have time to put on the suit that will delay its effects.

I also know, I just know, that I can survive this.

I step into the vestibule.

CHAPTER
FORTY-EIGHT

TOBIAS

FACTIONLESS HEADQUARTERS—BUT this building will always be Erudite headquarters to me, no matter what happens—stands silent in the snow, with nothing but glowing windows to signal that there are people inside. I stop in front of the doors and make a disgruntled sound in my throat.

"What?" Peter says.

"I hate it here," I say.

He pushes his hair, soaked from the snow, out of his eyes. "So what are we going to do, break a window? Look for a back door?"

"I'm just going to walk in," I say. "I'm her son."

"You also betrayed her and left the city when she

forbade anyone from doing that," he says, "and she sent people after you to stop you. People with guns."

"You can stay here if you want," I say.

"Where the serum goes, I go," he says. "But if you get shot at, I'm going to grab it and run."

"I don't expect anything more."

He is a strange sort of person.

I walk into the lobby, where someone reassembled the portrait of Jeanine Matthews, but they drew an X over each of her eyes in red paint and wrote "Faction scum" across the bottom.

Several people wearing factionless armbands advance on us with guns held high. Some of them I recognize from across the factionless warehouse campfires, or from the time I spent at Evelyn's side as a Dauntless leader. Others are complete strangers, reminding me that the faction-less population is larger than any of us suspected.

I put up my hands. "I'm here to see Evelyn."

"Sure," one of them says. "Because we just let anyone in who wants to see her."

"I have a message from the people outside," I say. "One I'm sure she would like to hear."

"Tobias?" a factionless woman says. I recognize her, but not from a factionless warehouse—from the Abnegation sector. She was my neighbor. Grace is her name.

"Hello, Grace," I say. "I just want to talk to my mom."

She bites the inside of her cheek and considers me. Her grip on her pistol falters. "Well, we're still not supposed to let anyone in."

"For God's sake," Peter says. "Go tell her we're here and see what she says, then! We can wait."

Grace backs up into the crowd that gathered as we were talking, then lowers her gun and jogs down a nearby hallway.

We stand for what feels like a long time, until my shoulders ache from supporting my arms. Then Grace returns and beckons to us. I lower my hands as the others lower their guns, and walk into the foyer, passing through the center of the crowd like a piece of thread through the eye of a needle. She leads us into an elevator.

"What are you doing holding a gun, Grace?" I say. I've never known an Abnegation to pick up a weapon.

"No faction customs anymore," she says. "Now I get to defend myself. I get to have a sense of self-preservation."

"Good," I say, and I mean it. Abnegation was just as broken as the other factions, but its evils were less obvious, cloaked as they were in the guise of selflessness. But requiring a person to disappear, to fade into the background wherever they go, is no better than encouraging them to punch one another.

We go up to the floor where Jeanine's administrative office was—but that's not where Grace takes us. Instead she leads us to a large meeting room with tables, couches, and chairs arranged in strict squares. Huge windows along the back wall let in the moonlight. Evelyn sits at a table on the right, staring out the window.

"You can go, Grace," Evelyn says. "You have a message for me, Tobias?"

She doesn't look at me. Her thick hair is tied back in a knot, and she wears a gray shirt with a factionless armband over it. She looks exhausted.

"Mind waiting in the hallway?" I say to Peter, and to my surprise, he doesn't argue. He just walks out, closing the door behind him.

My mother and I are alone.

"The people outside have no messages for us," I say, moving closer to her. "They wanted to take away the memories of everyone in this city. They believe there is no reasoning with us, no appealing to our better natures. They decided it would be easier to erase us than to speak with us."

"Maybe they're right," Evelyn says. Finally she turns to me, resting her cheekbone against her clasped hands. She has an empty circle tattooed on one of her fingers like a wedding band. "What is it you came here to do, then?"

I hesitate, my hand on the vial in my pocket. I look at her, and I can see the way time has worn through her like an old piece of cloth, the fibers exposed and fraying. And I can see the woman I knew as a child, too, the mouth that stretched into a smile, the eyes that sparkled with joy. But the longer I look at her, the more convinced I am that that happy woman never existed. That woman is just a pale version of my real mother, viewed through the self-centered eyes of a child.

I sit down across from her at the table and put the vial of memory serum between us.

"I came to make you drink this," I say.

She looks at the vial, and I think I see tears in her eyes, but it could just be the light.

"I thought it was the only way to prevent total destruction," I say. "I know that Marcus and Johanna and their people are going to attack, and I know that you will do whatever it takes to stop them, including using that death serum you possess to its best advantage." I tilt my head. "Am I wrong?"

"No," she says. "The factions are evil. They cannot be restored. I would sooner see us all destroyed."

Her hand squeezes the edge of the table, the knuckles pale.

"The reason the factions were evil is because there

was no way out of them," I say. "They gave us the illusion of choice without actually giving us a choice. That's the same thing you're doing here, by abolishing them. You're saying, go make choices. But make sure they aren't factions or I'll grind you to bits!"

"If you thought that, why didn't you tell me?" she says, her voice louder and her eyes avoiding mine, avoiding me. "Tell me, instead of *betraying* me?"

"Because I'm afraid of you!" The words burst out, and I regret them but I'm also glad they're there, glad that before I ask her to give up her identity, I can at least be honest with her. "You . . . you remind me of *him*!"

"Don't you dare." She clenches her hands into fists and almost spits at me, "Don't you *dare*."

"I don't care if you don't want to hear it," I say, coming to my feet. "He was a tyrant in our house and now you're a tyrant in this city, and you can't even see that it's the same!"

"So that's why you brought this," she says, and she wraps her hand around the vial, holding it up to look at it. "Because you think this is the only way to mend things."

"I . . ." I am about to say that it's the easiest way, the best way, maybe the only way that I can trust her.

If I erase her memories, I can create for myself a new mother, but.

But she is more than my mother. She is a person in her

own right, and she does not belong to me.

I do not get to choose what she becomes just because I can't deal with who she is.

"No," I say. "No, I came to give you a choice."

I feel suddenly terrified, my hands numb, my heart beating fast—

"I thought about going to see Marcus tonight, but I didn't." I swallow hard. "I came to see you instead because . . . because I think there's a hope of reconciliation between us. Not now, not soon, but someday. And with him there's no hope, there's no reconciliation possible."

She stares at me, her eyes fierce but welling up with tears.

"It's not fair for me to give you this choice," I say. "But I have to. You can lead the factionless, you can fight the Allegiant, but you'll have to do it without me, forever. Or you can let this crusade go, and . . . and you'll have your son back."

It's a feeble offer and I know it, which is why I'm afraid—afraid that she will refuse to choose, that she will choose power over me, that she will call me a ridiculous child, which is what I am. I am a child. I am two feet tall and asking her how much she loves me.

Evelyn's eyes, dark as wet earth, search mine for a long time.

Then she reaches across the table and pulls me fiercely

into her arms, which form a wire cage around me, surprisingly strong.

"Let them have the city and everything in it," she says
into my hair.

I can't move, can't speak. She chose me. She chose me.

CHAPTER
FORTY-NINE

TRIS

THE DEATH SERUM smells like smoke and spice, and my lungs reject it with the first breath I take. I cough and splutter, and I am swallowed by darkness.

I crumple to my knees. My body feels like someone has replaced my blood with molasses, and my bones with lead. An invisible thread tugs me toward sleep, but I want to be awake. It is important that I want to be awake. I imagine that wanting, that desire, burning in my chest like a flame.

The thread tugs harder, and I stoke the flame with names. Tobias. Caleb. Christina. Matthew. Cara. Zeke. Uriah.

But I can't bear up under the serum's weight. My body

falls to the side, and my wounded arm presses to the cold ground. I am drifting. . . .

It would be nice to float away, a voice in my head says. *To see where I will go . . .*

But the fire, the fire.

The desire to live.

I am not done yet, I am not.

I feel like I am digging through my own mind. It is difficult to remember why I came here and why I care about unburdening myself from this beautiful weight. But then my scratching hands find it, the memory of my mother's face, and the strange angles of her limbs on the pavement, and the blood seeping from my father's body.

But they are dead, the voice says. *You could join them.*

They died for me, I answer. And now I have something to do, in return. I have to stop other people from losing everything. I have to save the city and the people my mother and father loved.

If I go to join my parents, I want to carry with me a good *reason*, not this—this senseless collapsing at the threshold.

The fire, the fire. It rages within, a campfire and then an inferno, and my body is its fuel. I feel it racing through me, eating away at the weight. There is nothing that can kill me now; I am powerful and invincible and eternal.

I feel the serum clinging to my skin like oil, but the darkness recedes. I slap a heavy hand over the floor and push myself up.

Bent at the waist, I shove my shoulder into the double doors, and they squeak across the floor as their seal breaks. I breathe clean air and stand up straighter. I am there, I am *there*.

But I am not alone.

"Don't move," David says, raising his gun. "Hello, Tris."

CHAPTER
FIFTY

TRIS

"HOW DID YOU inoculate yourself against the death serum?" he asks me. He's still sitting in his wheelchair, but you don't need to be able to walk to fire a gun.

I blink at him, still dazed.

"I didn't," I say.

"Don't be stupid," David says. "You can't survive the death serum without an inoculation, and I'm the only person in the compound who possesses that substance."

I just stare at him, not sure what to say. I didn't inoculate myself. The fact that I'm still standing upright is impossible. There's nothing more to add.

"I suppose it no longer matters," he says. "We're here now."

"What are you doing here?" I mumble. My lips feel awkwardly large, hard to talk around. I still feel that oily heaviness on my skin, like death is clinging to me even though I have defeated it.

I am dimly aware that I left my own gun in the hallway behind me, sure I wouldn't need it if I made it this far.

"I knew something was going on," David says. "You've been running around with genetically damaged people all week, Tris, did you think I wouldn't notice?" He shakes his head. "And then your friend Cara was caught trying to manipulate the lights, but she very wisely knocked herself out before she could tell us anything. So I came here, just in case. I'm sad to say I'm not surprised to see you."

"You came here alone?" I say. "Not very smart, are you?"

His bright eyes squint a little. "Well, you see, I have death serum resistance and a weapon, and you have no way to fight me. There's no way you can steal four virus devices while I have you at gunpoint. I'm afraid you've come all this way for no reason, and it will be at the expense of your life. The death serum may not have killed you, but I am going to. I'm sure you understand—officially we don't allow capital punishment, but I can't have you surviving this."

He thinks I'm here to steal the weapons that will reset the experiments, not deploy one of them. Of course he does.

I try to guard my expression, though I'm sure it's still slack. I sweep my eyes across the room, searching for the device that will release the memory serum virus. I was there when Matthew described it to Caleb in painstaking detail earlier: a black box with a silver keypad, marked with a strip of blue tape with a model number written on it. It is one of the only items on the counter along the left wall, just a few feet away from me. But I can't move, or else he'll kill me.

I'll have to wait for the right moment, and do it fast.

"I know what you did," I say. I start to back up, hoping that the accusation will distract him. "I know you designed the attack simulation. I know you're responsible for my parents' deaths—for my *mother's* death. I know."

"I am not responsible for her death!" David says, the words bursting from him, too loud and too sudden. "I *told* her what was coming just before the attack began, so she had enough time to escort her loved ones to a safe house. If she had stayed put, she would have lived. But she was a foolish woman who didn't understand making sacrifices for the greater good, and it *killed* her!"

I frown at him. There's something about his reaction—about the glassiness of his eyes—something that he mumbled when Nita shot him with the fear serum—something about *her*.

"Did you love her?" I say. "All those years she was sending you correspondence . . . the reason you never wanted her to stay there . . . the reason you told her you couldn't read her updates anymore, after she married my father . . ."

David sits still, like a statue, like a man of stone.

"I did," he says. "But that time is past."

That must be why he welcomed me into his circle of trust, why he gave me so many opportunities. Because I am a piece of her, wearing her hair and speaking with her voice. Because he has spent his life grasping at her and coming up with nothing.

I hear footsteps in the hallway outside. The soldiers are coming. Good—I need them to. I need them to be exposed to the airborne serum, to pass it on to the rest of the compound. I hope they wait until the air is clear of death serum.

"My mother wasn't a fool," I say. "She just understood something you didn't. That it's not sacrifice if it's someone *else's* life you're giving away, it's just evil."

I back up another step and say, "She taught me all about real sacrifice. That it should be done from love, not misplaced disgust for another person's genetics. That it should be done from necessity, not without exhausting all other options. That it should be done for people who need your strength because they don't have enough of their own. That's why I need to stop you from 'sacrificing' all those people and their memories. Why I need to rid the world of you once and for all."

I shake my head.

"I didn't come here to steal anything, David."

I twist and lunge toward the device. The gun goes off and pain races through my body. I don't even know where the bullet hit me.

I can still hear Caleb repeating the code for Matthew. With a quaking hand I type in the numbers on the keypad.

The gun goes off again.

More pain, and black edges on my vision, but I hear Caleb's voice speaking again. *The green button.*

So much pain.

But how, when my body feels so numb?

I start to fall, and slam my hand into the keypad on my way down. A light turns on behind the green button.

I hear a beep, and a churning sound.

I slide to the floor. I feel something warm on my neck, and under my cheek. Red. Blood is a strange color. Dark.

From the corner of my eye, I see David slumped over in his chair.

And my *mother* walking out from behind him.

She is dressed in the same clothes she wore the last

time I saw her, Abnegation gray, stained with her blood, with bare arms to show her tattoo. There are still bullet holes in her shirt; through them I can see her wounded skin, red but no longer bleeding, like she's frozen in time. Her dull blond hair is tied back in a knot, but a few loose strands frame her face in gold.

I know she can't be alive, but I don't know if I'm seeing her now because I'm delirious from the blood loss or if the death serum has addled my thoughts or if she is here in some other way.

She kneels next to me and touches a cool hand to my cheek.

"Hello, Beatrice," she says, and she smiles.

"Am I done yet?" I say, and I'm not sure if I actually say it or if I just think it and she hears it.

"Yes," she says, her eyes bright with tears. "My dear child, you've done so well."

"What about the others?" I choke on a sob as the image of Tobias comes into my mind, of how dark and how still his eyes were, how strong and warm his hand was, when we first stood face-to-face. "Tobias, Caleb, my friends?"

"They'll care for each other," she says. "That's what people do."

I smile and close my eyes.

I feel a thread tugging me again, but this time I know that it isn't some sinister force dragging me toward death.

This time I know it's my mother's hand, drawing me into her arms.

And I go gladly into her embrace.

+ + +

Can I be forgiven for all I've done to get here?

I want to be.

I can.

I believe it.

CHAPTER
FIFTY-ONE

TOBIAS

EVELYN BRUSHES THE tears from her eyes with her thumb. We stand by the windows, shoulder to shoulder, watching the snow swirl past. Some of the flakes gather on the windowsill outside, piling at the corners.

The feeling has returned to my hands. As I stare out at the world, dusted in white, I feel like everything has begun again, and it will be better this time.

"I think I can get in touch with Marcus over the radio to negotiate a peace agreement," Evelyn says. "He'll be listening in; he'd be stupid not to."

"Before you do that, I made a promise I have to keep," I say. I touch Evelyn's shoulder. I expected to see strain at the edges of her smile, but I don't.

I feel a twinge of guilt. I didn't come here to ask her to lay down arms for me, to trade in everything she's worked for just to get me back. But then again, I didn't come here to give her any choice at all. I guess Tris was right—when you have to choose between two bad options, you pick the one that saves the people you love. I wouldn't have been saving Evelyn by giving her that serum. I would have been destroying her.

Peter sits with his back to the wall in the hallway. He looks up at me when I lean over him, his dark hair stuck to his forehead from the melted snow.

"Did you reset her?" he says.

"No," I say.

"Didn't think you would have the nerve."

"It's not about nerve. You know what? Whatever." I shake my head and hold up the vial of memory serum. "Are you still set on this?"

He nods.

"You could just do the work, you know," I say. "You could make better decisions, make a better life."

"Yeah, I could," he says. "But I won't. We both know that."

I do know that. I know that change is difficult, and comes slowly, and that it is the work of many days strung together in a long line until the origin of them is forgotten. He is afraid that he will not be able to put in that work, that he will squander those days, and that they will leave him worse off than he is now. And I understand that feeling—I understand being afraid of yourself.

So I have him sit on one of the couches, and I ask him what he wants me to tell him about himself, after his memories disappear like smoke. He just shakes his head. Nothing. He wants to retain nothing.

Peter takes the vial with a shaking hand and twists off the cap. The liquid trembles inside it, almost spilling over the lip. He holds it under his nose to smell it.

"How much should I drink?" he says, and I think I hear his teeth chattering.

"I don't think it makes a difference," I say.

"Okay. Well . . . here goes." He lifts the vial up to the light like he is toasting me.

When he touches it to his mouth, I say, "Be brave."

Then he swallows.

And I watch Peter disappear.

+ + +

The air outside tastes like ice.

"Hey! Peter!" I shout, my breaths turning to vapor.

Peter stands by the doorway to Erudite headquarters, looking clueless. At the sound of his name—which I have told him at least ten times since he drank the serum—he raises his eyebrows, pointing to his chest. Matthew told us people would be disoriented for a while after drinking the memory serum, but I didn't think "disoriented" meant "stupid" until now.

I sigh. "Yes, that's you! For the eleventh time! Come on, let's go."

I thought that when I looked at him after he drank the serum, I would still see the initiate who shoved a butter knife into Edward's eye, and the boy who tried to kill my girlfriend, and all the other things he has done, stretching backward for as long as I've known him. But it's easier than I thought to see that he has no idea who he is anymore. His eyes still have that wide, innocent look, but this time, I believe it.

Evelyn and I walk side by side, with Peter trotting behind us. The snow has stopped falling now, but enough has collected on the ground that it squeaks under my shoes.

We walk to Millennium Park, where the mammoth bean sculpture reflects the moonlight, and then down a set of stairs. As we descend, Evelyn wraps her hand around my elbow to keep her balance, and we exchange a look. I wonder if she is as nervous as I am to face my father again. I wonder if she is nervous every time.

At the bottom of the steps is a pavilion with two glass blocks, each one at least three times as tall as I am, at either end. This is where we told Marcus and Johanna we would meet them—both parties armed, to be realistic but even.

They are already there. Johanna isn't holding a gun, but Marcus is, and he has it trained on Evelyn. I point the gun Evelyn gave me at him, just to be safe. I notice the planes of his skull, showing through his shaved hair, and the jagged path his crooked nose carves down his face.

"Tobias!" Johanna says. She wears a coat in Amity red, dusted with snowflakes. "What are you doing here?"

"Trying to keep you all from killing each other," I say. "I'm surprised you're carrying a gun."

I nod to the bulge in her coat pocket, the unmistakable contours of a weapon.

"Sometimes you have to take difficult measures to ensure peace," Johanna says. "I believe you agree with that, as a principle."

"We're not here to chat," Marcus says, looking at Evelyn. "You said you wanted to talk about a treaty."

The past few weeks have taken something from him. I can see it in the turned-down corners of his mouth, in the purple skin under his eyes. I see my own eyes set into his skull, and I think of my reflection in the fear landscape, how terrified I was, watching his skin spread over mine like a rash. I am still nervous that I will become him, even now, standing at odds with him with my mother at my side, like I always dreamed I would when I was a child.

But I don't think that I'm still afraid.

"Yes," Evelyn says. "I have some terms for us both to agree to. I think you will find them fair. If you agree to them, I will step down and surrender whatever weapons I have that my people are not using for personal protection. I will leave the city and not return."

Marcus laughs. I'm not sure if it's a mocking laugh or a disbelieving one. He's equally capable of either sentiment, an arrogant and deeply suspicious man.

"Let her finish," Johanna says quietly, tucking her hands into her sleeves.

"In return," Evelyn says, "you will not attack or try to seize control of the city. You will allow those people who wish to leave and seek a new life elsewhere to do so. You will allow those who choose to stay to *vote* on new leaders and a new social system. And most importantly, *you*, Marcus, will not be eligible to lead them."

It is the only purely selfish term of the peace agreement. She told me she couldn't stand the thought of Marcus duping more people into following him, and I didn't argue with her.

Johanna raises her eyebrows. I notice that she has pulled her hair back on both sides, to reveal the scar in its entirety. She looks better that way—stronger, when she is not hiding behind a curtain of hair, hiding who she is.

"No deal," Marcus says. "I am the leader of these people."

"Marcus," Johanna says.

He ignores her. "*You* don't get to decide whether I lead them or not because you have a grudge against me, Evelyn!"

"Excuse me," Johanna says loudly. "Marcus, what she is offering is too good to be true—we get everything we want without all the violence! How can you possibly say no?"

"Because I am the rightful leader of these people!" Marcus says. "I am the leader of the Allegiant! I—"

"No, you are not," Johanna says calmly. "*I* am the leader of the Allegiant. And you are going to agree to this treaty, or I am going to tell them that you had a chance to end this conflict without bloodshed if you sacrificed your pride, and you said no."

Marcus's passive mask is gone, revealing the malicious face beneath it. But even he can't argue with Johanna, whose perfect calm and perfect threat have mastered him. He shakes his head but doesn't argue again.

"I agree to your terms," Johanna says, and she holds out

her hand, her footsteps squeaking in the snow.

Evelyn removes her glove fingertip by fingertip, reaches across the gap, and shakes.

"In the morning we should gather everyone together and tell them the new plan," Johanna says. "Can you guarantee a safe gathering?"

"I'll do my best," Evelyn says.

I check my watch. An hour has passed since Amar and Christina separated from us near the Hancock building, which means he probably knows that the serum virus didn't work. Or maybe he doesn't. Either way, I have to do what I came here to do—I have to find Zeke and his mother and tell them what happened to Uriah.

"I should go," I say to Evelyn. "I have something else to take care of. But I'll pick you up from the city limits tomorrow afternoon?"

"That sounds good," Evelyn says, and she rubs my arm briskly with a gloved hand, like she used to when I came in from the cold as a child.

"You won't be back, I assume?" Johanna says to me. "You've found a life for yourself on the outside?"

"I have," I say. "Good luck in here. The people outside—they're going to try to shut the city down. You should be ready for them."

Johanna smiles. "I'm sure we can negotiate with them."

She offers me her hand, and I shake it. I feel Marcus's eyes on me like an oppressive weight threatening to crush me. I force myself to look at him.

"Good-bye," I say to him, and I mean it.

+ + +

Hana, Zeke's mother, has small feet that don't touch the ground when she sits in the easy chair in their living room. She is wearing a ragged black bathrobe and slippers, but the air she has, with her hands folded in her lap and her eyebrows raised, is so dignified that I feel like I am standing in front of a world leader. I glance at Zeke, who is rubbing his face with his fists to wake up.

Amar and Christina found them, not among the other revolutionaries near the Hancock building, but in their family apartment in the Pire, above Dauntless headquarters. I only found them because Christina thought to leave Peter and me a note with their location on the useless truck. Peter is waiting in the new van Evelyn found for us to drive to the Bureau.

"I'm sorry," I say. "I don't know where to start."

"You might begin with the worst," Hana says. "Like what exactly happened to my son."

"He was seriously injured during an attack," I say. "There was an explosion, and he was very close to it."

"Oh God," Zeke says, and he rocks back and forth like

his body wants to be a child again, soothed by motion as a child is.

But Hana just bends her head, hiding her face from me.

Their living room smells like garlic and onion, maybe remnants from that night's dinner. I lean my shoulder into the white wall by the doorway. Hanging crookedly next to me is a picture of the family—Zeke as a toddler, Uriah as a baby, balancing on his mother's lap. Their father's face is pierced in several places, nose and ear and lip, but his wide, bright smile and dark complexion are more familiar to me, because he passed them both to his sons.

"He has been in a coma since then," I say. "And . . ."

"And he isn't going to wake up," Hana says, her voice strained. "That is what you came to tell us, right?"

"Yes," I say. "I came to collect you so that you can make a decision on his behalf."

"A decision?" Zeke says. "You mean, to *unplug* him or not?"

"Zeke," Hana says, and she shakes her head. He sinks back into the couch. The cushions seem to wrap around him.

"Of course we don't want to keep him alive that way," Hana says. "He would want to move on. But we would like to go see him."

I nod. "Of course. But there's something else I should

say. The attack . . . it was a kind of uprising that involved some of the people from the place where we were staying. And I participated in it."

I stare at the crack in the floorboards right in front of me, at the dust that has gathered there over time, and wait for a reaction, any reaction. What greets me is only silence.

"I didn't do what you asked me," I say to Zeke. "I didn't watch out for him the way I should have. And I'm sorry."

I chance a look at him, and he is just sitting still, staring at the empty vase on the coffee table. It is painted with faded pink roses.

"I think we need some time with this," Hana says. She clears her throat, but it doesn't help her tremulous voice.

"I wish I could give it to you," I say. "But we're going back to the compound very soon, and you have to come with us."

"All right," Hana says. "If you can wait outside, we will be there in five minutes."

+ + +

The ride back to the compound is slow and dark. I watch the moon disappear and reappear behind the clouds as we bump over the ground. When we reach the outer limits of the city, it begins to snow again, large, light flakes that swirl in front of the headlights. I wonder if Tris is watching it sweep across the pavement and gather in piles by the airplanes. I wonder if she is living in a better world than the one I left, among people who no longer remember what it is to have pure genes.

Christina leans forward to whisper into my ear. "So you did it? It worked?"

I nod. In the rearview mirror I see her touch her face with both hands, grinning into her palms. I know how she feels: safe. We are all safe.

"Did you inoculate your family?" I say.

"Yep. We found them with the Allegiant, in the Hancock building," she says. "But the time for the reset has passed—it looks like Tris and Caleb stopped it."

Hana and Zeke murmur to each other on the way, marveling at the strange, dark world we move through. Amar gives the basic explanation as we go, looking back at them instead of the road far too often for my comfort. I try to ignore my surges of panic as he almost veers into streetlights or road barriers, and focus instead on the snow.

I have always hated the emptiness that winter brings, the blank landscape and the stark difference between sky and ground, the way it transforms trees into skeletons and the city into a wasteland. Maybe this winter I can be persuaded otherwise.

We drive past the fences and stop by the front doors,

488

which are no longer manned by guards. We get out, and Zeke seizes his mother's hand to steady her as she shuffles through the snow. As we walk into the compound, I know for a fact that Caleb succeeded, because there is no one in sight. That can only mean that they have been reset, their memories forever altered.

"Where is everyone?" Amar says.

We walk through the abandoned security checkpoint without stopping. On the other side, I see Cara. The side of her face is badly bruised, and there's a bandage on her head, but that's not what concerns me. What concerns me is the troubled look on her face.

"What is it?" I say.

Cara shakes her head.

"Where's Tris?" I say.

"I'm sorry, Tobias."

"Sorry about what?" Christina says roughly. "Tell us what *happened*!"

"Tris went into the Weapons Lab instead of Caleb," Cara says. "She survived the death serum, and set off the memory serum, but she . . . she was shot. And she didn't survive. I'm so sorry."

Most of the time I can tell when people are lying, and this must be a lie, because Tris is still alive, her eyes bright and her cheeks flushed and her small body full of power and strength, standing in a shaft of light in the atrium. Tris is still alive, she wouldn't leave me here alone, she wouldn't go to the Weapons Lab instead of Caleb.

"No," Christina says, shaking her head. "No way. There has to be some mistake."

Cara's eyes well up with tears.

It's then that I realize: Of course Tris would go into the Weapons Lab instead of Caleb.

Of course she would.

Christina yells something, but to me her voice sounds muffled, like I have submerged my head underwater. The details of Cara's face have also become difficult to see, the world smearing together into dull colors.

All I can do is stand still—I feel like if I just stand still, I can stop it from being true, I can pretend that everything is all right. Christina hunches over, unable to support her own grief, and Cara embraces her, and

all I'm doing is standing still.

CHAPTER
FIFTY-TWO

TOBIAS

WHEN HER BODY first hit the net, all I registered was a gray blur. I pulled her across it and her hand was small, but warm, and then she stood before me, short and thin and plain and in all ways unremarkable—except that she had jumped first. The Stiff had jumped first.

Even I didn't jump first.

Her eyes were so stern, so insistent.

Beautiful.

CHAPTER
FIFTY-THREE

TOBIAS

BUT THAT WASN'T the first time I ever saw her. I saw her in the hallways at school, and at my mother's false funeral, and walking the sidewalks in the Abnegation sector. I saw her, but I didn't see her; no one saw her the way she truly was until she jumped.

I suppose a fire that burns that bright is not meant to last.

CHAPTER
FIFTY-FOUR

TOBIAS

I GO TO see her body . . . sometime. I don't know how long it is after Cara tells me what happened. Christina and I walk shoulder to shoulder; we walk in Cara's footsteps. I don't remember the journey from the entrance to the morgue, really, just a few smeared images and whatever sound I can make out through the barrier that has gone up inside my head.

She lies on a table, and for a moment I think she's just sleeping, and when I touch her, she will wake up and smile at me and press a kiss to my mouth. But when I touch her she is cold, her body stiff and unyielding.

Christina sniffles and sobs. I squeeze Tris's hand, praying that if I do it hard enough, I will send life back into her body and she will flush with color and wake up.

I don't know how long it takes for me to realize that isn't going to happen, that she is gone. But when I do I feel all the strength go out of me, and I fall to my knees beside the table and I think I cry, then, or at least I want to, and everything inside me screams for just one more kiss, one more word, one more glance, one more.

CHAPTER
FIFTY-FIVE

IN THE DAYS that follow, it's movement, not stillness, that helps to keep the grief at bay, so I walk the compound halls instead of sleeping. I watch everyone else recover from the memory serum that altered them permanently as if from a great distance.

Those lost in the memory serum haze are gathered into groups and given the truth: that human nature is complex, that all our genes are different, but neither damaged nor pure. They are also given the lie: that their memories were erased because of a freak accident, and that they were on the verge of lobbying the government for equality for GDs.

I keep finding myself stifled by the company of others

and then crippled by loneliness when I leave them. I am terrified and I don't even know of what, because I have lost everything already. My hands shake as I stop by the control room to watch the city on the screens. Johanna is arranging transportation for those who want to leave the city. They will come here to learn the truth. I don't know what will happen to those who remain in Chicago, and I'm not sure I care.

I shove my hands into my pockets and watch for a few minutes, then walk away again, trying to match my footsteps to my heartbeat, or to avoid the cracks between the tiles. When I walk past the entrance, I see a small group of people gathered by the stone sculpture, one of them in a wheelchair—Nita.

I walk past the useless security barrier and stand at a distance, watching them. Reggie steps on the stone slab and opens a valve in the bottom of the water tank. The drops turn into a stream of water, and soon water gushes out of the tank, splattering all over the slab, soaking the bottom of Reggie's pants.

"Tobias?"

I shudder a little. It's Caleb. I turn away from the voice, searching for an escape route.

"Wait. Please," he says.

I don't want to look at him, to measure how much, or

how little, he grieves for her. And I don't want to think about how she died for such a miserable coward, about how he wasn't worth her life.

Still, I do look at him, wondering if I can see some of her in his face, still hungry for her even now that I know she's gone.

His hair is unwashed and unkempt, his green eyes bloodshot, his mouth twitching into a frown.

He does not look like her.

"I don't mean to bother you," he says. "But I have something to tell you. Something . . . *she* told me to tell you, before . . ."

"Just get on with it," I say, before he tries to finish the sentence.

"She told me that if she didn't survive, I should tell you . . ." Caleb chokes, then pulls himself up straight, fighting off tears. "That she didn't want to leave you."

I should feel something, hearing her last words to me, shouldn't I? I feel nothing. I feel farther away than ever.

"Yeah?" I say harshly. "Then why did she? Why didn't she let you die?"

"You think I'm not asking myself that question?" Caleb says. "She loved me. Enough to hold me at gunpoint so she could die for me. I have no idea why, but that's just the way it is."

He walks away without letting me respond, and it's probably better that way, because I can't think of anything to say that is equal to my anger. I blink away tears and sit down on the ground, right in the middle of the lobby.

I know why she wanted to tell me that she didn't want to leave me. She wanted me to know that this was not another Erudite headquarters, not a lie told to make me sleep while she went to die, not an act of unnecessary self-sacrifice. I grind the heels of my hands into my eyes like I can push my tears back into my skull. *No crying,* I chastise myself. If I let a little of the emotion out, all of it will come out, and it will never end.

Sometime later I hear voices nearby—Cara and Peter.

"This sculpture was a symbol of change," she says to him. "Gradual change, but now they're taking it down."

"Oh, really?" Peter sounds eager. "Why?"

"Um . . . I'll explain later, if that's okay," Cara says. "Do you remember how to get back to the dormitory?"

"Yep."

"Then . . . go back there for a while. Someone will be there to help you."

Cara walks over to me, and I cringe in anticipation of her voice. But all she does is sit next to me on the ground, her hands folded in her lap, her back straight. Alert but relaxed, she watches the sculpture where Reggie stands under the gushing water.

"You don't have to stay here," I say.

"I don't have anywhere to be," she says. "And the quiet is nice."

So we sit side by side, staring at the water, in silence.

+ + +

"There you are," Christina says, jogging toward us. Her face is swollen and her voice is listless, like a heavy sigh. "Come on, it's time. They're unplugging him."

I shudder at the word, but push myself to my feet anyway. Hana and Zeke have been hovering over Uriah's body since we got here, their fingers finding his, their eyes searching for life. But there is no life left, just the machine beating his heart.

Cara walks behind Christina and me as we go toward the hospital. I haven't slept in days but I don't feel tired, not in the way I normally do, though my body aches as I walk. Christina and I don't speak, but I know our thoughts are the same, fixed on Uriah, on his last breaths.

We make it to the observation window outside Uriah's room, and Evelyn is there—Amar picked her up in my stead, a few days ago. She tries to touch my shoulder and I yank it away, not wanting to be comforted.

Inside the room, Zeke and Hana stand on either side of Uriah. Hana is holding one of his hands, and Zeke is holding the other. A doctor stands near the heart monitor, a clipboard outstretched, held out not to Hana or Zeke but to *David*. Sitting in his wheelchair. Hunched and dazed, like all the others who have lost their memories.

"What is *he* doing there?" I feel like all my muscles and bones and nerves are on fire.

"He's still technically the leader of the Bureau, at least until they replace him," Cara says from behind me. "Tobias, he doesn't remember anything. The man you knew doesn't exist anymore; he's as good as dead. *That* man doesn't remember kill—"

"Shut up!" I snap. David signs the clipboard and turns around, pushing himself toward the door. It opens, and I can't stop myself—I lunge toward him, and only Evelyn's wiry frame stops me from wrapping my hands around his throat. He gives me a strange look and pushes himself down the hallway as I press against my mother's arm, which feels like a bar across my shoulders.

"Tobias," Evelyn says. "Calm. Down."

"Why didn't someone lock him up?" I demand, and my eyes are too blurry to see out of.

"Because he still works for the government," Cara says. "Just because they've declared it an unfortunate accident doesn't mean they've fired everyone. And the government isn't going to lock him up just because he killed a rebel under duress."

"A rebel," I repeat. "That's all she is now?"

"Was," Cara says softly. "And no, of course not, but that's what the government sees her as."

I'm about to respond, but Christina interrupts. "Guys, they're doing it."

In Uriah's room, Zeke and Hana join their free hands over Uriah's body. I see Hana's lips moving, but I can't tell what she's saying—do the Dauntless have prayers for the dying? The Abnegation react to death with silence and service, not words. I find my anger ebbing away, and I'm lost in muffled grief again, this time not just for Tris, but for Uriah, whose smile is burned into my memory. My friend's brother, and then my friend, too, though not for long enough to let his humor work its way into me, not for long enough.

The doctor flips some switches, his clipboard clutched to his stomach, and the machines stop breathing for Uriah. Zeke's shoulders shake, and Hana squeezes his hand tightly, until her knuckles go white.

Then she says something, and her hands spring open, and she steps back from Uriah's body. Letting him go.

I move away from the window, walking at first, and then running, pushing my way through the hallways, careless, blind, empty.

CHAPTER
FIFTY-SIX

THE NEXT DAY I take a truck from the compound. The people there are still recovering from their memory loss, so no one tries to stop me. I drive over the railroad tracks toward the city, my eyes wandering over the skyline but not really taking it in.

When I reach the fields that separate the city from the outside world, I press down the accelerator. The truck crushes dying grass and snow beneath its tires, and soon the ground turns to the pavement in the Abnegation sector, and I barely feel the passage of time. The streets are all the same, but my hands and feet know where to go, even if my mind doesn't bother to guide them. I pull up to the house near the stop sign, with the cracked front walk.

My house.

I walk through the front door and up the stairs, still with that muffled feeling in my ears, like I am drifting far away from the world. People talk about the pain of grief, but I don't know what they mean. To me, grief is a devastating numbness, every sensation dulled.

I press my palm to the panel covering the mirror upstairs, and push it aside. Though the light of sunset is orange, creeping across the floor and illuminating my face from below, I have never looked paler; the circles under my eyes have never been more pronounced. I have spent the past few days somewhere between sleeping and waking, not quite able to manage either extreme.

I plug the hair clippers into the outlet near the mirror. The right guard is already in place, so all I have to do is run it through my hair, bending my ears down to protect them from the blade, turning my head to check the back of my neck for places I might have missed. The shorn hair falls on my feet and shoulders, itching whatever bare skin it finds. I run my hand over my head to make sure it's even, but I don't need to check, not really. I learned to do this myself when I was young.

I spend a lot of time brushing it from my shoulders and feet, then sweeping it into a dustpan. When I finish, I stand in front of the mirror again, and I can see the edges of my tattoo, the Dauntless flame.

I take the vial of memory serum from my pocket. I know that one vial will erase most of my life, but it will target memories, not facts. I will still know how to write, how to speak, how to put together a computer, because that data was stored in different parts of my brain. But I won't remember anything else.

The experiment is over. Johanna successfully negotiated with the government—David's superiors—to allow the former faction members to stay in the city, provided they are self-sufficient, submit to the government's authority, and allow outsiders to come in and join them, making Chicago just another metropolitan area, like Milwaukee. The Bureau, once in charge of the experiment, will now keep order in Chicago's city limits.

It will be the only metropolitan area in the country governed by people who don't believe in genetic damage. A kind of paradise. Matthew told me he hopes people from the fringe will trickle in to fill all the empty spaces, and find there a life more prosperous than the one they left.

All that I want is to become someone new. In this case, Tobias Johnson, son of Evelyn Johnson. Tobias Johnson may have lived a dull and empty life, but he is at least a whole person, not this fragment of a person that I am, too damaged by pain to become anything useful.

"Matthew told me you stole some of the memory serum and a truck," says a voice at the end of the hallway. Christina's. "I have to say, I didn't really believe him."

I must not have heard her enter the house through the muffle. Even her voice sounds like it is traveling through water to reach my ears, and it takes me a few seconds to make sense of what she says. When I do, I look at her and say, "Then why did you come, if you didn't believe him?"

"Just in case," she says, starting toward me. "Plus, I wanted to see the city one more time before it all changes. Give me that vial, Tobias."

"No." I fold my fingers over it to protect it from her. "This is my decision, not yours."

Her dark eyes widen, and her face is radiant with sunlight. It makes every strand of her thick, dark hair gleam orange like it's on fire.

"This is *not* your decision," she says. "This is the decision of a coward, and you're a lot of things, Four, but not a coward. Never."

"Maybe I am now," I answer passively. "Things have changed. I'm all right with it."

"No, you're not."

I feel so exhausted all I can do is roll my eyes.

"You can't become a person she would hate," Christina says, quietly this time. "And she would have hated this."

Anger stampedes through me, hot and lively, and the muffled feeling around my ears falls away, making even this quiet Abnegation street sound loud. I shudder with the force of it.

"Shut up!" I yell. "Shut up! You don't know what she would hate; you didn't know her, you—"

"I know enough!" she snaps. "I know she wouldn't want you to erase her from your memory like she didn't even matter to you!"

I lunge toward her, pinning her shoulder to the wall, and lean closer to her face.

"If you *dare* suggest that again," I say, "I'll—"

"You'll what?" Christina shoves me back, hard. "Hurt me? You know, there's a word for big, strong men who attack women, and it's *coward*."

I remember my father's screams filling the house, and his hand around my mother's throat, slamming her into walls and doors. I remember watching from my doorway, my hand wrapped around the door frame. And I remember hearing quiet sobs through her bedroom door, how she locked it so I couldn't get in.

I step back and slump against the wall, letting my body collapse into it.

"I'm sorry," I say.

"I know," she answers.

We stand still for a few seconds, just looking at each other. I remember hating her the first time I met her, because she was a Candor, because words just dribbled out of her mouth unchecked, careless. But over time she showed me who she really was, a forgiving friend, faithful to the truth, brave enough to take action. I can't help but like her now, can't help but see what Tris saw in her.

"I know how it feels to want to forget everything," she says. "I also know how it feels for someone you love to get killed for no reason, and to want to trade all your memories of them for just a moment's peace."

She wraps her hand around mine, which is wrapped around the vial.

"I didn't know Will long," she says, "but he changed my life. He changed *me*. And I know Tris changed you even more."

The hard expression she wore a moment ago melts away, and she touches my shoulders, lightly.

"The person you became with her is worth being," she says. "If you swallow that serum, you'll never be able to find your way back to him."

The tears come again, like when I saw Tris's body, and this time, pain comes with them, hot and sharp in my chest. I clutch the vial in my fist, desperate for the relief it offers, the protection from the pain of every memory clawing inside me like an animal.

Christina puts her arms around my shoulders, and her embrace only makes the pain worse, because it reminds me of every time Tris's thin arms slipped around me, uncertain at first but then stronger, more confident, more sure of herself and of me. It reminds me that no embrace will ever feel the same again, because no one will ever be like her again, because she's gone.

She's gone, and crying feels so useless, so stupid, but it's all I can do. Christina holds me upright and doesn't say a word for a long time.

Eventually I pull away, but her hands stay on my shoulders, warm and rough with calluses. Maybe just as skin on a hand grows tougher after pain in repetition, a person does too. But I don't want to become a calloused man.

There are other kinds of people in this world. There is the kind like Tris, who, after suffering and betrayal, could still find enough love to lay down her life instead of her brother's. Or the kind like Cara, who could still forgive the person who shot her brother in the head. Or Christina, who lost friend after friend but still decided to stay open, to make new ones. Appearing in front of me is another choice, brighter and stronger than the ones I gave myself.

My eyes opening, I offer the vial to her. She takes it and pockets it.

"I know Zeke's still weird around you," she says, slinging an arm across my shoulders. "But I can be your friend in the meantime. We can even exchange bracelets if you want, like the Amity girls used to."

"I don't think that will be necessary."

We walk down the stairs and out to the street together. The sun has slipped behind the buildings of Chicago, and in the distance I hear a train rushing over the rails, but we are moving away from this place and all that it has meant to us, and that is all right.

+ + +

There are so many ways to be brave in this world. Sometimes bravery involves laying down your life for something bigger than yourself, or for someone else. Sometimes it involves giving up everything you have ever known, or everyone you have ever loved, for the sake of something greater.

But sometimes it doesn't.

Sometimes it is nothing more than gritting your teeth through pain, and the work of every day, the slow walk toward a better life.

That is the sort of bravery I must have now.

EPILOGUE

TWO AND A HALF YEARS LATER

EVELYN STANDS AT the place where two worlds meet. Tire tracks are worn into the ground now, from the frequent coming and going of people from the fringe moving in and out, or people from the former Bureau compound commuting back and forth. Her bag rests against her leg, in one of the wells in the earth. She lifts a hand to greet me when I'm close.

When she gets into the truck, she kisses my cheek, and I let her. I feel a smile creep across my face, and I let it stay there.

"Welcome back," I say.

The agreement, when I offered it to her more than two years ago, and when she made it again with Johanna shortly after, was that she would leave the city. Now, so much has changed in Chicago that I don't see the harm in her coming back, and neither does she. Though two years have passed, she looks younger, her face fuller and her smile wider. The time away has done her good.

"How are you?" she says.

"I'm . . . okay," I say. "We're scattering her ashes today."

I glance at the urn perched on the backseat like another passenger. For a long time I left Tris's ashes in the Bureau morgue, not sure what kind of funeral she would want, and not sure I could make it through one. But today would be Choosing Day, if we still had factions, and it's time to take a step forward, even if it's a small one.

Evelyn puts a hand on my shoulder and looks out at the fields. The crops that were once isolated to the areas around Amity headquarters have spread, and continue to spread through all the grassy spaces around the city. Sometimes I miss the desolate, empty land. But right now I don't mind driving through the rows and rows of corn or wheat. I see people among the plants, checking the soil with handheld devices designed by former Bureau scientists. They wear red and blue and green and purple.

"What's it like, living without factions?" Evelyn says.

"It's very ordinary," I say. I smile at her. "You'll love it."

I take Evelyn to my apartment just north of the river. It's on one of the lower floors, but through the abundant windows I can see a wide stretch of buildings. I was one of the first settlers in the new Chicago, so I got to choose where I lived. Zeke, Shauna, Christina, Amar, and George opted to live in the higher floors of the Hancock building, and Caleb and Cara both moved back to the apartments near Millennium Park, but I came here because it was beautiful, and because it was nowhere near either of my old homes.

"My neighbor is a history expert, he came from the fringe," I say as I search my pockets for my keys. "He calls Chicago 'the fourth city'—because it was destroyed by fire, ages ago, and then again by the Purity War, and now we're on the fourth attempt at settlement here."

"The fourth city," Evelyn says as I push the door open. "I like it."

There's hardly any furniture inside, just a couch and a table, some chairs, a kitchen. Sunlight winks in the windows of the building across the marshy river. Some of the former Bureau scientists are trying to restore the river and the lake to their former glory, but it will be a while. Change, like healing, takes time.

Evelyn drops her bag on the couch. "Thank you for letting me stay with you for a little while. I promise I'll find another place soon."

"No problem," I say. I feel nervous about her being here, poking through my meager possessions, shuffling down my hallways, but we can't stay distant forever. Not when I promised her that I would try to bridge this gap between us.

"George says he needs some help training a police force," Evelyn says. "You didn't offer?"

"No," I say. "I told you, I'm done with guns."

"That's right. You're using your *words* now," Evelyn says, wrinkling her nose. "I don't trust politicians, you know."

"You'll trust me, because I'm your son," I say. "Anyway, I'm not a politician. Not yet, anyway. Just an assistant."

She sits at the table and looks around, twitchy and spry, like a cat.

"Do you know where your father is?" she says.

I shrug. "Someone told me he left. I didn't ask where he went."

She rests her chin on her hand. "There's nothing you wanted to say to him? Nothing at all?"

"No," I say. I twirl my keys around my finger. "I just wanted to leave him behind me, where he belongs."

Two years ago, when I stood across from him in the park with the snow falling all around us, I realized that just as attacking him in front of the Dauntless in the Merciless Mart didn't make me feel better about the pain he caused me, yelling at him or insulting him wouldn't either. There was only one option left, and it was letting go.

Evelyn gives me a strange, searching look, then crosses the room and opens the bag she left on the couch. She takes out an object made of blue glass. It looks like falling water, suspended in time.

I remember when she gave it to me. I was young, but not too young to realize that it was a forbidden object in the Abnegation faction, a useless and therefore a self-indulgent one. I asked her what purpose it served, and she told me, *It doesn't do anything obvious. But it might be able to do something in here.* Then she touched her hand to her heart. *Beautiful things sometimes do.*

For years it was a symbol of my quiet defiance, my small refusal to be an obedient, deferent Abnegation child, and a symbol of my mother's defiance too, even though I believed she was dead. I hid it under my bed, and the day I decided to leave Abnegation, I put it on my desk so my father could see it, see my strength, and hers.

"When you were gone, this reminded me of you," she says, clutching the glass to her stomach. "Reminded me of how brave you were, always have been." She smiles a little. "I thought you might keep it here. I intended it for you, after all."

I wouldn't trust my voice to remain steady if I spoke, so I just smile back, and nod.

The spring air is cold but I leave the windows open in the truck, so I can feel it in my chest, so it stings my fingertips, a reminder of the lingering winter. I stop by the train platform near the Merciless Mart and take the urn out of the backseat. It's silver and simple, no engravings. I didn't choose it; Christina did.

I walk down the platform toward the group that has already gathered. Christina stands with Zeke and Shauna, who sits in the wheelchair with a blanket over her lap. She has a better wheelchair now, one without handles on the back, so she can maneuver it more easily. Matthew stands on the platform with his toes over the edge.

"Hi," I say, standing at Shauna's shoulder.

Christina smiles at me, and Zeke claps me on the shoulder.

Uriah died only days after Tris, but Zeke and Hana said their good-byes just weeks afterward, scattering his ashes in the chasm, amid the clatter of all their friends and family. We screamed his name into the echo chamber of the Pit. Still, I know that Zeke is remembering him today, just as the rest of us are, even though this last act of Dauntless bravery is for Tris.

"Got something to show you," Shauna says, and she tosses the blanket aside, revealing complicated metal braces on her legs. They go all the way up to her hips and wrap around her belly like a cage. She smiles at me, and with a gear-grinding sound, her feet shift to the ground in front of the chair, and in fits and starts, she stands.

Despite the serious occasion, I smile.

"Well, look at that," I say. "I'd forgotten how tall you are."

"Caleb and his lab buddies made them for me," she says. "Still getting the hang of it, but they say I might be able to run someday."

"Nice," I say. "Where is he, anyway?"

"He and Amar will meet us at the end of the line," she says. "Someone has to be there to catch the first person."

"He's still sort of a pansycake," Zeke says. "But I'm coming around to him."

"Hm," I say, not committing. The truth is, I've made my peace with Caleb, but I still can't be around him for long. His gestures, his inflections, his manner, they are hers. They make him into just a whisper of her, and that is not enough of her, but it is also far too much.

I would say more, but the train is coming. It charges toward us on the polished rails, then squeals as it slows to a stop in front of the platform. A head leans out the window of the first car, where the controls are—it's Cara, her hair in a tight braid.

"Get on!" she says.

Shauna sits in the chair again and pushes herself through the doorway. Matthew, Christina, and Zeke follow. I get on last, offering the urn to Shauna to hold, and stand in the doorway, my hand clutching the handle. The train starts again, building speed with each second, and I hear it churning over the tracks and whistling over the rails, and I feel the power of it rising inside me. The air whips across my face and presses my clothes to my body, and I watch the city sprawl out in front of me, the buildings lit by the sun.

It's not the same as it used to be, but I got over that a long time ago. All of us have found new places. Cara and Caleb work in the laboratories at the compound, which are now a small segment of the Department of Agriculture that works to make agriculture more efficient, capable of feeding more people. Matthew works in psychiatric research somewhere in the city—the last time I asked him, he was studying something about memory. Christina works in an office that relocates people from the fringe who want to move into the city. Zeke and Amar are policemen, and George trains the police force—Dauntless jobs, I call them. And I'm assistant to one of our city's representatives in government: Johanna Reyes.

I stretch my arm out to grasp the other handle and lean out of the car as it turns, almost dangling over the street two stories below me. I feel a thrill in my stomach, the fear-thrill the true Dauntless love.

"Hey," Christina says, standing beside me. "How's your mother?"

"Fine," I say. "We'll see, I guess."

"Are you going to zip line?"

I watch the track dip down in front of us, going all the way to street level.

"Yes," I say. "I think Tris would want me to try it at least once."

Saying her name still gives me a little twinge of pain, a pinch that lets me know her memory is still dear to me.

Christina watches the rails ahead of us and leans her shoulder into mine, just for a few seconds. "I think you're right."

My memories of Tris, some of the most powerful memories I have, have dulled with time, as memories do, and they no longer sting as they used to. Sometimes I actually enjoy going over them in my mind, though not often. Sometimes I go over them with Christina, and she listens better than I expected her to, Candor smart-mouth that she is.

Cara guides the train to a stop, and I hop onto the platform. At the top of the stairs Shauna gets out of the chair and works her way down the steps with the braces, one at a time. Matthew and I carry her empty chair after her, which is cumbersome and heavy, but not impossible to manage.

"Any updates from Peter?" I ask Matthew as we reach the bottom of the stairs.

After Peter emerged from the memory serum haze, some of the sharper, harsher aspects of his personality returned, though not all of them. I lost touch with him after that. I don't hate him anymore, but that doesn't mean I have to like him.

"He's in Milwaukee," Matthew says. "I don't know what he's doing, though."

"He's working in an office somewhere," Cara says from the bottom of the stairs. She has the urn cradled in her arms, taken from Shauna's lap on the way off the train. "I think it's good for him."

"I always thought he would go join the GD rebels in the fringe," Zeke says. "Shows you what I know."

"He's different now," Cara says with a shrug.

There are still GD rebels in the fringe who believe that another war is the only way to get the change we want. I fall more on the side that wants to work for change without violence. I've had enough violence to last me a lifetime, and I bear it still, not in scars on my skin but in the memories that rise up in my mind when I least want them to, my father's fist colliding with my jaw, my gun raised to execute Eric, the Abnegation bodies sprawled across the streets of my old home.

We walk the streets to the zip line. The factions are gone, but this part of the city has more Dauntless than any other, recognizable still by their pierced faces and tattooed skin, though no longer by the colors they wear, which are sometimes garish. Some wander the sidewalks with us, but most are at work—everyone in Chicago is required to work if they're able.

Ahead of me I see the Hancock building bending into the sky, its base wider than its top. The black girders chase one another up to the roof, crossing, tightening, and expanding. I haven't been this close in a long time.

We enter the lobby, with its gleaming, polished floors and its walls smeared with bright Dauntless graffiti, left here by the building's residents as a kind of relic. This is a Dauntless place, because they are the ones who embraced it, for its height and, a part of me also suspects, for its loneliness. The Dauntless liked to fill empty spaces with their noise. It's something I liked about them.

Zeke jabs the elevator button with his index finger. We pile in, and Cara presses number 99.

I close my eyes as the elevator surges upward. I can almost see the space opening up beneath my feet, a shaft of darkness, and only a foot of solid ground between me and the sinking, dropping, plummeting. The elevator shudders as it stops, and I cling to the wall to steady myself as the doors open.

Zeke touches my shoulder. "Don't worry, man. We did this all the time, remember?"

I nod. Air rushes through the gap in the ceiling, and above me is the sky, bright blue. I shuffle with the others toward the ladder, too numb with fear to make my feet move any faster.

I find the ladder with my fingertips and focus on one rung at a time. Above me, Shauna maneuvers awkwardly up the ladder, using mostly the strength of her arms.

I asked Tori once, while I was getting the symbols tattooed on my back, if she thought we were the last people left in the world. *Maybe,* was all she said. I don't think she liked to think about it. But up here, on the roof, it is possible to believe that we are the last people left anywhere.

I stare at the buildings along the marsh front, and my chest tightens, squeezes, like it's about to collapse into itself.

Zeke runs across the roof to the zip line and attaches one of the man-sized slings to the steel cable. He locks it so it won't slide down, and looks at the group of us expectantly.

"Christina," he says. "It's all you."

Christina stands near the sling, tapping her chin with a finger.

"What do you think? Face-up or backward?"

"Backward," Matthew says. "I wanted to go face-up so I don't wet my pants, and I don't want you copying me."

"Going face-up will only make that more likely to happen, you know," Christina says. "So go ahead and do it so I can start calling you Wetpants."

Christina gets in the sling feet-first, belly down, so she'll watch the building get smaller as she travels. I shudder.

I can't watch. I close my eyes as Christina travels farther and farther away, and even as Matthew, and then Shauna, do the same thing. I can hear their cries of joy, like birdcalls, on the wind.

"Your turn, Four," says Zeke.

I shake my head.

"Come on," Cara says. "Better to get it over with, right?"

"No," I say. "You go. Please."

She offers me the urn, then takes a deep breath. I hold the urn against my stomach. The metal is warm from where so many people have touched it. Cara climbs into the sling, unsteady, and Zeke straps her in. She crosses her arms over her chest, and he sends her out, over Lake Shore Drive, over the city. I don't hear anything from her, not even a gasp.

Then it's just Zeke and me left, staring at each other.

"I don't think I can do it," I say, and though my voice is steady, my body is shaking.

"Of course you can," he says. "You're *Four*, Dauntless legend! You can face anything."

I cross my arms and inch closer to the edge of the roof. Even though I'm several feet away, I feel my body pitching over the edge, and I shake my head again, and again, and again.

"Hey." Zeke puts his hands on my shoulders. "This isn't about you, remember? It's about her. Doing something she would have liked to do, something she would have been proud of you for doing. Right?"

That's it. I can't avoid this, I can't back out now, not when I still remember her smile as she climbed the Ferris wheel with me, or the hard set of her jaw as she faced fear after fear in the simulations.

"How did she get in?"

"Face-first," Zeke says.

"All right." I hand him the urn. "Put this behind me, okay? And open up the top."

I climb into the sling, my hands shaking so much I can barely grip the sides. Zeke tightens the straps across my back and legs, then wedges the urn behind me, facing out, so the ashes will spread. I stare down Lake Shore Drive, swallowing bile, and start to slide.

Suddenly I want to take it back, but it's too late, I am already diving toward the ground. I'm screaming so loud, I want to cover my own ears. I feel the scream living inside me, filling my chest, throat, and head.

The wind stings my eyes but I force them open, and in my moment of blind panic I understand why she did it this way, face-first—it was because it made her feel like she was flying, like she was a bird.

I can still feel the emptiness beneath me, and it is like the emptiness inside me, like a mouth about to swallow me.

I realize, then, that I have stopped moving. The last bits of ash float on the wind like gray snowflakes, and then disappear.

The ground is only a few feet below me, close enough to jump down. The others have gathered there in a circle, their arms clasped to form a net of bone and muscle to catch me in. I press my face to the sling and laugh.

I toss the empty urn down to them, then twist my arms behind my back to undo the straps holding me in. I drop into my friends' arms like a stone. They catch me, their bones pinching at my back and legs, and lower me to the ground.

There is an awkward silence as I stare at the Hancock building in wonder, and no one knows what to say. Caleb smiles at me, cautious.

Christina blinks tears from her eyes and says, "Oh! Zeke's on his way."

Zeke is hurtling toward us in a black sling. At first it looks like a dot, then a blob, and then a person swathed in black. He crows with joy as he eases to a stop, and I reach across to grab Amar's forearm. On my other side, I grasp a pale arm that belongs to Cara. She smiles at me, and there is some sadness in her smile.

Zeke's shoulder hits our arms, hard, and he smiles wildly as he lets us cradle him like a child.

"That was nice. Want to go again, Four?" he says.

I don't hesitate before answering. "Absolutely not."

+ + +

We walk back to the train in a loose cluster. Shauna walks with her braces, Zeke pushing the empty wheelchair, and exchanges small talk with Amar. Matthew, Cara, and Caleb walk together, talking about something that has them all excited, kindred spirits that they are. Christina sidles up next to me and puts a hand on my shoulder.

"Happy Choosing Day," she says. "I'm going to ask you how you really are. And you're going to give me an honest answer."

We talk like this sometimes, giving each other orders. Somehow she has become one of the best friends I have, despite our frequent bickering.

"I'm all right," I say. "It's hard. It always will be."

"I know," she says.

We walk at the back of the group, past the still-abandoned buildings with their dark windows, over the bridge that spans the river-marsh.

"Yeah, sometimes life really sucks," she says. "But you know what I'm holding on for?"

I raise my eyebrows.

She raises hers, too, mimicking me.

"The moments that don't suck," she says. "The trick is to notice them when they come around."

Then she smiles, and I smile back, and we climb the stairs to the train platform side by side.

+ + +

Since I was young, I have always known this: Life damages us, every one. We can't escape that damage.

But now, I am also learning this: We can be mended. We mend each other.

ACKNOWLEDGMENTS

To me, the acknowledgments page is a place for me to say, as sincerely as possible, that I don't prosper, in life or in books, because of my own strength or skill alone. This series may have only one author, but this author wouldn't have been able to do much of anything without the following people. So with that in mind: Thank you, God, for giving me the people who mend me.

Here they are—

Thank you to: my husband, for not only loving me in an extraordinary way but for some difficult brainstorming sessions, for reading *all* the drafts of this book, and for dealing with Neurotic Author Wife with the utmost patience.

Joanna Volpe, for handling everything LIKE A BOSS, as they say, with honesty and kindness. Katherine Tegen, for excellent notes and for continually showing me the compassionate candy center inside the publishing badass. (I won't tell anyone. Wait, I just did.) Molly O'Neill, for all your time and work and for the eye that spotted *Divergent* from what I'm sure was a giant stack of manuscripts. Casey McIntyre, for some major publicity prowess and for showing me astounding kindness (and dance moves).

Joel Tippie, as well as Amy Ryan and Barb Fitzsimmons,

for making these books so gorgeous Every. Single. Time. The amazing Brenna Franzitta, Josh Weiss, Mark Rifkin, Valerie Shea, Christine Cox, and Joan Giurdanella, for taking such good care of my words. Lauren Flower, Alison Lisnow, Sandee Roston, Diane Naughton, Colleen O'Connell, Aubry Parks-Fried, Margot Wood, Patty Rosati, Molly Thomas, Megan Sugrue, Onalee Smith, and Brett Rachlin, for all your marketing and publicity efforts, which are far too substantial to name. Andrea Pappenheimer, Kerry Moynagh, Kathy Faber, Liz Frew, Heather Doss, Jenny Sheridan, Fran Olson, Deb Murphy, Jessica Abel, Samantha Hagerbaumer, Andrea Rosen, and David Wolfson, sales experts, for your enthusiasm and support. Jean McGinley, Alpha Wong, and Sheala Howley, for getting my words on so many shelves across the globe. For that matter, all my foreign publishers, for believing in these stories. Shayna Ramos and Ruiko Tokunaga, production whizzes; Caitlin Garing, Beth Ives, Karen Dziekonski, and Sean McManus, who make fantastic audiobooks; and Randy Rosema and Pam Moore of finance—for all your hard work and talent. Kate Jackson, Susan Katz, and Brian Murray, for steering this Harper ship so well. I have an enthusiastic and supportive publisher from top to bottom, and that means so much to me.

Pouya Shahbazian, for finding *Divergent* such a good

movie home, and for all your hard work, patience, friendship, and horrifying bug-related pranks. Danielle Barthel, for your organized and patient mind. Everyone else at New Leaf Literary, for being wonderful people who do equally wonderful work. Steve Younger, for always looking out for me in work and in life. Everyone involved in "movie stuff"—particularly Neil Burger, Doug Wick, Lucy Fisher, Gillian Bohrer, and Erik Feig—for handling my work with such care and respect.

Mom, Frank, Ingrid, Karl, Frank Jr., Candice, McCall, Beth, Roger, Tyler, Trevor, Darby, Rachel, Billie, Fred, Granny, the Johnsons (both Romanian and Missourian), the Krausses, the Paquettes, the Fitches, and the Rydzes—for all your love. (I would never choose my faction before you. Ever.)

All the past-present-future members of YA Highway and Write Night, for being such thoughtful, understanding writer buddies. All the more experienced authors who have included me and helped me for the past few years. All the writers who have reached out to me on Twitter or e-mail for camaraderie. Writing can be a lonely job, but not for me, because I have you. I wish I could list you all. Mary Katherine Howell, Alice Kovacik, Carly Maletich, Danielle Bristow, and all my other non-writer friends, for helping me keep my head on straight.

All the Divergent fansites, for crazy-awesome internet (and real-life) enthusiasm.

My readers, for reading and thinking and squealing and tweeting and talking and lending and, above all, for teaching me so many valuable lessons about writing and life.

All of the people listed above have made this series what it is, and knowing you all has changed my life. I am so lucky.

I'll say it one last time: Be brave.

SPECIAL THANKS

In the spring of 2012, fifty blogs helped spread their love for the **DIVERGENT** series by supporting the release of **INSURGENT** in a faction-based online campaign. Every participant was integral to the success of this series! Thank you to:

ABNEGATION: Amanda Bell (faction leader), Katie Bartow, Heidi Bennett, Katie Butler, Asma Faizal, Hafsah Faizal, Ana Grilo, Kathy Habel, Thea James, Julie Jones, and HD Tolson

AMITY: Meg Caristi, Kassiah Faul, and Sherry Atwell (faction leaders), Kristin Aragon, Emily Ellsworth, Cindy Hand, Melissa Helmers, Abigail J., Sarah Pitre, Lisa Reeves, Stephanie Su, and Amanda Welling

CANDOR: Kristi Diehm (faction leader), Jaime Arnold, Harmony Beaufort, Damaris Cardinali, Kris Chen, Sara Gundell, Bailey Hewlett, John Jacobson, Hannah McBride, and Aeicha Matteson

DAUNTLESS: Alison Genet (faction leader), Lena Ainsworth, Stacey Canova and Amber Clark, April Conant, Lindsay Cummings, Jessica Estep, Ashley Gonzales, Anna Heinemann, Tram Hoang, Nancy Sanchez, and Yara Santos

ERUDITE: Pam van Hylckama Vlieg (faction leader), James Booth, Mary Brebner, Andrea Chapman, Amy Green, Jen Hamflett, Brittany Howard, O'Dell Hutchison, Benji Kenworthy, Lyndsey Lore, Jennifer McCoy, Lisa Parkin, and Lisa Roecker

BONUS MATERIALS

BONUS MATERIALS

Q&A WITH VERONICA ROTH

Explain your design process for the dripping stone sculpture. Why water and stone?

The symbol is meant to be one of slow progress—one drop of water at a time can wear through stone, in time, but progress is slow, almost unnoticeable. I devised this sculpture, in particular, because I knew it was something that Tris would be at odds with. Tris is, at best, brave, and at worst, reckless—she doesn't understand the cautious approach that the Bureau prefers, and to some extent, she's right. They have become callous to the suffering of the people within the city, all because they prioritize this greater hope of progress.

But in another way, the sculpture brings out Tris's

immaturity. She is unable to look at the bigger picture, unable to fathom that sometimes change can't come in a huge wave, and has to come over time, through consistent effort. As the series progresses, Tris becomes more and more aware of how big the world is, and how complicated, and the Bureau is just another way to bring that out of her—its official symbol included.

How did the character David come to be? Is he based on anyone?

Well, I sort of . . . got rid of Tris's parents early on. So in *Allegiant*, I decided to create someone who knew Tris's mother in a different way than even her father did and could serve as a parental figure, helping her transition from her old world to her new one at the Bureau. But part of growing up is realizing that your parents aren't perfect, and Tris experiences this to a heightened degree with David, who first wins her trust by reacquainting her with her mother and then loses it by showing his dark side. He gives Tris the illusion of safety and comfort, but ultimately she has to take care of herself and her loved ones. She becomes her fully realized self—an adult, in the truest sense of the word—through David's connection to Natalie and his subsequent betrayal.

So no, he's not based on anyone—he's designed to be a

character who presents one identity that slowly unravels, showing the vulnerability (and darkness) beneath.

Tell us more about Amar and why he was an essential character in the series.

Amar! Amar, Evelyn, and George are (I think) the only characters I "resurrected"—something I avoid doing, as a rule, because it can take the emotional weight out of losing characters. (If you're always convinced they'll come back, you don't quite grieve for them the same way as you read.) Amar is important because he's the bridge between the city and the Bureau, as well as between past Tobias and present Tobias. I mean, there's something so interesting about talking to someone who knew your boyfriend or girlfriend before you met them! So I thought the dynamic between him and Tris was particularly interesting: they both have deep affection for Four, but they have different perspectives on him. It helps Tris to know Tobias more intimately, seeing him through Amar's eyes.

Amar also furthers Tobias's emotional journey, discovering that pretty much everyone in his life is lying to him. I mean, this is the second time someone important to Tobias has allowed him to grieve for them without actually being dead. Since Tobias is basically figuring out how to trust people and rely on them for help and strength, I wanted to put as many obstacles in his path as possible. Amar is an important obstacle.

Did anything surprise you while writing from the dual perspectives of Tobias and Tris?

How hard it was! I learned a lot from attempting dual perspectives for the first time, such as . . . that characters can sound far more different to you, the writer, than they do to readers! To me, Tris is really clipped, direct, and doesn't indulge in many descriptions. She withholds things from you—she knows more than the reader does. Tobias, on the other hand, is a little more descriptive, and he doesn't hide anything. I love that tension between how reserved and private he is as a character, and how open and vulnerable his voice is—that was another surprise.

It was also fun to play with traditional gender roles through Tris's and Four's voices. Tris has a stereotypically masculine "stiff upper lip" kind of voice, and Four's voice is more poetic and intimate, which we might consider stereotypically feminine. At least, that's what I was going for, and one of the things that kept me interested in the dual POV as I wrote.

Excerpts from

FACTION HISTORY
A TEXTBOOK
(REVISED EDITION)

Introduction

Decades ago, our ancestors realized that it is not political ideology, religious belief, race, or nationalism that is to blame for a warring world. Rather, they determined that it was the fault of human personality—of humankind's inclination toward evil, in its many forms. They divided into five factions that sought to eradicate those qualities they believed responsible for the world's disarray. Working together, these five factions have lived in peace for many years, each contributing to a different sector of society. In our factions, we find meaning, we find purpose, we find life.

OUR MOTTO
"FACTION BEFORE BLOOD"

The phrase "faction before blood" was coined several decades after the factions were formed, but gained popularity quickly thereafter. Its origin is unknown, but it expresses one of our core beliefs: the faction is the most important social unit, more important even than family. Some factions choose to cultivate this belief in their social structure; others merely teach it. But every faction holds this phrase true.

Some have theorized that the phrase came from the Choosing Ceremony, in which a young person literally gives some of their blood to the faction, thus forsaking their blood relationship. Others postulate that the Choosing Ceremony was instituted after the phrase became popular. Either way, "faction before blood" is one of the most important sentences ever spoken.

ABNEGATION
THE SELFLESS

CORE BELIEF: "Them before I."

VALUES

If asked, the Abnegation would insist that what they believe in, and the values they prize, are of little importance compared to what they think a person ought to do. Therefore, to say that the Abnegation value selflessness and self-denial is to fail to comprehend the faction as it comprehends itself.

Even the faction's name furthers this attitude. Left to their own devices, the Abnegation chose a name that is closely related to a behavior, rather than a quality (Candor, Erudite, Dauntless), or a goal (Amity), emphasizing action rather than identity. Most of their teachings involve the *how* of behavior and very little of the *why*. Even the *why* that exists serves only to inform the *how*, and not to explain the faction to outsiders—or even to members. Every faction norm, including ritual, language, and style of dress, is designed to encourage acts of self-denial.

FACTION NORMS

Jobs—The most prominent role the Abnegation play in city life is in government. A council of Abnegation leaders makes all political decisions, and all projects that extend beyond the reach of a faction must be submitted to them for approval. The Abnegation can train to be elementary school teachers, nurses (with permission from Erudite leaders), firefighters (with permission from Dauntless leaders), morticians, or to do administrative tasks or "background work" in a variety of sectors. Additionally, they often choose to work among the factionless to improve quality of life.

Family Life—The Abnegation adhere as strictly as possible to the traditional family model: husband, wife, and two children. If an Abnegation member of marriageable age cannot find a spouse, the faction will find one for him or her. Remaining single is an option for those who do not wish to marry, but it is an option that necessarily excludes intimate companionship, and requires dedication to serving the community. Single or widowed individuals live in group housing, separated by gender.

Clothing—The official color of Abnegation is gray; therefore, their wardrobe consists entirely of gray clothing. Most of this clothing is loose, so as to preserve modesty and discourage ogling, and made of synthetic fabrics, because they are easy for the factionless to produce and always available. No adornments are allowed except for those that serve a practical purpose: rubber bands and clips to pull back loose hair, watches, spectacles, and so on. The rumor that the Abnegation wear an arm band specifically designed to induce discomfort is false, and in fact reveals the other factions' lack of understanding of Abnegation teachings. (Constant discomfort would mean constant self-reflection, something the Abnegation discourage.)

Inter-Faction Relations—While the Abnegation would deny harboring resentment toward any other faction, it is well known that they exhibit an obvious distaste for Erudite. This is perhaps because they believe the Erudite lifestyle, which centers around the individual's pursuit of knowledge, creativity, and innovation, is inherently selfish, or because of Abnegation's discouragement of curiosity, something the Erudite promote among their members. The Abnegation have a particularly good relationship with Amity, and often work together on city improvement projects.

CHOOSING CEREMONY SUBSTANCE: STONES

The Abnegation view stone as the most useful and stable material available, since it forms our roads and the majority of our homes. Usefulness and stability are two qualities the Abnegation, in particular, appreciate. It also reflects the gray color of their faction, clothing, and even their sector of the city.

AMITY
THE PEACEFUL

CORE BELIEF: "Open arms, open eyes, forgiving hearts."

VALUES

Amity is the only faction without a prized quality; rather, they define their most valued traits, peacefulness and harmony, as the absence of aggression. In order to achieve this lack of aggression, the Amity teach trust, forgiveness, self-sufficiency, and kindness. They believe in peaceful (and often public) conflict resolution, and emphasize joy, beauty, and celebration more than any other faction. Like the Erudite, they also value creativity, but for the sake of beauty rather than technological innovation.

FACTION NORMS

Jobs—Amity is the other "essential faction" because they produce all the food for the city. Almost all of their members are required for there to be enough food, so most Amity do not seek other employment. Within the food production realm, however, an Amity can specialize in livestock, large crops, specialty foods, water purification, and other areas. There are a handful of Amity counselors, mediators, and caretakers of the sick, mentally ill, and elderly. Artists, writers, and musicians emerge almost exclusively from Amity, but these are defined as hobbies rather than jobs.

Family Life—The Amity in particular believe in the value of different kinds of community. They seek to balance family relationships with friendships. Thus, most of the Amity live in large groups according to specialty. These large groups are often comprised of several traditional families and a few untraditional families (couples/partners without children, single people, et cetera). The large group therefore defines a person's peer group, as well. All of the Amity eat together, though, so it is rare for one Amity to be unacquainted with another Amity, no matter how different their specialties are. The Amity believe strongly in communal living, such that they have no real leader, except the one they are forced to provide to advise the Abnegation political leaders.

Clothing—The colors of Amity are red and yellow (the colors most likely to produce joy), but they are less strict than other factions about how those colors must be worn. They prefer loose-fitting garments that foster ease and comfort, and encourage repurposing of old garments, because it requires creativity.

Inter-Faction Relations—The Amity seek to establish good relationships with all other factions. Historically, most of their conflicts (if they can be called conflicts) have been with the Dauntless, due to their disagreements about conflict resolution. They have a special relationship with Erudite, as noted earlier, and with Candor and Abnegation, in the realm of religion.

CHOOSING CEREMONY SUBSTANCE: EARTH

Aside from working extensively with the earth, the Amity also value a connection with nature because they believe it can bring peace to their lives. Therefore giving your blood to the earth is a way of committing yourself to peace from your first moment as one of the Amity.

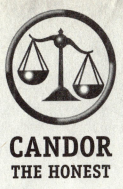

CANDOR
THE HONEST

CORE BELIEF: *"Truth makes us inextricable."*

VALUES

To say the Candor value honesty is an understatement. They instruct their members to be as open as possible in all areas of life, whether in praise or criticism, through boasting or confession, by invitation or interruption. There is no such thing as "private life" among the Candor; everything is public, and everything is the business of the community.

Impartiality, though not as prominent in Candor teachings as openness, is regarded as equally important. When evaluating a situation, the Candor are encouraged to disregard their own feelings about the people involved. A Candor who sides with his enemy rather than his friend about a particular issue is regarded as honest and fair.

"The true Candor," famous Candor leader Trevor Johnson once said, "is bold enough to be Dauntless, fair enough to be Amity, incisive enough to be Erudite, and wise enough to be Abnegation."

FACTION NORMS

Jobs—The realm of the Candor is law. The Candor therefore receive extensive training in the laws that govern society as a whole, as well as the laws that govern each faction. Some Candor decide either to be judges or to represent either side of a trial. Others work as reporters.

Candor is the only faction that regularly cooperates with other factions in their everyday work. They advise Abnegation political leaders, Amity mediators and counselors, and Erudite teachers. They act in a leadership capacity in schools. They work with Amity to distribute goods fairly among the factions. Though their roles are less clearly defined than those of other factions, if they were to vanish from the city, the glue that binds us together would vanish with them, and we would undoubtedly be left in chaos.

The Candor pursuit of truth often leads them to work closely with the Abnegation and the Amity in the realm of religion. There are as many Candor religious leaders as there are Abnegation and Amity religious leaders.

Family Life—Because there is no private life among the Candor, families are not as important. Peer groups, rather than family groups, dominate Candor society. The parents' responsibility is more protective than instructive. Children live with their parents until age ten, at which point they relocate to a dormitory until they turn sixteen and choose a faction. Young faction members also live in a dormitory until they find a spouse or partner and choose to live separately.

Clothing—Candor clothing is determined by color alone. They believe that the truth is black and white, so they wear black and white only, in any form, as long as both colors are represented. The Candor are less bold in their styling decisions than the Dauntless, but not nearly as conservative as the Abnegation.

Inter-Faction Relations—The Candor have a strained relationship with Amity (because "they will always lie to keep the peace," as Trevor Johnson once said) and Erudite (because of "their talent for subterfuge and craftiness"). They work closely with the Abnegation in government, but often publicly criticize the Abnegation's lack of openness. Faction transfers between Dauntless and Candor are common, however, so the factions are generally amicable toward each other.

CHOOSING CEREMONY SUBSTANCE: GLASS

The Candor selected glass for its transparency. A transparent person, they say, is an honest person.

DAUNTLESS
THE BRAVE

CORE BELIEF: "Freedom from fear."

VALUES

Without hesitation, any Dauntless would say that what they most value is courage. It is when the word "courage" is defined that they begin to disagree with one another. One subset of Dauntless would define "courage" as "fearlessness," and seeks to eradicate fear in all its forms among its members. Another subset would define "courage" simply as "boldness," and emphasize action in spite of fear rather than the elimination of fear itself. This difference, though minor, often leads to conflict among the Dauntless, particularly in the area of initiating new members. Those Dauntless who emphasize fearlessness advocate harsher and more extreme methods of training, which boldness-emphasizing Dauntless call cruelty and bullying.

Common to all Dauntless is a commitment to bravery that supersedes all other considerations, including safety, the opinion of others, and sometimes even peace itself.

FACTION NORMS

Jobs—The primary role of the Dauntless is city security. This extends both outside the city (along the fence) and inside the city (on the streets), although the latter has become less prominent in recent years. This role also includes a physical presence (guards) as well as a technological presence (security monitoring). The majority of firefighters are also comprised of Dauntless, although the Abnegation often contribute a small number as well. Paramedics and construction workers who work on high-rise buildings are also Dauntless jobs. Apart from these public roles, however, the Dauntless are largely self-contained, so a large number of jobs are available within the Dauntless compound, including positions for nurses, cooks, tattoo artists, and trainers, among others.

Family Life—Dauntless families are diverse, so it is difficult to pin down exactly what the average Dauntless family looks like. Some families reside together in large apartments in the Dauntless compound, and include grandparents as well as parents and children. Blood ties are often not well-defined, so a Dauntless "aunt" or "uncle" may not be related by blood.

Marriage is a peculiar institution among the Dauntless, defined differently depending upon who is asked. Many Dauntless couples opt not to marry at all. Young Dauntless often live together (irrespective of gender) until they find a spouse or partner. But for every generalization about

Dauntless families, there are half a dozen Dauntless families that contradict it.

Clothing—Black is the official color of Dauntless, which almost all Dauntless clothing reflects. Piercings and tattoos are common, as well as odd hairstyles and hair color. Due to their emphasis on physical fitness, most Dauntless prefer tight clothing to loose clothing. The Dauntless emphasize clothing style far more than any other faction, and those styles change too rapidly to be included in this textbook.

Inter-Faction Relations—Due to their reliance on surveillance and simulation technology, the Dauntless have developed a strong relationship with Erudite. They are also friendly with Candor, since there are semi-frequent transfers between the two factions. There is often tension between Dauntless and Amity, given their opposite natures and frequent contact at Dauntless patrol sites along the fence, and Dauntless and Abnegation, for more superficial reasons of differing lifestyles.

CHOOSING CEREMONY SUBSTANCE: FIRE

"Fire," the Dauntless say, "can be destructive, but can also bring warmth and vitality—just like bravery."

ERUDITE
THE INTELLIGENT

CORE BELIEF: "Knowledge eliminates conflict."

VALUES

"Knowledge, understanding, and innovation" are the three areas of emphasis in Erudite.

"Knowledge" includes the accumulation of information, or, simply put, learning about everything.

"Understanding" involves putting that information to use, whether through the practice of medicine, scientific experiments, or the act of writing, among other things. Understanding in relationships is also something that the Erudite value. Conflicts are often resolved by the offended party receiving instruction about the offensive party, and vice versa, until both parties empathize with each other.

"Innovation" requires a person to take their understanding and knowledge and push it beyond its original borders to create something new.

The Erudite also teach their members to develop curiosity, and to obey its impulses.

FACTION NORMS

Jobs—Erudite is one of the two "essential factions," that is, the factions without which our basic needs would not be met. They are our doctors, scientists, and teachers. Though we often think of a scientist as someone in a lab coat, the Erudite include titles like sociologist, psychologist, and mathematician in the "scientist" category.

Often those Erudite who lose their dexterity or have trouble interacting with others will choose to be researchers, and aid in important discoveries in medicine or technology. The "Low IQ" Erudite (those Erudite who scored the lowest on their initiation intelligence tests upon completing initiation) work as technicians or laboratory assistants.

Family Life—The Erudite believe that the traditional family unit is the most practical while children are young; however, they do not see the logic of marriage, so "couples" are bound only by their children, and sometimes do not live together. The most important relationship in Erudite is the mentor/mentee relationship, which a child often finds with one of his or her parents, but not exclusively. Some Erudite children live with their aunts and uncles, or older siblings.

Clothing—The Erudite wear blue—with the rationale that blue induces calm, and a calm mind is an absorptive one—and place almost no emphasis on clothing style. Pockets are seen as particularly useful, so it is rare to find an article of Erudite clothing without them. Spectacles are seen as a sign of intelligence, so many Erudite without vision-correction needs will wear glasses regardless.

Inter-Faction Relations—The Erudite have a strong relationship with the other "essential faction," Amity, because the Amity require technology to make their food production more efficient. They have a similar relationship with Dauntless, as noted earlier. The Erudite frequently criticize the Abnegation for being "illogically selfless and inefficient," particularly in the realm of government. Some selfishness, they argue, is necessary for an individual to live a fruitful life.

CHOOSING CEREMONY SUBSTANCE: WATER

While the Erudite traditionally reject symbolism as illogical and unnecessary, they chose water because it has knowledge's clarity—it is intelligible to all who seek it—and weight—it is of utmost importance.

THE FACTIONLESS

Those who fail to complete initiation into their chosen faction, or choose to leave their factions for whatever reason, become factionless. They live without support from their fellow factionless, and without community. They have high levels of crime and illness, both physical and mental.

Factionless parents are legally required to turn over their children to the government as soon as they are born so that every child is given the same opportunity to participate in and choose a faction. The children are temporarily housed in the Abnegation sector, but they can ultimately be adopted by members of other factions (though most remain in Abnegation). This mandate is difficult to enforce, however, so the children of the factionless often remain factionless themselves.

Though factionlessness is not necessary, it seems to be inevitable. Therefore we have developed a way of making factionlessness as useful as possible. The factionless perform important functions such as train and bus operation, textile production, janitorial duties, maintenance, and some construction work. We believe this restores some of the sense of purpose that these persons have lost by living without a faction.

ALLEGIANT DISCUSSION QUESTIONS

1. The third book in the **DIVERGENT** series opens with Tris being held prisoner by Evelyn, Tobias's mother. Describe the circumstances surrounding her imprisonment. What can you infer from the text about her situation? Explain how Tobias comes to her rescue.

2. Why is Tris angry with Caleb, her brother, and why does Tobias plan his escape from prison? Is Tris's anger justified? Why or why not?

3. Who are the Allegiants and what is their mission? How do Tris and Tobias become involved in their movement? Why does Cara choose Tris and Tobias as part of her team?

4. Describe Tobias's relationship with his parents. Who are they and why does his mother tell him about the Allegiants?

5. Why do Tris and Tobias want to go "outside the fence"? Describe the world of the compound and the work of the Bureau. How does this world differ from the lives

Tris and Tobias have known? What parallels, if any, can you draw with modern society and class systems?

6. Who is David and why does he want Tris to train to be a member of the council? Why is Tris interested in this role? What does she learn about her mother while living at the compound and how does this information affect her beliefs?

7. Both Tris and Tobias undergo genetic testing. What does Tobias learn about himself and how does this information affect his self-image?

8. Both Tobias and Tris visit the fringe. Characterize this community. How does it differ from their city? How does it differ from the compound? Why do they go there and what effect does it have on them?

9. Tobias asks Cara how she can forgive Tris for killing her brother. What answer does she give? What does her response say about her character?

10. Who is Nita and what role does she play in the story? Is she a likeable character? Why or why not?

11. What do Tobias and Tris learn about the work of the Bureau and why do they plot to secure the memory serum?

12. How does Tris save the Bureau? Are her actions characteristic of her personality? How is her brother affected by her choice?

13. Tobias has an unstable relationship with both of his parents. After watching video of both parents, he says, "I feel like what I have become is halfway between my mother and my father, violent and impulsive and desperate and afraid." Explain his thinking. Would you agree or not?

14. At the end of the story, Tobias says, "There are so many ways to be brave in this world. Sometimes bravery involves laying down your life for something bigger than yourself, or for someone else. . . . Sometimes it is nothing more than gritting your teeth through pain, and the work of every day, the slow walk toward a better life." Why does Tobias make this statement? What examples in your life or in the lives of those around you support this belief?

15. The freedom to choose is one recurring theme in the story. Use evidence from the text to discuss this theme.

ONE CHOICE BREAKS FREE OF HIS PAST
ONE CHOICE EMBRACES HIS FUTURE
ONE CHOICE EXPOSES THE DANGERS
ONE CHOICE CHANGES HIM—FOREVER
ONE CHOICE WILL FREE HIM

TURN THE PAGE TO READ AN EXCERPT FROM

FOUR

A DIVERGENT COLLECTION

FOUR STORIES IN THE WORLD OF DIVERGENT
TOLD FROM TOBIAS'S POINT OF VIEW

INTRODUCTION

I FIRST STARTED writing *Divergent* from the perspective of Tobias Eaton, a boy from Abnegation with peculiar tension with his father who longed for freedom from his faction. I reached a standstill at thirty pages because the narrator wasn't quite right for the story I wanted to tell; four years later, when I picked up the story again, I found the right character to drive it, this time a girl from Abnegation who wanted to find out what she was made of. But Tobias never disappeared—he entered the story as Four, Tris's instructor, friend, boyfriend, and equal. He has always been a character I was interested in exploring further because of the way he came alive for me every time he was on the page. He is powerful for me largely because of the way he continues to overcome adversity, even managing, on several occasions, to flourish in it.

The first three stories, "The Transfer," "The Initiate,"

and "The Son," take place before he ever meets Tris, following his path from Abnegation to Dauntless as he earns his own strength. In the last, "The Traitor," which overlaps chronologically with the middle of *Divergent*, he meets Tris. I wanted very much to include the moment when they meet, but unfortunately, it didn't fit into the story's timeline—you can find it instead at the back of this book.

The series follows Tris from the moment she seized control of her own life and identity; and with these stories, we can follow Four as he does the same. And the rest, as they say, is history.

—*Veronica Roth*

THE TRANSFER

I EMERGE FROM the simulation with a yell. My lip stings, and when I take my hand away from it, there is blood on my fingertips. I must have bitten it during the test.

The Dauntless woman administering my aptitude test—Tori, she said her name was—gives me a strange look as she pulls her black hair back and ties it in a knot. Her arms are marked up and down with ink, flames and rays of light and hawk wings.

"When you were in the simulation . . . were you aware that it wasn't real?" Tori says to me as she turns off the machine. She sounds and looks casual, but it's a studied casualness, learned from years of practice. I know it when I see it. I always do.

Suddenly I'm aware of my own heartbeat. This is what

my father said would happen. He told me that they would ask me if I was aware during the simulation, and he told me what to say when they did.

"No," I say. "If I was, do you think I would have chewed through my lip?"

Tori studies me for a few seconds, then bites down on the ring in her lip before she says, "Congratulations. Your result was textbook Abnegation."

I nod, but the word "Abnegation" feels like a noose wrapped around my throat.

"Aren't you pleased?" she says.

"My faction members will be."

"I didn't ask about them, I asked about you." Tori's mouth and eyes turn down at the corners like they bear little weights. Like she's sad about something. "This is a safe room. You can say whatever you want here."

I knew what my choices in the aptitude test would add up to before I arrived at school this morning. I chose food over a weapon. I threw myself in the path of the dog to save the little girl. I knew that after I made those choices, the test would end and I would receive Abnegation as a result. And I don't know that I would have made different choices if my father hadn't coached me, hadn't controlled every part of my aptitude test from afar. So what was I expecting? What faction did I want?

Any of them. Any of them but Abnegation.

"I'm pleased," I say firmly. I don't care what she says—this isn't a safe room. There are no safe rooms, no safe truths, no safe secrets to tell.

I can still feel the dog's teeth closing around my arm, tearing my skin. I nod to Tori and start toward the door, but just before I leave, her hand closes around my elbow.

"You're the one who has to live with your choice," she says. "Everyone else will get over it, move on, no matter what you decide. But you never will."

I open the door and walk out.

+ + +

I return to the cafeteria and sit down at the Abnegation table, among the people who barely know me. My father doesn't permit me to come to most community events. He claims that I'll cause a disruption, that I'll do something to hurt his reputation. I don't care. I'm happier in my room, in the silent house, than surrounded by the deferential, apologetic Abnegation.

The consequence of my constant absence, though, is that the other Abnegation are wary of me, convinced there's something wrong with me, that I'm ill or immoral or strange. Even those willing to nod at me in greeting don't quite meet my eyes.

I sit with my hands clenching my knees, watching the other tables, while the other students finish their aptitude tests. The Erudite table is covered in reading material, but they aren't all studying—they're just making a show of it, trading conversation instead of ideas, their eyes snapping back to the words every time they think someone's watching them. The Candor are talking loudly, as always. The Amity are laughing, smiling, pulling food from their pockets and passing it around. The Dauntless are raucous and loud, slung over the tables and chairs, leaning on one another and poking one another and teasing.

I wanted any other faction. Any other faction but mine, where everyone has already decided that I am not worth their attention.

Finally an Erudite woman enters the cafeteria and holds up a hand for silence. The Abnegation and Erudite quiet down right away, but it takes her shouting "Quiet!" for the Dauntless, Amity, and Candor to notice her.

"The aptitude tests are now finished," she says. "Remember that you are not permitted to discuss your results with *anyone*, not even your friends or family. The Choosing Ceremony will be tomorrow at the Hub. Plan to arrive at least ten minutes before it begins. You are dismissed."

Everyone rushes toward the doors except our table,

where we wait for everyone else to leave before we even get to our feet. I know the path my fellow Abnegation will take out of here, down the hallway and out the front doors to the bus stop. They could be there for over an hour letting other people get on in front of them. I don't think I can bear any more of this silence.

Instead of following them, I slip out a side door and into an alley next to the school. I've taken this route before, but usually I creep along slowly, not wanting to be seen or heard. Today all I want to do is run.

I sprint to the end of the alley and into the empty street, leaping over a sinkhole in the pavement. My loose Abnegation jacket snaps in the wind, and I peel it from my shoulders, letting it trail behind me like a flag and then letting it go. I push the sleeves of my shirt up to my elbows as I run, slowing to a jog when my body can no longer stand the sprint. It feels like the entire city is rushing past me in a blur, the buildings blending together. I hear the slap of my shoes like the sound is separate from me.

Finally I have to stop, my muscles burning. I'm in the factionless wasteland that lies between the Abnegation sector and Erudite headquarters, Candor headquarters, and our common places. At every faction meeting, our leaders, usually speaking through my father, urge us not to be afraid of the factionless, to treat them like human beings instead of broken, lost creatures. But it never occurred to me to be afraid of them.

I move to the sidewalk so I can look through the windows of the buildings. Most of the time all I see is old furniture, every room bare, bits of trash on the floor. When most of the city's residents left—as they must have, since our current population doesn't fill every building—they must not have left in a hurry, because the spaces they occupied are so clean. Nothing of interest remains.

When I pass one of the buildings on the corner, though, I see something inside. The room just beyond the window is as bare as any of the others I've walked by, but past the doorway inside I can see a single ember, a lit coal.

I frown and pause in front of the window to see if it will open. At first it won't budge, and then I wiggle it back and forth, and it springs upward. I push my torso through first, and then my legs, toppling to the ground inside in a heap of limbs. My elbows sting as they scrape the floor.

The building smells like cooked food and smoke and sweat. I inch toward the ember, listening for voices that will warn me of a factionless presence here, but there's only silence.

In the next room, the windows are blacked out by paint and dirt, but a little daylight makes it through them, so I can see that there are curled pallets scattered on the floor all over the room, and old cans with bits of dried food stuck inside them. In the center of the room is a small charcoal grill. Most of the coals are white, their fuel spent, but one is still lit, suggesting that whoever was here was here recently. And judging by the smell and the abundance of old cans and blankets, there were quite a few of them.

I was always taught that the factionless lived without community, isolated from one another. Now, looking at this place, I wonder why I ever believed it. What would be stopping them from forming groups, just like we have? It's in our nature.

"What are you doing here?" a voice demands, and it travels through me like an electric shock. I wheel around and see a smudged, sallow-faced man in the next room, wiping his hands on a ragged towel.

"I was just . . ." I look at the grill. "I saw fire. That's all."

"Oh." The man tucks the corner of the towel into his back pocket. He wears black Candor pants, patched with blue Erudite fabric, and a gray Abnegation shirt, the same as the one I'm wearing. He's lean as a rail, but he looks strong. Strong enough to hurt me, but I don't think he will.

"Thanks, I guess," he says. "Nothing's on fire here, though."

"I can see that," I say. "What is this place?"

"It's my house," he says with a cold smile. He's missing one of his teeth. "I didn't know I would be having guests, so I didn't bother to tidy up."

I look from him to the scattered cans. "You must toss and turn a lot, to require so many blankets."

"Never met a Stiff who pried so much into other people's business," he says. He moves closer to me and frowns. "You look a little familiar."

I know I can't have met him before, not where I live, surrounded by identical houses in the most monotonous neighborhood in the city, surrounded by people in identical gray clothing with identical short hair. Then it occurs to me: hidden as my father tries to keep me, he's still the leader of the council, one of the most prominent people in our city, and I still resemble him.

"I'm sorry to have bothered you," I say in my best Abnegation voice. "I'll be going now."

"I do know you," the man says. "You're Evelyn Eaton's son, aren't you?"

I stiffen at her name. It's been years since I heard it, because my father won't speak it, won't even acknowledge it if he hears it. To be connected to her again, even just in facial resemblance, feels strange, like putting on an old piece of clothing that doesn't quite fit anymore.

"How did you know her?" He must have known her

well, to see her in my face, which is paler than hers, the eyes blue instead of dark brown. Most people didn't look closely enough to see all the things we had in common: our long fingers, our hooked noses, our straight, frowned eyebrows.

He hesitates a little. "She volunteered with the Abnegation sometimes. Handing out food and blankets and clothes. Had a memorable face. Plus, she was married to a council leader. Didn't everyone know her?"

Sometimes I know people are lying just because of the way the words feel when they press into me, uncomfortable and wrong, the way an Erudite feels when she reads a grammatically incorrect sentence. However he knew my mother, it's not because she handed him a can of soup once. But I'm so thirsty to hear more about her that I don't press the issue.

"She died, did you know?" I say. "Years ago."

"No, I didn't know." His mouth slants a little at one corner. "I'm sorry to hear that."

I feel strange, standing in this dank place that smells like live bodies and smoke, among these empty cans that suggest poverty and the failure to fit in. But there is something appealing about it here too, a freedom, a refusal to belong to these arbitrary categories we've made for ourselves.

"Your Choosing must be coming up tomorrow, for you to look so worried," the man says. "What faction did you get?"

"I'm not supposed to tell anyone," I say automatically.

"I'm not anyone," he says. "I'm nobody. That's what being factionless is."

I still don't say anything. The prohibition against sharing my aptitude test result, or any of my other secrets, is set firmly in the mold that makes me and remakes me daily. It's impossible to change now.

"Ah, a rule follower," he says, like he's disappointed. "Your mother said to me once that she felt like inertia had carried her to Abnegation. It was the path of least resistance." He shrugs. "Trust me when I tell you, Eaton boy, that resisting is worth doing."

I feel a rush of anger. He shouldn't be telling me about my mother like she belongs to him and not to me, shouldn't be making me question everything I remember about her just because she may or may not have served him food once. He shouldn't be telling me anything at all—he's nobody, factionless, separate, nothing.

"Yeah?" I say. "Look where resisting got you. Living out of cans in broken-down buildings. Doesn't sound so great to me." I start toward the doorway the man emerged from. I know I'll find an alley door somewhere back there;

I don't care where as long as I can get out of here quickly.

I pick a path across the floor, careful not to step on any of the blankets. When I reach the hallway, the man says, "I'd rather eat out of a can than be strangled by a faction."

I don't look back.

+ + +